T0019767

'Few other novels of the war describe the grinding claustrophobia, violence and lethal danger of being in a tank crew with the stark vividness of Peter Elstob. It's possible to almost smell the fumes and sweat, while the intimate detail of operating such a beast and the camaraderie of the crew are utterly compelling. This is a forgotten classic that deserves to be read and read.'

JAMES HOLLAND, Historian, author and TV Presenter

WARRIORS FOR
THE WORKING DAY

Peter Elstob

IMPERIAL WAR MUSEUMS

First published in Great Britain by
Jonathan Cape Ltd 1960

First published in this format in 2020 by
IWM, Lambeth Road, London SE1 6HZ
iwm.org.uk

ISBN 978-1-912423-16-3

A catalogue record for this book is available from the
British Library.

Printed and bound in Great Britain by Clays Ltd, Elcograf S.p.A

Every effort has been made to contact all copyright holders.
The publishers will be glad to make good in future editions any
error or omissions brought to their attention.

Cover illustration by Bill Bragg
Design by Clare Skeats

FSC
www.fsc.org
MIX
Paper from
responsible sources
FSC® C018072

About the Author

Peter Elstob (1915 – 2002)

Born in London, PETER ELSTOB attended school in New York and New Jersey, whence his family had moved as a result of his father's job. He spent a brief period at the University of Michigan before a short stint in the Royal Air Force (RAF), and as a volunteer for the Republicans in the Spanish Civil War.

On the outbreak of the Second World War, following a rejection to re-join the RAF, Elstob volunteered for the army and joined the 3rd Battalion, Royal Tank Regiment. He served in a variety of theatres across Europe, the Middle East and further afield. *Warriors for the Working Day*, originally published in 1960, is a lightly fictionalised account of his time in a tank crew during the liberation of north-west Europe.

After the war Elstob pursued a variety of ventures and displayed an entrepreneurial spirit. His main success was the beauty mask Yeast Pac, which he and his business partner developed and marketed successfully for many years. He also co-ran the Arts Theatre Club in London, founded an artistic and writers' community in Mexico, and attempted a trans-Atlantic balloon flight in 1958. Elstob wrote a number of books including novels covering his experiences of the Spanish Civil War, the story of his balloon exploits (*The Flight of a Small World*, 1959) and a number of well-received military histories, including *Hitler's Last Offensive* (1971) about the Battle of the Bulge. *Warriors for the Working Day* – which was translated into several languages and reportedly sold nearly a quarter of a million copies – is regarded by many as his greatest literary work. He died in 2002.

Introduction

War novels are often associated with the First World War, with an explosion of the genre in the late 1920s. Erich Maria Remarque's *All Quiet on the Western Front* was a bestseller and was made into a Hollywood film in 1930. In the same year, Siegfried Sassoon's *Memoirs of an Infantry Officer* sold 24,000 copies. Generations of school children have grown up on a diet of Wilfred Owen's poetry, as well as the novels and memoirs of Sassoon and Robert Graves – so much so that in this novel of the Second World War, one of the tank crew aspires (and fails) to emulate this literary legacy: 'He read over some of it [his diary] but was not satisfied – it was flat and matter of fact, not at all like Siegfried Sassoon or Robert Graves.'

In contrast to the First World War, the novels of the Second World War – or certainly those written by individuals who had first-hand front line experience of that conflict – are often unfairly overlooked. *Warriors for the Working Day* is one such novel. It was written by Peter Elstob, who joined the 3rd Battalion, Royal Tank Regiment on the outbreak of the conflict. He served across a variety of theatres – including India, Iraq, Syria, Lebanon, Palestine, Egypt, Libya, France, Belgium, Holland and Germany. By all accounts quite a colourful character throughout his varied career, Elstob had previously been dismissed from the Royal Air Force after a brief five month stint in the 1930s. He then did a variety of jobs before volunteering in 1936 as a fighter pilot for the Republicans during the Spanish Civil War, where he was imprisoned in Barcelona as a suspected spy.

Warriors for the Working Day portrays the life of a tank crew during the north-west Europe campaign, from training to D-Day +5 (when the regiment leaves Aldershot), until they enter Germany. The novel reflects the reality of the situation at this stage in the war – British armour quickly stalled in Normandy, as the campaign differed from what was expected or trained for and much was 'unlearned gladly', in the words of one of the characters. The fighting continued for a long and unexpected period in the close terrain, although the armour eventually adapted to a role of providing close fire support.

The book's narrative is very closely based on Peter Elstob's own experiences as part of a tank crew. Tanks had a crew of five: a driver, a co-driver/bow machine gunner, a loader/wireless operator, a gunner and a tank commander. At the novel's opening, Paddy Donovan is the tank commander, a character based on the real Sergeant Buck Kite, who was awarded three military medals (M.M.). In the opening pages the reader learns: 'The youngsters had absolute faith in Sergeant Donovan because of his two M.M.s. They were not to know that when you got the second M. M. you were always past your best, on the slope that led to the condition called bomb-happy.' Donovan, like Buck Kite, is later awarded his third M.M. Elstob himself was Kite's radio operator, alongside Taff Evans the driver, when their tank was hit by an AP (armour piercing) shell during the battle for Caen (which features prominently in the novel). The crew bailed out. Elstob got lost but made his way back to the tank which was only slightly damaged, and drove it back to headquarters. He was promoted to command his own tank. In the novel Elstob is thinly disguised as Brook, who is depicted as in awe of Donovan, and once the older man is injured, Brook takes command of the tank. Then the story develops as he commands the tank for the remainder of the book, which features various actions in which Elstob himself was directly involved, including the advance into Germany.

Much of the novel thus concerns Brook's development as a tank commander and the necessary isolation, fear and sense of responsibility inherent in this role. Life within the tank was very precarious, as British tanks were noticeably inferior to German armour. The Sherman tank which the crew inhabit for the majority of the book (later switched to a Comet), has a tendency to catch fire when struck by German shells. These tanks were nicknamed 'Ronsons' by their crews at the time, as, similar to the advertising for the cigarette lighters, they lit 'first time, every time'. The Germans called them 'Tommy Cookers'. Although the tank is ostensibly 'home' while advancing, references throughout to burnt-out tanks, coupled with the surprising physicality of tank warfare, lend it a peculiarly claustrophobic quality and tone:

Brook was overcome by the most powerful feeling of sheer animal terror. It was as though his whole body and soul had suddenly rebelled against what he was doing and where he was. For a fraction of a second he wanted to scream and fly in panic, and only the physical impossibility of getting out of the tank stopped him.

Each tank was usually part of a troop of four tanks commanded by a lieutenant. There were four troops in a squadron (commanded by a major), and four squadrons to a regiment, which was in turn commanded by a lieutenant colonel. This is the level the novel is based at, with little mention of formations above the regiment and only occasional mention of supporting infantry. Although Field Marshal Montgomery talks about 'the part of the war they knew nothing about. He brought generals, prime ministers and kings before them, and they had a sudden inkling of the war as it would be written in the history books', service life revolves around the tank, the squadron and the regiment. Crews live in close proximity for long periods of time with little opportunity for rest, and come from all walks of life and differing parts of Britain, as is evident from their nicknames: Taffy, Geordie and so on. They are all young, except for the few remaining regular soldiers. Donovan, the old hand is 'amused… to realise that Brook and Hogg and Geordie had been only thirteen or fourteen years old when it all began'.

There is continuous banter between the men, and the novel is reminiscent of Alexander Baron's *From the City, From the Plough* in its depictions of the camaraderie – or otherwise – of army life. At the start of the book, the inexperienced Brook quickly adapts:

It was all unfamiliar to Brook, but he soon learned the unwritten rules: the abuse was kept within carefully understood limits – a man's honour, courage, honesty, truthfulness or morals could be torn to shreds with impunity, it was permissible to accuse another man of always avoiding work, to maintain that he would run like a rabbit at the sound of a pop-gun, to accuse him of lying, cheating or stealing, and no offence would be taken; but nothing could be said that reflected upon his social status, his ability to pay his share, his personal cleanliness, or his family.

Brook himself is well educated, and even considered becoming a conscientious objector at school. On his first leave home he buys a copy of a literary journal, as 'in his last year at school it was considered the mark of a Philistine not to read *Horizon*, and Brook bought it every month and tried to feel that it still had something to say to him'. Indeed 'he had been helped then by the attitude of *Horizon* to the war; here were intelligent, sensitive, and, he felt, good men, who recognised the need to kill'. His promotion to corporal and eventually to sergeant and command of his tank means that there is always a gulf between the men and him. He initially struggles with this, particularly where it concerns one of the novel's larger than life characters, the co-driver Geordie:

> *He knew now that he had to choose – either to keep his rank, or to be one of the boys; but then he knew that for him there was no choice. It was going to mean that his life in the army would be much lonelier, but there could be no question of his refusing to accept responsibility.*

However there does exist between 'Brookie' and the crew an intimacy that would not be apparent in the infantry, for example, due to the close proximity in which the men live and fight. As the story develops the reader sees the bonds between the men being both forged and broken, sometimes with shocking regularity as the advance into Normandy deepens.

Another important theme that recurs throughout the novel is the interconnectedness of the home and fighting fronts. Elstob makes the clear point that both are essential, juxtaposing the V2s dropping on Antwerp and London at the same time as the crew is fighting across the channel, resulting in a particularly poignant moment in the narrative regarding Donovan's family at home. Battle weariness also repeatedly occurs, with men and officers able to take a certain amount before fear becomes an overriding obsession. Both Donovan, Brook and several other characters suffer from it to varying degrees. Donovan tries to describe the symptoms to his wife, although they manifest themselves differently in different individuals:

> *You never know what it really is until you get it yourself. It's like something sitting on your stomach that you can't digest, that's making you feel sick and you can't be sick. You feel it in your heart – I mean your real heart in your chest. It's as though it's become separated from your body and its floating out by itself for a minute and then it's going to fall... But what's the use – you can't explain it to anyone.*

What does come across clearly is that there is only a limited time a soldier can take of being constantly in action – when that reserve is used up, battle fatigue sets in, and not even the diligent Brook is immune to it.

After the war Elstob co-ran the Arts Theatre Club but his main source of income was a beauty mask, Yeast Pac, which he and his business partner marketed. They also went on to found an artistic and writers' community in Mexico, followed by a failed balloon Atlantic crossing. Elstob wrote a number of books including novels covering his experiences during the Spanish Civil War, the story of his balloon exploits (*The Flight of a Small World*, 1959) and a number of military histories, including *Hitler's Last Offensive* (1971) about the Battle of the Bulge, which was very well received at the time.

Warriors for the Working Day is generally regarded as his greatest work. When it was originally published in 1960 it reportedly sold nearly a quarter of a million copies and was translated into five languages. This welcome reprint will make it available for another generation of readers as one of the finest fictional depictions of life in a tank during the Second World War.

Alan Jeffreys
2020

Let me speak proudly: tell the constable
We are but warriors for the working day;
Our gayness and our gilt are all besmirched
With rainy marching in the painful field:
And Time hath worn us into slovenry:
But, by the mass, our hearts are in the trim.

SHAKESPEARE: *Henry V*

BOOK ONE

FIRST LIGHT

First Light: When it is possible to distinguish
between and black and white

ONE

AS SOON AS the tanks stopped, Sergeant Donovan pulled the earphones off his head and rubbed his ears. The crackling of the wireless had given him a headache, and the pressure of the headset had made his ears ache too. He hung the headset from the open hatch, turning the earpieces towards him so that he could hear if his code letters were called. At the moment there was a lot of waffling going on between the colonel and his squadron leaders, and the regiment had come to a standstill with the tanks spread over the sandy common.

Donovan settled himself comfortably on the small saddle-like seat and propped his feet up on the circle of armour-piercing shells running round the inside of the turret. He lit a cigarette and listened for a few moments to the confusion on the wireless.

He decided there was just time for tea. 'Better get a brew on, Taffy,' he said to his driver.

He watched, as always with amusement and admiration, the swift, efficient way the four members of his crew worked together to make tea inside the tank. The petrol stove was lit and the big mess-tin filled with water, the tinned milk and the tea and sugar mixture were got out from the box that was supposed to hold spare wireless valves, the battered tin mugs were swilled out and wiped round with cleaning rag. Then the gunner spun the wheel to depress the gun fully, thus raising the breech inside the turret, to give them as much room as possible.

Sergeant Donovan absently watched the heavy gun-barrel go down until it was lying almost on top of the co-driver's escape hatch. He remembered suddenly quite clearly the time his tank was hit at Alam Halfa. He, the gunner and the wireless operator had got out of the turret all right and had waited for the driver and co-driver. The seconds had dragged by, then he had seen the hole right in front of the driver's place and at the same moment noticed that the gun was lying across the co-driver's hatch, stopping it from coming up more than three or four inches. The co-driver's arm had come out, trying to push the gun away, just before the ammunition exploded... He shut his eyes tightly.

'Traverse right!' he snapped, almost before he realised it.

Hogg, the gunner, was busy spreading cheese on biscuits, but his reaction was automatic and he spun the wheel which raised the gun and began to revolve it to the right.

'Steady... on,' Donovan said when it was pointing straight ahead, and the traversing stopped. 'All right, carry on.' He ignored the questioning look in Hogg's eyes, and after a moment the youngster went back to his cheese and biscuits.

He was pleased with the speed of Hogg's reaction. He'd got the gun traversing smoothly like an old-timer. By God, it might be possible to get these green kids sharp enough for the invasion yet – so that at least they'd stay alive through the first two or three actions. If they could do that, they stood a good chance. But this was the middle of May, and he knew there wasn't much time left.

'Isn't that brew ready yet?' he asked testily.

Taffy passed his mug up to him. 'Here you are, Paddy,' he said.

Taffy was one of the old hands from the desert days – the only one in his crew, and the only one allowed to call him Paddy. The other three were still too inexperienced to understand all that was implied by the old soldiers phrase 'On parade, on parade: off parade, off parade' – and Donovan didn't believe in rushing these things.

'What about some burgoo?' said Taffy.

Donovan gulped some of the hot, sweet liquid, warming his hands on the metal mug. 'All right,' he said. 'Have a go at it if you like, but be ready to pack it up in a hurry if we have to move.'

Taffy set about instructing the others in the niceties of making burgoo, which consisted of a mass of army biscuits dissolved in tinned milk, slowly heated in a mess-tin with treacle or plain sugar.

Donovan scanned the country around him slowly and carefully with his field-glasses, purely from habit; he knew that the Hussars, who had been the enemy on the day's scheme, were down on the Farnborough road out of sight waiting for the umpires' decision. As automatically as a sailor notices the wind and the weather, he picked out likely anti-tank gun positions and his best approach to the far ridge.

The crew were arguing about the value of the French as allies.

'You're bloody daft, mate, that's what you are – orf yer rocker,' said Geordie, the co-driver. He sat below, next to Taffy, and could only make his point to the others in the turret by twisting round and gesticulating from under their boots. 'If they was so brave,' he said, 'why did they pack up so quick in 1940, then?'

Brook, the wireless operator, started to reply. 'They were betrayed by their leaders – '

Geordie jeered.

'Betrayed by my Aunt Fanny,' he said. 'They was windy – that's what they was – windy. They seen a few Jerry tanks, and they said "Oo la la we've 'ad it", and they scarpered orf 'ome.'

'Now wait a minute,' Brook protested 'What about the holding action they fought so we could get away at Dunkirk?'

'What 'olding action? I never heard of no French fighting at Dunkirk!'

'Well that, I suggest, is because you haven't read the authoritative reports,' said Brook crushingly.

Brook, as a very new lance-corporal, was going to have to drop that superior tone, Donovan decided: that sort of tone was always resented. But all in all, Donovan was not dissatisfied with any of his own tank crew, nor with any of the others in his troop of four tanks. Most of the men were untried, but they were keen, and there was a good leavening of experienced men like Taffy. Lieutenant Grimshaw, the troop officer, was a good, steady officer who would do more than his share and look after his men – he wasn't after medals or promotion, and he and Sergeant Donovan understood each other.

'Don't blind us with science, Brookie boy,' Geordie was jeering. 'Put all them big words back.'

There was rather more annoyance in Geordie's voice than the argument warranted, and Donovan suspected it had something to do with Brook's recent promotion to acting unpaid lance-corporal. Donovan knew well that every soldier secretly hoped to find his own name in each new list of promotions. Geordie had done his basic training in the infantry, but had not been up to the required physical fitness. He had been sent to one of the new special training battalions for building up and then to the Tank Corps – so he had had longer in the army than the other new lads.

The wireless, which had been spluttering quietly in the background, cut into the talk with a call to all tanks.

Donovan replied with the conventional phrase that acknowledged both that he was listening and that he could hear clearly. The next tank to reply should have been Smudger Smith, his troop corporal, but Smudger didn't reply, and after a pause the rest of the tanks carried on. Donovan hoisted himself up and looked over towards the troop corporal's tank. Smudger was sprinting towards it holding something in his hand – eggs perhaps. Scrounging in England within a couple of miles of Aldershot barracks! – it was typical of Smudger.

There were more delays from other unwary tank commanders, and when the major came up on the air again he was fuming.

'*Hello* all stations George Able Baker – that was Christ bloody awful! Now get your fingers out and keep on your toes! I want you all – repeat *all* – reported in ninety seconds, next time! Now – *Orders* – there will be a Tank Commanders' conference at R.H.Q. in figures ten. The jeeps will be round to collect you all, so leave your boys where they are. All stations George Able Baker... *Over.*'

This time they were all waiting for it, and the replies snapped back.

'One minute and fifty seconds – that's better. Wireless silence from now – all stations George Able Baker – *Out.*'

The jeep from H.Q. arrived in a few minutes. It picked up the other three tank commanders, and then came for Donovan.

'You're in command of the Troop, Corporal Brook,' said Lieutenant Grimshaw.

'Yes, sir,' Lance-Corporal Brook replied smartly. He remembered he ought to salute, but the jeep was gone while he hesitated.

He had been acting unpaid lance-corporal for only a week, and except for a fatigue detail and twice on the barrack square he had never commanded anybody. His former close friends had not yet been able to make up their minds whether he was going to be an easy-going N.C.O. who would try not to allow the promotion to make any difference, or would move over to *their* side and so put an end to his old relationships. Brook himself was hardly conscious of the need to make such a choice; he thought his old, easy relations would continue, that he would be obeyed because he was liked.

'How about the B.B.C., Brookie? If there's wireless silence no one will call us up,' Hogg suggested.

'We're probably all right for the next fifteen minutes or so,' said Brook. He switched the 'A' set to the B.B.C. frequency, and they all settled back to listen to a Forces record programme.

Brook moved across the turret and climbed up to the commander's place, and sat there unconsciously imitating Donovan. God, how lucky he was to be in this tank, he told himself again. He had nearly burst with pride when Major 'Tommy' Johnson had sent for him after Eagle scheme and told him he was pleased with his showing and was making him wireless operator to the legendary Sergeant Donovan with the double M.M. Brook had written a long letter to his parents about it. His father had said it was a jolly good show, and Brook hoped it had made up a little bit for their disappointment when his application for a commission had been turned down. His father had been commissioned immediately in the First World War, but Brook felt that things must have been different then.

He knew the invasion would come in a few weeks now, and he wished he could discover some clues to his ability to stand up to it: Whether I am a *coward*, he said to himself, using the actual word deliberately. Up until now there had been few opportunities for him to find out. He remembered the fight during his last year at school, and how his fear had left him after the first punch on the nose, and how he had felt ill when it was all over. He wondered what would happen if he panicked completely. He couldn't get out of the tank without pushing Donovan out of the way – and that, somehow, didn't seem feasible. For a moment he pictured himself lying on the floor of the turret in sheer terror, unable to move... jamming the traverse... screaming... He pushed the scene away from him quickly.

He pulled the earphones off his head. 'I'm just going for a Jimmy Riddle – take over, will you, Hogg?' He dropped off the tank and walked towards a clump of young silver birch.

Hogg watched him go. The lance-jack tape had gone to his head, Hogg thought bitterly. If he was so damned clever why wasn't he an officer? Hogg was pretty sure that if it hadn't been for Brook with his accent and his public school, he himself would have been promoted. He'd even let his girl think he was going to be, on his last leave. Well, roll on the invasion – perhaps Brook would get killed, and he, Hogg, would get promoted. There was no limit to what could happen in action. He watched Brook sit down under the trees – dozy, that's what he was. Hogg picked up Donovan's field-glasses and scanned the hills, imagining himself coolly knocking out one German tank after another.

Vera Lynn was singing on the wireless, and they all joined in unmelodiously.

The late afternoon sun warmed the tank, and Geordie opened his hatch and climbed out to sit with his back to the turret. He scratched the scar on his forehead where the army doctors had cut his bump out. Funny now to think of how he hadn't wanted to let them do it. The medical officer had told him that it wouldn't hurt, but it hadn't been the thought of the pain that had made him refuse – for he had been beaten often enough by his mother's blokes in his time. He had known he could never tell the M.O. what his grandmother had told him about his bump. He knew it was barmy, of course – she'd said that all his brains were in it and that if he ever lost it he'd go loopy – and he couldn't explain that to the M.O., or to anyone: because he knew it couldn't be so... But just the same there was always the possibility that it was true. In the end the M.O. had bullied him into consenting to the operation, and he had gone down to the hospital in Aldershot in a state of terror. It had got progressively worse, until at the end he had fought like a wildcat against the anaesthetic. When he came round, his hand went up to his forehead and felt a flat bandage in place of the egg-sized growth he had had for so many years. Even when they took the bandage off and he saw how much better he looked he hadn't lost his resentment completely.

He thought of the tremendous changes the army had made in him. He had been called up to serve in the infantry, and on his first day he had sat on his palliasses in the barrack room with the pile of clothes given him at the quartermaster's stores and waited while all the other recruits changed from their civvies into uniform. He tried to remember the name of the bloke in the bunk next to him who had disappeared in the first few weeks to become an officer... Well, it didn't matter... But if it had been one of the others, he would probably have gone ahead and changed: but just as he was screwing up his courage, this chap had stood up in his posh underwear and held up the long woollen underpants they had been issued with, and caught Geordie's eye. 'My God!' he had said. 'They don't expect us to *wear* this, do they? It's positively shaggy. I'm not going to put it on – I shall tell them that I just can't wear wool next to the skin – it makes me scratch all day.' He had smiled in what was obviously a friendly overture, but Geordie had known then that it was impossible to strip in front of him.

He had sat there, with a slow, dumb defiance, feeling a dread at what they would do to him for refusing to obey almost the first order. The lance-corporal had asked him what the hell he was doing, and told him to get a move on, and when he had continued to sit without replying, had sent for the platoon sergeant. When Geordie had refused to answer him too, the sergeant had told him very quietly to pick up his kit and follow him. He had done so, convinced that he was going to be put in the Guard Room.

But the sergeant had taken him to his own small room and shut the door.

'Now lad, what's oop with thee?' the sergeant had said, firmly but kindly.

The familiar accent, and the obvious fact that the sergeant was someone he could recognise, had succeeded. Without a word, he had dropped his trousers and shown the sergeant the rags and newspapers tied round his legs.

'I didn't want them toffs to see,' he had said.

'There's no toffs in army, lad,' the sergeant had said. 'Only soldiers. Good 'uns and bad 'uns. You're not the first poor lad that's coom, you know, not by a long chalk. I didn't have too much moonie mysel' when I joined seven year ago. Times was bad then and I was lucky to get in. You'll say same thing when you get used to it. You can make oop parcel of your civvies and change in here and we'll post 'em home. Now hurry oop.'

The sergeant had walked out, leaving him there. Geordie had cut away the swaddling which had served to keep him warm while sleeping in the passage where his granny had a tiny room in Newcastle. Then he had pulled on the warm, unbelievably soft woollen underwear.

None of the lads had said anything to him when he walked back to the barrack room in uniform. The toff in the next bunk had been all right too, when he got to know him better. He'd given him picture magazines to look at, and once had taken a photograph of him dressed for his first guard. Geordie had posted it to his girl. And it was the toff who had talked to him about his bump. It was funny, but he hadn't minded at all when the toff talked about it, although he had always been ready to fight before. The toff told him that taking it off was a simple matter, and pointed out that it wouldn't cost him anything in the army.

'You'll probably have a Harley Street specialist or two do it for you, old boy,' he had said. Geordie had thought it over for a few days and had then asked the sergeant about it.

'Better see M.O., lad – that's what he's there for. If he says have it off, you do it.'

The M.O. hadn't asked him about it at all, but sent him to the hospital. After it was all over and he was ready for discharge the hospital doctor had told him that he was undernourished and underweight and probably couldn't stand up to the hard life in the infantry and they were sending him to be built up. Geordie had thought it was nonsense, but it sounded like a holiday.

In three months the food and exercise in the special battalion had put two stone on him. The P.T. instructors taught him unarmed combat, and when he went home for his first leave he felt like the bloke in the muscle-building advertisements who surprises everyone who used to push him around. He had gone to his granny, who, as much as anyone, had brought him up. He had given her a couple of quid which made him feel good.

His granny had told him that his mother had moved in with a chap that worked on the docks sometimes, and he had gone to see her. She was still in her dressing-gown, although it was three o'clock in the afternoon. She was not quite drunk – not as drunk as he had seen her, that is. They had quarrelled fiercely before he had left to join the army, but she seemed to have forgotten that and greeted him boisterously and told him that he was looking wonderful. She'd given him a Guinness, and then her bloke had come in.

'It's my son,' she'd said quickly.

'Oh, is it?' He was a big unpleasant-looking man, and he had glared at Geordie. 'Hop it,' he had said briefly.

His mother told him nervously that he'd better go, and he'd left. Most of his day-dreams since revolved about a scene in which he rescued his mother from drink and the docker, knocking him arse over tip like they did in the pictures.

His girl, Lillian, had been very impressed with the changes in him and obviously eager to hang on to him. With his pocket full of money for the first time in his life and the self-confidence of his uniform she had been easy. She struggled and scratched him and pulled his hair but she couldn't stop him, and as soon as it was too late to matter anymore she stopped trying and put her arms round his neck. Afterwards she had clung to him crying bitterly while he tried to comfort her. He swore that he would marry her, and he had meant it at the time.

Now he wasn't so sure. He'd been sort of promoted when they'd put him in the Tanks instead of the Infantry. He wasn't the same poor sod he'd been when he joined, he told himself – not knowing nothing, and scared to talk to a girl what worked in a shop or maybe didn't have to work at all. He'd been about a bit now; there was a girl in Farnborough whose dad worked in an office in London. She'd been pleased enough to go to the pictures with him and she hadn't said no to a bit of kissing and a feel or two either. After all, Lillian was ignorant and uneducated, and she wasn't improving herself like what he was. If he came through this lot all right, and he felt pretty sure that he would, then he'd wait a bit before making up his mind about marriage. Perhaps he'd travel a bit. Australia or even the States? Why not? Other blokes had done it, and what they could do, he could do.

He saw himself in New York driving a big car with some sort of a well-paid job. Or California. Hollywood.

A shout from Sandy, the troop officer's wireless operator, warned the other tanks that they were being called. Hogg shouted for Brook and then jumped into the turret and flicked over to the regimental frequency.

'... Sugar Able Baker over.' The major's operator had obviously asked for a reception report before he passed any message in order to give them all an opportunity to get on frequency. Brook clambered up on the turret in time to answer, and when all tanks were netted in, the order came.

'... Bring all your boys down here. Over.'

'Wilco out.' Brook felt tremendously excited at the prospect of leading four tanks down the road and over to the rest of the regiment.

'O.K., pack up, lads,' he said. Unconsciously he was imitating Sergeant Donovan's voice, and the others grinned. 'We've got to go down and join the rest. Get everything cleared up and put away and let's get weaving. Geordie – get the mess-tins and primus cleaned up.'

'It's not my turn,' said Geordie sourly.

'Whose turn is it, then?'

As soon as he had said it, Brook realised that that was a mistake.

'Yours,' said Geordie. Hogg giggled.

'Well, do it anyway.'

Brook tried to make his voice sound stern.

'B set for control,' he shouted to the other tanks, and the wireless operators nodded to show that they understood. He switched over to the special B set which had a range of only a thousand yards and was used for a few tanks in close contact with each other.

Geordie was sitting undisturbed in his co-driver's seat, and Brook saw he wasn't going to obey the order.

'Geordie.'

Geordie looked up at him.

'Get out and get those things, do you hear?'

'I got a name for lance-jacks to call me by,' Geordie said. 'My *friends* call me Geordie.'

'Here, I'll get the beggars,' said Taffy in disgust. He started to climb out of the driver's seat.

Brook stopped him. 'No, you won't. Get back in the tank.'

Taffy looked at him for a moment, and then got back.

'All right. Brunch, I'm giving you an order – get out of the tank.'

'Trooper Brunch,' Geordie muttered. But he got out of the tank.

'March round to the back of the tank and pick up the mess-tins and the primus.'

Geordie slouched round and picked them up.

'Scrape out the mess-tin with the spoon.'

Geordie stroked the caked biscuit mess once or twice.

'Stow them on the back and get back into your seat.'

Geordie pushed the two things under the tank sheet and got back into his seat with a triumphant leer at Taffy and Hogg.

'I'm putting you on a charge,' Brook said. 'Advance, Taffy.'

'I did it, didn't I?' Geordie grumbled. 'You can't put me on a fizzer.'

In a few minutes they came up to the rest of the tanks. The sergeant-major waved them to the back of the queue and came over to them.

'Smart bit of work that,' said the sergeant-major approvingly to Brook. As this was almost the first normal sentence the sergeant-major had ever addressed to him, Brook was rather at a loss.

'Thanks, Sergeant-Major,' he said. 'But it wasn't far.'

'Wasn't far?' The sergeant-major seemed puzzled. 'I mean your troop catching the Hussars with their slacks down this afternoon – the umpires gave us six tanks destroyed.' He looked closely at Brook. 'What did you think I meant?'

Unable to pass off the situation, Brook said miserably, 'I thought you meant my getting the tanks down here.'

'Oh.' The sergeant-major put his hand up to his mouth. 'Oh, yes. That was pretty smart too,' he said, and earned Brook's devotion. He turned to go.

'... Sergeant-Major,' said Brook. 'Just a minute, sir.'

'Yes?'

'I want to put Brunch on a charge, sir.'

'All right. Come and see me about it when we get back tonight.' He walked away.

No one in the tank spoke. Brook felt he had suddenly lost their sympathy. He sat on top of the turret, determined to make no concessions to them, and feeling very much alone.

Soon the tank commanders came back.

'Well, we won that battle anyhow,' said Donovan wryly. 'I wish they were all like that. Back to barracks, Taffy.'

Taffy had started up and swung out into the road without waiting for orders; Hogg had elevated the gun to the proper travelling position, and Brook was checking the wireless. They were good lads, Donovan told himself again. And in some ways it wasn't a bad thing that they were so inexperienced. If he'd had a whole crew of veterans they'd have indulged in time-honoured pessimistic forecasts about the coming invasion – and he knew that in his present state he couldn't take much of that. As it was, there was an unspoken understanding between him and Taffy to let them keep some of their illusions of invulnerability for a while. The youngsters had absolute faith in Sergeant Donovan because of his two M.M.s. They were not to know that when you got the second M.M. you were nearly always past your best, on the slope that led to the condition called bomb-happy.

Donovan had often been frightened, as had very nearly everyone he'd known, certainly all the best ones. At first his control had been exceptionally good and he'd never brought the fear back with him when they pulled out. He'd probably earned his first M.M. as much as most earned them. He'd certainly been very pleased to get it, and for a little while had had dreams of a V.C., but that had soon worn off. After three years of tank warfare he was still a first-rate tank commander, but it had become the automatic response of his training and experience. He found that now he was thinking more and more of staying alive, with the growing conviction that he wasn't going to. He was no longer able to leave his fear up at the sharp end, but took it back with him to keep him awake in his tent at night. In North Africa, Rommel's surrender had come none too soon for him; he knew he wouldn't have lasted much longer. They'd made him a troop sergeant, and while the regiment was waiting for orders outside Tunis the other M.M. had come along. He had been surprised, but it wasn't the first time a decoration had been given for no specific cause, and no one seemed to begrudge him it. He had allowed himself to boast a little to his wife when he wrote to her about it. He had felt ashamed, and told her the truth in a second letter – that he didn't know why he had got it and a number of the lads deserved it at least as much; but of course she had believed his first letter and had thought the second one was only his trying to be modest. Oh well, if it made her happy to think he was a hero it didn't do any harm... Then, to his relief, the regiment had been ordered home. They had thought it was a reward for their desert record and their casualties, but soon discovered it was for the invasion. In England a lot of the battle experienced tank crews were sent to untried regiments to stiffen them, and had been replaced by youngsters from the training battalions, like Brook and Hogg and Geordie.

It amused Donovan to realise that Brook and Hogg and Geordie had been only thirteen or fourteen years old when it all began – still in school when it had looked as though the Eyeties were going to get right through to Cairo.

The youngsters lapped up everything they were told. They took his and the other senior N.C.O.'s word as gospel. They were eager to believe that everything they had been forced to learn at the training battalion was nonsense, and in this they had been indulged a bit, out of the fighting soldier's contempt for the non-combatant instructors. It was true that along with their valuable training they had been told some arrant nonsense out of the book. They had been taught that tanks went into battle with hatches closed down and the commander peering through the periscope as though he were in a submarine; they had thought that crews wore their steel helmets inside the turret and that tanks exchanged shots like boxing blows; they had thought that the Bren gun on the turret was for shooting down dive bombers, and they had even been told how to do it; they had been taught tank warfare on the assumption that a thirty-ton tank could creep up unseen to the enemy. All these things they unlearned gladly. Now they knew that a tank with hatches closed was like a blind monster at the mercy of a fast sharp-eyed enemy, and that, dangerous as it was for the commander to keep his head out, it was not so dangerous as shutting himself in. They realised that if anything pierced their armour their steel helmets would not be of much use to them; that when a tank was hit by an armour-piercing shell those who were still alive and able to move got out fast before the next one hit it; the whole thing was as unlike a boxing match as it could be, because in a tank battle the first hit was the winning one. They learned with dismay that the dive bombers shot down by tanks could be counted on the fingers of one hand. After a few weeks they had lost a lot of their over-optimism, but had gained in its place a tremendous confidence in their experienced tank commanders.

When they got back to barracks, Brook went immediately to find the sergeant-major.

'Oh yes, Corporal Brook – now what happened with Brunch?'

Brook told him.

The sergeant-major rubbed his chin. 'You did quite right,' he said. 'Every junior N.C.O. has to make a stand sooner or later. But the good ones don't have to do it more than once or twice – in other words, you shouldn't get obeyed just because they're afraid you'll put them on a charge. Now Brunch is a difficult man, but basically he's all right. How would it be if I was to have a talk with him and we were to forget about the charge this time?'

Brook was tempted to accept the sergeant-major's offer; but he felt it was the easy way out – and besides, Geordie's not being charged might be misinterpreted by the others.

'If you don't mind, sir, I think I ought to go through with it.'

The sergeant-major looked surprised, and was evidently not pleased. 'He'll be on Squadron Leader's orders in the morning, then. Charge him under Section Forty.'

As Brook came into the barrack room the horseplay stopped.

'Brunch?'

'Corporal!' shouted Geordie in parade-ground style, coming to attention with a crash of his boots.

'You'll be on Squadron Leader's orders in the morning.'

No one spoke.

'You'd better get your kit blancoed.'

He turned and walked out.

As soon as the door shut behind him he heard the buzz of talk break out.

'I've done more jankers than he's got service,' he heard Geordie say clearly and the others laugh.

Later that evening he went to the pub where One Troop usually met. Seven or eight of them were there, and he greeted them as a body. No one replied to him. He bought his pint of beer and went over to the dart board where Hogg and Sandy, the troop officer's operator, were playing. He picked up the chalk and stood by the score slate.

'I'll take chalks,' he said. It was the customary way of getting into the next game.

'We can't have an N.C.O. working for us,' Hogg said. 'It's against regulations.'

Brook put the chalk down and walked over to the bar.

'You want a game?' said a voice beside him. It was Nobby Clarke, Corporal Smith's driver and one of the old desert rats.

'Yes, Nobby.'

'Right – we'll play after them, then. What you drinking – mild and bitter?'

When Nobby had beaten him at three games of darts they walked back to the barracks together.

'I had a tape once meself,' Nobby said casually. 'But I didn't keep it long.'

'What happened?'

'Old Smudger and me got copped trying to flog an Eyetie staff car in Cairo. Smudge got busted down to trooper and I got twenty-eight days over the wall.'

'He's quite a lad, isn't he?'

'Old Smudger? He's the greatest shitehawk what ever lived. He always gets his tapes back – he's too good a tank commander. I suppose they thought my tape was a mistake anyway.'

As they parted at the bottom of the barrack stairs, Nobby punched him gently.

'Don't let 'em get you down, Brookie boy.'

The next morning Sergeant Donovan put his head in the barrack room while they were waiting to go on parade.

'Come out here a minute, will you, Brook?' he said pleasantly.

Brook walked out, and significant looks were exchanged in the barrack room. The two of them walked down to the end of the corridor, where they could not be overheard.

'The sergeant-major tells me that you put Brunch on a charge.'

'Yes. He acted up a bit when you left yesterday – refused to obey an order, and generally tried to make me look foolish.'

'I see. Why didn't you tell me about it?'

Suddenly Brook realised that he had been guilty of a gross breach of army etiquette in not telling the troop sergeant that he had put one of the troop on a charge. He felt himself blushing deeply.

'I'm awfully sorry, Sergeant. I can't think how it happened. I just forgot.'

'Forgot?' Donovan looked at him keenly. 'You don't *forget* things like that. I'm the troop sergeant – how do you think it feels to find out that one of my men is up on a charge and I don't even know about it? The Colonel himself would have made sure I knew about it.'

Brook felt too miserable to reply. Donovan waited for a few moments, then he said, more kindly: 'We'll forget about it this time, Brook. Next time, use your head. Now, make sure you're looking smart when you go in front of the Major. He doesn't like frivolous charges. That's all.'

Brook walked round to the squadron office at nine forty-five. Geordie was already there, looking very much the old soldier in his best battledress with razor-sharp creases and his boots a dazzling black that Brook had never been able to achieve. The sergeant-major came up almost immediately and spoke to Geordie. Geordie snapped smartly to attention. The sergeant-major examined Geordie meticulously, and was evidently satisfied. He got the two clerks out of the office to act as escorts, and stood the three of them in a row. He called them to attention once or twice and then told them to stand easy. He walked away and indicated that Brook was to come up to him. Brook marched quickly over and stood to attention.

'Stand easy, Corporal.' Brook knew that he too was being inspected, though not as obviously as Geordie had been. 'You fall in on the left and follow my orders. When I say "Halt – Right Turn", I want you about an arm's length from the escort so that you'll be standing half left from the squadron leader. Have you got that?'

'Yes, sir.'

'Right. Go and fall in with the others, then.'

The four of them stood together in silence.

After a few moments the sergeant-major came out of the office. 'Atten-shun! Left Turn! Quick March! Right Wheel! Hat Off!' He whipped off Geordie's beret as they marched quickly into the office. 'Mark time.'

The four soldiers marked time in front of the squadron leader's desk, raising their knees grotesquely high.

'Halt. Right Turn.'

They were now in a row, facing the desk, with Geordie directly opposite the squadron leader and Brook at one side.

'78351245 Trooper Brunch,' said the squadron leader in a quiet voice.

'Sir!'

'You are charged that whilst on active service you did behave in a manner prejudicial to the maintenance of good order and discipline in that you did, 1, refuse to obey an order given to you by your superior officer until it had been repeated three times, and 2, you replied in an impertinent and disrespectful manner. Do you plead Guilty or Not Guilty?'

'Guilty, sir.'

'Tell me what happened, Corporal Brook.'

'Sir! On the fourteenth of the fifth nineteen forty-four at about six fifteen p.m. I ordered the accused, Trooper Brunch, to get out of the tank and pick up the mess-tin and primus stove. He replied that it was not his turn. I ordered him to do it anyway and he still did not obey. I then ordered him the third time and this time he obeyed.' Brook had memorised the words, but he was glad to get them out without stumbling.

'What have you got to say, Brunch?'

'Nothing, sir.'

'Why did you refuse to obey an order?'

'I thought it was the Corporal's turn to put the stuff away, sir.'

'What do you mean – the Corporal's turn? If you are ordered to do something you do it. Just because the corporal or the tank commander or your troop officer sometimes choose to do certain tasks themselves doesn't mean that you have a right to demand that they do it. How long have you been in the Army?'

'Eighteen months, sir.'

'Well, you're not a recruit any longer, and you know better than that, don't you?'

'Yes, sir.'

'What about the second part of the charge, Corporal Brook?'

For a moment Brook's mind went completely blank, as he struggled to remember the second part of the charge. He must have looked panic-stricken, for the squadron leader repeated it. Brook tried to remember what Geordie had said that seemed impertinent and disrespectful, but he could remember nothing.

'Well, Corporal?' The squadron leader sounded annoyed. 'What did he say?'

'I don't remember, sir.'

'You don't remember?' There was silence in the room for some seconds. 'Do you want to withdraw that part of the charge then?'

'I think I had better, sir.'

'All right. Now you, Brunch. You have admitted refusing to obey an order, which is one of the most serious crimes you can be charged with, and one that can get you a court martial. I don't care what you think about the order, nor who gives it to you – you will obey it immediately, without argument, and without lip. If after you have obeyed it you have any complaint, you know what the proper channels are for making it. As you did obey the order in the end, and because I haven't had any trouble with you before, I will this time take a lenient view; but if I ever get you up before me again on this sort of charge I'll see that you find out just how unpleasant a place the Army can be. Reprimanded. March him out, Sergeant-Major. Corporal Brook to remain here.'

Brook remained standing at attention while the sergeant-major roared out the commands that took them outside. He heard 'Hat on... Dis-miss!' Then the sergeant-major came back.

'Stand at ease, Corporal,' said the squadron leader.

'Now, you got exceptionally high marks on your cadre course, and I had hopes that you might prove to be one of my more responsible N.C.O.s in time; but this demonstration has made me wonder if I'm wrong. In this squadron, putting a man on a charge is a serious thing: and I do not expect my N.C.O.s – even the most junior – to use it to lend weight to their authority except in the most necessary circumstances. I expect you to handle men so that it is almost never necessary to put them on a charge. Do you understand?'

'Yes, sir.'

'All right. You may go.'

Brook marched out into the air, and drew a deep breath. He tried to think where he had gone wrong, but it seemed that what had happened had proceeded inevitably from the circumstances. He realised that he had expected obedience founded on something personal, and that the essence of the system was that it must be impersonal. He knew now that he had to choose – either to keep his rank, or to be one of the boys; but then he knew that for him there was no choice. It was going to mean that his life in the army would be much lonelier, but there could be no question of his refusing to accept responsibility.

TWO

ON THE FIRST Monday in June Brook drew a forty-eight-hour leave. He knew that he ought to go home, that his parents would be hurt if he didn't, that Jennie would expect to see him again if possible; but he had told them all last time that it was unlikely he would be able to get home again before the invasion, and he preferred to leave it at that. Anyway, he thought, he had often promised himself a holiday alone in London.

At the station he bought a copy of *Horizon*. In his last year at school it was considered the mark of a Philistine not to read *Horizon*, and Brook bought it every month and tried to feel that it still had something to say to him. At school he had been much attracted to the principle of Conscientious Objection, and his final decision to obey his call-up had not been an easy one. He had been helped then by the attitude of *Horizon* to the war; here were intelligent, sensitive, and, he felt, good men, who recognised the need to kill.

He still sometimes felt that perhaps he had not had the moral strength to take the hard, unpopular way: but having made his choice, he allowed himself no reservations. He had an uneasy feeling that a clever pacifist would make short work of his own carefully constructed case – which was, simply, that this war was an exception; that if there was a situation which he would honestly rather die than accept (and he had decided that Nazi domination was such a situation) then it was right to recognise the necessity of killing. But, because of his youth, he still had misgivings. Mixed in with his doubts about his physical courage were others, about his ability to maim and kill when ordered to.

Just before the train was due to start the carriage door opened and a white pigskin bag was thrust at him. He took it, and then another. They were followed by a young, pretty woman clutching a third. The train started before she could sit down, and she lurched against him. He helped her stack the suitcases on the rack above. She thanked him, and sat in the opposite corner. There was no one else in the carriage.

He settled down to attack *Horizon*, but after the first few pages his attention wandered. He raised his eyes until he could see over the magazine.

She had long slim legs, very smart shoes with unbelievably high heels, and expensive-looking silk stockings of a sheerness hardly ever seen in that fifth year of the war. She was holding her newspaper high and he couldn't see her face, and this emboldened him to examine the lines of her body more closely than he would otherwise have dared. It was a warm day and she had put her light summer coat on the rack and was wearing only a yellow dress. There was a line across her thigh made by the top of her stockings, and a little bump where it was attached to her suspender belt. Although she was slim, her hips seemed rather large, and there was a slight roundness about her belly like the nudes in the Art section of the encyclopaedia at home. By slumping slowly in his seat he could see under her folded paper to where her breasts were clearly defined. At that moment she put down the paper and looked at him with a half smile.

In complete confusion he began to stammer something quite incomprehensible, but she interrupted him.

'If you've finished with your magazine, may I look at it?' she said.

Without a word he handed it over. She offered him her paper, and he took it, immersing himself in it immediately.

In a few minutes she put the magazine down.

'Have you been in the army long?' she said.

He told her how long, and where and what he did. He talked, and seemed to go on talking, and a few minutes later – or so it seemed – they were pulling in to Waterloo.

'Can I help you with your bags?' he said. 'Are you going on somewhere else?'

'Yes – I'm going on to the United States.' He showed his surprise and she laughed. 'But not until tomorrow – I'm staying in London for tonight. You can carry my cases to a taxi, if you like.'

There was a long queue for taxis, and it moved slowly, giving him time to summon up his courage. He felt the seven pounds nine shillings in his pocket. Just as they reached the front of the queue, he plunged.

'Could you... I mean would you... have lunch with me?'

She looked at him squarely, and he felt that he was ridiculously young and she immeasurably old.

She said: 'On one condition.'

'Any condition.'

'I know you're not paid very much in the army, and I'll only come if you let me pay half.'

He protested that he had plenty of money, but she was adamant. She told him to meet her at Claridges Causerie at a quarter to one.

He spent the morning walking round central London. He had intended to spend several hours in the National Gallery, but it seemed to have lost its attraction. He looked up Claridges in the telephone book and in his street map, and at about twelve o'clock began to walk there. It was just on half past when he arrived. He walked down one side of the building, wondering whether the main entrance was the one for the Causerie or whether there was another way in. He turned into Davies Street and saw the sign. He decided he would look foolish hanging about outside the door, so he walked up Grosvenor Street, past what seemed hundreds of American soldiers, and back again. By that time it was twenty to one. Just as he was about to set off again a taxi drew up, and she got out.

'You're early,' she said. 'How nice. I was just going in to make myself pretty for you.'

He knew he ought to make some gallant reply, but by the time he had composed a suitable sentence, the moment had passed, and she was walking ahead of him, obviously expecting him to follow.

He thought they would be greeted by a head waiter and shown to a place, and he had made up his mind to object if they were put at a small out-of-the-way table: he must show her that he was not completely inexperienced. But there were no waiters in sight. In the middle of the room was a huge circular table covered with dishes full of strange things. The rest of the room was filled with small tables, some already occupied. He was very conscious of the red tabs of some young staff officers. It occurred to him that it might be Out of Bounds to Other Ranks, like some of the hotels in Aldershot. But she was already at the mass of food, and had picked up a plate from a pile.

'Do you like Smörgäsbord?' she said. She indicated that he should take a plate too.

'I've never had it.'

'Well, there's quite a choice, and you're bound to like some of it. Try those little sausages and that red stuff. It's beetroot and apples.' They moved round the table, putting what he thought was an enormous amount of food on their plates, then sat down at one of the small tables.

'I'm going to have a Pimm's,' she said brightly. 'What about you?'

'I'll have a beer.' He rose to go to the bar he had just noticed at the end of the room.

She put a hand on his arm. 'There's a waiter to get the drinks – I expect the bar's too small. But a beer doesn't sound very exciting. Why don't you have a Pimm's? – they make delicious ones here.'

'All right,' he said, wondering what he was letting himself in for.

The Pimm's, served in half-pint pewter beer mugs, tasted rather like the fruit punch his mother made in the summer, except that it was ice cold and there was a certain astringency his mother's punch never had.

'It's awfully nice, but not very strong,' he said.

'I think you'll find it strong enough,' she smiled. 'Now – tell me your name. Do you realise we've been calling each other "you" up to now?'

'Michael Brook.'

'My name's Julia. Julia Henderson. Mrs Julia Henderson to be precise.'

'Where's your husband?' he asked, then realised it sounded gauche.

She laughed. 'He's an instructor in the United States – I've finally wangled to go and join him.'

They spent an hour and a half over lunch, and had three Pimm's each. When he tried to stand up he found they were rather stronger than they tasted. The room seemed to slope, and he gripped on to the table. He was aware that she was paying the bill, and he tried to protest.

'Oh, we can settle that up later,' she said casually. 'Come on, or we'll be late.' She took his arm and steered him outside into a waiting taxi.

'Late for what?'

'God knows, darling, late for life – late for anything.'

He sat back in the taxi and closed his eyes, but that was worse. He hoped he wasn't going to be sick.

'How old are you?' she said.

'Twenty – practically twenty-one.'

She laughed. 'You're sweet. I'm thirty-five – nearly old enough to be your mother.'

'Some mother,' he giggled foolishly, groping for her. She took his wrist firmly and placed it in his lap.

'I'm sorry,' he said solemnly.

'You're squiffy, my boy. Where are you staying?'

'The Union Jack Club.'

'But isn't that rather dull? I'm at a little hotel just the other side of Oxford Street. It's only twenty-five bob a night – why don't you stay there?'

'S'marvellous idea,' he said enthusiastically.

When they walked in the woman at the desk looked up and smiled.

'Oh, you found your cousin all right, Mrs Henderson?'

'Yes,' Julia said cheerfully. 'He was there right on time. Have you got the room?'

'Yes, number twenty-three – just down the corridor from you.' She handed over a key. 'You will remember to sign the register, won't you Mr...'

'Brook,' said Julia. 'Michael Brook. You'd better sign it now, Mike.'

Brook signed his name and army address, and followed her meekly upstairs. The room was small, but very light, and the bed looked comfortable.

'Haven't you any luggage?' Julia asked. 'Not even a toothbrush?'

'Yes. I've got it in my battledress pocket – this one. It's supposed to be for a field dressing, but a toothbrush and razor and things just fit.'

'That really is travelling light.' She stood in the open doorway. 'Well, I expect you want a wash. I know I do. Come along to my room when you're ready. I'm in twenty-eight.' She shut the door.

Brook sat down on his bed and closed his eyes. The room was still a little unsteady, but it wasn't as bad as it had been. He laid his washing things out on the shelf, took off his battledress blouse, and splashed water over his head. After he had dried himself and drunk a glass of water he felt much better.

He was very pleased with his adventure. It was turning out almost exactly as he had often imagined it. Except, of course, that she was thirty-five, and married. She had been extraordinarily kind to him. It was wonderful how she had known instinctively that she was safe with him. He would have to warn her, though, that she should be more careful about inviting men she met on trains to come to her hotel. Some of them might take advantage of her kindness. He put that picture from him sternly. He dressed, and walked briskly along the corridor and knocked at the door of twenty-eight.

'Who is it?'

'Brook,' he said. 'Mike.'

'Oh. Just a minute.' She opened the door and glanced casually along the corridor. 'Come in. I've just had a shower. You *were* quick.'

'Er... shall I come back a bit later?'

'No, of course not. Come in, silly.'

She was wearing a bright blue silk dressing-gown. He stood awkwardly in her room, which was much larger and better furnished than his.

'Sit down,' she said. 'No, not in the chair on top of my things.' He jumped up as though he had sat on a needle, and she laughed. 'On the bed. Here – do you want to read the paper? Oh, of course, you read it in the train. Well, you'll just have to wait while I get dressed. I won't be a minute.'

She picked up the little pile of underwear from the chair and went into the bathroom. He carefully kept his eyes from the half-open door. She appeared again almost immediately and came over to him and reached behind him for her small suitcase.

She seemed to be having difficulty with the lock. A little gold key wouldn't turn. She was half leaning across the bed and had one knee on it. The blue dressing-gown was caught under her knee, but half of it followed the line of her body and it separated at the opening. He saw that her upper leg was a deep tan.

He felt a tightening of his throat and chest which seemed to prevent his breathing deeply. He knew now that she wanted him to make love to her: but for the moment his muscles seemed paralysed.

'Here – you try,' she said, handing him the key.

He took it and tried to put it in the lock, but his hand was shaking so badly he couldn't get it in.

'I can't do it,' he said, and hardly recognised his own voice. They looked at each other for a few seconds, and then he clutched her, pressing his face to her breasts.

'Wait a minute, wait a minute,' she said gently, and moving away from him went to the door and locked it. She crossed quickly to the windows and drew the blackout curtains.

The room was in almost complete darkness. He felt the bed give under her weight, and he pulled her to him again and kissed her.

'Get your things off,' she whispered, and now her voice too was hoarse.

He struggled with his heavy army boots, and got off his gaiters and socks. There seemed to be more buttons than he had ever noticed, but he pulled off his things and turned to her. She had thrown back the covers and was lying naked in the bed.

'Wait a minute,' she said. 'You're too excited. Calm down. Please, Mike. It's much better if you do, Mike!'

But he was quite incapable of waiting.

When he woke she was sitting up in bed with the reading light on, smoking a cigarette. He rolled over and looked at her.

'I'm sorry,' he said.

She ran her fingers through his hair. 'Was that the first time?'

'Yes.'

'Well, never mind.' She kissed him softly. 'It'll be better tonight.'

Next morning when he woke she was sleeping deeply beside him. He looked at her little jewelled wrist-watch and saw that it was just seven o'clock. His waking time in the army had already become a habit. He slipped quietly out of bed and pulled on his battledress.

There was no noise in the corridor, and he opened the door and got quickly back to his own room.

Deciding he didn't want any more sleep, he washed and dressed and went out into the early morning streets. There were a few people about, all hurrying even at this early hour. He got to Oxford Street and walked along it looking in the shop windows. Outside Bond Street Underground station there was a small crowd of people, and he crossed over to see what was happening. He got on the outside of the crowd, and saw they were all buying newspapers. He pushed his way to the centre, where a frenzied little paper seller was trying to deal with the rush of trade. He put a penny in his hand and got out of the crowd again. When he was clear of them he opened the paper. There were only two words on it, in huge letters: 'WE INVADE.'

His first feeling was one of guilt. He pictured the regiment already on the road to the coast and a blank place in his tank. He knew that wasn't the case, but he thought the invasion might mean his leave pass was automatically cancelled.

In the Underground station there were a number of telephones. Without much difficulty he got on to the regimental Orderly Room. He asked to speak to the orderly officer.

'Orderly Officer speaking.'

'My name is Brook, sir, Lance-Corporal Brook of A Squadron, and I'm in London on a forty-eight-hour pass.'

'Yes?'

'Well I was wondering if I should come back, sir.'

'Come back? Why? – Oh I see – the invasion. No, you don't have to come back before your leave's up – I think they're getting along quite nicely without you, Corporal.'

He bought copies of all the papers and carried them back to the hotel. He knocked on Julia's door, and a sleepy voice said 'Come in.'

'It's on!' he said, and couldn't keep the excitement out of his voice.

'Damn,' she said, scanning the headlines. 'They might have waited a few days – I hope this doesn't mean my passage is off.' She lit a cigarette. 'I suppose you're glad?'

'It's what we've been waiting for – for so long!'

'Is it?' She sounded weary. 'All right, little boy, go off to your damned war.'

At the barracks there was an air of intense and controlled excitement, and a dozen conflicting rumours. They had been given five days to get ready to move on one hour's notice. This meant five days of concentrated work, for many of the tanks had not finished the waterproofing necessary if they were to make the run ashore from the landing craft to the Normandy beaches.

Every crack, up to an imaginary line around the belly of the tank, had to be filled with a black, sticky substance which soon got in their hair and their mouths and ingrained in their pores. So that the engines could continue to draw in air and expel the exhaust gases a large foghorn-shaped bit of metal was welded on the back to clear the water. The driver and co-driver were to be sealed in their compartments in case the water proved deeper than expected.

The whole troop was working, and Brook had been put by Sergeant Donovan to work with Geordie sealing up every small crack in the 'breathers'.

It had been three weeks since the scheme and Geordie's charge; during that time Geordie had given no trouble, and Brook had been particularly careful not to give him any reason to feel victimised, but at the same time he made sure that Geordie did his work. Geordie, after a day or two of suspicion, had accepted the new situation. Brook was pretty sure that Donovan had deliberately put the two of them to work together on terms of equality to get rid of any bad blood there might be remaining.

'Do you want to take the scraper or the brush, Geordie?' he said.

'It's all the same to me,' said Geordie.

'Well, I'll start with the scraper and we'll switch about.'

They worked quietly together until the tea break, and then walked over to the Naffy with the rest of the troop. Geordie shoved his way into the queue.

'Tea and a wad, Brookie?' he said over his shoulder. It was the first time he hadn't called him Corporal – with emphasis – since the charge. Brook nodded, and Geordie brought the two mugs of tea and heavy slabs of yellow cake over to his table. Brook handed over the coppers for his, and Geordie pocketed them.

In the Sergeants' Mess, Donovan sipped his tea and listened to Sergeant Brass holding forth about the stupidity of unloading tanks into the water.

'How do they know how deep the water is?' said Sergeant Brass, in the voice that always sounded as though he was on the parade ground and in a rage with some awkward recruit. He had had nine years in the cavalry, and thoroughly disapproved of tanks. He was round, red-faced, as hard as saddle leather. 'The water can't be the same depth all over. It's four or five feet deep at one place and ten or twenty a few yards away. Some of our tanks'll go off and right down and I wouldn't want to be no poor sod of a driver sealed in, neither...'

Donovan finished his tea and walked outside. He knew that Gee-gee was talking arrant nonsense, but he was too jumpy to allow himself to listen to it. Ever since he had heard the calm, measured voice of the announcer on the radio he had known that he couldn't face a German 88-millimetre gun again. He had been unable to sleep since he heard the news, and he knew that only the unaccustomed activity of the regiment explained why his state hadn't been noticed. He didn't know what to do about it. The medical officer, whom he knew well from the desert, had a reputation for toughness – for him, a man didn't crack until he was unable to stand up. He hesitated to go to the squadron leader. He had known Tommy Johnson since he was a troop officer, and they respected each other, but Tommy had as much on his plate as any man could handle, and Donovan didn't want to add to his worries. Nevertheless his nerves were getting worse: something must be done about it.

After lunch, when he saw that the troop were working well, he spoke to Lieutenant Grimshaw. 'Do you mind if I go off for about half an hour?' he said.

Grimshaw looked at him but asked no questions. 'Go ahead, Paddy,' he said.

31

Donovan caught up with Major Johnson walking briskly back from R.H.Q.

'If you're not too busy, I'd like a few words with you, sir.'

Major Johnson was about to say that he was indeed too busy; then he remembered that Donovan was the last man to waste his time.

'All right, Paddy, what is it?' He slowed down and they walked along together. For a few moments nothing was said. At last Donovan squeezed the words out.

'I've had it, Tommy, I've had it!'

The major stopped by a huge First World War tank sitting in a square of whitewashed stones.

'Let's inspect Milly,' he said.

They stepped over a whitewashed low rope fence and stood against the tank.

'Have a cigarette... Now, how long have you been feeling like this?'

'I couldn't have gone on much longer in Tunis.'

'You're not the only one, you know.'

'I know – I thought it would pass like it has before, but this time it's got worse. There's thousands of blokes who could go in my place. I've had enough.'

'There's not thousands of blokes with your experience, and you know it. Christ, Paddy, we *all* feel windy – you know that, but it's all right when you actually get in.'

'I know, but this time it's different. If you've never felt it you can't know what I mean. But I *know* that I can't go in again – it isn't that I *won't*, it's that I *can't*. I'm sorry, but that's the way it is.'

The major looked sharply at him and then away. For a half a minute neither of them spoke. Donovan felt a tremendous relief at having got it out.

'We've got about five days or a week yet, Paddy. I'm going to send you home on Compassionate Leave – you'll have to cook up a dying relative or something, because I'm not supposed to let anyone away. Have a few days at home with your wife and the kids, and I'll have a telegram sent when I want you. How is Annie, by the way?'

'She's fine, thanks.'

'Good – well, give her my regards, Paddy. You can leave this afternoon.'

'All right. Thanks.' Donovan decided to take the leave and simply send word that he was ill and unable to come. He'd get into his bed and refuse to get up. Perhaps that was what Tommy was suggesting. For the benefit of any of the troops who might be watching he came smartly to attention and saluted.

'Your pass will be in the squadron office,' Major Johnson said, returning the salute.

Donovan packed a few of his personal things in his haversack and went to find his troop officer.

'I've got a couple of days compassionate leave, sir,' he said. Lieutenant Grimshaw looked surprised.

'How did you wangle that?' he asked. 'Sorry – I hope it isn't anything serious?'

'No sir – just a scrounge.'

'Good show – get one for me while you're about it. Well, I expect Corporal Smith can manage things all right. Don't forget to come back, will you?' He laughed.

Donovan walked to the office where the squadron sergeant-major handed him his pass. 'I don't know how you do it,' said the sergeant-major admiringly. 'I swear to Christ I don't. I wish it was me – only I might not come back.' And he too laughed.

Donovan came up out of the Underground at Hammersmith station, as he used to do when he was working as a joiner in the furniture factory before the war. He stopped at the Irish house where he was known, for a Guinness. The publican's wife looked surprised to see him.

'We all thought you must be in France by now,' she said, drawing his pint before he asked for it. 'You always seem to be in the thick of it.' She called her husband from the other end of the bar. He shook Donovan's hand warmly.

He drank his Guinness and smacked his lips, but in fact it didn't taste as good as usual. He told them he'd drop in for another later, and went out. When the door shut behind him the publican turned to two of his regulars who worked in an aircraft factory.

'Double M.M., that bloke – he's knocked out more Jerry tanks than you could count.'

They pushed their glasses forward to be filled.

'He can have his medals,' said one. 'Give me a quiet life.'

'Too bloody true,' said the other.

Donovan slowly walked the quarter of a mile or so to his house. He hadn't had time to let Annie know he was coming, but with the kids to get into bed she'd be bound to be home. He lived on the third floor of an old house that had been converted into flats before the war. With rent control it had not been worthwhile for the landlord to spend any money on it; he had always been able to plead that materials and labour were unobtainable anyway. The whole street was looking very shabby.

He let himself in, and trying to shake off his low spirits, shouted a hello for Annie and the kids.

Young Michael got to him first. He was five years old, snub-nosed, stocky, and looked ridiculously like his father. His mother had made him a pair of short trousers from some old ones of Donovan's and they were held up by braces that were too big for him. He looked like a miniature man, held in Donovan's arms. Kathleen, the seven-year-old, and Annie, came running to him next. Everybody spoke at once. He walked into the little living-room with a child sitting on each arm. He dropped them on the old corduroy sofa, which gave out a great cloud of dust.

'Now be quiet a minute, you two,' Annie said. 'Pat, what is it? Is there anything wrong?'

'No, of course not. They don't need us right away, that's all, so we're getting a few days at home first.'

'Oh, thank God. It's marvellous. What a surprise.' She kissed him, then shrieked, 'There's nothing to eat in the house and I bet you're starved!'

'No, I'm not. Come on, sit down and relax. We'll go out for some fish and chips later.'

'I want to come,' both children said at once.

'No, not tonight,' Donovan knew they would be bitterly disappointed, but he wanted to get them to bed so that he could be alone with Annie. 'Perhaps tomorrow night, though.'

'Come on, you two,' Annie said, and led them protesting away.

Donovan stretched his legs out in front of him and took off his web belt. He wished he had thought to buy a couple of quarts of beer at the pub. He got up and crossed to the window. It needed cleaning. The evening was grey and gloomy, and although it was only half past seven and the sun wouldn't set for some hours, there was so much cloud that it looked like a dull autumn day instead of high summer. The street seemed particularly forlorn, and the houses opposite old and decrepit. The gap in the row where the bomb had fallen four years before was overgrown with weeds. Eleven people had been killed in that house, and Annie and he hadn't known any of them although they had been living there for three years then. He had wanted Annie to go and live in the country for the duration, but she had firmly refused. In the worst of the bombing she and the two children had slept down in Hammersmith Underground station. She had steadfastly refused to leave. He had managed to get her to spend one summer with his mother in Ireland, and he had rather hoped his mother would persuade her to stay, but it hadn't worked out that way. Now he was glad; the bombing seemed over, and they still had their home. He had been able to see much more of her and the children since he had returned from the Middle East than he would have been able to if she had been in the little village in Cork.

He pulled the blackout curtains and switched on the light. Of the three bulbs in the standard lamp only one lit. The lamp had been one of their first pieces of furniture. The pink celluloid of the shade was cracked, and many of the glass beads of the fringe were missing. The fluted metal of the stand had become tarnished and it was wobbly at the base. He moved the bulbs round and found they were all right; the fault was in the wiring. He decided to dismantle the whole thing the next day and rewire it. He'd clean it up, too. He sat in his chair next to the radio, and after some searching found the *Radio Times*. There was nothing on that he wanted to listen to, but he left it on the Forces programme anyway, filling the flat with dance music.

Annie poked her head into the room. 'Put it down a bit till the kids get to sleep,' she said. 'I'll just ask Mrs Smith to keep an eye on them, then we can go out.'

He realised he should have bought an evening paper. In the old days he always had a glass of beer and a look at the paper when he got home at night while Annie was getting his supper on the table.

He prowled about the room. On the mantelpiece were several photographs. There was one of himself. He remembered having it taken in Cairo when he had first got his sergeant's rank. The stripes had been chalked, and they glared white in the photograph. He looked young and keen. He remembered it was at the beginning of the leave, before he went to the birkha with the boys and drank that foul Cyprus brandy and paid a small fortune to the rough old whore who had told him she was French. He remembered the four of them walking back to Cairo in the dawn without a penny among them. Now two of them were dead.

'Pat?'

He turned to see Annie looking at him with a little frown.

'Do you really feel like going out?' she said. 'I've got a kipper, and there's some rice pudding.'

'No – let's go and have a couple of beers and some fish and chips.' He tried to sound light-hearted. 'We can celebrate a bit of unexpected leave.'

In the pub they went to the saloon bar. The publican's wife came out to wait on them herself, exchanging a few commonplaces with Annie: she liked Annie, and she only saw her when Donovan was on leave. They knew two or three other people in the bar slightly and exchanged greetings with them. One was a fat, red-faced man who was a local builder and was thought to be making thousands from bomb-damage repair for the council. He was with his wife, a stout, over-dressed woman, and another couple, also middle-aged.

'Thought you were in Normandy,' said the builder, raising his voice for it to carry over to them. 'You'd better hurry up or it'll all be over.' His party laughed. Paddy waved hello to him, hoping he wouldn't come over, but over he came.

'Isn't the news grand?' said the man jovially. 'Our boys are going through them like a knife through butter. Very light casualties we've had, too; it's wonderful, isn't it?'

'Yes.'

'That fellow Montgomery's a genius, by God. More than a match for the Jerries – if only Eisenhower doesn't try to hold him back. That's the only danger – the damn Yanks will want all the credit to themselves and won't let our boys get a crack at them.'

'Cock,' Donovan said.

'What did you say?'

'I said that's all cock. What you were saying – it's a lot of *cock*.'

'Oh – you think the Yanks are all right, do you?'

'Some of them are and some of them aren't – just like some of our lads are and some aren't, and for that matter some of the Jerries are and some aren't.'

Donovan felt the anger leave him to be replaced by weariness.

The fat man looked at him keenly. 'If I didn't know you, Paddy, I'd think you might be a fifth columnist,' he said solemnly.

Donovan laughed shortly. 'That's right,' he said. 'Fifth columnist, that's me.'

'I didn't say you were – but there's something wrong with you tonight.' He went back to his group and in a low voice repeated his version of the conversation.

Donovan drained his pint. 'Come on,' he said. 'Let's get out of here.'

Annie's glass of light ale was three-quarters full. She made a brave effort to drink it. She finished about half, and they left. Outside she took his arm.

'Hungry?' she said. 'I am.'

'Yes. I could do with a nice big plate of fish and chips.' He tried hard to sound as though the scene in the pub had meant nothing.

There was a queue in the fish and chip shop. They waited for nearly half an hour, and when they got to the counter they were told there was only rock salmon left.

'What's rock salmon?' Donovan asked.

'The muck they used to throw back,' said the man sourly.

They laughed, and had two portions.

Afterwards they walked to Hammersmith Bridge and along by the river, stopping in two pubs on the way. It was a walk they used to take every Sunday in peacetime. Leaning over a brick wall they watched the river swirl darkly by beneath them. Against the sky, to their left, they could see the shadow of Hammersmith Bridge.

They stood side by side, not talking, for a long while. She held his hand tightly and tried to draw close to him, but she knew she was not succeeding. She was about to suggest that they start for home, when in a low intense voice he said:

'I'm not going back, Annie.'

She understood immediately. She put her arm through his. 'All right, Pat,' she said gently.

'It's because I *can't*, you see. I can't do it, Annie. I'd be useless and they'd have to take me out. It's better that I do it this way.' He turned her to him. 'You don't understand, do you?'

'Of course I do. Many a time I've wondered how you stuck it so long, Pat. I know how you've been feeling; you can't sleep next to a man and not know that. Don't *worry* about it, Pat; they'll understand. Have you spoken to anyone yet?'

'Only Tommy Johnson.'

'What did he say?'

'Oh, the usual stuff about everybody feeling that way, and how it'll pass as soon as we get up the sharp end. All the stuff I've said myself a dozen times. Only you never know what it really is until you get it yourself. It's like something sitting on your stomach that you can't digest, that's making you feel sick and you *can't* be sick. You feel it in your heart – I mean your real heart in your chest. It's as though it's become separated from your body and it's floating out by itself for a minute and then it's going to fall... But what's the use – you can't explain it to anyone.'

'Oh, but I know, Pat, I know! When I've heard the German bombers' engines in the sky and the noise of the guns firing at them and then the bombs in the distance and then when one whistles...' She stopped suddenly.

'But you stuck it, eh?' he said.

'No, Pat, no, I didn't mean that. Of course, it's nothing like you've been through – I just wanted you to know that I knew how you felt, that's all.'

He put his arm round her and they started to walk back slowly. She knew she had said the wrong thing.

'No one can say you haven't done more than your share, Pat. You've got the proof of that.'

'They can have 'em back. I'll turn 'em in.'

'You can't do that, Pat! You won those medals, and they're yours by right.'

'You don't think I'd refuse to go in, and keep wearing them, do you?'

'I don't see why not,' she said stubbornly. 'You won them. The King himself gave you the second one.'

'You don't understand, Annie. Let's stop talking about it.'

'All right, darling.' It was a name she saved for their most intimate moments. 'Do what you like with the medals. As long as I have you home with me, I don't care.'

He slept late the following morning and woke feeling better than he had for a long while. Annie had left the bed, but the pillow still carried the impression of her head, and when he pulled it to his face he could smell her. They had come together last night as they used to do, and with a completeness they only rarely achieved now. He stretched his legs luxuriously in the bed and called her.

She came in and sat on the bed and ruffled his hair. He pulled her to him and kissed her.

'What's for breakfast?'

'Finnan-haddock and poached egg. Do you want a cup of tea before you get up?'

'No, but I certainly could do with a nice bit of haddock.' He swung his legs out and retrieved his pyjama trousers from the bottom of the bed. 'Go along and get it ready and I'll be in in two minutes.'

He washed quickly, feeling amazingly light-hearted, and allowed himself the luxury of not shaving. He knew that the butter on the haddock and the poached eggs would take all of his emergency ration card, but Annie always told him that the shopkeepers gave her extra when he was on leave. In fact they allowed her to draw against the future.

The weather had cleared a bit, and with the sun in the sky the street didn't look half as bad as it had the evening before. He settled himself in his chair with the papers which Annie had brought in from seeing the children off to school. He read one or two about the progress in Normandy, but he soon saw that in fact there was almost no information.

He pottered about the house all morning – fixing the lamp, oiling the doors, putting a new washer in the tap in the sink. The children came back for lunch, and afterwards they decided to go to Richmond for the afternoon.

They caught a 73 bus at Hammersmith Broadway and went upstairs, luckily getting the two front seats over the driver.

'Could you drive a bus, Dad?' Michael asked.

'Of course he could!' said Kathleen scornfully. 'He can drive *anything*. Can't you, Daddy?'

'Well I don't know about that, but I expect I could manage a bus with a bit of practice.'

When the conductor came for the tickets Michael said to him, 'My dad can drive a bus.'

The conductor smiled, and glanced down at Donovan, taking in the black tank corps beret and the double M.M., as almost all men did. He himself was wearing a set of miniature First World War campaign ribbons on his uniform.

'Can he, nipper? Well, perhaps he will, after the war.'

'Couldn't stand the stomach ulcers,' said Donovan with a grin.

'You're right, there, mate. Some of 'em suffer something cruel with 'em. Richmond two and two halves? Havin' a day on the river? Well, have a good time.' He punched the tickets and handed them to Michael, who held them tightly with importance. 'And good luck when you get over there, too,' he said.

'Thanks,' said Donovan.

'What did he mean, Mummy? What did the conductor mean?' Kathleen asked.

'You don't miss much, do you, my girl? Never mind what he meant – just watch where we're going.'

When they got off the bus they walked up the hill towards the gates of Richmond Park and past the Star and Garter Home for disabled soldiers. A number of soldiers in wheelchairs were outside enjoying the sun. Donovan carefully kept his eyes away from them, but one called to him.

'Hi, tankie, got a minute?'

Donovan turned and saw a man without legs waving cheerfully at him. He walked over to him dry-throated and trying to keep his eyes up to the level of the man's face.

The man held out his hand and shook Donovan's firmly.

'I was at Cambrai,' he said proudly. 'November 21st 1917. I always say hello to any tankies I see go by.' He proffered a cigarette.

'No, have one of mine,' said Donovan, getting them out. He pulled himself together. 'Cambrai, eh? That must have been quite a do.'

'Ran like rabbits, the Jerries did,' said the man, with a chuckle. 'Ran like rabbits. Couldn't believe their eyes. What mob you in?'

'The thirty-third.'

'Oh. Since my time. Since my time.' He drew on the cigarette, and looked over to where Annie and the children were waiting by the gate. 'Well, I expect you want to get on with your kids. Embarkation leave?'

'Yes.'

'Oh. Well, I won't keep you. Come and see us when you're this way.'

They shook hands again. Donovan walked away.

The man shouted after him, 'Keep your head down!' and he waved acknowledgment.

Annie and Donovan lay in the warm grass while the children roamed around them, approaching as near as they dared to the deer and then racing back in delighted terror as one raised its antlered head to look curiously at them. Kathleen was slim and fast, and easily outdistanced Michael, whose fat little legs worked like pistons as he projected himself along with a look of fierce concentration on his miniature man-like face.

Annie and Donovan talked about the children... about his job after the war... about the past. They didn't mention the subject that was uppermost in both their minds.

The telegram came on the third day of his leave. Tommy had not put anything personal in it.

'REPORT BACK TO UNIT IMMEDIATELY JOHNSON.'

He handed it to Annie. She read it, and said nothing, but just looked at him. Her face was paler than usual, and her dark eyes seemed very large to him.

'Pack my kit for me, will you? I'd better have a shave.'

It was understood between them that she never walked to the Underground station at the end of his leave. He buttoned his tunic right to the top and made sure that his beret was at the correct angle.

He opened the front door and turned to look over her shoulder through the tiny hall into the living-room. The heather he had brought from Yorkshire three months before was still standing in the old 75-millimetre shell in the fireplace. He had meant to throw it out, because it was dusty. He kissed her.

'Goodbye, Annie. Kiss the kids goodbye for me.'

She kissed him hard and stepped back dry-eyed. 'Goodbye, darling,' she said.

THREE

ON D-DAY plus five the regiment moved out of Aldershot and strung out along the road leading south to the Channel coast, making a line about two miles long. The noise made by fifty-seven tanks disturbed the quiet countryside, and people came out of houses and shops and lined the road. The occasion was momentous enough to permit a quite un-English show of emotion. Elderly gentlemen in the uniform of the Home Guard, wearing the campaign ribbons of forgotten wars, stood to attention and saluted endlessly. The older women, remembering watching other men go off to France, openly wept, but the young women waved excitedly.

The prevailing mood was one of high hope. The landings had been accomplished with but a fraction of the expected losses, and it looked as though everything was going smoothly in accordance with some long-prepared master plan. On this fine June day, watching the armour roll towards the coast, it was easy for them to believe that the end was in sight. The long-awaited Second Front was a reality; the defeat of Germany was probably only a few months, perhaps weeks, away.

Donovan had allowed Brook to sit outside on top of the turret, and Hogg's white face showed just above the hatch. Geordie sat half out of the co-driver's seat and scrupulously returned every salute. Taffy had his driver's hatch open and smiled at the pretty girls.

The column moved in a series of jerks as the head was stopped or slowed down by traffic control. The rear tanks fell behind on the long stretches and then speeded up to close the gaps, making clouds of dust. The spectators thoroughly approved of the spectacle of huge tanks dashing madly towards the ports.

In one small village A Squadron were halted, with Donovan's tank directly in front of the village school. All the school-children were lined up in charge of a young schoolteacher – a very pretty girl who was trying to fulfil her role of leading the children in singing and cheering and to ignore the frankly admiring stares and complimentary remarks of the tank crews as they passed. She was exceedingly attractive, and every tank commander turned round to watch her until his tank turned the corner. Donovan was no exception, and he enjoyed the opportunity of the halt to stare at her. Now that the tanks had stopped she became a little flustered. The children were cheering enthusiastically, having a wonderful time participating in the general excitement. Many of them had small Union Jacks which they shook with great vigour. Their shrill shrieking drowned out the noise of the idling motors. Lieutenant Grimshaw was about twenty-five yards ahead, and turned round to admire the girl. Smudger Smith in the tank behind shouted his opinion of her in explicit terms to Donovan. She blushed deeply.

'Now children – all together!' she shouted desperately. 'God Save Our Gracious King. God Save Our Noble King...'

The children took it up with a will, quite drowning her voice.

'Send Him Victorious...' their childish trebles rose to a painful pitch. The tanks started again. Brook, emboldened by his complete anonymity, caught her eye and blew her a kiss. She looked away quickly. As they swung round the corner they could still hear the children's voices unthinkingly shouting the words of the anthem.

As the tank got up to thirty miles an hour, Taffy enjoyed the chance to use his skill. With his foot hard down on the accelerator and a lever in each hand for braking and steering, he felt that his tank was alive. Each lever braked one track, and at speed only the slightest pull was needed to slew from one side of the road to the other. The tank ahead was throwing up a good deal of dust, and there was a fine coating all over Taffy's face and hair except where the goggles fitted closely over his eyes.

The feel of the grit on his skin and tickling his scalp brought back to Taffy the memory of the pit in Wales where he had worked until he was called up. He knew now that the mining village where he had been born and had lived until he was nearly twenty was ugly and poor by the standards of most of the other men in the army and that his life was thought to have been exceptionally hard. It had not seemed that way at the time, though. He came from mining stock on both sides, and although he often heard his father and his uncles complain, it was never thought that he would do any other kind of work or want to live anywhere else. He had first gone down as his uncle's 'boy', and after a year of learning the job had been allowed to work at the coal face. The work had been hard, but, he thought, well paid, and he had enjoyed the hot showers at the pithead, the Rugby football on Saturday afternoons, and the social life of the chapel. There was a cinema in the village, which he went to weekly, whatever the picture, and when he started at the coal face he was able to get his beer in the pub although he was only seventeen.

He enjoyed the hard physical work, and had no trouble at home, where there were three sisters and two elder brothers. He didn't want to leave the village and the pit and go into the army, and he knew vaguely that he could probably get exemption, but his father and his uncles had all been in the First World War and it seemed to be accepted that it was something that happened to a young man, like going down the pit, getting married, and having children. When he went to register he was interviewed and asked if he had any particular preference. He thought of the stories he had heard of the marching and the mud of Flanders, and said he didn't want to go into the infantry. When the tank corps was suggested – principally because of his shortness – he agreed, without considering much what it meant.

He was sent to a tank training regiment in Yorkshire, where they tried to teach him wireless and gunnery, in which he took no interest at all. But the first morning that they took him down to the tank park and let him get in the driver's seat and handle the controls, he knew that this was the job he wanted. He paid strict attention to everything that was told him about driving a tank, and he watched every move the instructor made as he demonstrated it.

On the day he had got into the driving seat for his first attempt, the rest of the class were draped over the tank waiting for their turns and the bored sergeant instructor was sitting on the top of the turret with his legs dangling inside. Taffy had adjusted his headset and listened to the sergeant reciting the instructions. When the droning voice finally stopped he shut his ears to it, and went through the motions he had memorised. He pressed the heavy starter button firmly, and the five aero engines exploded immediately into a smooth roar. As he engaged the gears the huge mass of metal lurched ponderously forward. He had pulled his right hand instinctively to avoid a small bush, and had been delighted with the feeling of the right track biting into the ground and the whole tank pivoting on it. He heard none of the corrections or encouragements, and the instructor had to lean over and tap him on the head before he realised that he had done enough.

He was an instinctive, natural driver, and the instructors in the school had enough sense to realise it. But he was weak on theory; the written paper at the end of the course had been sheer torture to him, and he had been astonished at the high marks he had scored – he never knew that the instructors had rewritten his paper for him. The instructors were sensible men, who had often saved the army from losing a good driver.

He had been sent to the Middle East in time for the chase through Libya and Tunisia, but had been wounded during the last week of the fighting and had spent five months in hospital, rejoining the regiment when they returned to England. Now he was driving his tank towards the enemy again – this time to finish the war. The sooner they got stuck in, he thought, the sooner it would be over.

But it was five more days before the four tanks of One Troop were loaded into a tank landing craft and moved into the queue of vessels flowing across the Channel like a production belt. Even then they seemed to move only a few hundred yards at a time, and spent a whole night crawling through the dark. When dawn came they were still in mid-channel.

By the time they had rolled up their bedding and stowed it away on the tanks and cleaned up after breakfast, it was full daylight. The day was cold, grey, and unpleasant, and they could see nothing ahead or behind but the other ships. There was a general feeling of flatness after the excitement of embarkation.

'I never knew this bloody Channel was so wide,' Geordie said disgustedly. 'I thought we'd be over in a couple of hours. Blimey – they swim across it, don't they?'

Before anybody could explain to Geordie, the captain's voice came from the bridge.

'A couple of battleships ahead, you chaps. The *Ramillies* and the *Nelson*... rather a good sight.'

They all climbed on the nearest tank to get a good view. Their queue of little boats was threading its way between the two battleships, which seemed an enormous size when seen from the deck of the small tank landing craft. The huge guns were elevated for maximum range, their muzzles burnt and blackened for a quarter of their length by the hundreds of shells they had fired. For Brook and all the other new soldiers, it was the first authentic note of war. The leading ships of their group had already dropped off their tanks, and the tanks were pushing through the shallow sea like hippos coming to land. The foghorn-shaped breather at the rear magnified the sound of their engines, sending it over the water as a roar.

'Everyone in his place' Lieutenant Grimshaw ordered. 'Start your engines.'

Brook borrowed Donovan's field-glasses. The beach was covered with shell craters; there were several wrecked landing craft inshore, one tank knocked out and half submerged, two more on the beach. Up against a block-house there was a burnt-out Sherman. Brook inspected it minutely, but apart from its black colour there was nothing unusual about it.

The Atlantic Wall of concrete dragon's teeth and coils of heavy barbed wire had been breached in half a dozen places. Through two of the gaps white tapes ran, to show they had been cleared of mines.

Brook turned his binoculars on the village, and saw for the first time that not one of the houses was whole. Some were no more than outside walls, others leaned drunkenly, looking as though a push would topple them over. The peculiar-shaped building in the centre was the church, with the steeple knocked off.

The landing doors that formed the blunt bow of their craft were lowered noisily, and Grimshaw's tank waddled slowly down and into the water. Although they had practised this many times, a feeling of apprehension gripped them as the water crept up the tank's sides. They listened acutely for any change in the note of the engine, which the driver kept going a little faster than was strictly necessary. Water was not their element, and no one felt safe until his tank began to rise out of the sea, and, shaking the water from itself, bear them up on to the beach.

In the village some of the shops were already open again, and there were people in the streets, who looked at them without much interest – for armour, soldiers and guns had been moving steadily past their shattered houses for days. The tank crews stared at them curiously, for they were the first Frenchmen many of them had ever seen. The people looked hard and unsmiling, and it did not seem possible that contact could be established with them: but then someone made the attempt – and suddenly there were tired smiles and friendly waving. Lieutenant Grimshaw saluted, and two old men queueing for bread stood to attention and returned the salute.

A Squadron was assigned a large field about seven miles out of the town, and they tucked themselves into the borders and tried to make the tanks look like hedgerows. They were told they were probably to be there for two or three days while the rest of the division were landing.

After a lunch of bully beef stew Sergeant Donovan suggested that they have a look round the nearby countryside. All of his tank went along.

Just over a hill to the south of them, not more than a few hundred yards away, was the wreckage of an aircraft, and half-way down the slope three burnt-out Sherman tanks. As they got near to them Brook saw with horror that there was a hole straight through the turret of one – it looked as though it had been drilled, and apparently the armour-piercing shell that had gone in at the front had not been blunted, for the hole where it had come out was just as clean. They stared at it in silence; suddenly their tanks no longer seemed so huge and powerful.

'Those goddamned 88s,' said Donovan bitterly, and Brook thought he heard a note almost of fear in his voice. In a way it was a comfort to know that there was some excuse for the sick feeling of apprehension at the bottom of his own stomach.

'Well, come on lads,' said Donovan in his usual cheerful, optimistic voice. 'Let's find some of theirs to buck us up a bit.'

But all they found on the other side of the hedge was another burned-out Sherman at the bottom of the field. A few yards from it was a mound of newly-dug earth like a flower bed. On it were four small, roughly made crosses.

'There couldn't have been much left of them to bury,' Geordie said, unnecessarily. They continued to stare for a minute or two longer.

'We'd better get back,' said Donovan, and they retraced their steps without speaking. It was a relief to hear the babble of noise when they reached their lines again.

That night it rained, and the rain continued without a break for three days. Donovan and his crew spent almost all their time either inside the turret listening to the wireless, or on the ground under the tank tarpaulin which they had stretched from the tank to the hedge. It was dark and warm like the inside of an igloo, with a small bulb for light running off the tank's batteries, and the petrol stove for warmth and cooking.

Sometimes most of the rest of the troop squeezed in under their tarpaulin. The other tanks contributed something from their supplies, and a huge mess-tin of tea would be made and they would sit around while two of them engaged in a heated argument or, more simply, a slanging match. It might be the Scots versus the English, the North versus the South, Old Soldiers versus New Soldiers, or any of many other popular combinations.

It was all unfamiliar to Brook, but he soon learned the unwritten rules: the abuse was kept within carefully understood limits – a man's honour, courage, honesty, truthfulness or morals could be torn to shreds with impunity, it was permissible to accuse another man of always avoiding work, to maintain that he would run like a rabbit at the sound of a pop-gun, to accuse him of lying, cheating or stealing, and no offence would be taken; but nothing could be said that reflected upon his social status, his ability to pay his share, his personal cleanliness, or his family.

Threats to do each other serious bodily harm were freely exchanged, seldom leading to anything more serious than a wrestling match, puppy fashion. Much of the banter was stereotyped:

'I've spent more time on a troop-ship than you've got service – stand to attention when you talk to a senior soldier.'

'Senior soldier? Saturday night soldier – a bloody Territorial.'

'I'll put you on a charge...'

'You wouldn't know how to make one out.'

'I'd put you on a charge for disobedience, if I could spell it.'

This went on sometimes for an hour or so, but the only result, so far as Brook could see, was to knit them all together in a strange kind of camaraderie.

On the morning of the third day they awoke to find that the rain had stopped and the sun was shining. The country looked as though it had been spring-cleaned: the leaves, which had been heavy and dull with the dust raised by the tanks, now shone in their young greenness; the heavy Normandy soil in the farmers' fields was a well-polished black; the crops of new potatoes were splashes of the lightest green.

They emerged from the tanks, from their holes and burrows everywhere, like ants coming out after rain. Lines were rigged from tank to tank, and blankets and wet clothes hung up to dry. Kit-bags were dumped out, sorted, and repacked. Some of the men made a real job of washing – fetching buckets of water from the river and heating it over a fire of diesel oil mixed with earth, and then washing all their dirty clothes and themselves.

Brook did his laundry, then wrote a letter to his mother, and one to Jennie. It was the first time he had ever written knowing it would be censored by one of the unit's officers, and it made the letter sound stiff and unreal. He could not speak directly of his feeling of fear and apprehension, nor even of the high excitement he had felt in these last hours; but he thought probably his father would understand what he was trying to say.

He felt he must get away from the tanks, if only for an hour. He went over to find Nobby Clarke, to suggest they go for a walk.

Nobby was peeling tiny new potatoes and dropping them into a large tin.

'Hello, Brookie,' he said. 'I dug 'em up early this morning. They're young ones, but potatoes is like women – when they're big enough they're old enough. They'll be smashing with a big lump of butter.'

'Where will you find the butter?'

'I've got it.' He turned up the corner of the tarpaulin to show a two-pound tin. 'You got to keep your eyes open, Brookie boy. Give me a hand with these, and bring your bully beef stew over later. There's enough for all.'

After a few minutes Corporal Smudger Smith came up to them. He nodded to Brook without warmth.

'I'm goin' have a scrounge round,' he said to Nobby. 'You want to come?'

'Right.' He jerked his head towards Brook. 'What about him?'

'I'm easy, if you want him.' He was obviously not enthusiastic. 'You want to come?' he said to Brook.

'Yes, I'd like to. Where are you going?'

'I don't know. We're goin' for a scrounge. Up towards the sharp end. Lookin' for loot. If you're comin' you'd better go and get your gun on.'

'Right, I won't be a minute.' Brook hurried off to his own tank.

When Brook had gone, Smudger turned to Nobby. 'What do you want that toff along for?'

'Brookie? He's all right. He can't help the way he talks, can he? He's green, but he's game – you'll see.'

'All right,' Smudger grumbled. He and Nobby had been troopers together on the desert, and had achieved a rare intimacy; but, following his promotion and their move to England, they had grown apart. His searching out of Nobby to come with him had been a deliberate attempt to get their relationship back on its old footing. It was for this reason as much as any that he resented Brook.

They cut across the fields to the main road and turned south. A few minutes later they passed through the forward positions of their infantry support regiment. As they left the last sentry he shouted something to them about watching their step or they'd end up in the bag.

'A lot he knows about it,' Smudger said contemptuously. 'There's a good three mile or more between us and Jerry.'

'I hope you're right,' said Nobby cheerfully. 'Because if a bloody great Jerry sticks his head over the hedge and says "Tommy, for you the war is over," I'll go quietly, I warn you. What about you, Brookie?'

This was an obvious attempt to ease the slight tension between Brook and Smudger, and Brook laughed nervously. He was excited, and a little afraid of the way they were walking nonchalantly beyond their own lines towards the enemy's. His palms were sweating, and he envied the other two their casual ease and tried to imitate them.

He knew he was there only because Nobby had asked for him; he had no idea what they were going to do, but he knew that he was to be tested, and he was determined that whatever it was he would enter into it with a will. Smudger's reputation as king of the scroungers was fabulous.

Brook tried to remember some of the exploits which he had heard detailed a dozen times in the Naffy or the barrack room, but he only remembered one. When the regiment came out of Burma, Smudger carried a kit-bag full of what everyone else thought were useless Burmese rupees but which he changed at the first bank they came to in India. He had sent three thousand pounds back to Wigan. There had been many such stories, and now Brook was about to take part in the legend himself.

After a mile or so they forked off down a farm track, and came into sight of a typical Normandy farmhouse. They stopped, listening intently for any signs of life. Straining his ears, Brook could hear the others breathing, but nothing else at all. There were none of the usual farmyard noises – no dogs barking, none of the individual sounds that together make up the distinctive hum of a farm.

After a few minutes they went slowly and cautiously towards the house. In the bright sunlight it looked as though its lack of sound and movement were only momentary. Brook almost expected the back door to open and a big red-faced farmer to come out and stamp across the cobbled yard into the barn. But nothing moved as they approached. The only sound was the ringing of their boots on the stones.

'Let's have a shufti inside,' said Smudger gruffly.

Brook moved forward to be the first to enter, but Smudger held him back.

'Wait a minute, lad. You never know about Jerry. He's a cunning beggar, and he loves booby traps.'

He walked over to the barn and leapt lightly across the open threshold, reappearing immediately with a long wooden rake.

'Keep well away, just in case,' he said, and standing against the side of the house, he pushed the back door with the side of the rake head. It swung open creakingly.

'Seems all right,' said Smudger, 'but we'll just make sure of the steps.'

He brought the rake down hard on them. Nothing happened.

'Right – now we can have a look.'

He went inside, and Nobby and Brook followed respectfully. In the kitchen, in the centre of a stone-flagged floor, stood a wooden table, with a long bench on either side, and chairs at the ends. Against the wall was an old sideboard. There was a wood-burning stove, and a large open fireplace with swinging hooks, from one of which hung a black iron pot. On the table were full plates of food covered with green fungus, pieces of mouldy bread, and other signs of a meal suddenly abandoned.

They ransacked the house thoroughly. Following Smudger's expert instruction they slit open the mattresses, pulled all drawers right out, rolled back the carpets, tested the floors for loose boards. They even looked behind the heavy-framed pictures of wedding couples. But they found nothing of any value to them, except a supply of Calvados, a bottle of which they took back to the kitchen.

Smudger shook his head. 'There's something wrong somewhere – something bloody wrong.'

'Looks to me like they just buzzed off in a hurry, taking everything with 'em,' said Nobby cheerfully.

'No they never.' Smudger was positive. 'Why would they leave their meal in the middle? What about all them suitcases upstairs – they wouldn't have many more suitcases than that, and they would have taken as many as they could carry – and that lot hasn't been touched for years. Then the drawers full of clothes. And the house wide open. No – there's something fishy, I tell you.'

Smudger emptied his glass and filled it up again with the fiery white spirit. It apparently had no effect on him, though Brook could feel his own head begin to swim.

'Come on,' said Smudger, getting to his feet. 'We'll have a real good shufti outside.'

They walked slowly around the silent house, looking at the ground for any signs of digging. Then they searched the barn, and finally went round to the back of it. There was a long mound of earth like a winter's supply of cattle fodder. Smudger hit it with a spade he'd brought from the barn, and a trickle of sand appeared. He reached down, and after some effort pulled away a piece of half-rotten sandbag.

'Looks like a shelter...' he started to stay, but Brook had already climbed on top and found the trapdoor.

'Here it is!' Brook shouted excitedly, pulling up the wooden door. 'Oh Christ...' He suddenly felt sick.

The midday sun was overhead and shone right down into the shelter. It was a trench some fifteen feet deep and only three feet wide. Running along one side was a bench – and on it, five people were sitting.

Directly under the trapdoor was a black-haired, heavy-set man sitting with his arm round the shoulder of a chubby, middle-aged woman. She in turn was pressing close to her a blue-smocked boy of about twelve, and next to him a girl of about sixteen clung to an old woman in black. They were all sitting upright, and for the first second seemed alive. Then it was obvious that they had been dead for days.

The three of them stared down into the dark hole lit by the sun. Brook was unable to let go of the trapdoor or to look away. Smudger took it out of his hand and let it fall shut.

'Let's have a drink,' said Smudger.

They went back to the kitchen and drank full glasses of Calvados.

Suddenly Brook felt he was going to vomit. He hurried outside, but nothing would come. He stood out in the sunshine for a minute or so, until he felt better. When he got back to the kitchen he could see that the others were all right again.

'I've been telling Nobby here,' said Smudger, in a new and more friendly tone as though the experience had broken down a barrier between them, 'that that's where the money is.'

'Where?' said Brook, though he knew with dread what Smudger was going to suggest.

'Why, the old man's got it, of course. It stands to reason. It probably happened about ten days ago when we was bombing all around here before the landings. There must have been a close one and they went down the shelter in a hurry. You can bet the old man wouldn't leave the family fortune in the house.'

'How do you know he didn't keep it in the bank?'

'Because they don't – that's why. Banks aren't for them. He'd keep it in a sock, or under the bed – and we haven't found it, so it must be on him. Now how are we going to fetch it out?'

There was a long silence.

'Someone'll have to go down and get it,' said Nobby at last.

'We'll toss for it – that's fair,' said Smudger. 'Odd man goes down.'

'No,' said Brook. 'I'll go.'

He knew that he had to be the one: that this was going to happen to him. It had nothing to do with the tossing of a coin. He was the odd man, and the whole morning had been moving towards this moment. He knew it was not only to impress Smudger or to justify Nobby's recommendation of him, though those things were important too. It was somehow that this stood for all the things that were going to happen to him. He had to do this thing which disgusted him so much, because of the other things that he would soon be called upon to do. The lives of the family down in the shelter were finished and nothing that he could do to their bodies could hurt them: but it would not always be so.

'All right,' said Smudger approvingly. 'Nobby said you was ready to have a go and now I believe him. Let's have a look and see what we've got to do.'

With the bravado of the Calvados in them they opened the trapdoor carelessly. They could see the ladder that the family had used to get down. It was lying in the bottom of the trench, under their feet.

'There's no mark on them. What do you suppose killed 'em?' Nobby asked.

'I don't know – the concussion perhaps, or bad air,' said Smudger vaguely. 'Anyway we'll get that rope out of the barn and lower you down – all right, Brookie?'

'Right,' Brook said. He looked away through the apple orchard to the fields.

They tied the rope around his chest under his arms and led the free end up from his back like a continuation of his spine. He sat on the edge of the hole, clenching his teeth. He felt them take up the slack. He took the weight on his hands, and slid his legs and body down into the hole.

'For Christ's sake, don't let go.' He was unable to keep a tremor out of his voice.

'Don't worry, Brookie lad,' said Smudger confidently. 'You'll be up again in a minute.'

Slowly they lowered him down. He felt quite helpless dangling from the end of the rope like a spider. He avoided looking down, until he felt his feet touch something and saw that he was standing on the farmer's shoulders like an acrobat. He pushed himself violently off the earth wall, and continued inexorably down. The rope was biting painfully into his chest, and he groped for the ground with his feet, to support his weight. The trench was so narrow that he had to stand between the farmer's legs.

Steeling himself he slipped his hand inside the buttoned-up coat. He felt like a pickpocket, afraid that the burly man would suddenly seize him. He tried to avoid looking into the face, but the wide-open eyes caught his own, and he nearly pulled his hand away.

The farmer was about fifty, with a full black moustache. His lips were drawn slightly back, showing yellow teeth; but there were no other signs of pain. His coat was tightly stretched over a body as hard as stone.

Brook couldn't get his hand inside the coat. He pulled hard on the lapel, and the cloth, made rotten by the damp, tore away. In the inner breast pocket were some papers, a letter, a stub of pencil, and a crushed packet of cigarettes. Nothing else.

The stench was dreadful. He had held his breath for as long as he could, but it only made it worse when he was forced to breathe again. He was about to shout for them to pull him up, when in the empty waistcoat pocket he felt something bulky through the material, evidently sewn inside the shirt. But he couldn't stand the awful smell any longer.

'*UP!*' he shouted. 'Pull me up!' He was glad to feel the rope bite painfully into his chest.

They hauled him quickly to the top, and he drew in great breaths of fresh, sweet air and expelled it forcefully to drive the foulness from his lungs.

'What did you get?' said Smudger eagerly.

He handed over the papers, letter and cigarettes.

'Is that all there is?'

He nearly lied, to avoid going down again, but then knew he must not. 'No. He's got something sewn inside his shirt.'

'Ahhhhhhh!' said Smudger. 'That's it! That's it!'

'There's a God-awful smell down there. I need a mask or something.'

'Soak your handkerchief in Calvados and tie it round your face,' said Smudger. 'You won't smell nothing through that.'

They lowered him down once more, with the Calvados soaked handkerchief tied over his nose like a brigand's mask, and an open knife in his hand.

He braced himself firmly against the farmer's body, and sawed at the waistcoat quickly to get it over with. The knife hit the metal buckle of the braces, and he pushed hard against the obstruction. The sharp blade slipped, and went into the body like a walking-stick breaking through a crust of mud. He pulled his hand away in horror, and a cloud of foul gas followed it. The body shrank in front of him like a punctured child's balloon, and he realised that the farmer had not been a big man after all. Before he was overcome with revulsion he ripped the wallet from the woollen shirt and screamed to them above. As he went up, and his legs ceased to support the farmer's body, the body tottered slowly forward, face downwards, into the mud, dragging the other bodies after it like a collapsing house of cards.

There were ninety thousand-franc notes folded neatly in the wallet, and they divided them equally. Brook put his thirty quickly away in his back trouser pocket.

'Of course they smell a bit,' said Smudger, sniffing them. 'But just lay them out in the sun for a couple of hours and they'll soon lose that.' He folded them again and put them in his breast pocket, and buttoned it and patted the little bulge they made. 'A good morning's work, that; a good morning's work.'

That night, Brook had difficulty in getting to sleep, and when he did get to sleep he woke suddenly with the awful stench in his nostrils. The rest of the crew were sleeping in the same narrow space under the tarpaulin, and the smell obviously was not going to wake them. He had folded his battledress trousers with the notes in the back pocket and laid them on top of an empty petrol tin. Now he got up, slipped on his trousers and boots and went outside.

It was a beautiful clear night. He walked down to the river, stumbling over the rocks in the field and making what he thought was a lot of noise, but the guard did not challenge him.

At the river's edge he took the notes out of his pocket. He tore them into small pieces, and scattered them into the water. Then he held his hands in the water until they began to feel numb with the cold. He sluiced the water over his face, and sniffed it up his nose to get rid of the smell.

On the way back to bed he heard the muffled thud of bombs and the far-off crackling of anti-aircraft fire. He climbed on top of the tank and looked towards the coast. The sky was criss-crossed with lines of anti-aircraft shells floating lazily up, and on the horizon was the red glow of fires. It all seemed very unreal. He went back to bed and fell asleep immediately.

FOUR

A FEW NIGHTS later the Germans made their heaviest bombing attack on the bridgehead. The tank crews sat on the turrets and watched. The lines of tracer bullets were glowing red necklaces flung across the dark background of the sky; the bursting shells were flashing diamonds. One of the bombers started to burn: it writhed and turned and then plunged to earth like a spent rocket. All this was in dead silence, for the beachhead was eight miles away, and by the time the sound reached them the sky was black again. The bombers came back again and again.

Just after midnight their own artillery started a barrage.

'Twenty-five pounders,' said Donovan. 'That means an attack must be coming off. Hear them going over our heads! They sing differently when they're coming at you.'

'My God, they make a hell of a noise,' said Brook. He had a bad headache but didn't want to say so.

'Those?' said Taffy in surprise. 'Why they're nothing – wait till you hear the Long Toms or the five-fives – they'll shake you, by Christ.'

All that night the road was jammed with vehicles as the Scottish division moved up into battle position. The tanks had been moved off the road, and the crews watched the trucks filled with quiet men moving up to the fighting. Dispatch riders carrying messages kept roaring by; they were going too fast, as they had always done on schemes in England, but now there was an air of reality about it which made them, bent over the handlebars and cutting in and out, look most impressive.

After breakfast Lieutenant Grimshaw came back from a troop commanders' conference and called them together.

'This is it, chaps,' he said. 'The Jocks are putting in an attack of two-brigade strength. They are going to take two villages between here and the river Odon. Then we push through them and take the high ground covering the bridges, and if all goes well we cross the

Odon. We'll set up on the high ground on the other side, then the Jocks will go through us again. Then we'll go through them so that we keep up a continuous attacking advance without giving Jerry a rest.

'We move off this afternoon, so get cracking now. Test your guns, pack your kit away, and prime your grenades. Any questions?'

'Yes sir,' said Brook. 'How are the Yanks doing over on our right?'

'Very well indeed. They're twenty miles inland at places, and they've joined up with Fifty Div and Thirty Corp, so we've got a continuous front with them. Jerry has decided to concentrate his armour against us, though, and he's bringing all he's got here and leaving the Yanks alone. So if we can smash him or even hold him, they should be able to break out. I think if the RAF and the Gunners keep pounding at Jerry he'll be ready to crack when we attack. Any more questions?'

Sanderstead, Lieutenant Grimshaw's operator, spoke up. 'Why have we been waiting all this time before we put in an attack?' he said. Everybody looked at him in some surprise. He was a quiet youngster from Aberdeen; no one had suspected him of being a fire-eater.

'The main reason has been the weather. There was a hell of a gale that went on from last Monday until Friday – it mucked up the prefab harbours and made a mess of the boats that were bringing over the troops for the build-up. But never mind about that – we're all ready to go now.'

As there were no more questions, Lieutenant Grimshaw said, 'Right, let's get on with it. Sergeant Donovan – stay behind, will you?'

When the others had scattered back to the tanks he took Donovan to one side.

'It's not going to be a picnic, Paddy. There's an airfield on our flank with twenty 88s covering us...'

'Twenty! ...'

'Yes, and when I said that Jerry was concentrating against us I meant just that – there's seven Panzer divisions on our immediate front – seven in twenty miles. There's only ten or eleven Panzer divisions in all France, and we've got seven of them in front of us

– and among them are our old friends the 21st Panzer Grenadiers. It's going to be a real rough do. I'm telling you, because I'm afraid that some of these youngsters aren't going to like it at all. It's bad their first battle should be one like this – it ought to be a nice tidy one to give them confidence but it can't be helped. Are you sure of everyone?'

'I'm as sure as I can be before they've been in. Some of them are nervous, but that's not such a bad thing. There's no one I want to change.'

'Right. Well, there's one good thing. The RAF are going to start bombing at two a.m. in front of us, and give Jerry the pounding of his life – with particular emphasis on the aerodrome; so let's hope they knock out some of those damned 88s. You can tell any of the experienced ones some of the real griff if you think it wise, but I'd handle the youngsters carefully for a bit.'

Donovan walked slowly back to his tank with a weak feeling in his legs. His crew were getting things ready with enthusiasm. Their spirits were high, and he tried his best to match them.

About nine-thirty it started to rain. At ten-thirty word came that the R.A.F. attack was off.

'Is that serious, Sergeant?' Brook asked.

'Well, it would have been better if the RAF could have softened him up a bit for us, but it won't make much difference really,' Donovan said, with forced cheerfulness. Taffy looked at him sharply.

They moved off the next morning at half past eight. It was raining heavily and they didn't reach the ridge where the big guns of their own artillery were firing until about eleven. One Troop spread out as they approached the ridge, and they breasted it together. Almost immediately they came under heavy German shell fire, but as the shells were high-explosive and not armour-piercing, one of them would have to land practically on top of the tank to do them any harm.

Brook kept his eye stuck to his periscope, watching the shells burst in front of them. The nearest, landing about twenty yards away, rattled the side of the tank with bits of shrapnel. Brook was glad to find that though his heart was beating faster and his stomach fluttering he was not unduly afraid. They were not yet firing, as they could see no targets. The guns that were shelling them were on the other side of a high ridge. They continued to work towards it in a long line.

There were a number of cows still in the fields, bewildered by the noise and the sight of tanks. As Brook watched he saw a shell burst in the midst of four of them, and when the smoke and dust cleared away one cow was lying on its back with its four legs pointed to the sky and another was gazing at it curiously.

A few minutes later Donovan touched him on the shoulder.

'Here's your first dead one.'

Brook squeezed past him and got his head out of the turret.

A Canadian soldier was sprawled on his hands and knees in front of them, his face pressed to the earth. He was held balanced in a crouching position by his elbows. Someone had stuck his rifle in the ground by its bayonet, to mark the place for the burial party. Brook could see the soldier's face quite clearly, and for a moment he thought he was a Negro: but then he realised that his skin had turned black. He looked enormously fat, but Brook remembered the dead farmer, and knew that the soldier too was swollen with gases.

A bit farther on were two burnt-out Sherman tanks just like their own. Brook felt the beginnings of a sick dread creeping over him. There was a tremendous explosion, and he saw that one of Two Troop's tanks had gone up on a mine. When the smoke cleared away he was surprised to see the crew, apparently unhurt, waving cheerfully at them.

Before they reached the ridge they lost two more tanks on mines. As they got to the top and began to fire back, one of their ammunition lorries blew up with a tremendous roar, then a petrol lorry caught fire. All around them shells were landing, but Brook was busy loading the gun and wasn't able to see. He knew someone had fired on their own armoured cars by mistake, for the wireless crackled furiously.

Brook hadn't the least idea of what was really going on. He kept looking at Donovan and listening to him calmly ordering Hogg to fire at targets, but try as he could he was not able to distinguish anything ahead of them at all. The noise of the shells landing around them, of their own guns firing, of the exploding of ammunition from the burning lorry, made everything very confusing. But somehow it didn't seem so very different, yet, from the realistic schemes in England.

Then suddenly the voice of the medical officer came up on the air.

'M.O. speaking. Get the blood wagon over here as quick as you can. Out.'

The ambulance had never been called 'the blood wagon' on schemes, and the name made Brook shiver. He looked round for the M.O., and saw him bending over some of the men from the petrol lorry about five hundred yards behind. As he watched, a shell landed nearby, but the M.O. didn't look up from his task.

At dusk the Scots Greys relieved them, and they pulled back to their area for the night. It took several weary hours to replenish their stocks of ammunition and fuel and to cook a meal; it was half past twelve before they got down to sleep.

Reveille was four thirty in the morning. At five they moved off back to the ridge. Brook and Hogg had slept in the turret under the gun, but Donovan and the others had slept outside, covering themselves with the tank sheet to protect them from the rain.

Things were fairly quiet on the ridge; the heavy shelling of the day before had stopped. They got in hull-down positions and tried to search out the enemy gun emplacements.

Suddenly Donovan reached for his microphone and began reporting the position of an 88-millimetre gun which he had seen fire from a ridge well out of his range. The colonel acknowledged his report and relayed it to the artillery liaison officer, who had a tank of his own. It was the liaison officer's job to travel with them and report back artillery targets. In a few minutes he appeared and came up alongside them. He was very young, and rode with one leg hanging casually out of the turret. He wore the striped red and blue scarf of the Gunners and looked almost as though he was dressed for the part of the dashing young officer in an amateur production.

'Where is this 88, Sergeant?' he asked cheerfully.

Donovan explained it to him and pointed out the situation on his map.

'Ah – yes. And you actually saw it fire, did you?'

'Of course I did!' Donovan snapped.

'Yes. Sorry, Sergeant, but I have to be careful about laying on a stonk, you know. I think I'd better get up on top and have a good look myself.'

'It's pretty exposed up there, sir – if there's an 88 within range he'll be bound to have a go.'

'Yes, I suppose so – but we can't see anything from down here, can we? All right, driver – advance.'

As the young artillery officer started to move up to the top of the ridge, Donovan ordered Taffy to follow him. He kept half a tank behind, and glued his eyes to his binoculars. He kept sweeping the country immediately ahead, in an attempt to find the camouflaged gun before it fired, knowing that the chances were a hundred to one.

He said softly, 'Put an H.E. on delay up the spout.'

Brook took out the armour-piercing shell in the gun and replaced it with a high-explosive that would detonate two seconds after it touched anything.

The artillery observation officer had been on top of the ridge for about a minute, when an 88, not more than twelve hundred yards away, fired and hit his tank square. The tank was enveloped in a sheet of flame, and at the same instant the survivors shot out.

Brook was conscious of Donovan's cold, clear voice giving instructions to Hogg to bring their gun to bear. '... Steady... on... range... twelve hundred... *Fire!*' He sounded as though he was firing at targets in England. Brook looking through his periscope saw the shell burst. Without realising it he found himself jerking the used shell-case out of the gun and pushing home another one. They fired again.

'A.P. this time.' Donovan's voice was still quiet and unruffled. Brook put in an armour-piercing shell.

'Can you see him, Hogg?' The exploding shells had blown away the camouflage. 'Right. Take your time, now. Put the A.P. in his middle. Geordie, start spraying around there with Browning to keep the beggars quiet.'

Geordie's machine gun chattered immediately. A few seconds later Hogg fired, and they saw a flash of flame leap up from the target.

'Reverse, Taffy,' said Donovan urgently.

Instantly they backed off the ridge. A second or two later a shell screamed angrily a few feet above them. The time from the artillery officer's tank being hit, to their reversing back after destroying the 88, was just over a minute.

Brook heard Donovan's voice slowly and carefully reporting the artillery officer's tank hit and the destruction of the 88, and looked at him with admiration. He was astonished to see that Donovan's face was green: he was sweating, and his eyes were dilated, but his calm clear voice went on. Brook turned quickly away, not wanting to look at him.

The artillery officer's tank had, for some reason, not burnt out. There were four survivors – three burnt by the flash, and the officer with a broken leg. They were huddled on the ground twenty yards behind their tank. An ambulance drove up to them and the M.O. jumped out. He gave them shots of morphine, and then the stretcher-bearers carried them into the ambulance. The M.O. crossed swiftly to the knocked-out tank, peered in the driver's compartment, and came away.

A little later their own artillery laid down a very heavy barrage on the next ridge ahead, and they went up with the rest of the squadron's tanks and fired too. When the barrage stopped they stopped also, but remained on top of the ridge. There was no reply from the enemy.

When things were quiet, Brook asked for permission to get out of the tank.

Donovan looked at him. 'What do you want – a piss?'

'Yes – and to stretch my legs a bit.'

'Well, don't stretch them too far.' Donovan still looked ill, but he had lost the green colour in his face.

Brook walked over to the knocked-out tank and climbed up to look in the driver's seat. The driver was there, slumped forward, still holding the driving sticks. The shell had come in just in front of him, a bit to the left, and travelling diagonally, had come out behind his right shoulder, tearing out the shoulder blade so that Brook saw straight into the chest cavity. He looked like a trussed chicken.

His eyes were closed and his expression was peaceful, though his complexion had already turned greyish-black. Brook found that the sight did not upset him very much. His worst moment had been when the tank got hit and the flame shot out of it: when they were firing he had not felt afraid, and the torn corpse of the driver did not make it worse. He began to feel that perhaps he was going to be all right.

When he got back to the tank, Donovan said to him, 'What did you do that for?'

'I thought he might still be alive,' he lied.

At ten o'clock they moved back, and were glad to think they were going to get some sleep a bit earlier that night; but it was only to replenish fuel and ammunition, and this done they got on the move again. Brook was tired, but full of confidence, and pleased at the way he had reacted to his first experience of real war.

A little after midnight Lieutenant Grimshaw came over to Donovan's tank.

'Everything all right, lads?' he said.

Full of tea and bully beef they assured him that everything was.

'Good. Get Corporal Smith and Corporal Knight, will you, Paddy? Bring your maps and come over to my tank.'

The three tank commanders met at the troop leader's tank. His map was spread out on top of the turret, illuminated by the extension light from the tank.

'Give us the griff,' said Smudger. 'I bet it's bad.'

Grimshaw smiled. 'Not too bad. Come on and gather round and I'll picture you.'

They climbed on the tank and looked at his map, which had been elaborately marked with different-coloured map pencils.

'See this river – the Odon? Well, the Hussars and the infantry found a bridge unblown yesterday and put two squadrons over to make a bridgehead, and by midnight last night the other brigade in the division was over the river and it looked fine. But unfortunately it turned out that the unblown bridge wasn't an oversight on Jerry's part: it was probably left because he still had a lot of his own stuff on this side of the river. Anyway, it got very warm around there last night and there was a bit of a flap. Our infantry, who were protecting this side of the bridge, got spread out a bit too much and Jerry knocked off half of them. This morning they're all feeling a bit windy and our brigade has got the job of expanding the bridgehead. Now here it is on the map.'

He drew a red ring round Hill 112 on his map.

'This is where we are going now to relieve the Hussars. As you can see, it's an obvious defensive position – it dominates the bridgehead and the whole valley. Needless to say it was strongly held, and as a matter of fact it's doubtful who holds it now. The Hussars and a company of infantry had a hell of a time getting up it, and when they'd pushed Jerry off the top some Tigers in a wood on the southern slope opened up and knocked them off it. The infantry and what's left of the Hussars are dug in at the crest, and we're to relieve them and play king of the castle tomorrow.'

'I said it was going to be grim, and by Christ it is!' said Smudger, sounding rather pleased with the accuracy of his forecast.

Donovan said nothing. He knew Grimshaw well, and he could see that the officer was depressed, which was unusual for him.

Back at the tanks the men were waiting eagerly for the news. Each tank commander briefed his crew in his own way.

Smudger Smith was met by Nobby, who was boiling a chicken inside the turret.

'How much time we got?' Nobby asked anxiously. 'This needs another half-hour at least.'

'I don't know. It won't make much difference anyway, because as far as I can see we'll all catch a packet tomorrow. There's about a thousand Tigers over the other side of the river just waiting for some silly beggars like us to stick our head up over the hill. It's going to be bloody awful. Did you put the spuds in?'

'Yes, and some carrots I found. It'll be lovely.' Nobby stirred it briskly.

Hunter, the young co-driver, wanted to know more, but didn't dare ask. Collins, the wireless operator, who had been glued to his set, offered some information.

'Did you know Jerry was attacking with twenty tanks a couple of miles behind us?' he said.

'Of course he is,' said Smudger lugubriously. 'We'll be cut off, that's what we'll be, and not one of us'll get out alive. Did you put *all* the butter in the spuds?'

'Well, if it's as bad as you say there's no use saving butter, is there?' said Nobby.

'Don't be bloody silly – what'll we do tomorrow? You know I can't eat them horrible biscuits dry – they give me indigestion something cruel.'

'Well, you remember when we passed the Q stores a few miles back?' said Nobby. Smudger nodded. 'Well, as it happened, a tin of butter fell into me driving seat – and two tins of bully beef.' He stirred the chicken, and the delicious smell filled the tank.

When Donovan had told his crew briefly what it was all about, he stretched out on the back of the tank and tried to sleep. He could hear sounds of shelling behind them and machine gun fire on their flanks. He distinguished the sound of their own Brens, and the answering, silk-tearing noise of the much faster German Spandau. But he knew that what was keeping him from sleeping was not the noise of guns but the tight knot of fear in his belly. The duel with the self-propelled gun was the sort of thing that he would have taken in his stride at one time, but it had left him feeling sick and shaken, although they had not been fired on at all. The day had been nothing but a rehearsal for the real battle, which would begin in a half-dozen hours: but he was already feeling badly shaken. In fact it had done his inexperienced crew good to have a little shoot and come under a bit of light shelling, and, of course, to see an enemy gun knocked out. It had steadied them, and their morale was now high. It was not them that he had to worry about but himself. He kept his eyes shut and tried to forget what was coming.

Brook had been left in charge of the tank, and he sat up in the turret watching the flashes of bursting shells behind them and listening to the confused noises of the fighting. He felt tremendously excited at the prospect of heavy fighting the next day, and he envied Sergeant Donovan's nerves of steel which enabled him to curl up and sleep at a time like this. Sitting on top of the turret in the tank commander's position he indulged in a little reverie in which he saw himself, older and battle-scarred, leading tank in a set-piece tank battle, knocking out two of the enemy and dashing forward to complete the rout. He would be decorated and commissioned on the field – well, decorated anyway. He saw himself refusing a commission gracefully: 'No sir, I feel I can be of more use as a troop sergeant. The men trust me...' He was at the bottom of a deep, dark, warm hold, and someone was rocking the boat.

'You'd better get down for a kip,' Donovan was saying, shaking his shoulder.

'I'm sorry, Sergeant, I must have dozed off.'

He felt terribly guilty. You could be shot for sleeping on duty.

'That's all right. Get down to it.'

Donovan took over his position, and Brook lay down on the engine covers and went back to sleep immediately.

When he woke up they were jogging along the road. As he climbed in the turret he saw the shadowy figures of the supporting infantry walking stolidly along beside the tanks.

One Troop went off the road and climbed up a steep slope. Near the top were the tanks which had taken the hill in the day's fighting, waiting to be relieved. Donovan took over a position not more than fifty yards from the crest. The attack was scheduled for dawn, three hours away.

At half light Major Tommy Johnson called his tank commanders to him.

'Here's the form. The Jocks have forced another bridgehead over on our right and we're all going forward together. Jerry has a very strong position on the next ridge, from which he can knock anything off the top of our hill. As long as he's there we can't go forward, so he has to be winkled out. The infantry are putting in an attack with us in support, and our artillery will keep pounding him while we get over the top of that hill and during the critical period going down the southern slope. When we move off I want One Troop up, followed by Three and then Two. Stay together, though, so we go down the other side in battle line. That's all. The new call-sign for today is Oboe. Operators to net in immediately. Good luck.'

Lieutenant Grimshaw and his three tank commanders walked briskly back to their tanks, which were the highest position on the northern slope of the hill.

'You'll lead, Paddy,' said Grimshaw. The orders were that troop officers were not allowed to be leading tank in a situation like this. Grimshaw didn't like it, but it was obviously sensible. 'Then me, then you, Corporal Smith, and you bring up the rear-guard, Corporal Knight.'

Donovan climbed heavily into his tank and adjusted his headset. His crew were all looking up at him waiting for the news.

'We're putting in an attack with the infantry to get Jerry out of a wood on the other side of the hill. The gunners are going to paste him hard to make him keep under cover, so it shouldn't be too bad. A Squadron leading, with One Troop up.'

'Who's leading tank?' asked Taffy.

'We are.'

Brook felt a lump in his throat and a weakness in his stomach.

'Hello all stations Oboe. Advance. Out.' The major's voice was strong and confident.

'Start up, Taffy. Advance slowly to the crest.'

The noise of tank engines starting up was everywhere. The infantry were all around them. Donovan's tank swung out and started slowly up the last fifty yards of the hill, Lieutenant Grimshaw followed close behind, and behind him Smudger and Lance-Corporal Knight fell into their positions. Three Troop moved up level with them only a few yards behind Donovan. Two Troop, on their right, took up the same position. Just behind, as though herding them, came the four tanks of Headquarters Troop. As Donovan's tank arrived at the top of the hill all the rest were in a wave just behind him.

He waited on the crest. Nothing happened. Brook could see one of the knocked-out Hussar tanks a few yards to their left. The top of the hill was almost flat, and about as big as a football ground. Just in front of them was a cluster of small trees, and as they moved towards them they could see two more derelict tanks and a number of dead bodies of their infantry who had tried to hold the place the day before.

Donovan stopped right up against the trees and carefully examined the country ahead with his field-glasses. The ground sloped away from them to a shallow valley and then rose to make another ridge about three thousand yards away. Any German 88-millimetre gun on that ridge could just about destroy them, and it would be quite useless for them to reply until they had shortened the distance by at least a thousand yards. Donovan was used to their inferiority in fire power from his fighting on the desert, but Brook and the others, though they had been told about it on their courses, had not really comprehended what it would mean until now. They all kept their eyes glued on the far ridge.

As Donovan combed the country in the improving light the rest of One Troop took up their positions alongside him. Three Troop had stopped about thirty yards behind, still protected by the ground, and the rest of the squadron had not yet come up the hill. All One Troop's tank commanders were trying to discover where the danger lay: everyone was waiting for the enemy to fire. There was a strange feeling of absolute quiet, despite the noise of the tank engines. The infantry between and in front of the tanks were not moving or talking. Every man was peering ahead in the lightening dawn, trying to spot some movement or anything suspicious.

Down the hill, a little to their right and only twelve hundred yards away, was a small, thick copse. The three German Tiger tanks in it were so skilfully concealed it wasn't likely that even the most experienced tank commander could have discovered them with field-glasses alone. The positions had been prepared before the invasion with just this situation in mind, which was why they had succeeded in driving the Hussars off the flat, exposed hilltop the day before with a concentrated, withering fire.

The young Panzer Grenadier officer in command had been waiting all night for the attack to be renewed. He was sure that infantry would be used this time to find him, and he was prepared for them. He had loaded his guns with high-explosive shells and had taken his Spandau machine guns out of his tanks and sited them to give him covering fire. He was brave and determined, but he had been awake all night expecting to be attacked hourly and was getting a bit jumpy. He knew his crews did not like the feeling of having been left out as a last-ditch defence while the rest of their regiment had retreated. If he had not been so young, and had had the coolness and patience to change his shells again to armour-piercing and to wait for the last minute, he could have knocked out most of A Squadron. But he could see four tanks in his sights and the infantry supporting them getting ready to move down the hill towards him. He decided to fire his salvo of high-explosive into the midst of the infantry and follow that up immediately with armour-piercing shells to knock out the tanks. One of his targets, the tank on his extreme left, was partly shielded by some trees, but the other three were like clay pipes on a fairground shooting range. He gave the order to fire.

To One Troop it seemed as though an 88 fired three shots in two seconds. Two high-explosive shells hit Lieutenant Grimshaw's tank, shaking it and the crew but not doing any damage to them. The blast and shrapnel killed three of the infantrymen standing near and wounding others. The third high-explosive shell hit the front of Smudger Smith's tank, killing and wounding more of the infantry.

Immediately the two tanks that had been hit began backing blindly away. Donovan had returned the fire, and Taffy had moved towards the trees without being ordered. Only Lance-Corporal Knight didn't move, but gave orders to bring his gun to bear on the wood. Before he could fire, the second salvo came over and he took the armour-piercing shell, which was low, right into his full petrol tanks. The explosion blew him out of the turret, and Cohen, his wireless operator, badly burned, followed. Dusty Rhodes, the driver, had come out like a jack-in-the-box unhurt, but there was no sign of either the co-driver or the gunner.

By this time Lieutenant Grimshaw's tank had thrown a track, which had probably been broken by the high-explosive shell, and he and his crew had baled out. Donovan was still firing towards the wood as fast as Hogg could fire or Brook could load, and at the same time reversing in a zigzag path, which was why the second shot missed them. Donovan was soon able to put a rise in the ground between them and the Tigers.

They were now near Lance-Corporal Knight's burning tank. Brook stared at it in horror as Johnson, the gunner, dragged himself half out of the turret. His legs had been shattered but he had hauled himself off the turret floor badly burned and tried to pull himself out by his arms. But the bone of his leg sticking out had caught under the commander's seat and he could go no farther. The flames were all around him and it did not seem possible that he was still alive. Brook looked for a split second straight into his eyes and saw him screaming, and then almost immediately Johnson slipped back into the turret. Seconds later, the ammunition inside exploded.

Brook was overcome by the most powerful feeling of sheer animal terror. It was as though his whole body and soul had suddenly rebelled against what he was doing and where he was. For a fraction of a second he wanted to scream and fly in panic, and only the physical impossibility of getting out of the tank stopped him. A moment later it passed, and he found himself obeying Donovan's orders automatically.

Some 88s on the far ridge opened up and knocked out two of Two Troop's and one of Three Troop's tanks, all of which began to burn. Those of the crews who were not killed or too badly wounded got out and ran. Part of the squadron tanks that were left turned to meet this new threat, while the others faced the woods from where the first shots had come. Some tanks reversed blindly, colliding with others that had been knocked out. The infantry had got a grip on themselves and begun to advance grimly down the slope.

Donovan moved his tank diagonally across the hill to support them, waving to Smudger Smith to follow him. Both tanks fired rapidly into the wood, which was now also being heavily shelled by their artillery.

Suddenly the major's voice cut through all the confusion.

'Hello – all stations. *Oboe* – stop milling and swanning about or there'll be a massacre. Form battle line and fight back. Keep firing. Form battle line.'

The 88s on the far ridge had gone over to high-explosive now, to kill or pin down the infantry advancing doggedly towards the Tigers in the woods.

Smudger watched the infantry moving down the slope with shells and mortars falling all around them.

'All right, Nobby, let's give the poor beggars a little support – down you go.'

As Smudger's tank advanced from the top of the hill to join the infantry, Donovan saw it was the only thing to do, and ordered Taffy to follow. He was in command of what remained of One Troop now.

'Hello Oboe One Able,' he called up. 'The infantry are putting in an attack on the wood where the Tigers are, and we are supporting them. Out.'

'Hello One Able. Good show. Hello Oboe Two and Three. Follow One and get those Tigers out of there! We can't do anything until you do.'

Two and Three Troops acknowledged the order and swung across and down the slope towards the wood, which was being pounded heavily by their own artillery. There was no answering fire from the wood until they were within three or four hundred yards of it, and then two guns fired and Smudger's tank and one from Three Troop were knocked out.

The shot that hit Smudger's tank was very low, and passed under the co-driver's seat without touching him and knocked out the bogie-wheel on his side.

As soon as it hit, Smudger shouted 'Bale out!' and all five of his crew were out in a matter of seconds and round to the back of the tank, where they threw themselves flat on the ground.

Donovan was on the extreme right flank, and apparently out of the radius of fire, for nothing came at him. He continued to advance slowly as their infantry disappeared into the wood. At the same moment the artillery barrage was lifted, and all the tanks stopped firing as they could not see where their own infantry were.

Donovan had a chance to look around. He saw Smudger's tank abandoned and the crew on the ground behind, and he shouted to them. Smudger raised his head and waved.

'Get back up the hill now,' Donovan shouted, 'while it's quiet for a minute.' There was a noise of rifle fire from the woods which told of close fighting, but no one came out. Smudger and his crew stood up and ran crouched over back up the hill and disappeared over the crest.

Donovan moved his tank over towards Two Troop. As he was the only tank left in One Troop he knew he would be put under the command of one of the other troops.

In a few minutes the infantry reappeared, and the young officer in charge of them reported that the wood was now clear. 'Three Tiger tanks destroyed and no prisoners,' he said grimly.

At the tank commanders' conference about nine o'clock that night, Major Johnson told them that their advance had been stopped by a heavy German counter-attack behind them.

'The infantry will try to hold the bridge as long as they can, and we're all pulling out. We've been elected to do the rear-guard, so we don't move until about midnight.'

When Donovan came back from the conference he told his crew the worst, without any trimmings. By now, nursing them was either unnecessary or useless.

By evening Brook had lost the feeling of unreasoning terror that had been so awful earlier in the day; but he was still badly shaken, as most of them were. The mathematics of the situation were a little terrifying. This was their first real battle, and *in a day* the regiment had lost fifteen tanks and had had eleven men killed outright and many others wounded. It looked as though there was a one-in-four chance that his tank would get knocked out next time and an almost equal chance that he would be killed when it did. If there are three days like this a week, he thought, I shall be dead or injured within a month almost certainly. Then he looked over at Donovan, and immediately felt better. No one knew how many tanks Donovan had lost, and he was still alive and whole. Brook told himself he must try somehow to keep calm as Donovan did, for he knew that the one reason they hadn't been knocked out was simply Donovan's cool, fast thinking.

Donovan's legs were badly swollen, as he had been standing for most of four days. He was lying on the back of the tank now massaging them, but it didn't seem to be doing much good. He saw

Brook looking at him and smiled.

'How do you like tank fighting, Brook?'

'I don't like it at all,' Brook said promptly. I think it's bloody awful. I want to go home.'

Donovan laughed. 'You were all right: you were all, all right, lads. Don't worry – we came out of that one, and if we get away with it tonight we'll be pulled out for a rest. And today was particularly bad; it's not often like that, is it, Taffy?'

'We wouldn't be here now if it was,' Taffy said calmly, and they all felt better.

'I wonder what happened to Smudger and his lot?' Taffy said.

'I think they're all right. I saw them get over back of the hill this afternoon. They're probably back in echelon now having a good scoff – you know how echelon always gets the best rations.'

They cursed echelon, and all headquarters staff, and everyone whose job was a little safer than theirs; and that also made them feel better.

About midnight they moved down on to the road. The expected counter-attack had not developed and most of the troops in the bridgehead had been withdrawn safely, although there was still a solid column stretching from the bridge a mile or so up the road to them. They were intended to act as a rear-guard and so would go no faster than the slowest. It took them over an hour to cover the mile, but eventually they reached the bridge and got over it, to be followed by the last of the infantry. A small force was left on the other side as a token, with orders to withdraw if they were attacked.

About half a mile north of the river they pulled off the roads into the fields. By this time they felt they were walking in their sleep, but before they could rest they had to discard their empty shell-cases, take on new ammunition, and fill their fuel tanks. Brook handed up the heavy 75-millimetre shells to Geordie standing on the back of the turret, who passed them in to Hogg, who stowed them in their proper positions. They moved as though they were drugged, and the task seemed never-ending; but at last they had their complement of shells again, and the fuel tanks were full. The cookhouse brought up tea and bully beef sandwiches.

Brook sat on the ground leaning against a pile of empty shell-cases and drank his tea. He took one bite out of the thick sandwich and fell into a deep sleep on top of the shells. They were in the middle of a battery of heavy guns which fired all the rest of the night, but not one of them even stirred.

FIVE

THE REGIMENT WAS RESTING. The bridgehead was so crowded there was nowhere out of the way to put them, and they had been squeezed into some fields right in front of their heavy artillery batteries. After two weeks of rain the sun had come out strongly, and on the same day their mail had caught up with them. There had been several sacks for A Squadron, and everyone had had a letter or two. The rumour that they were to move the next day was very strong and everywhere that hot afternoon were men writing letters, concentrating on the effort to reach out from their strange world to a more familiar one.

Letter-writing did not come easily to Geordie. The stub of a pencil he had scrounged seemed to have difficulty in forming the letters, but he struggled for nearly an hour and then read it over with satisfaction:

Dear Mum,
I been hoping to get a Letter from you, Granny wrote but she never said nothing about You. Did you get the letter what I sent before we come over? If you never then I will say again what I said in it I said that the Troop Officer told me that I could get an Allowance for you from the Army if I could say that I was supporting you. It would only mean a few Bob off my Pay and I got more than I want anyway and then you wouldn't have to depend on nobody else and you could tell him to sling his Hook if you wanted. I learned a lot in the Army and I wont have no trouble getting Work when I come out maybe Lorry Driving if the Money is good and I dont see me getting Married for Years so I thought maybe if you wanted we could have a place together like a Home. But if you dont want to please write and tell me.
Hoping this finds you as it leaves me, your ever loving Son
GEORDIE.

Lieutenant Grimshaw had had five letters from Jamaica which had been chasing him around, and he had been writing steadily all morning to get the replies off before they went in again. He had saved the one to his wife until the last and he found that he had let his pent-up longing for her and his son run away with him. It read more like a letter from a love-lorn adolescent, he told himself wryly, than a middle-aged warrior. He wondered what he could tell her about his troop, for she always asked him questions about them.

... I am very pleased with them. First of all, good old Paddy Donovan. He has completely fulfilled all my hopes and I know how lucky I am for a good Troop Sergeant makes all the difference. He's done remarkably well again and quite lived up to his reputation. I was very happy to be able to recommend him for the Military Medal – his third, and I should think that there is every chance that he'll get it for Tommy Johnson endorsed the recommendation and I know the Colonel thinks he deserves it too. I can't really tell you what he did without risking saying something that I shouldn't but just over two weeks ago we had rather a bad time when we were caught on top of a hill. I was very lucky as my tank was disabled fairly early on and so I missed the worst of it. Well the situation showed signs of getting out of hand with the infantry going off one way and the tanks another when Donovan on his own responsibility put in a determined attack on the main source of the danger, taking Corporal Smith along with him and by his example rallying the entire squadron who then set about doing things the right way. He's amazingly lucky and came out with a whole skin. Corporal Smith is a good chap too, but rather an old soldier and a terrible chap for looting which is not really taken very seriously I'm afraid. When we do get to Germany I'm sure he'll finish up with all Goering's medals or something equally fantastic. You remember Lance-Corporal Knight the serious one I have rather poked fun at once or twice? Well I'm sorry to say that he has died of wounds as well as two others of the original troop. He has been replaced by a Corporal Hilton who is forty-five if he is

*a day and has a son of twenty who is an officer in the infantry.
He seems most conscientious but is not exactly a dashing type.
I recommended that one of my lance-corporals, a youngster
named Brook, be promoted and given a tank but the Major
ruled that he is not yet experienced enough. He is Donovan's
wireless operator who speaks very highly of him. I expect that
he will get his chance soon enough.*

His small son had asked him to bring a tank back with him – 'not
a toy one – a real one'. He sent a message saying that if he couldn't
manage an actual tank he would bring something extra-special to make
up. He sealed the letters and looked round for Sergeant Donovan.

'Better collect all letters and send them down to the squadron office,
Paddy – I don't think we've much time left.'

Donovan had been putting off writing, but at this he nodded and
then climbed into the turret and got down to it:

*My darling wife,
I got two of your letters today and I am sorry if you have
been worried but you know that I am not much of a one for
writing every day like some of the blokes do. I do not know
what they find to write about. Anyway I am all right and
I have not had much bother from what was bothering me
when I was home on leave. It has not been too bad. There
was one sticky do but we came out all right. Major Johnson
told me there was a Course coming up at Bovey for one tank
commander from each Squadron to learn about some new
stuff and that he will put me in for it. But don't bank on it
too much because you know what it is with these courses,
half the time they don't come off or some wailer back at Div.
wangles on it instead and anyway Johnny says that it won't
be for a month yet. If it does come off I can get up from
Dorset for the week-end and I'll wangle to come and see
you on the way through of course. Maybe you could come
and stay down there at Wool or Lulworth Cove. It is very
pretty country round there and it wouldn't hurt the kids to*

have them miss a week's school and we could spend a lot of time together. How much have you got in the savings? I've got about eight quid back pay to come so I should think we could manage it all right but as I said don't go looking forward to this because you never know.

Well I can't think of anything more to say. Give the kids my love. We are having it cushy just now and listen to the wireless a lot. I heard some girl sing 'Red Sails in the Sunset' last night and of course I thought of you like I always do when I hear that song.
Your loving husband
PADDY

Geordie collected all the letters from the troop and carried them down to the lorry which served as squadron headquarters. The squadron clerk pointed to a box to drop them in. Two young officers on censorship duty were struggling through the sudden mass of letters, cutting out with a razor blade occasional indiscretions.

The clerk handed Geordie a typewritten sheet of paper. 'Here you are, Geordie, Orders. Save the runner going up to One Troop. Give it to Mr Grimshaw.'

Geordie waited until he was out of sight of the lorry, then sat down by the side of the road and spread out the paper on his knee. He picked out the words slowly, syllable by syllable.

'*Operation Goodwood...*' What did they always give such fancy names to things for? Goodwood had something to do with racing, didn't it? Maybe it was going to be a race. '*Movement order. Rev. 0230 hrs; move off 0330 hrs.*' He groaned. '*The regiment will move to the area...*' he skipped the unintelligible map references. He could make nothing of the rest of it, but that was enough. He folded up the paper again and hurried back to the troop with the news that they were going in again.

There was no need of the guard to wake them up at two-thirty in the morning, for an air raid did that half an hour before. They rolled out of their blankets and climbed up on the tanks to get a good view. The Germans were bombing the beachhead again.

The dark sky was cut up into segments by the crossing of anti-aircraft searchlights; pathfinder flares on parachutes floated slowly down in brilliant clusters; every now and then the whole area was lit for a second by an enormous flashlight flare as the enemy photographed the activity underneath. Now the sky was mottled with air bursts and further crisscrossed by the thinner lines of tracer bullets; the star shells completed the fantastic design, while below, the pink glow of the spreading fires lit up the smoke which seemed to grow mushroom-like from the ground.

The raid was short and sharp, and by the time they were moving down the road it was already in its last stages.

They arrived at the assembly area at four o'clock in the morning. Donovan woke them all and set them to work covering the tank with brushwood. Then they all got down to sleep again and slept until midday. They awoke and had an enormous meal.

It was hot again and they took off their shirts and sunbathed all afternoon. About five Taffy made some tea and they finished off the bully beef; Donovan came back from a tank commanders' conference at regimental headquarters.

'Over to the troop officer's tank, you shower,' he said. 'He's going to give you the griff.'

'What's it going to be like, Sergeant?' Brook couldn't help asking.

'Well, the Colonel said it was a "to win or lose it all" effort,' Donovan said cynically. They all groaned.

Lieutenant Grimshaw began by indicating a map that he had made out of sticks and stones on the ground.

'This stone,' he said, 'is Caen: and as you know, it has been the main stumbling block in the way of our breaking out of the bridgehead. Since the invasion we have kept almost all the German armour engaged on our front, and as a result the Americans over on our right have been able to regroup and reorganise themselves. This is going to be the heaviest attack of the war. We're going to throw three armoured divisions at Jerry with no infantry support. First the bombers are going to paste the whole area with the heaviest and most concentrated bombing there has ever been, and after that the artillery are going to have a go, and then we advance behind a creeping barrage and finish the knock-out.'

'Sounds cushy,' said Smudger.

'So long as Jerry plays his part,' Lieutenant Grimshaw added. 'He's not noted for being very co-operative, though.'

'How do we advance?' asked Corporal Hilton, the new tank commander. 'A brigade up, or a division?'

'Our brigade up, and we are leading regiment.' There was a pause as that sank in. 'But we're advancing line abreast – no point-tank. A huge force of American heavies are going to drop big bombs first in front of us, and then some mediums are coming in low and fragging a path for us.'

'What's fragging?' several of them asked at once.

'Bombs that burst fifty feet above the ground, kill everyone underneath except the ones in deep shelters, and leave no craters. They'll be followed by a big artillery barrage: actually there are twenty-four field regiments supporting us – that's about six hundred guns on a path two thousand yards wide – and we advance behind that as it lifts. It doesn't seem likely that Jerry will be feeling like a fight after that lot. Now details: we move off from here at one forty-five in the morning, cross the river, and get up to the start line. The heavy bombers are due at five-thirty, and they should finish bombing at seven-thirty; then the artillery starts, and we move off at eight as the barrage lifts. If all this comes off according to plan the war may be over quicker than any of us think.'

Brook felt a tremendous excitement. It might prove to be an historic battle like Alamein or Stalingrad. The weight of the air and artillery attack sounded so impressive that it didn't seem possible that human beings could stand up against it. Morale was very high.

By first light they were in position. Eighty-four tanks line abreast fifty yards apart; behind them, as far as they could see, more tanks and all the impedimenta of an armoured division. They heard the concentrated hum of the heavy bombers approaching before they saw them, and then they came from out of the northern sky like a swarm of locusts.

The ground in front of them was a flat plain stretching south. A thousand yards or less away was a small village on a slight rise of ground silhouetted in the clear light of early morning. For a moment it hung against the still clear sky like a picture on glass, and then, as the enormous weight of bombs dropped, the entire landscape shivered and the picture collapsed into fragments.

For over two hours the planes passed overhead without a break and they watched the bombs bursting until it did not seem possible that a tree could still be standing. At a quarter to eight the last plane disappeared, and immediately the artillery began. Some of the shells dropped short, bursting fifty yards or so in front of them, but they saw that the whole force of the explosion was carried forward. At five to eight the order came to advance.

'It's five minutes early,' Donovan said. 'We'll go straight into our own barrage.' He looked over at Lieutenant Grimshaw in the next tank and pointed to his wrist-watch. Grimshaw nodded his head to show that he knew it was too early, but the whole long line had begun to move forward in obedience to the radioed command, and they moved too.

'The old man wants a bar to his D.S.O.' Donovan said bitterly. 'And we're going to pay for it.'

The artillery barrage was due to start lifting at eight o'clock exactly, and it still lacked two or three minutes of that when they passed over the start line. For perhaps half a minute no shell landed near them, and they began to think that perhaps they were going to get away with it. Lieutenant Grimshaw waved the thumbs-up signal. Just at that moment a hundred-pound shell burst ten yards behind him. A piece of shrapnel caught him between the shoulder blades, and his headless body dropped inside the turret. His gunner stared at him in horror for a moment, and then pushed past the wireless operator and plunged unthinking out of the turret. He jumped off the tank and began to run blindly. He and another shellburst seemed to merge. Donovan and Smudger had gone down inside their turrets and closed their hatches as soon as the first shell landed among the tanks, but Corporal Hilton had kept his hatch open and he also was killed. When the tanks halted they had lost five tank commanders in three minutes. They waited until the barrage began to creep forward, and then followed behind it. Donovan and Smudger opened their hatches and came out again.

The ground ahead of them was a picture of devastation so complete that it could not have been imagined. Every tree, every building, almost every bush, looked as though it had had its own bomb. For the first five miles there was no resistance and it seemed as though the tremendous barrage had been an unqualified success. Their spirits rose as dazed German soldiers came out of their slit trenches and surrendered. They came across a dreaded 88-millimetre anti-tank gun in the shattered village and fired at it point-blank range even though it was not manned. Another one, seven hundred yards in front of them, was destroyed before its shaken crew could bring it to bear. There was a heady feeling of triumph.

And then about ten o'clock the enemy began to hit back hard. From well-concealed positions dominating the plain his tanks and anti-tank guns opened fire, knocking out twelve of the regiment's tanks in the first half-hour. The other regiments of the brigade were having an equally bad time, and although they fought back as well as they could they suffered from the disadvantage of being exposed to good defensive positions and to the great superiority of the German tanks and guns. The advantage which was supposed to be theirs from overwhelming numbers disappeared as they were steadily whittled down throughout the day.

By four o'clock in the afternoon A Squadron's sixteen tanks were reduced to five, and the regiment had only twenty-four left out of an initial fifty-seven. They had been continuously engaged for six hours. Donovan and Smudger were still all right, but besides them there was only Major Johnson the squadron leader, one tank of Two Troop, and one of Three Troop. They were all very tired, and morale was low.

There had been a lull in the fighting, and they had taken the opportunity to get behind the shelter of a railway embankment. C Squadron, which had so far escaped the heaviest fighting, had thirteen tanks left and were engaging some Panthers and Tigers on a far ridge.

They were all listening to the battle on their radios. There was little talk. Brook had gone through every possible stage of terror, and now felt numb. It seemed a miracle to him that they had not been knocked out, for at one time everywhere he looked he saw tanks burning. Donovan had been quietly magnificent, but it was obvious that he also was near the end of his endurance. His voice had broken once or twice, which had never happened before, and Brook had been terrified to see him lay his head on his arm at one point and ignore everything that was going on for half a minute or so. But Donovan had dragged his head up and continued to give his slow clear commands to Hogg, returning their light shells against the terrible German heavy ones.

C Squadron were caught between two groups of Tigers, and were being steadily destroyed. The order came for the remaining five tanks of A Squadron to go to their assistance, and was acknowledged by Major Johnson.

'All stations Love. All right, chaps. Advance line abreast over the embankment and keep firing. Out.'

The five tanks moved to the railway line and started up one side of it. Every tank commander felt that the position was nearly hopeless, but there was no shelter anywhere. As they reached the top an 88 fired, and hit Smudger's tank. Brook and the others saw Smudger come out of his tank like a scalded cat followed by his crew, and they counted them: one, two, three, four – Nobby didn't come out. The next moment they were down the other side and firing back blindly at where they thought the Tiger was likely to be. It made the mistake of firing again, and not only missed but gave away its position, and three of them put armour-piercing shells into it immediately. There was a great sheet of flame, and the noise of its ammunition blowing up. They continued to engage the enemy while what remained of C Squadron extricated themselves from the exposed position – then A Squadron's last four tanks retreated again over the railway tracks. As they passed they saw Smudger's tank burning fiercely. Donovan spotted Nobby, who had somehow got out and dragged himself a few feet away.

'Come on, lads, quick. Get Nobby up on the back of the tank.' He jumped down followed by Brook, Hogg and Geordie, and the four of them lifted Nobby up and as gently as possible laid him on the bedding on the back of the tank. Both his legs were smashed, but he was conscious, and groaning. As they were getting back into the turret he opened his eyes and recognised Brook.

'Put me out of it, mate, please,' he begged.

Donovan pushed Brook down inside the turret and ordered Taffy to continue to reverse to join the other surviving tanks. At the same time he got out the morphine and hypodermic needle issued to all tank commanders and gave Nobby a stiff shot. He put a large M on his forehead with a special pencil to let the doctor know he had had a morphine shot. A few minutes later the ambulance arrived and Nobby was loaded into the last remaining space.

At nine o'clock that night, thirteen hours after the attack had begun, they advanced over the railway line again and took up positions about two hundred yards in front of it. Nothing fired at them this time.

About five hundred yards ahead of them was the spot where the regiment had been caught by the enemy and lost most of its tanks. They could see forty or fifty knocked-out tanks of their own and of the regiment which had been sent in to support them. Many were still burning, and the engine of one was roaring. No ambulance had been able to get up to this area, and they could only guess at the dying and wounded, praying for darkness. At ten o'clock the light began to fade, but it was a cloudless day and last light would not be until eleven. They were all sick with exhaustion, and only fear kept them awake.

Major Johnson looked at the other three tanks left in his squadron and hoped that nothing else would happen that day. At ten-thirty he decided they could pull back beyond the protecting railway line.

'All stations Love. Start pulling back now. Out.'

'Thank Christ!' Donovan said. 'You heard, Taffy – start up.'

The four tanks started their engines and began to crawl backwards, keeping their guns towards the enemy. When they were fifty yards from the embankment six 88s fired together in the fading light. Three of the shells were armour-piercing and two went through Two Troop's tank, killing the commander and the driver. The other A.P. missed, but two of the high-explosive ones hit Donovan's tank.

The noise and the concussion felt as though a shell had exploded inside the tank, but no real damage was done. Brook, coiled and ready to leap out, waited for the order to abandon tank, but it didn't come. Instead he heard Donovan's clear, calm voice giving directions to Taffy.

'Full Throttle... Left Stick... Right Stick... Left Stick... Right Stick.' The voice went monotonously on and the tank reversed in a zigzag pattern like a dancing elephant. The 88s fired again, but the tank's irregular movement saved it. The remaining two tanks of the squadron reached the railway line well ahead of them and got safely over, and it seemed they were going to, too. At the last moment they turned round, because it was necessary to advance to get over the embankment. Just as they reached the top a high-explosive shell hit the back of the tank, and the engines stopped abruptly. At the same moment a bright pink flare landed twenty yards from them. An armour-piercing shell screamed a foot or so over their heads.

Donovan reacted quickly, but still spoke quietly.

'Well, blokes, we've had it. Abandon tank.'

Donovan moved instantly out of the turret, followed by the others. They ran down the safe side of the railway embankment and threw themselves on the ground, expecting their tank to be hit and the ammunition to blow up at any moment; but the flare went out, and left them in darkness.

They could not see anything of the remaining two tanks of A Squadron. They began to walk towards where they supposed the regiment to be. A few minutes later a stick of mortar bombs landed near them, and they all ran in different directions looking for a German slit trench. Brook fell into one about six feet deep and hugged the bottom while more mortars fell all around. Following the mortars came shellfire, and he decided not to get out of his little hole until things were quiet.

The barrage continued spasmodically for ten minutes or so. Then he put his head cautiously out of the hole and called to the others. There was no reply. He started to crawl out of his trench and heard aeroplanes. There had as yet been little sign of the German air force, but after the beating the regiment had taken that day he was quite prepared for the planes to be the enemy's as well. The first bombs fell a thousand yards or so to the rear and were followed by flares, and he knew that the reserves and retreating tanks were being bombed. There didn't seem to be much sense in wandering around alone in no man's land during an air raid, so he got back in his hole and lay down.

When the stick of mortar bombs straddled them Donovan felt as though he had run full tilt into a low iron fence. There was a heavy blow across the front of his thighs and he went down hard. Almost immediately he felt the warm sticky feeling of blood and a dull pain, and he knew he had been hit. A feeling of tremendous relief overwhelmed him, and he could have shouted for joy. Over and over again he thought: 'A Blighty one; a Blighty one! Thank God I copped a Blighty one!' He didn't try to move, and when the mortaring was finished and the others got up he called to them. All except Brook came over to where he was lying.

'I been hit,' he said. 'Give me a hand, will you?'

The three of them lifted him upright, and suddenly the pain came sharp and hot in waves and he wanted to scream. They manhandled him across a hundred yards or so of broken ground to a tank of another regiment in the division, and with their assistance got him up on the back of it. There were two more wounded already there.

'If you blokes keep walking down this track you'll come to the main road which takes you back to echelon,' the tank commander said. 'I'm sorry I can't give you a lift.'

Donovan raised his head. 'What happened to Brook?'

'I seen him run off to the right when the stonk started,' said Geordie.

'Go find him, Geordie, and show him the way back,' said Donovan.

As he ran back the hundred yards or so they had come, Geordie grumbled, 'Someday I'll learn to keep my trap buttoned up.' At that moment the mortaring started again, and they saw Geordie go to ground as they did themselves. The tank started up and left Taffy and Hogg in the ditch.

When it was once more quiet Taffy stood up. Hogg was still lying on the ground, and for a second Taffy thought he'd been hit.

'Hoggy – you all right?'

Hogg groaned, and Taffy knelt beside him.

'What's the matter, mate, you been hit?'

'No, but I can't go on, Taffy. I can't go on any more. You go on and leave me here. I've had enough, Taffy.'

'Come on, don't be stupid – you'll cop it for sure if you stay here. Come on – get on your feet and we'll be back in echelon in no time. They won't have a tank for us, and we'll have a rest.'

'Do you think so? We won't have to go in again tomorrow?'

'No, of course not. What do you think they keep that shower of three-and-fourpence for? You couldn't go in again tomorrow if you wanted to.' He got Hogg to his feet, and half-bullying, half-cajoling got him walking back. When the air raid came they crouched in a ditch for half an hour, and it took all Taffy's ability to get Hogg moving again; but in the end they got to the road, and were picked up by one of the lorries which had taken reinforcements up to the tanks and was now returning to the rear area. When they got there they found that the air raid had scored a direct hit on it and had killed and wounded as many tank crews again as the day's battle. They had some food, and lay down in dead men's blankets.

Three hours later Taffy was awakened by a motor cycle starting up a few feet from his head. He sat up and saw the dispatch rider adjusting his helmet and racing his motor.

'Where you off to, chum?' he said.

'Up to the Thirty-Third tanks.'

Taffy threw off his blankets. 'Give me a lift, will you?' he said, pushing his swollen feet back into his boots.

'I can't. It's against orders.'

'Orders be blowed – who'll know? Come on, be a pal.'

'What do you want to go for?'

'Because that's my mob, that's why.'

'All right, but if we get stopped you say I found you wandering about – all right?'

Taffy agreed and climbed on the back of the motor bike, and the D.R. roared out of the camp and along the road as though he were in a race.

SIX

BY MIDNIGHT the air raid was over and everything was comparatively quiet. Brook climbed out of the slit trench and sat on the edge with his legs dangling inside, and tried to decide what to do next. He felt a little light-headed, and talked aloud to himself.

'We've lost about ninety-five per cent of our tanks today, and by some fluke I'm still alive. Whether I stay alive depends on luck and on me. I can't push my luck much further. If I try to keep on like this I'm bound to be killed, or at least injured.'

The sound of his voice made him feel better.

'Now, I can walk towards the German lines shouting "Kamerad!" at the top of my voice, or I can get back in this hole and stay there for the rest of the night, or I can make an honest effort to find our own lines. If I get back into the hole no one will blame me when they come up and retake this ground tomorrow. If Jerry takes it instead, then I'll finish out the war in a prison camp – and it can't be more than a few months now.'

He tried seriously to contemplate giving himself up. Then he thought that probably the Germans wouldn't be too happy themselves after the heavy fighting of the day before, and it might not be too easy just to surrender. He suddenly thought of his father and mother – it was not so much that they would mind his being taken prisoner but there was bound to be a long period of uncertainty when he would be posted 'Missing Believed Killed', and he knew what torture that would be to them.

He tried logically to present the alternatives to himself, and he suddenly realised that in thinking this was a question of cold logical choice, he was deluding himself. It became crystal clear to him that he wasn't going to give himself up. He was going to be all right, and the mathematical probabilities didn't have anything to do with it. He was going to go on as long as he could; and if a time came when he couldn't go on then that would be that, but he certainly wouldn't be arguing the alternatives with himself.

He nearly laughed aloud with relief. Feeling much better he stood up, and decided to climb the embankment and have a look at the battlefield.

From the railway line he could see seven burning tanks. Every now and then some ammunition in one or other of them exploded. He looked up the railway line until he could just make out the dark shape of his own tank still balanced on the top. He realised that he was cold – he was wearing nothing but slacks, a shirt and gym shoes. He had had a 'bale-out bag' packed and alongside him in the turret, but when the time came he had thought of nothing but getting out. He walked along the railway line towards the tank.

He was no more than fifteen yards from the tank when suddenly all his new-found bravery left him, and he froze to the spot. He could hear someone talking, inside the tank. He thought it must be German infantry who had come forward to explore, and he wondered how he was going to escape. Then he realised that the voice was coming over the wireless, and that his earphones were hanging over the side where they had pulled off his head as he leapt out.

He went up to the tank and listened.

'I say again...' It was the colonel's voice, heavy with fatigue. 'I want fifty. Figures fifty. Over.'

A very faint voice answered. 'Fifty men? You want fifty men? Over.'

'No. Fifty tanks. Fifty tanks. I need fifty tanks to make up my strength.'

The faint voice acknowledged the request, and the wireless went silent.

Brook stared fascinated at the headset dangling from the tank, and almost without realising what he was doing picked up the microphone and pressed the pressle switch. He heard the hum of the wireless change, which told him he was broadcasting.

'Love four. Love four,' he said. 'Report my signals. Over.'

The answer came almost immediately: 'Love Four. Strength five. Where are you?'

'Love Four. I have come back to my tank which is on the railway line. Shall I destroy it? Over.'

'Love Four. Is it all right – can you get it going? Over.'

'I don't think so but I will have a try. Out.'

He walked round and got into Taffy's seat. He pressed the big starting button, not expecting anything to happen, but the motors started instantly. He reached for the driver's microphone. Then he stopped.

He suddenly realised that if the engines started that easily, they had probably only stalled when the shell hit the back of the tank, and the tank should not have been abandoned. He knew that Donovan had done the right thing for they had been a helpless target perched on the railway line with a flare lighting them up: but it might not seem that way to the colonel. On the other hand if he reported that the engines would not start he would be ordered to destroy the tank, and he knew that every tank would count when light came. He could not be responsible for the regiment not having this tank, but he could not be the cause of Donovan's record being spoiled.

The solution came to him. The tank was powered by five aero engines but would move on three. If he were to put two out of action by smashing something with a spanner he could get the tank back that night, and Donovan would be absolved from abandoning it without cause. He could make sure that it was the kind of damage that REME could quickly repair. He spoke into the microphone.

'Hello, Love Four. Two or three engines are not working but I think I can get it crawling on the others. Over.'

'Love Four. Right. Bring it in. We need it. Over.'

'Love Four, Wilco, can you tell me how to find you? Over.'

There was a pause, and he wondered if his set had failed to broadcast: but then the colonel's voice came up again:

'Give me your name, rank and number.'

He was puzzled, for he had often been told for security reasons not to use any names over the air: but he recognised the colonel's voice, and thought it best to obey.

'79913915 Lance-Corporal Brook M. R.,' he replied in the army manner.

'Your troop and squadron?'

'One Troop, A Squadron.'

'Where and when did you join the regiment?'

Then it registered on him that the colonel was satisfying himself that he was not talking to the enemy. 'February this year at Bridlington,' he said promptly.

'Who was second-in-command of A Squadron at that time?' the colonel asked quickly.

'Captain Macdonald.'

'Right. Now you are doing remarkably well, but I want you to carry on with another task. From where you are you should be able to see a number of tanks burning – about five hundred yards to your front. Do you see them?'

He climbed out of the driver's seat and up on top of the turret. The burning tanks lit up the battlefield like a nightmare.

'Yes, I can see them,' he reported.

'Can you hear one of the engines racing?'

It had been going on since they were first knocked out. He reported that he could.

'Now I want you to take your tank over there to that one, where you will find a badly wounded driver and a wireless operator staying with him. We haven't been able to get the blood wagon up there. Get him up on your tank and bring him in. Bring them both in and anyone else you see wandering about out there. Understood?'

'Love Four. Wilco. Out.'

He got down off the turret, and was about to get into the driver's seat when a voice spoke out of the darkness a few feet from him, and his heart nearly stopped with fright.

'Brookie?' it said plaintively. 'Is that you, Brookie?'

'Yes. For Christ's sake who is it?'

Geordie Brunch's face appeared.

'Oh you, Geordie! Thank God! You can drive this damn thing now.'

'What!' Geordie backed away. 'Are you bloody mad or something? What do you think Jerry's going to do when he sees it move off? Come off of there – I got a nice warm slit trench over here.'

'Wait a minute, Geordie, listen to this...' He got hold of the microphone again. 'Hello, Love Four. The co-driver has just turned up and will drive while I command – over.'

Geordie gasped.

'Hello, Love Four.' The colonel sounded pleased. 'First class. You're doing well – both of you. Now get on with it and bring in those other chaps. Out.'

Geordie was swearing bitterly.

'Why the hell I didn't bloody well stay where I was and not come sticking my nose in, I don't know. When I heard the tank start up I might have known it was you – anybody else would have more sense. I'm getting out of here, and you can bloody well go driving around on your own.'

'Now Geordie, you heard what the Colonel said – he said you were doing well, and you'll probably get promotion and a medal for this bit of work.'

He tried to calm Geordie.

'Jerry doesn't know we're here, because he can't see beyond the burning tanks. And anyway he's not going to be watching the battlefield now, he's going to be getting what kip he can before morning. There's a badly wounded bloke over there and we might save his life – you'd expect him to try and fetch you in, wouldn't you? Come on, now – you're not windy, are you, Geordie?'

'Of course I'm not windy. I just don't believe in playing silly buggers, that's all. I done my job all right today and I don't have to do nothing like this.'

'Yes you do, Geordie – you do now, because the Colonel knows about you being here and he's ordered you to; and if you don't get in and drive I'll report that you refused, and you'll be court-martialled and probably shot.'

'Don't be bloody silly,' Geordie said uneasily. 'They don't shoot you for that these days.'

'Come on, Geordie – it's going to be all right.'

'Where is this bloke, then?'

'Over by that tank with the engine revving. It's not far.'

'All right, but if anyone fires at us I'm shoving off without waiting for you.' He climbed into the driver's seat and reversed off the embankment, turned the tank round and started forward.

'A bit over to the left,' said Brook. 'And go slowly, because I can't see much.'

'Don't worry. I'll go so slow they won't think we're moving at all.'

After a minute or so Brook's eyes became accustomed to the light and he saw that the way was clear. There were a few tanks between them and the ones that were burning, and he hoped that one of these near ones was the one with its engine going. But as yet he couldn't see; he could just hear the noise getting louder as they approached.

'Geordie,' he said, over the wireless, 'what happened to Donovan and the rest?'

'He got hit by a bit of mortar.'

'Dead?'

'No. Hogg and Taffy carried him to one of the Hussars' tanks. He sent me back to find you and then the stonk started and I got down in a slit trench. Where were you?'

'I was down in one too, and I stayed there until things got quiet. I hope Paddy's all right. Where did it get him?'

'Across the legs. He'll be all right. He's tough.'

A few minutes later they were able to detect the tank with its motor running, and headed for it.

When they were a few yards away a small figure seemed to rise out of the ground and run towards them.

'Stop, Geordie!' said Brook.

'Doctor, Doctor!' cried the figure. 'Over here, Doctor.'

It was 'Tich' Morris, a B Squadron wireless operator whom Brook knew by sight.

'I'm not the doctor, I'm Brook of A Squadron. We'll get your bloke to the doctor as soon as we can. Where is he?'

'Over here by the tank. Thank God you've come. I thought I'd go out of my head if someone didn't come! It's Tom Moore, Sergeant Whitaker's driver. It's smashed both his legs and the pain is awful. I gave him all the morphia I could find but it doesn't seem to do him any good. He's my mate.'

Morris was obviously on the verge of collapse.

They stopped the tank and walked over to where Tom Moore lay groaning on the ground. Brook had not known the name, but he recognised him now. He was one of the biggest men in the regiment, and always stood out on parades. He knelt beside him.

Moore opened his eyes.

'I'll live, Doc, won't I?' he said.

'Of course you'll live,' said Brook, trying to sound like a doctor. 'We'll have you right as rain in no time.'

'I know I'll never walk again but I don't give a damn about that so long as I live. I will live, won't I?'

'If you've lived this long then it means you're going to be all right,' Brook said, illogically. 'And we'll probably fix up your legs too.'

'You'd better have a look at them before you say that, Doc.'

Tich Morris handed him a torch and he turned it on Moore's legs.

From the knees down they looked as though a steam roller had crushed them. It was impossible to tell one leg from the other. There was a mass of splintered bone and pulped flesh, ending incongruously in two army boots which didn't seem to belong to the rest at all.

Brook flicked off the light. Tich Morris began to moan like an animal.

'How the hell did he get out of the tank?' said Geordie hoarsely.

'I got him out,' Tich Morris said. 'I don't know how, but I got him out. He's my mate.' He began to cry, uncontrollably.

'Well, come on and let's see if we can get him up on the back of the tank.' Brook knew that if he could get little Morris working he would probably hang on a bit longer.

He got his hands under Moore's shoulders with the head on his lap. Geordie and Tich put their hands under his hips from either side, and they all heaved up together. Moore was very heavy and they staggered to their feet.

As they moved a pace or two forward Brook stepped on something which seemed to tug at them, and Moore screamed and fainted. Brook looked down and saw that he was stepping on Moore's foot which had been left behind and was attached to the rest of his body by a long tendon.

They put him down again.

'We need to make a splint,' said Brook.

'The cleaning rods,' Geordie suggested.

'That's it. Get them off the tank, Geordie, and a couple of blankets.'

Tich was sitting on the ground holding his head in his hands, making little whimpering noises.

'Come on, Tich.' Brook put his hand on the other's shoulder. 'It won't be long now.'

'I've been here with him since two o'clock this afternoon. I can't stand it anymore. I can't stand it.'

'As soon as we get his legs wrapped up in the blankets and tied to the cleaning rods we can hoist him up on the tank and then we'll take him to the M.O. and he'll be all right. You've got to hang on for a bit more.'

'All right. I'll be all right. Let's get on with it.'

Geordie came down off the tank with the sections of cleaning rod used to pull-through the big gun, two blankets, and some clothes-line from someone's bed-roll. Moore was still unconscious. They scooped up the mess that had been his lower legs and got it on to a blanket, which they wrapped round, making a bundle. Then they tied a cleaning rod to each side of him, and put another blanket round that and roped him up like a mummy. It was not then too difficult to get him on the back of the tank. Tich sat holding Moore's head in his lap. Geordie got in the driver's seat and started up, and Brook got in the turret. As they moved off Moore regained consciousness again and Tich tried to soothe him.

When they moved away from the light of burning tanks it was too dark to see, and Brook got out and walked ahead of the tank, directing Geordie with the torch. He felt, as he walked slowly across the battlefield shining his torch up and down, that it was all now completely unreal. It seemed so obvious that one of the enemy would see a torch bobbing around in front of them and fire at it, that he just felt a numb terror, waiting for the bullet. But nothing at all happened. When they got over the railway embankment they found a road running north, and he was able to get back into the turret again. When a few minutes later they came across a convoy of reinforcements, they knew they had pulled it off.

Brook saw the tanks leaguered up just ahead of him. There were pitifully few. He reported on the wireless, and was told to come in to the centre of the leaguer, where the M.O. and stretcher-bearers were standing by.

In a matter of moments they had Moore off, and on to the stretcher. He opened his eyes and recognised the doctor.

'I'm going to live, aren't I, Doc? I'm not going to die, am I, Doc?'

The M.O. looked as though he was ready to drop to the ground with fatigue. He put his hand on Moore's forehead for a moment.

'You're going to be all right now,' he said. 'Don't worry.'

Tich Morris had dropped off the tank and fallen to the ground, where he lay still. Brook tried to lift him up thinking that he had fainted, but Tich resisted. Brook looked at the doctor. The doctor had seen it and now crossed over and tried to raise Tich's head from the ground.

Tich looked up, and recognising the doctor, clutched his ankles with both hands.

'Don't make me go in a tank again, sir, don't make me go in a tank again, don't make me go in a tank again sir, don't make me go in a tank.'

Brook felt the other's panic chill him. He stared in horror at the small man gibbering at the doctor's feet.

The doctor stooped and gripped Tich's shoulders, and bent him back forcing him to look up. Tich's eyes were as wild as a frightened colt's.

'Listen to me, Morris, *listen* to me,' the doctor commanded. 'Do you know who I am? Who am I, Morris?'

All this time Tich had been mumbling the same words over and over, but now he stopped and said dully, 'Yes sir, you're the M.O.'

'Right. Now listen carefully. I give you my *word of honour* that you will never have to go in a tank again. Do you understand?'

'I don't have to go in a tank again?'

'Never.'

For a moment, neither spoke. Then Morris shuddered, and dropped his head.

The doctor went on. 'Now you're going to be all right. Get up and walk with me, and I'll give you something to make you sleep and then we'll take you back out of here.'

The doctor got to his feet, and Tich slowly rose too. They walked off together towards the ambulance.

'By Christ,' said Geordie fervently, 'if I ever hear anyone say a word against the M.O. again I'll beat his bloody head in.'

Major Johnson came over and congratulated them and told them to get some food and sleep.

'You won't get much sleep, because it's two-thirty now and we go back in at four-thirty; but take what you can.'

'How many tanks will we be, sir?' said Brook.

The major looked at him for a moment, and then, evidently satisfied, answered, 'We had forty-two tanks knocked out today; with reinforcements we think we can mount twenty-five tomorrow.'

When he had gone, Brook and Geordie looked at each other.

'Christ!' said Geordie. 'Forty-two out of fifty-seven. I wish to hell I'd stayed in my warm slit trench.'

'You and me both.'

After they had eaten their fill of bully beef stew they went over to the casualty post to inquire about Sergeant Donovan and Nobby.

'Nobby Clarke died,' the medical sergeant told them. 'Paddy Donovan caught a nasty lot of shrapnel in both legs, and nobody can tell what'll happen. He had a blood transfusion here, and he seemed to be not too bad – but he may lose a leg, or even both legs.'

They went back to their tank, on which the mechanics were hard at work. Brook realised that he had forgotten to do anything to the engines. As they dragged their bed-rolls off, the corporal in charge looked up.

'Don't worry – we'll have this one ready in time,' he said.

'Don't split yourselves for our sake,' Geordie said bitterly.

They pushed their ground-sheets and blankets under the tank and stretched out on top of them.

Brook dragged himself from the bliss of deep sleep when the sound of his name being shouted pierced his consciousness. It sounded like the sergeant-major's voice... It was the sergeant-major's voice!

He opened his eyes and sat up, banging his head on the

underside of the tank. He crawled hurriedly out, wondering what he had done wrong.

'Here I am, sir, over here,' he shouted. The sergeant-major appeared.

'Ho – there you are. Come on, look lively – the Colonel wants to see you, lad.'

He hurried over to the colonel's tank wondering if they had found out that there was nothing wrong with the tank's engines. The colonel looked years older, and as though he had had no sleep for days. When Brook saluted he looked up from his map and turned his red-rimmed eyes on him.

'Yes?' he said wearily.

'You wanted to see me, sir – Lance-Corporal Brook of A Squadron.'

'Oh yes, of course – Brook. You did very well yesterday, Corporal, and we're proud of you. I'm promoting you to full corporal immediately, and I'm going to give you a tank to command for today's show. I'm sure you'll do well. That's all.'

'Yes, sir. Thank you, sir.'

Brook turned away filled with an awful pride. He couldn't remember ever having felt like it before. He was ready to take on any task that was set him.

Geordie asked, 'What did the old man want?'

'He said I'd done well and he promoted me to full corporal. He's going to give me a tank of my own for today's do.' He tried to keep the exultation from his voice, but failed.

Geordie was obviously delighted.

'That's the stuff, Brookie boy; a King's Corporal – that's what you are – a King's bloody Corporal, and nobody can't bust you only the King. You can tell the sar'nt-major to stuff hisself and he can't do nothing about it.'

'He didn't say anything about that...' Brook started to object, but Geordie overruled him.

'Of course you are,' he said. 'Stands to reason, don't it? If you're made up in the field like that?'

'Well we'll see about that, but now we've got to get over to the three-and-fourpence and pick out the rest of the crew – a co-driver for you, and a gunner and operator for me.'

'Now wait a minute, Brookie,' said Geordie, 'wait a minute. *I* haven't been promoted – only you. And I had a basinful yesterday. No, you go on and get yourself a medal – but if you don't mind, not me.'

Brook began to protest, and then realised that what Geordie said was true. There was no lack of crews, for there had been a full complement of reinforcements sent up with the new tanks, and there were the uninjured ones from the day before.

'All right, Geordie,' he said, 'but come on over with me while I get them anyway, will you?'

They walked over to where the reinforcements and tankless crews were eating breakfast. It was just getting light in the east.

Brook asked the sergeant-major for a complete crew for his tank. The sergeant-major congratulated him on his promotion, and he felt the glow of pride come again. They went down the list of names together looking for any they recognised.

'Sanderstead – Mr Grimshaw's operator,' Brook said. 'I'll take him.'

'Sanderstead!' the sergeant-major shouted.

Sanderstead came over immediately, and greeted Brook.

The sergeant-major said, 'You're to be Corporal Brook's operator today.'

'If you don't mind,' Sanderstead said with his soft Scotch burr, 'I'd rather be the gunner. I'm a pretty good gunner,' he added modestly.

'All right,' Brook agreed. They took the next wireless operator on the list, who was named Wilcox. He was young and studious looking, and reminded them a bit of Lance-Corporal Knight. He listened carefully to his instructions and seemed very conscientious. They picked a driver and co-driver they didn't know, and went back to the tank. Geordie was packing his gear and preparing to go back to the reinforcements, trusting to his knowledge of the routine to keep out of the way.

They got the new ammunition in and the petrol and oil replenished, and were about to move off, when Taffy came up.

'Hi, wait for me,' he said.

'Taffy! I thought you were back with Paddy and Hogg.'

'I was,' said Taffy, 'but I got a lift up with a D.R. this morning. I heard about your promotion, Brookie – congratulations. The Major said I can have my tank back if you want me.'

'Don't be bloody silly,' said Brook. 'Hi, you – I'm sorry, I forget your name. This is Taffy's tank, so you'll have to go back to the reinforcements...'

The new driver got out grinning. 'Suits me,' he said. 'I don't want no medals.'

Taffy eyed Geordie with his small pack on his back.

'Where you think you're going, Geordie?' he said.

Geordie stopped, with a mock scowl.

'Oh, all right, all right, I'll get me bloody self killed like the rest o' you. Come on, mate, out o' there.'

The new co-driver climbed out and caught up with the other.

'Right,' said Brook. 'Now we'll just keep our heads down and we'll be all right. And Taffy, you're more experienced than I am, so if you see me doing something silly just tell me, will you?'

'Well if it's *bloody* silly, I will; but you're going to be all right, Brookie – just like Nobby always said. How is he, do you know?'

'Yes. He's dead.'

Taffy's face fell.

'Poor old Nobby,' he said. 'Smudger'll take it hard. They were mates up on the blue, you know. Well, a good few blokes got it yesterday. Let's hope it's not so rough today.'

That day the atmosphere was one of caution. Their objectives were the villages immediately in front of them, and now that the strength of the enemy was understood they moved forward slowly and in great strength – and, what was more important, with supporting infantry. It had been proved yet again that the infantry was indispensable.

Brook, over-anxious to do the right thing, gave too many orders and was too much inclined to use the wireless. He was told once by the major not to waffle – which filled him with shame, and his triumphs of the day before seemed ashes. Taffy wisely ignored many of his orders to move, and, the only two times that they were unnecessarily exposed, got the tank into a protected position almost before Brook knew where the danger was. But by the end of the day Brook had learned a lot. He was beginning to have a tank commander's eyes, and had learned to appreciate how much he could trust Taffy.

Sandy, the new gunner, was first-class. He was cool and quick, though he always waited until he saw exactly what he wanted to hit. The principal event in the day was their suddenly being switched from their objective and swung in to the assistance of another regiment of the brigade who were being shot up from a village to their right. The colonel realised the situation, and acting independently swung his regiment in from the other side so that they came in behind the enemy's guns. Sandy kept firing fast, and when the guns' crews broke and ran he raked them with machine gun fire. Then their supporting infantry, who were small, tough Welsh miners, went in with bayonets and finished the job.

'That was grand,' said Sandy. 'I always wanted to be a gunner but they made me an operator. I told them I'd rather be a gunner but they wouldn't listen.'

'I was an operator myself,' said Brook. 'Why do you prefer a gunner's job?'

Sandy looked at him with clear, innocent eyes, and smiled. 'I just like killing the bastards,' he said.

It was Wilcox's first action, and Brook, already feeling something of an old-timer, could guess at his feelings. But Wilcox showed little sign of strain, apart from keeping his eyes glued to his periscope and trying to see everything that was going on. He did his job well, and without fuss. The wireless was kept right on net the whole time, and the gun was loaded quickly and calmly. Because of Brook's inexperience he was kept in a supporting role and not given any of the important and dangerous tasks he had become used to with Sergeant Donovan.

The squadron lost seven more tanks that day, of which five were in action for the first time. When they pulled back again at last light Brook had gone through the state of fatigue in which it didn't seem possible to keep his eyes open and he was moving like an automaton. Food had been prepared and brought up to them, and they sat round eating it without talking, dreading the physical work that was to follow of throwing out the empty shell-cases and loading in the heavy new ones, lifting up the full jerricans, and the many other little jobs that had to be done. When they were told that they had had enough and were being pulled out for a rest, they were too tired to cheer.

They slept where they were, and in the morning moved to the edge of a completely shattered village to await new tanks and new men to rebuild their torn regiment.

Brook walked over to the ambulance to find out about Tom Moore and to see if there was any news of Donovan.

'Can you tell me about that chap we brought in, sir – Tom Moore?' he asked the M.O.

'He didn't pull through, I'm afraid. I don't know how he stayed alive as long as he did.'

'And Sergeant Donovan?'

'He's lost his left leg. He's going to be all right, though. I saw him last night, and he's as cheerful as a cricket. He asked about you, and was very pleased that you'd brought the tank in. I expect you'll be able to see him when we get settled – unless they fly him back to England, of course.'

When Brook got back to the tank the rest of them were already getting all their kit out and spreading it on the ground. Wilcox, the new operator, was conscientiously doing the maintenance on his set and running the little petrol motor inside the turret which charged the wireless batteries.

'Another hard worker, just like you, Brookie,' said Geordie with a wink.

Major Johnson was catching up on his paper work. Squadron strength returns, confidential reports, a query about wastage of diesel oil and another about smoke flares, a missing gallon of rum – he grinned to himself – a note from the colonel asking for medal recommendations and another confirming that Sergeant Donovan M.M. and bar, had been awarded the second bar to his M.M. for the action on Hill 112.

'Sergeant-Major.'

'Sir?'

'Donovan got his third M.M. See that it goes on orders tonight, will you?'

'Yes, sir. Good old Paddy. Christ knows he earns them.'

Good old Paddy, thought the major. And now safely out of it with no worse than a leg off. He'd go down and see him that evening and tell him about his third gong.

He opened a letter addressed to 'The Commanding Officer, A Squadron' which was a bit unusual. It was inexpertly typed, on a sheet of plain paper.

Dear Sir,
I regret to inform you that on the night of Sunday the 16th inst. at about 1145 hrs a flying bomb scored a direct hit on No. 38 Ebers Road, Hammersmith. Among those killed were Mrs Patrick Donovan and her two children, Michael and Anne. Will you please inform Sergeant Donovan of this.
I am, Sir, Your Obedient Servant,
C. R. TRASK
Captain
Hammersmith Home Guard

SEVEN

AFTER TWO WEEKS of idleness the division had been suddenly moved like a chessman right across the bridgehead from east to west. Here the country was heavily wooded; the narrow roads ran between high, thick hedges, and there seemed to be a natural anti-tank position every hundred yards or so. The ground rose and fell like a washboard, and every ridge could have concealed an anti-tank gun. It would have been difficult, they told each other bitterly, to find worse tank country.

For two frustrating days they crawled about like blind beetles. They had to carry supporting troops with them everywhere, advancing a few hundred yards and then waiting while the infantry went ahead of them to clear the woods on either side of the road. When this was done the Engineers walked down the road carefully, covering every foot with their detectors, marking where the mines had been buried, and finally lifting them delicately. Only then were the tanks allowed to lumber on. The big, clumsy vehicles seemed more trouble than they were worth.

And then, it seemed in a moment, everything changed. One of the fast, light reconnaissance regiments roaming far out in front of them in armoured cars stumbled on an unmined, unguarded track. It ran through the woods, straight as the flight of a bullet, into the heart of the enemy-held country. Reconnaissance exploited it recklessly, finding that it led to an undamaged bridge over the river which formed the enemy's defence line.

The opportunity was seized boldly. The armour funnelled through the hole as fast as it could be pushed, fanning out behind the German lines. The whole picture of the campaign changed in a few hours.

B Squadron led the regiment against hastily organised and generally ineffective opposition and took the first little hillside town, which had looked so formidable an obstacle on the map, after a few minutes' sharp fighting. They swept on to gain as much ground as possible while the enemy were still off balance.

A Squadron was right behind B, One Troop up and Corporal Brook leading. He got to a little cobblestoned market square just as the last tank of B Squadron's H.Q. Troop disappeared down a narrow street on the other side. As twenty tanks had already crossed the square there didn't seem any need for particular caution, and it certainly didn't seem possible that there could be an undetonated anti-tank mine still there; but half-way across, the ground heaved under them, a solid wall of noise smacked them, and cobblestones and earth spewed over the houses as though from a volcano.

It was all over in a few seconds. Brook, his head ringing, knew what had happened, and wiping the dust from his eyes looked anxiously round for the damage. The right-hand track had been cut and was now stretched straight out behind them.

Lieutenant Henderson, the new troop officer, stopped by them.

'Everyone all right?' he shouted.

They were all shaken but unhurt. Brook gave the thumbs up sign.

'Wait for REME then – see you in a day or two.'

He gave the order and the squadron started to move on.

Smudger, who was now troop sergeant, stopped.

'Looks like the town's deserted – lots of lovely loot,' he shouted over the noise of the engines.

Brook nodded, Smudger and the rest of the regiment swept by them, and after a few minutes the familiar noises of tank engines, gears changing and tracks chewing up the road could no longer be heard. The silence of the countryside flowed back. Brook pulled his headset off his aching head and clambered stiffly out of the turret.

'Geordie – get up here and man the Bren just in case there are any odd Jerries swanning about. Sandy, get cracking with a brew. Wilcox, stay on the air and keep in touch with them for as long as you can still receive. Taffy, let's have a look at the damage.'

A piece of the track had been blown to bits; the bogie-wheel which carried it round was badly bent; the mechanism for revolving the turret had jammed. There was nothing to do but wait for the repair gangs to come up. Normally they were not far behind the armour, but this time only fighting vehicles had been put across the bridge. It was then about nine o'clock in the morning, and Brook knew the repair gang was not likely to get there before that evening. He looked round for a comfortable place within reach of the tank to put his crew.

The building immediately in front of them was a wooden-framed hotel in a pleasant garden. Brook walked round the back and found an apple orchard not more than fifty yards from the tank. The green grass looked inviting. Leaving Wilcox on duty in the tank listening to the wireless, they carried their cooking things and bed-rolls over to the orchard and in a few minutes made a comfortable bivouac.

They had acquired in their travels a side of bacon, a crate of eggs, and an enormous old black-iron frying-pan. Taffy got a fire going, and cut five large ham steaks which were soon sizzling; then he methodically broke eggs into the pan until the entire surface was covered with them. It took about forty eggs to do this, but Brook knew they would all be eaten without difficulty. After five years of regarding eggs as semiprecious they enjoyed wallowing in them, and apparently without ill effect. They had now been sleeping out for about six weeks, and during most of the time it had been raining, so they had been soaked and dried out many times: but they were all healthier than they had ever been before.

About ten o'clock in the morning the people of the village began coming in from the countryside, where they had been hiding during the attack. First they hurried to their shops and houses, surveying the broken windows with amusement, and they were obviously pleased that the damage was not worse. Then they came to the tank, and each formally shook hands with every member of the crew.

Wilcox, Sandy and Brook all managed schoolboy French phrases, which quite delighted them; Taffy and Geordie solemnly shook hands and spoke in English, which delighted them no less. They seemed to queue up for the handshaking ceremony as though it was a necessary part of the important day's events. Brook was questioned about the campaign. What parts of France had already been liberated? Where were the Allies now? Where would they go next? How long would the war last? Was it certain that the Germans would not return?

Would other landings now be made? He explained that he was only a corporal and that he knew almost nothing about the higher strategy of the war. They thought he was being discreet, and praised him for it.

The tank was surrounded by a group of twenty or thirty people all talking at once and all eager to show their appreciation. Bottles of Calvados were shoved at them, and Brook realised that if he didn't do something his entire crew would soon be completely drunk. He handed the bottles back to their owners, who laughed but took them away.

About twelve o'clock, when the crowd had mostly drifted away except for a couple of dozen children, the proprietress of the hotel came out and formally invited them all to a lunch with the mayor, the gendarmes, who were also officers in the Maquis, and the leader of the local resistance movement, who had been notified and was hurrying into town. Brook accepted with thanks.

The lunch tasted fantastically good to them, for they had been living for too long on army rations and what they could scrounge. The cutlets cooked with garlic, the new potatoes and little peas, the sliced tomato in oil and vinegar sprinkled with parsley, the little, unbelievably tasty omelettes, the farm cheese and the wine all seemed to be of a mythical quality.

'It's a bloody banquet, that's what it is,' Geordie said with his mouth full. 'What is this meat – some kind of chicken?'

'It's veal, you great gormless clot,' Sandy said pleasantly.

There was still no sign of the infantry fighting in front of them or of the reinforcements and supplies. Brook decided they must be using another road. From what Wilcox was able to hear on the wireless it seemed that their brigade were still out by themselves and were getting worried about their exposed flanks. Brook realised that their own position would be very uncomfortable if an attack should come in from the flanks, for the town was a logical objective.

About four o'clock they heard the noise of a tank approaching from the way they had come.

'Here comes REME, lads. Get your kit ready in case we have to go back to the reinforcements.'

But it was not the breakdown crew. It was a single tank from divisional headquarters with a young staff officer in it. It stopped just in front of them and the officer jumped down and came over.

'Who's in command here?' he asked.

Brook saluted. 'I am, sir.'

'Right. What's wrong with your tank?'

'Broken track, bent bogie-wheel, and turret jammed.'

'I see. Anyone else here?'

'No, sir.'

'Now listen carefully. There are fifteen Tigers swanning around about two to three miles east of here. They've broken through your chaps and are now behind the Guards Armoured. They've been quiet for the last hour or so and are probably waiting for dark. We don't know which way they'll go when they move, but it looks as though they'll only have two choices. They'll either go south, in which case they'll run smack into the Guards Armoured, or they'll come west – through here. Do you follow that?'

'Yes, sir. Were there many casualties in our regiment when they broke through?'

'What? Oh. About ten, I think. Now, two things are important: one is that we know quickly which way they are coming, and the other is that if they *do* come through here we want them held up as long as possible. Now I'm going to tow your tank down the road to where you can cover the approach from the east. If they come this way you must first report the fact and make sure that the report is received, and then you must engage the leading elements and hold them up for as long as you can. Is that clear?'

Brook swallowed. 'Yes, sir. But haven't you forgotten that my turret is jammed? I can't traverse my gun.'

'Won't it move on hand at all?'

'No, sir. The gun will elevate or depress, but not traverse.'

'In that case we shall have to put you in position so that your gun is pointing down the road. Anything else?'

'No, sir.'

'Right. Let's get on with it, then.'

They put a steel hawser to the front of their tank, and the other tank hauled it slowly up the road with the crew feeding the broken track in by hand under the wheels. About two hundred yards from the village was a slight rise, from which they could get a fairly good hull-down position. Here Brook asked them to stop, and sent Geordie down the road to the position where the front of any approaching vehicle would first appear. They pulled the tank about until the gun was pointing at Geordie, and then wedged it with large rocks in that position.

The young officer seemed impressed. 'Good show. Now do you understand your orders?'

'Yes, sir. If they come this way I'm to report it – what they are – and then we're to hold them up as long as we can.'

'Right. Good. My wireless operator will give yours all the gen. Use your own call sign. Now are you sure you've got your gun lined up all right?'

'I think so. But as soon as it gets a bit darker I'll send someone down the road to the exact spot and we can sight on a match through the firing-pin hole.'

'Oh yes. Most ingenious. What's your name?'

'We're Thirty-Third Tanks, sir.'

'I know that. What's *your* name?'

'Corporal Brook, sir.'

'Right. Well, I know you lads will put up a good show. Now I'm going to tell the villagers what's up, so they can get ready to evacuate. We'll send some three-tonners for them in an hour or so and get them back to a safe place just in case Jerry does retake this town temporarily. Good luck to you.'

He strode briskly back to his tank, and it disappeared towards the town.

No one spoke for a minute.

Geordie spat. 'I don't want no bloody V.C.'

'One of these do-or-die wallahs,' said Taffy. 'Only we do the dying.'

'Don't worry,' said Brook, 'I'll see that you don't get killed that easily.'

'So you say,' Geordie grumbled. 'But I don't like it. This is a job for volunteers.'

The laughter eased the tension a bit.

'Now come on.' Brook tried to sound confident. 'Let's get organised, and don't flap. Geordie, get the Bren gun out and fix the tripod, and then get a couple of boxes of ammo and set it up alongside the tank.'

'Why?' said Geordie.

Brook restrained his impatience.

'Because it's no bloody good in the tank and it gives us an extra fire point and it may possibly persuade Jerry that we're a little stronger on the ground than we are.'

'Where am I going to be, then?'

'Get the gun out and I'll show you. Come on, that's enough nattering. Give him a hand, will you, Taffy? Wilcox – have you got any matches? Right. Come with me, will you? Sandy, take over the set for the time being.'

They pulled and jerked the gun about while Wilcox patiently lit matches, until finally Sandy could see the match flame through the firing-pin hole. They wedged it in that position.

'Now we're bang on,' said Brook. 'We'll knock out anything that gets to that point anyway.'

'Aye,' said Sandy. 'And then what happens, may I ask?'

'Well, perhaps we'll give them a belt of Bren and a bit of Browning, and even one or two H.E.s for a minute or so. Then we'll buzz off and take to the country. We'll have done what we can and we'll still be alive.'

'Sounds easy the way you tell it,' Taffy said.

'I've got a better idea,' said Geordie. 'Let's get the hell out of here now. If Jerry comes along this road he'll knock out the tank, and if he don't we'll just come back early in the morning.'

'No. That's out,' said Brook. 'We may be windy, but we're not as windy as that.'

'I'm not windy, but this is just bloody silly.'

'All right, Geordie, it's bloody silly but that's the way it's going to be.'

No one spoke.

'All right, Geordie, pick up the Bren and come with me.'

He walked about twenty yards in front of the tank and chose a piece of level ground off the road to the left.

'Now this is where you put the Bren. When our tank fires you lace the whole road from that tree to the curve there and up the other side, just in case they've got supporting infantry out with them. Also fire at anyone you see coming up the road or the ditch. You take first trick, and I'll have Taffy relieve you in an hour. Have you got that?'

'You're bloody mad,' said Geordie lugubriously. 'If I see any bloody Jerry infantry coming up that road I'm off quick before they see me.'

'Now listen, Geordie – a joke's a joke, but this is no time for pantomime. I'll be up there in the turret, and by Christ I promise you one thing – Jerry may miss you, but I won't.'

Geordie looked at him in disbelief.

'You *are* a bloody V.C. wallah,' he said in disgust. 'Just my luck to get stuck with a goddamned V.C. wallah. I'm putting in for a transfer.'

Brook laughed. 'All right, Geordie, but you'll get no transfer tonight.'

He went back to the tank and got hold of Taffy.

'Look, Taffy, you're no good in the driver's seat since we can't move, so I'm going to take you up ahead and put you in a position where you can see the bit of the road on the other side of the bend we're covering. I want to know what's leading so we can have an A.P. ready for a tank, H.E. for soft shell, and so on. So we'll rig up some signals. One long whistle for infantry; two for soft shell; and three for tanks. Got that?'

Taffy nodded.

Brook walked two or three hundred yards down the road with Taffy and selected a spot in a slight hollow, about fifty yards off the road, from which there was a view of the road running down some way into the valley.

'Now you don't need any arms, because I don't want you to fire at anything. Just blow the whistle and then lie perfectly still until we fire, and then cut over that way, away from the line of fire, and make your way round and meet us back at the hotel. O.K.?'

'You're the tank commander,' Taffy said quietly.

'You mean you don't like it?'

'Seems a bit like Cowboys and Indians – only they're not playing games.'

'Look, Taffy. I know they're bloody good soldiers and all that, but this isn't an ordinary situation. Think how they're feeling. They're not advancing in a battle – they're *cut off* behind the enemy lines, and if they do come this way it'll be because they're trying to get away. They'll be expecting to run into plenty of trouble, and as soon as we fire they'll think that's it. They won't know it's one crippled tank. When we put a few H.E.s among them and some cross machine gun fire, they're going to flap, just as we would, and it'll take them anything from ten to fifteen minutes to get going again. By the time the report gets back from their leading stuff to their H.Q. they'll think they've run into at least a squadron of tanks. You know what it's like at night – remember Caen?'

'Yes, I remember all right, and you were bloody good that night. Only I've had a lot more experience than you have, and I don't think it's going to be so easy. Anyway, you're the tank commander, and if you want to do it like this then this is the way we'll do it.'

'Thanks, Taff. I knew you wouldn't let me down.'

When he got back to the tank Sandy and Wilcox suddenly stopped talking. He felt that they too didn't like the job.

'Look, you two – let's get this straight. I'm not going to sit here and get us all killed. But on the other hand we've got a job to do. After we've fired he won't come forward again for ten minutes or so, and that gives us plenty of time to get well off the road. They won't have infantry out very far from their flanks and they certainly won't stop and look for us. We'll have made our report, delayed him and got away with a whole skin. It's a damn sight safer than an ordinary tank battle. Now buck up, will you?'

'You've got us wrong,' Sandy said. 'We were just saying we think it's a good plan.'

'Oh.' He felt a bit foolish. 'Well – thanks.'

They could hear the noise of the three-ton lorries driving to the square to take the villagers back.

Just before it was completely dark they saw three figures coming down the road from the town. The figures resolved themselves into the mayor, one of the gendarmes, and the patronne of the hotel.

'We have come to wish you good luck on your watch tonight,' said the mayor. 'Whatever may befall our little town we shall always remember you as the first representatives of the liberating army. We salute you.'

'Thank you. I don't imagine anything very much is going to happen. The Germans are defeated, and I expect tomorrow you will all come back to your homes.'

The patronne of the hotel stepped forward. She was a tall, gaunt figure, and only her face and hands showed in the dark. She held out something to him.

'It is the key to my hotel,' she said. Brook took the big iron key from her. 'If the dirty boches come back – I never want to see it again. Those swine have fouled it for four years and I cannot stand it anymore. Before you go will you put a match to it? I have prepared some wood and oil in the cellar. It will burn quickly. Will you do this for me?'

Brook was about to explain that he would have no time for burning hotels, but he realised that in the state she was in there was nothing he could say.

'I will burn it for you, madame,' he said.

The three of them walked back to the square, and a few minutes later he heard the noise of the last three-tonner driving off.

By midnight the noise of the far-off guns had died away, and they were all in position in the pitch dark waiting and listening for the first sounds of the enemy approaching. Wilcox had prepared a bully beef stew in the turret, and they all had some, except Taffy, who was still out in the forward observation post.

Brook ordered Wilcox to take over the Bren gun from Geordie, and then he took Geordie to relieve Taffy. Geordie kept up a continuous complaint which got more and more vehement as they got farther away from the tank.

When Brook had sent Taffy back for his supper, he gave Geordie the same instructions about the whistles.

'But, Brookie – ' Geordie was completely dismayed. 'Brookie, look, for Christ's sake *listen* a minute. This is a job for an infantry *platoon*, Brookie, not for one poor bloke on his lonesome. I've *been* in the infantry and I know. You never had no infantry training, Brookie, and it looks cushy to you, but it's not, I tell you, it's *not*. The first thing they'll do when they hear my bloody whistle'll be to lob a bloody great grenade over here, and that'll be the end of me and my bloody whistle. I know me rights – I'm in the Tank Corps and you can't make me do infantry work.'

'Now listen, Geordie.' Brook tried to keep his voice calm and reasonable. 'I'm only asking you to use your whistle *once*. You know it's impossible to tell where a whistle came from in the dark, and besides, as soon as you whistle we'll be firing, and they won't be thinking about you. Now if you do exactly what I tell you you'll be all right. Blow the signal and then lie low. *Don't move* until you hear us firing. You'll be in the safest spot of all, because all their fire'll be directed up the road away from you and you'll be as safe as if you were in Piccadilly Circus.'

'I'll be lucky if I ever see Piccadilly Circus again, with a bloody V.C. wallah like you for a tank commander. What do you want with a medal anyway?'

'Don't be a bloody fool. There's no medals in this. It'll be as safe as a scheme back home.'

He was glad to see that Geordie was lying down in the hollow.

'Now I'll have you relieved after a bit. Meanwhile don't move from this spot. You're safe here – but you won't be, wandering around.'

Back at the tank everything was quiet. Wilcox was sitting quietly by the Bren gun, Sandy had cleaned and oiled the breech, and Taffy was washing up the mess-tins. Brook told Taffy to get some sleep, intending to alternate during the remaining four hours before dawn with one of his crew resting.

He sat on the small commander's seat with his head and shoulders out of the turret peering through binoculars down the road. The night was quiet and dark. Despite his resolve his attention wandered, and he felt his eyes growing heavy.

Suddenly he was wide awake.

Wilcox had made a little sound to attract his attention.

'What is it?' he whispered.

'Someone coming down the road in the ditch,' Wilcox whispered hoarsely. 'He's ducking from tree to tree.'

'O.K. Wait until I fire, and then lace the whole road.' Brook strained his eyes trying to see through the darkness, examining every tree and bush through the binoculars, but he could distinguish nothing. He was just about ready to think it was a false alarm when he saw a shadowy figure run from one tree to another. He kept his glasses on the spot to see if there were any others following, but after a few seconds the figure moved again to the shelter of the next tree, about a hundred yards from the tank. There were half a dozen more trees between them. If it was a German with a bazooka he would have to get a good deal nearer to make sure. Brook decided to let him get to the fourth tree and then cut him down as he ran for the third. He sighted his Tommy gun on the space he had selected, and waited keeping his finger just off the trigger, remembering how easily the Tommy gun fired.

A high voice squeaked. 'Brookie... Brookie... don't fire – it's me, Geordie.'

Brook put the safety catch on the Tommy.

'Come in – you bloody fool,' he shouted.

Geordie came out from behind the tree and walked down the road towards them. 'Don't shout,' he whispered hoarsely. 'Do you want to bring the whole Jerry army down on us?'

Brook waited till he had got up to the tank.

'Well?' he said. 'What the hell do you think you're on?'

'I couldn't stick it out there, Brookie. It wasn't the Jerries – it was being all alone out there in the dark.'

'I'm putting you on a charge for deserting your post,' Brook said. 'Now get in the co-driver's seat and stay there. You'll stay there until I tell you to bale out, and if you try and get out before, I'll shoot you. We'll see how you like it in the tank instead.'

Geordie got in the hull without a word.

'Taffy – you awake?'

'Yes.'

'Go out to the forward position, will you?'

'O.K.'

Taffy got the whistle from Geordie and disappeared up the road. No one spoke for the next hour.

Suddenly Geordie said: 'I'll go back now, Brookie.' His voice told how much effort it had been for him to get the words out. 'I'm all right now,' he said.

'Take over Wilcox's job, then,' Brook said shortly.

Geordie changed places with Wilcox at the Bren, and Wilcox came in to the tank.

'Get yourself a bit of kip in Taffy's blankets,' Brook said to Wilcox.

There was silence for a time, while Brook fought with the desire to go to sleep. He noticed Sandy's head nodding in the turret, and poked him. 'What can you see through your periscope, Sandy?'

'Precious little. Blackness is about all.'

'Well, come up here for some fresh air.' Sandy squeezed past him and sat on top of the turret.

'Keep a sharp look-out down the road,' said Brook. He dropped off the tank and walked up ahead to the Bren gun. Geordie was sitting cross-legged behind the gun. He didn't say anything at Brook's approach.

'You know what you're supposed to do here?'

'Yes – when you fire I'm to lace both sides of the road down to the bend.'

There was a pause.

'You all right now?'

'Yes, I'm all right. It was that damn officer got me jumpy. He made it sound like a bloody cavalry charge. I'm all right when it comes. You know that, Brookie.'

'Up to now you always have been.'

'And I will be again. I just get a bit worked up beforehand, that's all. And I never have liked the dark. It's silly, I know, but I don't like it.'

'All right. Keep awake.'

'I will... and, Brookie?'

'Yes?'

'You really going to put me on that charge?'

'It depends on what happens.'

'Let 'em all come,' Geordie said, without conviction.

Suddenly the whistle sounded, loud and clear.

Three short blasts.

It was tanks, then.

Brook leapt back on the tank. Sandy was already inside and had the breach of the gun open and was removing the high-explosive shell. He placed it carefully back in the rack and shoved in an armour-piercing one.

'Good,' said Brook. 'Wilcox?'

'Yes?' Wilcox sounded dazed.

'Get up here quickly.'

Wilcox tumbled past him inside the turret.

'Taffy has just signalled tanks approaching.'

They listened intently but could hear nothing.

'They must be a hell of a long way off or we'd hear them,' Brook said.

They heard a shout from up the road.

Brook called, 'Is that you, Taffy?'

'Yes. I'm coming in down the middle of the road.'

'O.K. Come on in,' Brook shouted back. 'Did you hear that, Geordie?'

'Yes – all right.'

Taffy appeared running.

'I heard a flock of Tigers starting up,' he said. 'They sounded as though they were just over the next hill.'

'I'll come back with you. Take over, Sandy.'

They ran back the three hundred yards or so, and as soon as they got round the curve Brook could hear it. A faint, far off humming noise which was the unmistakable sound of the heavy diesel engines of the Tiger tank. There seemed to be a great many of them, and by the rise and fall of the note he guessed they were getting away from a leaguer, backing out from woods or fields on to the road. It was difficult to estimate exactly, in the quiet night air, but he thought they were not less than one, and not more than one and a half, miles away. He left Taffy there with the same instructions, and ran back to be ready for them.

Everyone was alert and excited. Within a few minutes they could all hear the noise of the motors alter as the drivers changed gear for a hill. Brook had studied the map carefully and he now decided on which road they were approaching. If he was right, they would soon come to a 'T' road under a mile away. If they turned left there, they would go south and run into the Guards Armoured division. If they came straight on, they would be upon them in four or five minutes. He suddenly realised he had better report quickly. He called Divisional H.Q. and the duty operator answered him almost immediately. He gave the approximate position of the Tigers, and his guess at the directions they could take. The duty operator got quickly on the job of relaying the report to the Guards Armoured.

By now the noise of the heavy engines was very loud, and they could even hear the sharper and faster noise of the motor bikes: which told them that it was a mixed group. This meant that it was almost certain that the leader would not be a tank but a fast, lightly-armoured reconnaissance vehicle – perhaps a half-track with an anti-aircraft gun. If they could knock that out they could afford to wait and see what came next. He kept his eyes glued to his binoculars, trying to pierce the darkness. The noise increased until it seemed to them, waiting tensely, that the enemy could only be a few yards away. Brook detected the significant change in the rhythm which told him that some of the tanks were moving away while others were still approaching the point nearest to them. It could only mean that they had turned left at the T road. He came up on the air immediately and reported it.

'Thank you. Good show. Keep us informed if you see anything.' It was a different voice now, older and more authoritative. Brook pictured the messages going out on other frequencies; the Guards Armoured in picked positions, waiting in the dark.

The sky was beginning to lighten, when at about half past four they heard the far-off noise of tank guns firing.

'Those bloody Guardsmen wish they was back in front of Buckingham Palace now,' Geordie said.

'I bet Jerry doesn't feel too happy about it,' Brook said. 'The

Guards would have waited until he was sitting in their sights.'

He sent Wilcox to bring Taffy back. They stayed by their guns until all noise of firing had stopped.

All at once they felt very tired.

'Let's have breakfast and then get some kip,' Brook said.

The huge black frying-pan came out, and again thick chunks were hacked off the ham and set frying, and the whole covered with eggs. It was a clear, bright morning, and the sun rose in a cloudless sky. They dragged their personal kit out of the tank and spread their blankets in the shade by the side of the road. Four slept while the fifth sat in the turret listening to the wireless to keep awake.

By half past ten they had all had four or five hours' sleep and were feeling much better. Brook got them up, as he expected the recovery crews to arrive and wanted to be ready for them. He decided to walk back to the village to see if there was any sign of the people returning.

'Come with me, will you, Geordie?'

They walked in silence until they were out of earshot of the tank.

In the clear sunlight the incident of the night before didn't seem so important, and Brook wanted to tell Geordie he was going to forget it; but Geordie spoke first.

'I been thinking about why I don't like the dark. It's because I was never out in it alone like last night. There's always the street lights, see? You wouldn't believe it, but stuck out there on my tod I could see things moving all around me and I was more worried about them than the Jerries, to tell the truth.'

'All right, Geordie, let's forget it.'

They had reached the square, and it was obvious that the village was still quite empty.

'Let's take a look in the hotel...'

The scream of a Moaning Minnie, the German nine-barrelled mortar, and the explosion of the first shell, occurred simultaneously. Brook and Geordie clutched each other as though for a waltz and fell to the cobblestones, each trying to burrow under the other and into the cracks between the stones as the remaining eight mortars burst all round them. They heard the white-hot bits of metal singing past them and wanted to turn themselves inside out.

Twenty seconds later it was all over.

The quiet came back, and only the strong smell of explosive remained. They stopped trying to dig themselves into the solid cobblestones. They were still entangled together, and pushed away from each other.

'You all right, Brookie?'

'Yes – you, Geordie?'

'Yes. Christ, I don't know why, though – they was all around us.'

'They certainly were. We were dead lucky.'

They walked quickly to the hotel and sat down inside.

'I threw meself on top of you to protect you, Brookie,' Geordie said earnestly. 'I thought to meself, "He's more valuable than what I am," so I tried to cover you.'

Brook looked at him to see if he was joking, but he seemed quite serious.

'What was that *under* me, then?'

'I wasn't under you, Brookie.' Geordie sounded hurt. 'I might have got me arms round you to turn you over but I was trying to cover you... Of course if you don't believe me...'

Brook decided that he believed him. 'All right, Geordie. Thanks. Only next time look out for yourself – we can't afford to lose you, you know.'

'Right.' Geordie seemed satisfied. 'And you don't have to say nothing to the others about it.'

Brook promised to keep his heroism quiet.

The deserted village square looked like a theatre set waiting for the actors, and Brook thought he could hear music.

'Listen!' said Geordie. 'It sounds like a fair.'

In a few moments it came quite clearly – the aggressively gay, raucous music of an English fairground. It seemed to be coming from the hills to the north. They walked to where they could see the road on the far side of the valley.

A small van was coming towards them. It disappeared for a few moments and then crested the near hill, and they could see four trumpet-shaped loudspeakers on the roof, from which the sound was welling. In a few moments it came round the corner and stopped in the middle of the square; its trumpets sending forth a great blast of sound which echoed around the empty houses.

Two figures got out – one a short, stout captain dressed rather dapperly, the other a typical, grime-encrusted old soldier, who was already getting out the primus stove and brew tin.

The officer acknowledged Brook's salute with a friendly wave.

'Where is everyone, eh? This usually wakes 'em up.'

'What is it?' Brook asked, in wonderment.

'Psychological Warfare. Morale Stiffener. We go ahead of Military Government to prepare the civilians for liberation – explain things to them. Tell them not to be frightened. The occupation is over – they're free. I've got some French records to play a little later. Sometimes they break down then. Very touching. But where are they?'

'They've all been evacuated,' Brook said. 'Last night when the Tigers broke through.'

'When the Tigers *what?*'

'Broke through. Down there...' He pointed vaguely down the road. 'They're behind the Guards Armoured, I think.'

'*Behind* the Guards Armoured?'

He turned to his driver, who had the primus going nicely.

'Turn that damned thing off!' he shouted.

The driver looked pained, but reached inside the van, and the music stopped in the middle of a stirring passage on the drums.

The officer started to move backwards towards his van.

'Well, we're obviously not supposed to be here yet,' he said. 'We're not armoured, you know... Psychological only...'

'Yes, sir,' said Brook.

'This place hasn't been cleared,' he said urgently to his driver. The primus and mess-tin disappeared instantly into the van in a matter of seconds and the driver was in his seat and turning the van round.

'Good luck, you chaps!' shouted the officer, and the van shot away.

An hour later the lorries came back with the townspeople, and the town became alive again.

Following close behind was a car full of war correspondents, who cross-examined each of the crew for possible stories. One of them, from a Northern daily, got hold of Geordie and seemed to have no trouble in getting him to talk, for Geordie was soon squatting on the ground behind an imaginary machine gun and going through all the motions of repelling an enemy attack.

EIGHT

'NOW WHERE the hell are we?' Taffy asked. All day they had been moving, well back in a long column, eating the dust raised by the tanks ahead. Now a halt had been ordered, but the dust took a long time to settle. Brook could feel it trickling down the back of his neck.

'We're about seven miles from the Seine,' he said, pushing his map down in the turret. 'We cross at a place called Vernon and push on to the Somme – if Jerry doesn't have other ideas.'

'My dad was in the fighting there in the First World War,' said Wilcox. 'The Retreat From The Somme – we lost four hundred thousand men. It used to give me the willies just to hear him talk about it.'

'If they'd just stop we could kill about that many of them,' Sandy said. 'Do you suppose the war's over, Brookie, and we won't get a chance to kill any more Jerries?'

'More likely he's decided this isn't good country to make a stand in. He's probably digging in somewhere up ahead... one of these days we'll find out where.'

'Twenty minutes' stop for a brew-up,' Wilcox reported.

In a minute or so there was water on the boil in the ditch by every tank in the column. When after half an hour the order to move still hadn't come they walked ahead to the troop sergeant's tank for some grousing.

'We ought to stop for at least a couple of days,' Taffy said to Smudger. 'The tanks have done over two hundred miles of this "clearing the Falaise pocket" lark and the tracks are as slack as clothes-lines. If we don't take a link out soon they'll all start breaking down at the same time.'

'That's probably what Jerry's waiting for,' Smudger said happily. 'He's diggin' in somewhere up ahead and one of these fine days when we're staggering along he'll have a bash and we'll all catch a packet.'

'They're not bloody supermen,' protested Hopper, the new troop corporal. He had joined them one night after the squadron had lost three tanks, and had been bracing himself ever since for his first battle. Now he was beginning to think it was all a bit exaggerated. 'Why shouldn't they crack like anyone else? How long can they go on taking the bashing they've been getting these last weeks – rocket-firing Typhoons all day and an artillery barrage all night?'

'That's just what we thought at Caen,' Brook said. He had been disappointed not to be promoted to troop corporal when their new one had been killed, and was jealous of Corporal Hopper who had come from England and had never been in action.

'Yes, but now we've got him on the run,' Corporal Hopper insisted. 'Look at all the stuff he's abandoning – tanks, half-tracks, self-propelled guns, ack-ack pieces, lorries. If we keep on he soon won't have anything left.' There was a chorus of disbelieving jeers, and he flushed.

Lieutenant Henderson walked over to them. 'Any char going?' he said.

'It's cold but we'll soon get it heated up,' said Smudger. 'Get cracking, Turner – and shift your bloody self.' He glared at Ben Turner, whom after a month he still thought of as his 'new' driver. Ben jumped up and got the primus stove going under the dixie of warm tea. He knew he could never replace Nobby Clarke in Smudger's eyes, but he wondered why he never seemed able to please the troop sergeant about anything.

Lieutenant Henderson sat down on an empty jerrican and sipped his tea. He had replaced Lieutenant Grimshaw after Caen and, after a trial period, was now accepted by the troop. He had transferred from one of the other armoured regiments in order to join his brother-in-law, Captain MacDonald, the second-in-command of A Squadron, and the move had evoked a good deal of criticism among the officers, who felt that preference should have been given to one of the wounded and recovered old officers in the regiment. It had been pretty obvious that Captain MacDonald had wangled the transfer.

But Lieutenant Henderson had done his job cheerfully and conscientiously, and as it was soon seen that the only favour he wanted was a chance to command a troop of tanks in a fighting regiment, he had become generally liked. He was a happy man.

'Want the latest griff?' he asked them. Most of the crews from the other tanks in the troop had wandered over. 'The war's going unbelievably well, touch wood.' He spread his map out on the ground. 'The Yanks have been doing wonders – they've got bridges over the Seine on both sides of Paris and are pouring men over. General Bradley has pushed right across our line of advance with a hundred thousand troops and is chasing Jerry up towards the Channel, where the Air Force is having a lovely time with them.'

'So what are we waiting for?' said Sammy Cohen. 'Let's go home.'

Sammy Cohen was a tailor's apprentice from Stepney who had got out of three burning tanks and always seemed to turn up again with the first reinforcement. He liked to pretend that he was in the army by accident, but he had in fact volunteered for armour. He was the troop comedian, and they all laughed at his look of happy expectancy now.

'It shouldn't be long anyway,' Lieutenant Henderson said. 'The Free French are already in Paris and the whole Allied front is about to cross the Seine all along from the Channel to Paris.'

'What's our next job?' Brook asked.

'Well, I expect you're all fed up with this Corps Reserve role we've been in – that's over now. We get ammoed up at Vernon, and then tomorrow we pass through 43 Div and go forward on a two-prong advance with the Guards Armoured on our right.' He paused.

'Who's leading?' asked Ben Lyon. He was Smudger's operator and one of the veterans from the desert. He didn't approve of tanks in close country.

'Our brigade.' Lieutenant Henderson grinned. 'Our regiment leading the brigade.' He let them wait a few seconds. 'And A Squadron leading the regiment.'

'What he's going to say next, I already know,' said Sammy Cohen. 'I must by psychic or something.'

'Sorry, Sammy – you're wrong. It's Three Troop leading, and us in reserve. I know you're all disappointed, and I'll ask the Colonel to keep you in mind.' They shouted him down good-humouredly.

Vernon was a pleasant little town with rows of holiday houses along the bank of the Seine. It was now crammed with vehicles of all kinds: tanks, half-tracks, lorries, staff cars and motor cycles. They moved slowly past all this and down to the river, where they took on food, fuel, water and ammunition, and got two weeks' back-log of letters.

Brook had two from his parents and two from Jennie. He read hers twice, trying to see if there were signs that she was beginning to feel differently about their relationship. She was two years younger than he, still at school, and they had known each other since they were children. The last time he had taken her to the pictures they had talked on the way home and agreed solemnly that they were just friends, that they were both too young to think of anything else, and that they wouldn't allow the war to stampede them. It had all been very sensible, and although Brook had agreed with her he had been a little disappointed.

The latest was the fourth letter he had had from her, and there was no doubt that it was more affectionate than friendly: but then so had been his earlier replies, and he thought unhappily that perhaps she was just being nice because she was sorry for him.

'Did you get one from your tart, Brookie?' said Geordie, standing in front of him with a letter in his hand.

'Yes,' Brook said, folding his letters and putting them in his battledress pocket.

'Nothing wrong, is there? No trouble?'

'Trouble?'

'I mean she's not in the family way, is she?'

Brook laughed and felt better. 'No, Geordie, I don't think so.'

'You never can tell with tarts,' Geordie said. 'The chaps sitting back in England having all the women and drinking all the beer while we're doing the fighting – it's not right. I've had a letter from my tart, too.'

'Is she in the family way?'

'No – at least she don't say nothing about it if she is. She mostly talks about what people are saying about me. Everybody's talking about that story in the paper – they put me picture in, you know...'

'I know – you showed it to me: "*Trooper Brunch – one of our Tank Men*".'

'Yes. Well, she cut it out and took it to work with her and stuck it on her machine and the gaffer come along and read it and told her she was a lucky girl.'

'Fine. I'm glad, Geordie.'

'I told you about how pleased me mum was, didn't I? She says she's going to have it framed and hang it on her wall no matter what no feller says.'

'Who'd be likely to object?'

'Her bloke. He don't like me much, and I hate the sod. He's got a cushy job on Tyneside – exempt, he is – and he don't like hearing about me, see? But she says she don't care what he says. After this lot is over she's coming to live with me.'

'What about her bloke?'

'She'll tell 'im to sling 'is 'ook – anyway I think she will. She didn't actually say nothing about it yet but I don't see why not.'

'Well, I hope so, Geordie.'

'Yes... Brookie?'

'Yes?'

'I know that newspaper bloke made it all sound better than what it was, but nobody will ever know, will they?'

'No, of course not – it was in the paper, wasn't it?'

'That's what I keep telling myself. If anyone ever does say anything I'll just show him the clipping out of the paper and that'll stop his gob. Anyway if it ever happens again I'll show you I could be like that.'

'Forget it, Geordie. You've been all right these last few weeks.'

'Well, it was pretty cushy going.'

'Not so cushy as all that – what about that bazooka wallah?'

'Yes – I got 'im all right, didn't I?' Geordie said. Then he added guiltily, 'But you know I really fired before I knew what I was doing.'

'You're not the first bloke to do that, Geordie. Anyway, you only think you did. It was really your training and experience that made you fire.'

'It was?'

Geordie thought that over for a few moments. Then he said:

'Thanks, Brookie. And don't worry, you won't never have no

more trouble with me.'

Sandy came over with a letter. 'Listen to this,' he said. 'It's from my headmaster: "... while I naturally deplore this dreadful war we must remember that there are always compensations, for there is no doubt but that it offers an unrivalled opportunity for young men of high spirits like yourself to work off their surplus energy".' Sandy laughed. 'So that's what you've been doing these last weeks, lads – working off your surplus energy.'

'I wish I 'ad my tart 'ere,' Geordie said, looking up from his letter. 'I'd work off me surplus energy – get up them stairs!'

Wilcox had made himself snug in the turret on the pretext of doing his wireless maintenance and was breaking a Standing Order – he was keeping a diary. He read over some of it but was not satisfied – it was flat and matter of fact, not at all like Siegfried Sassoon or Robert Graves. He pushed his head out and looked around him. The rest of the crew were sprawled comfortably about on the grass waiting for the water to boil for tea and reading their letters. Wilcox looked appraisingly at the countryside and then went back to his diary:

The trees have a peculiar beauty of their own; tall and slender, yet misshapen and unbalanced too; they harmonise remarkably well together. There is a line of them in front of me as I write. By ordinary, symmetrical standards of beauty the shapes are all wrong but somehow, silhouetted against the pale blue of the evening sky, they look like a Chinese painting. They are like those Dwarf Chinese trees at Kew Gardens, if I squint the whole scene looks a little like a landscape on a blue and white plate. The trees dark green, almost black green in this light; the sky a clean pale blue shot with delicate shell rose...

''ere you are, Wilkie, get this down your gut.'

Wilcox jumped and dropped his diary. He glared at a grinning Geordie holding out a cup of tea to him. He wanted to say something cutting, but instead he took the mug with a 'Thanks' – Geordie couldn't help being a crass, insensitive brute. He picked up his diary, but it was no use – the mood had fled.

By nightfall of the next day they had advanced seventy-two miles and had still not come across any organised defence in depth. They had outdistanced their supplies and had to wait until late at night for the R.A.S.C., exhausted by the long distances back and up again to the tanks. It was after one in the morning before the tank crews were able to sleep; the advance was to continue at four o'clock.

They moved off just before dawn and rumbled towards another village. Brook felt as though he had had no sleep at all, and he knew his crew were not rested either – the Allied advance was being led by sleepy men, in tanks badly needing attention. The only consoling thought was that any enemy they were likely to meet would almost certainly be in a worse state of exhaustion. Brook felt his eyes closing despite himself, and slapped his face vigorously to wake himself up.

'See that farmhouse over on the left?' said Taffy over the intercom.

Brook saw a small house with two horses hitched to a wagon, quietly grazing.

'That's Jerry horse transport,' said Taffy. 'It looks as if they've only just abandoned it, so we'd better be careful.'

Brook reported it to Lieutenant Henderson, and One Troop swung off the road towards the farm.

Everything seemed very quiet in the early morning light. They approached the farmhouse from several directions at once: some crashing through hedges and the others on the farm roads. As they got near, Brook could see that the wagon was a heavy ammunition caisson fully loaded, which indicated that it had been abandoned in a hurry. He examined the house and its surroundings carefully through his binoculars, but everything seemed quiet.

Suddenly the front door burst open and a tight knot of German soldiers ran out and, crouching low, made for some woods about a hundred yards away. They put the house between them and Brook's tank, but when they got into the clear he was ready for them.

'Traverse right, Sandy!' he shouted. 'Open up with the Browning as soon as you're on them.'

The turret swung round to the right and the machine gun began to chatter. Every third bullet was a tracer, so Sandy was quickly able to check a tendency to fire over their heads and the running soldiers started to go over like ninepins. Then Smudger bounced a high-explosive just behind the main body of them and it burst a few feet off the ground. When the smoke had cleared no movement could be seen.

They closed on the farmhouse, Brook taking his tank round to the front. The two horses, terrified by all the noise, had run across someone's sights and had both been hit. One, a grey, was slumped in the traces, while the other, a magnificent brown animal, apparently not badly wounded, dragged the heavy wagon round and round in a mad race.

It had not occurred to Brook, as it certainly would have to Donovan, that there might be more Germans still in the farmhouse. He was busy watching the horses and wondering how he could put them out of their misery without firing in the direction of his own troops, when a slight noise above his head attracted his attention. He glanced up as a figure darted back from an upstairs window; at the same moment he saw that something was caught in the branches of a big tree about ten feet over his head. It looked like a large tin with a stick projecting from its centre, or an oversize potato masher. He was about to call Taffy's attention to it, when it exploded and he was swatted to the floor of the tank as if he'd been shot from a sling.

His first thought was that he was dead; the next, in the same second, was that he had been hit on the head by a large piece of shrapnel. But he was already struggling to his feet and up to the commander's hatch before he realised what he was doing. He knew exactly what had happened, then. A German soldier still in the farm had opened a window and thrown a grenade at him. He grabbed a Mills bomb from the rack and pulled the pin. The window seemed to be revolving slowly, and he realised that Taffy was reversing the tank away from the building. His head was splitting but he held on and took careful aim. It was not more than twelve or fifteen feet from him and even in his stunned state he could hardly miss. The glass shattered and the hand grenade went into the room, as he dropped down inside the turret again the grenade went off. Taffy backed about twenty-five yards away from the farmhouse and then swung the tank round so that the hull machine gun was covering the door.

Someone was pressing a wet handkerchief to his head and asking him over and over again if he was all right. He opened his eyes and saw it was Wilcox. Sandy had left the gun and taken over tank commander.

He pushed the soggy, smelly handkerchief away and struggled up.

'Yes, I'm all right. Christ, that was stupid. You blokes all right?' They all said they were. 'O.K. Thanks, Sandy. I'll take over now.'

He climbed painfully back to his seat and looked around. His head felt as though a thousand red-hot needles had been driven into it, and he wanted to be sick. It was a fantastic chance that a grenade had exploded so near to him and not one piece of metal had touched him. He shuddered.

The horses were still revolving like circus animals, but now the grey had collapsed completely and one of the wheels had become bent. The other horse was still keeping the wagon moving but was visibly tiring, and after a minute or so came to a halt about thirty yards from him. Brook got out of the tank with his Tommy gun and walked slowly over to them. The horse eyed him suspiciously, but it was covered with sweat and quite blown, and allowed him to approach without bolting. He could then see the wounded grey. It looked as though it had been gored by a bull. There was a long deep slash running across its belly, and the intestines had been forced out by the galloping. It raised its head and looked at Brook miserably. He placed the muzzle of the Tommy gun behind its ear and pressed the trigger, letting half the clip go. The horse dropped dead in the traces. The other reared up but was unable to budge the dead weight. Brook could not see that it had any serious wounds: it was spattered with blood, but he thought that had probably come from the other one.

'Who do you think you are – the R.S.P.C.A.?'

It was Smudger, shouting at him.

'Come on. Get back to your tank.'

He ran back to the tank and they caught up with the others. The stretcher-bearers went into the house for the German wounded.

Brook's head got worse. He tried closing his eyes but it didn't seem to help.

'I've got some aspirin if you want it,' said Wilcox.

Brook stared at Wilcox as he produced a small bottle from his pocket.

The rest of the day was a nightmare. There was not much action, but enough to keep them jumpy, and the aspirins did no more than damp down his headache. He thought last light would never come, and he kept looking at his watch and shaking it to make sure it hadn't stopped.

They took one small village after another, and by late afternoon were only about thirty miles from Amiens. Here they were told they could have a twenty-minute break for tea. Smudger came over to Brook's tank.

'How're you feeling, Brookie?'

'Bloody awful.'

'I thought you was a goner when that potato masher went off. What was you doing – holding it to your ear to hear it tick?'

'Bloody nearly. I remember wondering what it was and thinking that it *looked* like a potato masher.'

Smudger laughed. 'Well, you'll know next time, by God. You were dead lucky to get nothing worse than a headache. Anyway it won't be long before we pack up now. I don't think we'll go any farther today – we're low on petrol and ammo. I wonder where the echelon is? The way we've been going these last few days they must be strung out from here to Aldershot.'

The twenty-minute halt stretched into an hour, and then Lieutenant Henderson came back and gave the signal for all tank commanders to come to his tank.

Brook climbed wearily out.

'That's probably the gen for tomorrow,' he told his crew. 'As long as I get more than three hours' sleep tonight, I don't care what happens tomorrow.'

Lieutenant Henderson waited until the three of them were standing in front of his tank.

'All here, Sergeant?' he said. He was given to sudden little bursts of formality.

'Looks like it, sir,' said Smudger cheerfully.

Lieutenant Henderson frowned slightly. He cleared his throat.

'It has been decided to try something quite unprecedented. We are going to advance through the night to Amiens.'

They stared at him in disbelief.

'What us?' Smudger asked.

'Yes – us. It will be a gigantic gamble, we know, but just because it's never been done it *might* come off. Jerry won't believe it and we've only thirty miles to do.'

'*Only* thirty miles?' Smudger exploded. 'Blimey, you don't think we'll get *three* miles, do you? It's bloody mad, that's what it is – moving tanks at night. We won't be able to see a bloody thing, and they'll hear us coming *and* be able to see us too. They'll knock out every tank. We might as well be blindfolded.'

'Well, it's not my idea,' Lieutenant Henderson said testily. 'It's the General's...'

'Go on the brave boys,' said Smudger bitterly, 'push on regardless.'

'Well, we'll have a shot at it anyway, and if we run into too serious opposition we'll have to stop and wait for light.'

'And the Jerries all around us – will they wait for the light, too?'

'Maybe not, but orders are orders. Who knows? – it might come off. He's been pretty disorganised lately. Anyway, here's the griff. There's only one really bad position, and that's leading troop.'

He paused, and they held their breath.

'The order of march is a single troop of tanks leading, followed by the infantry in their half-tracks, and so on down the column. Two Troop are going to lead...'

'Three bloody cheers,' said Smudger.

'... and then the rest of A Squadron. We're going to push on now until last light and then wait for petrol and ammo to come up. Then we start off again, probably just before midnight, for the last twenty miles or so to Amiens. Any questions?'

They could think of none. They walked slowly back to their tanks. When Brook told his crew, they thought at first that he was joking. When they realised that it was a serious proposal, they cursed everyone from the brigadier up to Field-Marshal Montgomery. Afterwards Brook found that his headache was gone and that he felt much better.

'Perhaps it's going to be all right, lads,' he said cheerfully.

'It's such a daft idea that Jerry won't believe it – he'll think we're his own tanks going back,' said Sandy. They all laughed.

'Anyway we're not point tank, or even leading troop,' said Brook. 'Think how those poor beggars must be feeling.'

At last light they were some twenty miles from Amiens. There they had a meal and waited for the petrol lorries to come up. The lorry drivers looked as though they were walking in their sleep.

At half past ten it began to rain, and clouds obscured the full moon. They were divided about whether total darkness was better or worse for them than the moonlight they had expected.

At eleven o'clock the infantry, in several half-tracks, came up armed with Bren guns. Two Troop moved out on the road, the infantry fell in behind them, then the rest of A Squadron. Behind them were the remainder of the infantry regiment, then another Squadron of tanks, and so on – a slender probing thread leading back in an unbroken line to the Seine, getting heavier and more compressed to the rear.

Orders were to show no lights at all, but Brook had to keep switching on the turret light, as did the other tank commanders, to make an attempt to follow their route on the map: for if a battle did develop it was essential that each commander knew where he was. The night was very black and the rain came down in torrents. Bushes looked like enemy tanks, and fallen trees like dreaded 88s.

For the first half-hour they advanced steadily, and then the leading tank suddenly left the road. Immediately all the others followed it. Brook ordered Taffy to take the ditch, and the tank went in at a steep angle from which they had some difficulty in getting out. Brook decided that after all it was probably just as safe on the road and told Taffy not to get off again.

Two Troop's officer in the leading tank kept reporting what he thought he saw and then correcting it; no one else was using the air at all, since it was from him that the first report of the enemy would come. Suddenly he came up excitedly.

'There's a long column of horse transport moving from west to east at the crossroads. We've cut it in half and are having a go at it.' His gun sounded unusually loud.

'Never mind about that – push on,' came the colonel's voice. 'We've plenty of stuff behind to take care of them. Push on.'

A minute or so later Brook's tank came to the crossroads and he traversed the turret to the left and fired down the road as they passed. Several wagons were burning, and men could be seen jumping from them and running off. A couple of hundred yards farther on they passed one of Two Troop's tanks that had broken down, and shouted friendly insults to them. A little later another broke down, and a few minutes after that the third, and then the column stopped.

'Now what?' said Sandy. Then the voice of the officer in the one remaining tank came up on the air.

'I've had a word with our flat-footed friends and they seem to think there ought to be more than one big boy in front of them,' he said.

The infantry in their open half-tracks had been told there would be a troop of four tanks ahead of them, and now there was only one. They were not unnaturally a bit worried lest that one should break down too, for they were sitting ducks to any defensive position covering the road, while it would take an anti-tank gun to stop the tanks.

'Righto,' came the colonel's voice. 'Hello, Love Able – did you hear that? Do something about it.'

'Hello, Love Able. Wilco, out to you.' It was the voice of the A Squadron leader.

'Wait for it, wait for it,' said Smudger lugubriously to his crew. 'Here we go.'

'Hello, Love Able *One*, Hello, Love Able *One*, Move up and take over the lead. Over.'

'Love Able One Wilco Out,' came Lieutenant Henderson's voice. 'All stations Love Able One move up front, over.'

'Love Able One *Able* Wilco out.' Smudger managed to put all his disapproval of the whole manoeuvre in the formal phrasing.

'Love Able One Baker, Wilco Out. Brook felt his heart thumping and a dryness in his mouth. 'This is it, lads,' he said. Taffy had already started towards the infantry, who were pulling off the road to let them by.

Corporal Hopper had also acknowledged the order, and had even sounded keen. For a moment nothing was heard but the noise of the four tanks moving past the infantry, and then Smudger's voice came over the air. He was singing to himself, and it was obvious that he was pressing his microphone switch without knowing it.

'We're going to catch a packet, We're going to catch a packet,' he sang.

Brook turned round and shouted at him, pointing to his microphone – and the broadcasting stopped.

The column got under way again, and now it seemed to Brook, in number two position, that it was not possible that the enemy hadn't been alerted. He must be drawing them into a trap, and any minute guns would start firing and tanks would go up like fireworks. But nothing happened.

Lieutenant Henderson in the leading tank stopped abruptly at one point as a car came rattling down the road towards them. It only just managed to stop before running head on into the tank, and a very irate, very stout, German staff officer climbed out and began to dress the tank commander down for driving without showing any lights.

'Shut up!' Lieutenant Henderson shouted at him. 'Surrender, you swine, surrender!'

But the German officer was so furious at the dangerous driving that he heard nothing, and carried on dressing him down.

'All right, Jones,' Lieutenant Henderson said to his co-driver, 'put a burst into his radiator.'

The hull machine gun fired, and the German officer stopped in the middle of a particularly long word and gaped at them.

'Push on Jones, shove the car into the ditch.'

The tank moved forward ponderously and the small car seemed to disappear into its maw. Another officer had staggered out of the car when the machine gun fired. He collapsed by the side of the road, and watched as the track crawled up and the little car was squashed beneath it. Then the tank backed off and passed the wreckage.

'Hello, One Baker – push that mess off the road as you go by,' Henderson ordered, and then reported two prisoners. He had indicated by signs that the fat officer was to wait by his wounded companion.

As Taffy expertly nosed the wreckage into the ditch Brook caught a glimpse of the German standing in the road with a completely dumbfounded look. He still wore his Luger at his belt, and Brook wondered who would get that prize.

A little later they passed a camp of German infantry, all of whom seemed to be asleep, and raked it with machine gun fire as they went by. Just before dawn they arrived at the outskirts of Amiens.

Half an hour later, when it was light, the startled and delighted Maquis appeared with armbands and rifles and led the tanks into Amiens, walking fearlessly ahead down the middle of the road and pointing out the houses where German soldiers were billeted. The infantry then went in and routed them out. On occasion the German soldiers would make a dash for it and the Maquis shot them down like rabbits. One of the Maquis leaders ran back and climbed on Lieutenant Henderson's tank. He pointed excitedly at a large house on the right-hand side of the road, telling him that it was the headquarters of the local S.S. As he was talking, a long, grey-green lorry came out of the driveway packed with German infantry. It was broadside on to the leading tank and not more than thirty yards away. Lieutenant Henderson's gunner fired immediately, and the high-explosive shell shattered the driver's cab. The next moment the big gun fired again, and the shell burst in the back of the lorry among the men. At the same time the door of the house opened and six or seven soldiers led by a blond young officer came charging out. The infantry had been covering the house with a Bren gun and were glad of the opportunity to join in the slaughter. The group were cut down before they were well clear of the door. The blond young officer ran into a burst of bullets and catapulted in a heap not twenty feet from the door. The men in the lorry who were able to move were falling out on to the street. It looked as though every one of them was injured. The Maquis were delighted and were cheering lustily, and the atmosphere of killing was like a fever. Brook clutched his Tommy gun hoping for more targets, and Sandy had his gun trained on the house and his finger on the trigger. But no one else appeared, and the fever left them suddenly. At the same time the groans of the dying men in the lorry could be heard. Brook put his Tommy gun down, and waited while the report went back and the doctor came up in the ambulance.

By midday enough reserve troops had arrived to take over, and the tank crews were billeted in houses in the town and told to get some sleep. After a meal they got down to their blankets about three in the afternoon. They had had eight hours' sleep in the last eighty-four and were sure they could sleep the clock round.

But by midnight most of them were awake. They had found that they were in the middle of the brothel district of Amiens, and the girls had come out of hiding, liquor had been produced, musicians found, and the celebration of the Liberation of Amiens was going with a swing.

The girls were at great pains to explain that they were for the French only and had never been available to the Germans, and the soldiers pretended to believe them. It was a long time since they had relaxed with a woman, and the girls were kept very busy. There were six in the house where Brook and his crew had been billeted, and by one o'clock in the morning there were over thirty soldiers competing for their favours. The soldiers all had plenty of money, and the girls were obviously determined to give money's worth.

Brook drank the fiery liquid labelled 'Cognac' as it was poured into his glass, and after a while he grabbed one of the girls and went upstairs with her.

Her room was untidy and looked as though it hadn't been cleaned for a month or so. The bed was wrecked, but she pulled the sheet straight and patted out the pillow. He found his boots awkward to get off and realised that he was drunk – but he wasn't too drunk to do what was expected of him. Then he fell into a deep sleep.

He woke about six with a thick head. The noise was still going on downstairs.

He found Taffy and Geordie and tore them away from their girls. Geordie, in particular, objected.

'Aw, Brookie. I've got a smashin' bird here. What do you want to go for?'

'We've got to be at the tank at seven ready to move off. Come on.'

Geordie kissed the bedraggled, exhausted female heartily, and then produced a handful of notes from his pocket.

'For vous,' he said grandly, 'because you give me a good time. Bon. Tray bon. For vous.'

He drained both glasses on the table and hurried out after the others. 'Well,' he said, 'it's true what they say about the French tarts, isn't it?'

When they got to the tank Sandy and Wilcox were already there and had done all the necessary preparation. They exchanged stories of the remarkable girls each of them had discovered.

Wilcox did not join in all this.

'What about you, Wilkie?' said Geordie. 'Did you get yourself a nice bit?'

'I was too tired,' Wilcox replied quickly, 'I never woke up.'

Geordie was sympathetic. 'Wait till the next place and I'll see you're taken care of, old chum. Just you stick with me.'

'Thanks,' Wilcox said without enthusiasm.

They had hoped they would be rested for a few days, and all sorts of rumours had been flying about, but at seven o'clock the orders came that they were to push on again.

They crossed the Somme and carried on, meeting no resistance at all. About midday they came to a high ridge and waited, before they advanced, to see if it was held, for it seemed a natural place for anti-tank guns. But they could see nothing, and the order came to advance up to it.

They got to the top of the ridge expecting to see the familiar countryside with another ridge a mile or so ahead, but instead there was a flat plain dotted with slag heaps as far as the eye could see. Brook had not been following the map and was startled at the sudden change.

'Where are we, Brookie?' Taffy asked. 'What's that town down there?'

Brook got the map out and traced their route from Amiens.

'That's Bethune,' he said. 'And we're at…' He found the name on the map. 'Vimy Ridge.'

Then they realised that in front of them lay the battlefields of the First World War. They picked out the names on the map – Ypres, Armentières, and, off to the right, Cambrai – where they all knew the tanks had come of age twenty-seven years before them.

A few minutes later a cloud of wildly cheering French descended on them and over them. They found themselves pulled and pummelled, thumped on the back, and kissed heartily. The tanks had to slow down to a crawl in order not to run over people.

Bottles were pushed at them and they took a swallow from a dozen different kinds of drink. Finally Brook told his crew not to drink any more. A few minutes later he saw Geordie accept a bottle.

'Geordie – I told you to pack it in.'

'I'm not drinking it, Brookie, I'm saving it for later – look.'

Brook ducked down inside the turret and Geordie showed him a large bottle on his lap with a funnel. He was adding a generous dollop to it from every bottle he was given. It promised to be a potent mixture.

As they got deeper into the industrial north of France, where the towns ran into each other, the welcome got more and more wild. These people had felt the weight of the German occupation much more than those on the rich farms of Normandy, and they let off steam with tremendous gusto. All along the ugly roads the people were packed, cheering wildly and continuously so that the noise sounded like the roar of the surf. The tanks were pelted with flowers, pears, apples and plums, and every time they stopped the crowd surged forward offering their precious coffee and the inevitable Cognac and bottles of wine. The noise and enthusiasm seemed as great after twenty-four hours as it had been in the beginning, as they moved steadily on towards the Belgian frontier.

When they stopped at night Brook and his crew were seized by a fine-looking woman and taken to a small café which she owned. Two of the café tables had been pushed together and covered with a white tablecloth that was evidently a prized heirloom. The table had been laid as for a party with an enormous bowl of flowers, but the sight that startled them was a bottle of Guinness at every man's place.

'Where on earth did you get those?' Brook asked.

She laughed. 'My 'usband buy them from the Naffee when the English soldiers leave in 1940 and 'e say to me "Marie, we will keep them and give them to the *first* English soldiers we see when they come back." Sometimes I think that we will drink the English beer but he always say that you *will* come back and now you are come back and I 'ave save the beer.'

'And your husband?'

'They have killed him, monsieur.'

The Guinness was flat and bitter, but they got every drop down, smacking their lips and praising it highly.

The next day they continued their headlong advance and ran into a cluster of self-propelled anti-tank guns. But the impetus of their advance swept them on, and the fight was short and sharp. They lost three tanks in C Squadron, and knocked out seven 88s, which greatly heartened them. But by this time the tanks had really reached the limit they could go without extensive maintenance. They had done nearly six hundred miles on their tracks almost non-stop, and now they began breaking down all along the way.

They crossed the Belgian frontier at midday and were told to push on to Antwerp, which was a further eighty miles, without delay. Every now and then they would catch up with the tail end of the retreating Germans and shoot them up, but there was very little real resistance.

Just outside a small Belgian town they sighted some German horse transport and speeded up to try and catch them. As they swept through the town the tank suddenly slowed down and stopped. The engine roared uselessly for a moment or two, and then died away.

'Looks like this is it, Brookie,' said Taffy. He got out and inspected the track. 'All the bolts on the off-side bogie-wheel have sheared off. This is as far as we go.'

The rest of the regiment was passing them tank by tank. When the colonel came by he stopped, and Brook pointed to the useless track. The colonel frowned as though the breakdown was their fault.

'Wait here for the fitters and then catch us up,' he ordered. 'Push on, driver, push on.'

The colonel's tank disappeared over the hill after his regiment, and a few moments later they heard the noise of firing and then the voice of the commander of the leading tank reporting that they had caught up with the tail of the retreating German column.

When the noise of the armour crashing through the narrow cobblestoned streets of the village had died away the people began coming up from their cellars and rushing over to the crippled tank, which seemed to have been left behind as evidence that the Liberation was a fact. The retreating Germans had machine-gunned the houses on both sides of the roads so that no one would be tempted to hinder their retreat, and the people had very sensibly gone to shelter; but now, suddenly and dramatically, the Germans and the Occupation were gone, and they were wildly excited, eagerly looking for someone to thank personally, someone to cheer, someone they could offer food and drink to. The exhausted tank crew shook hands ceaselessly, accepted the bottles thrust on them, and tried hard to match the people's enthusiasm.

NINE

THEY WERE EXTREMELY tired, dirty, hungry and thirsty, and there was an almost irrepressible urge to let off the pressure now that they had for the moment stepped out of the game. Brook felt it himself, and it was obvious that the others had already let go in varying degrees. All they wanted now was to get out of the tank, and to get their clothes off and wash themselves all over: then a good hot meal and the chance to lie down, as far away as possible from the tank, which they had not left for days. They wanted to stretch and relax, and to close their eyes and hear something other than the noise of the engines and the grating of the tracks.

Brook knew they ought to stay with the tank and make it as formidable a weapon as possible in case it was needed; he knew it would be unjustifiable carelessness to relax in a country which had only just been overrun by a few fast moving armoured columns and which was not in any sense successfully cleared of the enemy. But although these things were important, he seemed to have difficulty in thinking clearly; his mind moved very slowly, and then jumped erratically. Obviously he ought to be doing something now, but it was too much effort to decide just what.

So they sat in the tank and smiled wearily at the cheering crowd. They were still in wireless touch with the regiment, and listening was an excuse for doing nothing. The leading tanks were moving at top speed, having smashed through the German transport column, and had not yet encountered any serious resistance.

When the wireless began to fade, Brook roused himself from his almost hypnotic state.

'Well, we can't sit here all night. Better get the bedrolls and tank sheet off and see about a bivvie nearby.'

They lowered themselves heavily off the tank like arthritic old men.

The crowd was getting larger and was still milling excitedly about the tank. Brook looked around him over the heads. Just across the road he saw a huge pair of iron gates, swung from massive stone pillars; on top of the pillars were grinning stone lions, sitting upright and propping up large shields. The gates were open and led to a wide drive, which soon divided and swung out and back in a large figure 8 up a gentle hill. The holes in the '8' were two lily ponds, each containing a cluster of stone figures in awkward postures, which were obviously fountains in normal times. All this led and pointed to an unbelievable building on top of the hill – a miniature, many-towered castle.

Brook had often seen pictures of these elaborate, fairy-book castles perched on pyramids of rock high above the Rhine. This was about one-eighth the size, and looked not only freakish but a little indecent in this sober, respectable countryside.

As he stared, he saw someone hurrying down the drive towards the crowd. It was a tall, regal-looking woman of fifty or so, who carried herself superbly and obviously had once been very beautiful. Her hair was piled up in the most elaborate coiffure he had ever seen, and was a strange blue-white colour. She walked briskly through the crowd towards them. She did not speak, yet people seemed to sense her coming and they parted for her magically. She walked up to Taffy, who was the nearest to her, and grasped his hand firmly.

'Welcome,' she said in English. 'We are most happy to see you. Are you the Commander?'

'No, ma'am.' Taffy grinned and pointed up at Brook. 'That's the Commander up there.'

'Ah! Welcome, Commander, welcome to our village and my chateau. It is at the disposal of you and your brave men.' She held her hand up and Brook nearly fell off the turret stretching down to shake it.

'Thank you, Madame... Madame...?'

'Countess,' she said. 'The Countess...' and then followed a string of names he was completely unable to sort out.

'Thank you, Countess. We *would* like some fresh water.'

'Of course, of course. But you must be weary and in need of food. Will you not come up to the château and refresh yourselves before dining with us?'

The rest of the crew had been staring at her in fascination, and at the mention of food Brook felt his grip on them slacken perceptibly. Geordie was already moving.

'I'm sorry, Countess, but we cannot leave our tank...' he began.

'But surely some of you can come. Two at a time for example?' She smiled. Brook knew he had lost, and was not sorry.

'You are very kind, Countess. I will allow two of my men to go, and when they return, two more.'

'And yourself?'

'When the second two come back, I shall be delighted.'

'Ah yes, of course. That is the tradition of your army, is it not? The men are cared for first and then the officers. It is very noble, very British. Then, Commander, until later?'

'Thank you.' He turned to the others. 'Taffy, you go first and...'

'Me,' said Geordie firmly. 'Then when we get back I can give Taffy a hand, see?'

'Right. Now hurry up, you two, remember the rest of us are waiting down here.'

'We'll be back before you know we've gone,' said Geordie, moving away quickly. They watched the countess walk up one of the S-shaped paths between Taffy and Geordie, holding each of them by the arm and talking animatedly.

'And very nice too, Commander,' said Sandy. 'I hope you've got your full dress uniform in your kit-bag, Commander.'

'I wonder what she'll have to eat?' Wilcox sighed.

'I don't expect it'll be much; they've probably had a pretty rough time here under the Jerries,' said Brook.

At the end of half an hour Brook sent Sandy to find the other two and chase them back. Another twenty minutes passed, and he dispatched Wilcox after Sandy.

'Tell them *all* to get back here at the double!' he raged. 'I don't care if they're in the middle of eating or if they haven't eaten at all. Do you understand?'

'Right, I'll get them,' Wilcox promised, and disappeared up the drive.

Brook sat alone in the turret, seething with anger as the minutes ticked by. When he realised that Wilcox wasn't going to return either, he locked the driver's and co-driver's hatches from inside, stowed all the stuff they'd taken off the tank back into the turret, closed the commander's hatch, and then asked one of the more responsible-looking men in the group who were still there not to allow anyone to touch anything. He promised he would be back in five minutes. Then with mayhem in his heart he started up the path.

At close quarters the château looked even more unreal than from down in the road. It was covered with small towers, fake stone balconies and elaborate scroll work, most of which was plaster over brick. There were no lights showing from the front, but he could hear noises round at the back. As he came through the shrubbery on to a lawn he could make out the noise of a gramophone, playing a waltz, and the sound of someone talking. As he got closer he recognised the voice as Geordie's. He stopped and looked through an enormous pair of windows at the scene inside.

Sandy, fresh and clean looking, was dancing with a very pretty girl. Taffy, who had also had a good wash, was leaning back in an enormous chair, holding a glass of champagne. Geordie was standing at the end of a long table, with a glass of champagne in one hand, and gesturing with the other. There were several bottles on the table. There were about eight other people in the room, including the countess, all listening enthralled to Geordie.

Brook pushed open the door ready to blister them. Before he could get a word out, the countess had stepped to his side and taken both his hands in hers.

'The Commander!' she exclaimed delightedly. 'Now we are *all* here and the party is complete. Champagne, Commander?' She produced a glass magically and placed it in his hand, then picked up a bottle from the table and filled it.

'Come right in and make yourself at home, Commander,' said Sandy without stopping his dance.

'I was just telling them about you and me and them Tigers,' said Geordie.

Brook glared at them. They were all clean and relaxed looking, and he felt hot, dusty, tired and irritable.

'You, Taffy, and you, Geordie – get down on the tank.'

Taffy got up immediately and moved towards the door. Geordie began to say something, and then thought better of it. He moved towards Taffy.

At that moment a door opened, and Wilcox came in carrying a large tray, followed by a uniformed maid carrying another tray.

'Ham and eggs, coffee, rolls, butter and...' Wilcox stopped as he saw Brook, and finished lamely, 'I was just going to have a quick bite, Corporal...'

'But they haven't eaten *anything*, Commander,' the countess protested. 'Your poor men are *starved*. The girls from the kitchen had all gone down to welcome our liberators and I had to send for them. Surely they can stay and eat a little? Your tank will be perfectly safe, I assure you. No one would dare touch it standing in *my* property.'

Taffy and Geordie were waiting hopefully in the doorway. The smell of ham and eggs and coffee was very strong. Brook surrendered unconditionally.

'All right. Come on back, you two. We'll probably all be court-martialled.' Geordie was back and pulling a chair up to the table before he'd finished.

'Would you like a bath, first, Commander?' the countess asked.

'That sounds wonderful,' said Brook.

'Of course. But first you must meet the others. This is my sister, Madame Lachaise. Pola, may I introduce Commander – '

'Brook. And it's Corporal, not Commander. I'm a corporal tank-commander.'

'Corporal-Commander Brook, then.'

The countess's sister held out her hand, and with his grimy one he took it. It was small and cool. She was about ten years younger than the countess, and she also had been a beautiful young woman. She was dressed for a cocktail party, and looked as though she had just finished getting ready. There was a faint scent about her, and after the first few moments Brook forgot her age completely. She put him at ease with an air of easy familiarity, as though they had met before and were taking up the relationship where it had been left off.

'The maids are nowhere to be found,' she said. 'I will show you to your room.'

'My room?'

'But yes, of course. You are spending the night with us, are you not?'

'Why, yes, of course, but I think we should really sleep near the tank.'

'If it is necessary to guard the tank cannot you each take turns?'

'Why not?' said Brook. 'Yes, I would certainly like to sleep in a bed for a change.' We might as well go the whole hog, he thought to himself.

She took him upstairs and showed him a room overlooking the lawn at the back. The first thing he noticed was that the bed was a four-poster, with a dark green canopy over it.

'But it's wonderful! I've never slept in a four-poster before. Who else is in here with me?'

'I beg you pardon. What *are* you proposing, monsieur?'

Brook was overwhelmed with confusion. 'No. Good God, I don't mean that! I mean, which of my crew – there aren't separate rooms for all of them, are there?' He felt himself blushing.

She laughed. 'I am sorry. I was only teasing you. You are a nice boy. No, you have this room *quite* to yourself. The rest of your crew share two rooms.'

'But are you sure there are enough rooms? I mean, there are quite a few of you. Are you sure you're not giving up your own room? You will have somewhere to sleep all right...?' he trailed off, as again she laughed at him.

'I shall begin to think that perhaps you are not quite so innocent,' she said. 'No, do not distress yourself – I have a room of my own too, but your consideration is very gallant. My room is there – just across the hall. Would you like to see it?'

Brook felt dry-throated and foolish. He knew she was laughing at him, but he also knew she was flirting with him. He didn't know why. Determined not to be put out of countenance he followed her into her room. It was pink and blue and very feminine. He hadn't been in many women's bedrooms, and this one was quite unlike any he'd seen in England. It looked more like a sitting-room with a bed in it than a bedroom, he thought.

'Very pretty,' he said. 'But you don't have a four-poster like me.'

'No. But the mattress is much softer than yours. Feel it.' She sat down and bounced on it, and he sat beside her and felt it sink beneath their weight.

He cleared his throat. 'It's very soft,' he agreed.

'Yes. And now we must go, or they will begin wondering downstairs what we are up to, eh?' She laughed.

He got up and followed her out, feeling like an oaf.

'The bathroom is here. There is plenty of hot water, and the towels are in your room. If you want anything pull the bellrope, and if the maids have come back one of them will come. I'll see you downstairs.'

'Yes. Thank you very much.'

'You are a nice English boy. And very good-looking too,' she laughed, and left him standing in the bathroom doorway.

The bath was enormous and the water hot. The soap was a huge lemon shape, purple-coloured and strongly perfumed. He washed his hair and soaked luxuriously. Afterwards his clothes seemed dirtier than when he had taken them off.

He had some clean clothes in his kit-bag in the tank, and he determined to get them as soon as he had eaten. None of them had been out of their clothes since leaving Amiens. When he went down to the tank he took Sandy with him, to take the first trick on guard.

It was a black night and they stumbled down the curved path and felt their way out of the gates on to the road. They could hear voices coming from where they had left the tank, and see the glowing ends of cigarettes. As they drew near they were suddenly and sharply challenged in French.

'It's all right,' Brook shouted in English A torch was shone on him; he was recognised and welcomed. The tank was being guarded by two young men with white armbands armed with rifles.

'We are the Brigade Blanche. Our commandant has ordered us to stand guard over your tank until you are ready to do so yourselves. He says that naturally he understands that you are very fatigued and that if you desire to rest elsewhere you may leave it in our charge with perfect confidence.'

'Thank you. But I don't quite understand who you are. Are you like the Maquis in France?'

'Exactly. We have taken over the jurisdiction of this whole area – both civil and military. We are engaged at present in seizing and imprisoning the known collaborateurs. Our commandant says that he will be delighted to see you tomorrow at the Caserne and show you our little organisation.'

It was tempting.

'What do you think, Sandy?'

'Well I don't know, Brookie – isn't it a bit like the village in Normandy? Jerry might put in a counter-attack during the night – shouldn't we try and cover the road? The gun's all right this time.'

Brook thought of the bed at the château and of Madame Lachaise in the next room. He knew Sandy was right, but he and the crew were exhausted, and the Brigade Blanche seemed very competent.

'Let's forget it for tonight,' he said. 'After we've had a good rest we'll all feel better – tomorrow.'

'You're the tank commander,' Sandy said.

'You'd better pop inside and take out the firing-pins from all the guns – just in case anything should go wrong.'

Sandy disappeared into the turret. Brook turned to the Brigade Blanche.

'Thank you, gentlemen. I'll see you in the morning, then.'

The Brigade Blanche returned his salute very smartly.

As they trudged back up the hill Brook realised just how exhausted he was, now that the effects of the champagne were wearing off.

'I'm going to get some kip, Sandy. Tell the others to pack it in pretty soon, will you? We ought to take this chance to get a decent night's sleep.'

'Och, you can always sleep, but you don't get a chance to spend an evening with a beautiful girl that often,' Sandy protested. 'Have a heart, Brookie – we're not all old men, like you.'

'Don't worry about that – her mother'll see she gets out of your clutches soon enough – and bags I the mother, so hands off.'

'That's taking advantage of your rank, Corporal,' said Sandy sadly. 'I thought better of you.'

As soon as they got back he said his good nights to the countess and her sister. The youngest girl had claimed Sandy immediately, to join the others dancing. Brook watched Wilcox whirling expertly about, and really did feel like an old man.

'That reminds me that I am very tired too,' said Madame Lachaise. She clapped her hands, and to the disgust of the rest of the crew, sent her daughters to bed. Then she held out her slim hand and Brook took it – it felt delightfully cool, and his own hot and clumsy.

'Until tomorrow?' she said, with the slightest of inflexions so that it could have been a statement or a question.

In the four-poster bed, when he closed his eyes and tried to relax, he could feel the tank lurching under him. He started to think about Pola, and instantly all desire for sleep left him. He could easily summon up how she looked, and even how she smelled – a mixture of scent and her own flesh. Her dress had been of green silk, and in the dark he could see how tightly it had fitted round her thighs, buttocks and waist, and how the line of it when she had been sitting down had run up between her legs and then split into a Y at the slight protuberance of her belly. Her neck and shoulders were large but firm, and her breasts big, but not flabby. He tasted a pool of saliva at the tip of his tongue just behind his lower teeth.

He got up and opened his door. He could hear nothing in the house, not even the sound of snoring. A breath of cold air made him shiver and he went back to bed, but the excitement had not left him.

Suddenly he made his decision. He got up and walked firmly to the door. She had said she was going to lock it, and surely if she did not, that meant she was expecting him? He stood for a few moments with his fingers lightly on the handle, then gritting his teeth he turned it. The door opened noiselessly.

Immediately a light was switched on. It was a small one on the table next to her bed.

'Shut the door,' she whispered.

He pushed it shut behind him and sat down on her bed.

She was dressed in a baby-blue nightdress that seemed to be all bits of lace and ribbon. It was quite transparent, and the dark rings of her nipples showed through.

She smiled. 'I thought perhaps you weren't coming. I would have been disappointed.'

'Of course I was coming.' His voice was husky and he tried to control it. 'I was just waiting for everything to be quiet.'

She held out her arms. 'Kiss me.'

She didn't switch the bedside lamp off, and Brook thought he oughtn't to, though he didn't like making love to her in the light. He had an uneasy feeling, as though he was being watched.

Afterwards she pushed his arm away, and got her head underneath it in what he thought was a peculiar position. Then he realised that she was looking at something over the foot of the bed. He put his head down on the pillow and turned his face to see what it was. There was a triple dressing-mirror pushed right up against the end of the bed and so arranged that it reflected their bodies.

Its effect on Brook was like a cold shower. Her large flabby body was a dead white, and he was suddenly filled with revulsion and wanted to flee. He rolled over and covered his eyes with the back of his hand.

'What is the matter?' she said.

'Nothing. It's just rather hot in here.'

'Yes, of course. You English always open the windows on the trains,' she giggled. 'I think perhaps I shock you?'

'No, of course not. Of course you don't. But look here, hadn't I better be getting back? I'd better not be here in the morning, had I?'

'My daughters always come in to wake me at eight o'clock. I don't think they would like it if you were here.'

'Good God, no!' He was relieved that he was going to be able to escape. He got out of bed and found a towel. She shone the torch on him and he wrapped it round his waist. Then, dutifully, he leant over and kissed her.

'Good night, funny boy.'

'Good night, Pola.' He opened the door quietly and waited a minute. There was no noise. He walked quickly back to his own room. He got into bed, and this time there was no difficulty in relaxing. He slept soundly at first, and then he was back in his tank and crawling up a ridge towards a huge anti-tank gun on which it was no use to fire. He could feel the sweat running off his body in a stream and the tank seemed to be getting hotter every second. He looked down on the turret floor and saw flames licking his feet. He tried to get out of the tank but a weight was pressing down on his shoulders. He remembered he must give the order to abandon tank but he couldn't make a sound. It got hotter and hotter and the flames were creeping up his legs. He tried once more to scream the order to abandon tank.

'Bale out! Bale...'

He woke covered with sweat and pushed the heavy eiderdown from him. The room was hot and foul-smelling. He got up and opened one of the large windows and sucked in the cool night air.

It had been an extraordinarily vivid dream and had left him shaken. It was the first time he had dreamt of being in action, but he had a feeling it wouldn't be the last.

In the morning they had breakfast on the terrace, at about ten o'clock. The sun was shining. They were all talking animatedly and Brook was about to drink his third cup of coffee, when a British captain walked round the corner of the building. Brook stared at him in amazement, then scrambled to his feet. The others turned round and then got to their feet.

The officer looked at them distastefully, but spoke first to the countess, greeting her in French. Then he turned to Brook.

'Are you the tank commander?'

'Yes, sir.'

'Have you forgotten how to salute?'

'Sorry, sir.' He saluted. The officer returned it stiffly.

'Have you any explanation for leaving your tank unguarded?'

'The Brigade Blanche was looking after it for us, sir. It couldn't move and we had removed the firing-pins from the guns...'

'You can save those explanations. Consider yourself under open arrest. Go down to your tank.'

'Right, sir.' He saluted again. Then he turned to the countess. 'We are most grateful for your hospitality.'

She shook hands with him. 'Thank you. Thank you. You have been very kind. I hope you do not get into too much trouble.'

He turned to Pola, and heard the officer cluck impatiently. He ignored it. I might as well be hung for a sheep as a lamb, he thought to himself. He said his goodbyes to Pola. She said he must come back as soon as he could get some leave. He promised to, and then walked down to the tank.

The recovery crews had already loaded it on to a huge tank transporter. He climbed up on the lorry and then on to the tank. His crew got quietly into their places.

A few minutes later the officer and sergeant came down and climbed into a jeep and set off towards Antwerp. The tank transporter started with a jerk and then rumbled after them. Brook sat in the turret and kicked himself for having been so stupid.

The streets of Antwerp were filled with smiling crowds who waved excitedly as the huge transporter carried their tank past. Most of the people had taken shelter as the Allies approached, expecting that the Germans would defend the port fiercely, but there had been almost no fighting, and liberation had come with startling suddenness. Now they cheered every Allied soldier they saw.

Everyone they passed thought that the tank had been knocked out in battle, and the crew played up a little to this false impression, for at their age it was very pleasant to be thought heroes. Geordie leant wearily against the turret and managed to wave weakly at the prettiest of the girls.

The jeep led them to the Mercedes-Benz works on the outskirts of town, which had been converted into emergency repair shops. The Engineers were working round the clock to get the many broken-down tanks going again.

As soon as they were off the transporter the officer in the jeep came up to them. Brook saluted smartly.

'I shall make a formal report, Corporal, and your commanding officer will deal with you when you re-join your regiment. Is that clear?'

'Yes, sir.'

The officer turned and strode away without another word.

'A fire-eater,' said Sandy disgustedly. 'A Div. H.Q. fire-eater. If he ever got up to the sharp end he'd frighten Jerry to death.'

TEN

AN HOUR LATER they were strolling in the centre of the town. Although the shops were shut and the people had been warned to stay inside because the Germans were still desultorily shelling from just across the Scheldt, most of them ignored the danger and enjoyed walking freely about the streets of their city for the first time in over four years.

Brook and the others were greeted everywhere with friendly smiles and were dragged into bars and had drinks thrust on them. In one they were taken over by an enormous man speaking English well who insisted on giving up the rest of his day to entertaining them.

'But first you must drink,' he boomed, indicating a row of bottles behind the bar. 'What'll you 'ave, eh? Schnapps? Bols? Pernod? Elixir d'Anvers? Anything you want – we have *good* drink in Antwerp.'

'Schnapps, please,' said Brook. He didn't know what it was, but it sounded right.

'The same,' said Taffy cautiously, and Wilcox nodded his head. Geordie had been examining the bottles with interest.

'What's that yellow stuff?' he said.

'That is Pernod – very nice.'

'I'll have a basinful of that, then.'

'A basin full?'

The big man looked worried, until they explained it to him. They laughed and began to relax.

'My name is Carl,' said the big man, pouring the drinks out himself and giving them enormous portions. 'Today and tonight – you are all my guests.'

'Hey, no water in mine!' Geordie protested. 'I never take no water with it.'

Carl looked a little surprised. 'You drink Pernod without water?'

'Never had it no other way,' said Geordie. His glass was about half full and he swallowed a large gulp and smacked his lips. 'Very nice – bit weak, of course, but very nice. Tastes like cough medicine and I always did like that.'

Carl looked at him respectfully.

Not to be outdone, Sandy chose the Elixir d'Anvers, and was obviously disappointed when he got it in a thimble-sized glass; but he sipped it and a look of pleasure came over his face.

'It's very sweet, but it burns right the way down,' he said approvingly.

Brook found the Schnapps fierce, but managed not to show it. Taffy drained his at one go, and Carl immediately filled his glass again.

Within a few minutes they were telling the story of the advance across France and their welcome in the small Belgian town.

'But not everyone in Belgium was glad to see you come in,' said Carl. 'There are plenty of people who have made money out of the occupation and didn't want the Germans to go. They are the collaborateurs and they were afraid of what would happen to them – and it *will* happen.' He made a pistol with his hand. 'Do you know where most of them are now?'

'In prison?'

'No, the prisons are full. We have put them in the zoo.'

'With the animals?'

'No, there are no animals. They were all killed because there was not enough food for them. Now there are just men in the cages. We have put the Burgomaster in the lion's cage and all day long people who have suffered from the Germans, or from him walk past and look at him.'

'But that's barbarous,' said Wilcox a little unsteadily.

Carl roared with laughter. 'That's right,' he agreed. 'That's what we are going to be to them now – barbarous.'

Geordie pushed his chair back and drained his third glass of Pernod.

'Do you know what I'd like now?' he said dreamily. 'A nice bit of crumpet.'

'Crumpet?' said Carl. 'What is crumpet?'

Geordie made a shape in the air with his two hands, at the same time making a loud sucking noise.

'Oho!' said Carl, understanding immediately. 'Crumpet! If that is all, come along and I will find it for you. Come – come.' He got up and beckoned to them. 'We have fine girls in Antwerp – clean and beautiful girls.'

The small café-cum-nightclub that Carl took them to was named the Piccadilly Bar: two days before it had still been known as the Unter den Linden, but Carl assured them it was under entirely new management. They didn't believe it and they didn't care. It was brightly lit, there was a raucous sound of music, and they could hear women's laughter. They didn't ask for anything else.

There were only two girls, Greta and Yvonne, and they were beginning to tire, but after a few more drinks they didn't look too bad. Geordie saw the girl sitting on Sandy's lap laughing at him and he filled her glass unsteadily.

'You wanna drink? What you want – Cognac? Tray bon, Cognac?' he leered at her.

'Oh no you don't,' said Sandy. 'After me, perhaps, but this is all arranged. We're just finishing our drinks, aren't we, you beautiful creature you?'

'Oui, Tommee.' She giggled.

'All right. I'm next.' Geordie glowered at the rest of them, and then focused with difficulty on Wilcox. 'Ah, Wilkie, I nearly forgot – I'm going to fix you up, aren't I? Don't worry, old mate, I'll fix you with Yvonne – after me.'

'No *thanks*,' said Wilcox with some heat.

'Why not. You mean you don't want to go after me? All right then you can go *before* me – that's me, anything for me mates. You can have her next, old friend. All right?'

'I don't *want* her.'

'What's the matter with her? She looks all right to me. You can't be too fussy, you know. What do you expect her to look like – a film star?'

'Leave me alone, Geordie, I just don't want one, that's all.'

'You must be sick.' Geordie shook his head dolefully. 'You gonna have a go, Taffy?'

'Maybe I will and maybe I won't, but if I do I can arrange it myself, thanks.'

Sandy came back in a surprisingly short time, and Geordie staggered uncertainly towards the room at the back. Yvonne now came over to their table and the glasses were filled again. She kept making overtures to Wilcox, but apparently without effect; but suddenly he threw back his head and began to sing, which startled them because he was usually so quiet. He sang a modern, sentimental song in a very bad imitation of Bing Crosby, but they applauded, and he was very pleased and sang even louder. Suddenly he stopped, and grabbed Yvonne by the arm and dragged her towards the back. They all cheered his exit.

Later the girls came back and said that both Geordie and Wilcox had passed out and couldn't be wakened. They went behind to a small, untidy room with an old iron bed, on which Wilcox was sleeping peacefully. Geordie was curled up like a cat in the corner of the room. They managed to get Wilcox on his feet and conscious, but could get no response at all from Geordie, and had to take turns carrying him all the way back to the tank.

At the echelon where they arrived about three days later there was mail for everyone. Brook got several letters, but none from Jennie. Taffy had three from his girl, and climbed into the driver's seat to savour them in peace.

Wilcox heard from his mother.

Dear Arthur,

It was so nice to get your nice letter from Amiens and know that you are all right. Your father says that he remembers it from his war and that it is a nice town. I hope that you were able to get some good solid food there because I sometimes worry about you getting enough to eat when you are in your tank for such a long time. Do they bring food up to you regularly and is it hot? I do hope that the French people are nice to you and invite you into their houses as we should certainly do if there were French soldiers over here. If they do, I hope that you remember your manners because I know it is easy for soldiers to get rough and uncouth but I know that my Arthur never would. Another thing, dear, is that French people drink rather a lot and they don't think it is bad to do so. If you just say firmly – but politely – that you don't want wine and would rather have water I know they will understand. I didn't quite understand where you stayed in Amiens – was it some kind of hotel or boarding house and who were the girls that the other boys in your tank spent the evening with? Why didn't you stay too? You must try and get over your shyness dear and be nice to people who are nice to you. Dear me, this letter does sound as though I'm telling you what to do, doesn't it? Dad tells me that I mustn't treat you like a baby because you are a man now and doing a man's work and of course I know you are doing splendidly but, after all, you are only nineteen and although that may seem old to you it seems only yesterday that you were a little thing always getting under my feet. I expect that boys always seem younger to their mothers and older to their fathers so you must forgive me if I don't want to let you grow up completely. You're all I've got, Arthur dear, and I pray God that He will look after you particularly even though I know that He has a lot to do in these awful times. Well how your silly mother does run on! Dad went to the football game on Saturday and as soon as he came in with a face as black as thunder I knew that silly team had lost again and I remembered how only you ever could get him in a good temper again on Saturdays. Take care of yourself, darling, and don't worry about us. The bombing isn't bad now at all and I think that Dad actually likes his fire watching.

Don't forget to change out of wet clothes as soon as you can because you're not as strong as the other boys and please, for my sake, don't forget your prayers and go to see the padre before you do anything dangerous.

All my love, MOTHER

Wilcox knew he wasn't going to weep like a girl, at his age, but even so he was glad there was no one else in the turret.

The regiment were engaged in cleaning up some towns on the other side of the Scheldt. They were to re-join A Squadron at Helmond the next morning. They started off just before first light and got up to the positions by six-thirty. Major Johnson seemed glad to see them, and Brook thought that perhaps the report of his leaving his tank unguarded hadn't come through.

'One troop are just here, Brook,' said the major, pointing to a factory on the canal's edge on a small-scale map of the town. 'A bit later we're going to push on through these factories and houses and make sure that we've winkled all the Jerries out. I expect the Colonel will want to see you some time, but not until we've pulled back. You know what it's about, don't you?'

'Yes, sir.'

'Righto. You can find your way to the factory can't you? I'll tell Lieutenant Henderson that you're re-joining him.'

Lieutenant Henderson's tank was in a narrow street between some small houses. Brook drew up behind him, and got out to go over and report personally.

'Hello there, Brook. You've been having a holiday I hear.'

'I'm afraid so,' said Brook glumly. 'I never thought Recovery would get up to us so quickly.'

'No, I know. I don't know what came over them. Well – never mind – you won't be the first bloke to be busted and you'll get your tapes back if you watch your step.'

Brook's face fell. 'Do you really think I'll be busted, sir?'

'Got a good chance, I should think. Still, doesn't do to cross your bridges before you come to them.'

Henderson picked up his map.

'Speaking of bridges, I want you to nip down, when we move in alongside the factory, to here.' He indicated a point on the map. 'There's a foot-bridge shown there, and if there are any characters still swanning about they'll probably try to get across on that bridge. Have you seen Sergeant Smith in your travels? His tank broke down too.'

'Yes, he came in Brigade Workshops just as we left.'

'Good. Corporal Hopper is acting troop sergeant. I would have given you the job, except that I think we'd better wait and see what the Colonel does with you. We've been given another tank in your place. It's commanded by Corporal Cadey – from the Hussars. He was clanged at Caen. Seems like a good chap.'

Brook went back and moved his tank into position a few streets to the right of Lieutenant Henderson. On the way he called out to Corporal Hopper:

'How's it going?'

'Cushy.' Corporal Hopper made the thumbs-up sign. 'Like shooting rabbits. It'll all be over inside a month.'

Brook waved at him and they moved on past the new tank in the troop. Corporal Cadey was a tall, lean-faced man who looked strangely white. He had had a month in hospital, a week's convalescence, and a fortnight's leave, before finding himself back again in a tank. He gave Brook a friendly mock salute, which Brook returned.

About half an hour later the order came for them to move forward and mop up any resistance between them and the canal, which included clearing out the factory immediately in front of them.

'O.K. Taffy, advance.' Brook knew that they had all heard the orders in detail as they had come over the wireless, and he wanted to give his full attention to the job.

He always found it difficult, when he had been out of action for several days, to get back into the state of cat-like awareness that was so necessary if they were to stay alive. It was like playing yourself in against a spin bowler – the first few shots, like the first few balls bowled at you, were the most dangerous.

The three tanks arrived at the same time, about seventy-five yards apart, at the street running along in front of the factory. Corporal Hopper's tank, in the centre, rolled up against the big wooden gates of the main entrance. For a moment the gates resisted its thirty tons, but then burst open with a loud crack. At the same time Corporal Cadey's tank nosed through the brick wall.

Brook led Taffy along a narrow path leading down the side of the factory to the canal. The factory wall was on his left, but he couldn't see over it to find out what was happening to the other two tanks. Then they all heard the noise of a German Spandau machine gun, and almost at the same time the heavier, slower sound of their own

Brownings, then the crash of high-explosive shells bursting inside the factory. Brook kept his eyes glued ahead, where he could see the towpath of the canal and two small black houses.

'Keep those houses covered, Geordie.'

The bow machine gun swung obediently to the right to its fullest extent.

'We've got an H.E. up the spout, Sandy, haven't we?'

'Right – on delay.'

'Well, save it for something worth shooting at. When we get to the end of the wall we may see some infantry trying to get away. If so, open up with the Brownings. I've got the Bren mounted up here on the turret, so I can have a go too.'

Wilcox was plucking Brook's sleeve and pointing to his headset, which had slipped off as he got the Bren gun in its mounting.

'Corporal Hopper's been sniped,' he said.

'Dead?'

'I think so.'

Brook put his earphones on and listened. Lieutenant Henderson was ordering Sammy Cohen, the wireless operator, to take over Corporal Hopper's tank.

'Wilco – out,' Cohen replied; but his set stayed broadcasting, so they heard his next words: 'Martin – give me a hand to shift him. He's as heavy as an elephant. Get hold of his feet and pull. That's right – now let him down on the floor. Of course he's dead – can't you see the bloody great hole in his head?' Then he must have discovered that he was broadcasting and switched off.

Brook slumped down in the commander's seat as far as he could get. His head felt three times its normal size and his scalp tingled. A tank commander's head was the only target offered to a sniper, but it was impossible to command a tank with the turret closed. The periscopes were all right for playing war games in England, but would be suicide in action. He knew the steel helmet that was issued to them was of no use against a rifle bullet, but he huddled down in the turret and groped for the helmet and put it on anyway.

At that moment a number of German infantry broke from cover and ran down the towpath. Sandy had been alert, and his Browning fired at once. Two of them went down. Geordie's machine gun in the bow had been pointing the other way, covering the houses Brook had ordered. He now swung it round but was too late, for the rest of the soldiers had dived over the bank into the canal. Brook also had been caught napping – he was putting on his steel helmet – but he dropped the helmet and made a grab at the Bren gun swinging uselessly on its tripod.

'Quick, Taffy – down to the canal!' Taffy had already got the tank moving, and they roared down to the end of the path.

The German infantry were crouched in some barges. Brook swung the Bren gun to cover them, but one, evidently the leader, raised his hands above his head and shouted something. Brook didn't understand the words, but he held his fire. The other Germans then stood up with hands raised, and Brook gestured that they were to climb back up on to the towpath. As soon as they had done so and were standing in an uncertain group in front of the tank, he ordered Sandy to come up and hold the Bren gun on them.

Sandy had not been able to depress his turret periscope enough to see down into the barges, or he probably would have fired on them. He held the Bren gun now, hoping for an excuse to fire.

'I'm going to see what they've got, Sandy. Keep your finger off that trigger.' He jumped down. 'Geordie – pop out and help me search them.'

Geordie scrambled out of the co-driver s seat, and together they emptied the pockets of the Germans, at the same time taking their wrist-watches. Only their leader, a hard-bitten corporal, was armed, and Brook took a small-calibre pistol from him. The others had evidently thrown their rifles away.

When they had made sure that the prisoners were left with nothing of value for the rear troops to get, Brook told Wilcox to report the prisoners and ask what he was to do with them.

'Hold them here until our infantry come along to pick them up,' Wilcox relayed.

Brook waved them over to the factory wall, making signs that they were to sit down.

The corporal was about forty, and wore an Iron Cross. He looked exactly like the popular idea of a tough German N.C.O. The rest of them were just boys – some of them looking no more than sixteen or so – and they ignored Brook, keeping their eyes on the corporal, whom they were obviously much more afraid of than they were of their captors. He said something, and they trooped over to the wall and sat down. The corporal remained standing, looking at Brook defiantly.

At that moment came the noise of Moaning Minnies whining through the air, and habit was so strong that the prisoners, and Geordie and Brook, began to throw themselves flat on the ground. Brook checked this instinctive reaction, as it occurred to him that the mortaring would be an opportunity for his prisoners to make a break. As he checked himself he saw that the German corporal was watching him carefully. He straightened himself up against the side of the tank, hoping that the mortars would land on the other side. The German, who had also been about to throw himself flat, checked himself too and stood up against the factory wall some ten feet or so from Brook, still looking at him with defiance.

The screaming of the mortars got louder. Brook saw the young German soldiers trying to press themselves into the ground and Geordie expertly rolling under the tank. A stick of six mortars fell in a line about fifty yards from them. The explosions jarred them, the air was full of white-hot casing – and then it was all over and no one had been hurt. Brook and the corporal continued to watch each other for signs of fear.

'What's the matter with you, man?' said Sandy's voice disgustedly. 'Are you tired of living, or something?'

Brook felt a little foolish that his gesture of bravado had been seen. 'I didn't want this character to get any ideas,' he said.

'Och, I had the Bren pointing at him all the time,' said Sandy.

The German corporal barked a couple of orders and his men got to their feet again sheepishly. Geordie crawled out from under the tank, but no one laughed.

Brook borrowed Geordie's cigarettes and offered one to the German corporal. The German looked at the packet for a moment, then at Brook; then he took one.

'Danke schön,' he said, and nearly smiled.

A few minutes later a platoon of their own supporting infantry arrived, with a number of other German prisoners in tow. The sergeant in charge took the cigarette out of the German's mouth and threw it on the ground, pushed the corporal into the ranks and trotted the whole party off at the double.

'That's the way to treat those bastards,' said Sandy approvingly. 'D'you think he'd have offered you a cigarette?'

'Orders, Brookie,' Wilcox reported. 'We're to go back and rejoin the troop. Somebody's found an unblown bridge across the canal and they're putting us over.'

When they got back Lieutenant Henderson ordered Brook to come over to him.

'Now that Corporal Hopper is dead you'd better take over troop sergeant until Smudger gets back,' he said. 'Hopper's tank will wait here for a new commander to come up...'

'What about Cohen, sir?'

'I don't think so – he's a good man but not ready to command a tank yet. Anyway we would still have to wait for an operator. No, they'll rejoin us tomorrow. Meanwhile we have a little job to do. Jerry has left one bridge unblown and he's pulling out of a little village on the other side where we expected him to make a stand. We have to go over and see if it's all as easy as it looks.'

An hour or so later they picked their way across the bridge carefully, half expecting it to blow up even though the Engineers had assured them that it wasn't going to. They approached the village carefully, but all they could see were shattered and smoking houses. It had been very thoroughly shot up by a retreating German armoured column, who had no doubt been nervous of any possible resistance and had fired their heavy shells wantonly into the houses and had followed them up with thousands of rounds of machine gun.

When they had found the place quite clear of Germans they reported back, and ambulance and doctors were sent hurriedly to them.

There was hardly a house which did not bring out either dead or wounded. The dead were laid on the street for a burial party and the injured were given first aid on the spot and the worst of them taken back to the casualty clearing station for operations. It was obvious that the retreating Germans had, quite unnecessarily and with great brutality, done as much damage as possible in a small and defenceless village. Most of the dead and injured were women and children, because the able-bodied men had either fled or been sent as forced labour to Germany.

It was the first direct evidence of the atrocity stories they had often heard but had hardly believed. None of them ever again after that felt quite the same about the young, scared-looking German soldiers who surrendered to them.

They moved on and leaguered that night in an apple orchard bright with fruit. 'Windfalls only,' they were told, but the tanks grazed the trees and a surprisingly large number of apples fell.

They got rid of their spent ammunition cases and took on new, replaced the petrol they had used, and drew three days' rations. They made an enormous bully beef stew with apples, which at least changed the taste.

About midnight, when they had finished eating, Lieutenant Henderson came back from a troop officers' conference.

'Well, lads, it looks as though we'll be here for a couple of days – maybe longer. They're working out some sort of do with the airborne troops. The Guards are going to drive a corridor up north and then we're going to widen it. It doesn't sound too bad at all. But get some sleep while you can, just in case they change their minds.' He got up to go. 'Corporal Brook – here a minute.'

Brook knew what he was going to say.

'The Colonel wants to see you at his tank at ten o'clock tomorrow morning. I'll go with you.'

The colonel had made his headquarters in the front of a farmhouse. Brook saw the regimental sergeant-major in the R.H.Q. lorry and wondered if he would be marched in before the colonel bareheaded as Geordie had been so long ago in Aldershot. Then he remembered from his N.C.O.'s course that on a charge one never went straight to the colonel but always through the squadron leader. At that moment Major Johnson approached briskly. Lieutenant Henderson called Brook to attention and saluted. Major Johnson returned the salute, and hurried inside. Brook and Lieutenant Henderson walked up and down in silence, then Henderson was called inside as well.

Brook waited about, wondering what was going on and what was to become of him. If he lost both his tapes he could not continue as a tank commander, which would mean he would become a wireless operator again. They would probably move him to another squadron, which would be as much punishment as losing his rank. The door opened and Lieutenant Henderson called him.

He marched in, stood to attention in front of the colonel, and saluted smartly.

'Stand easy, Corporal.'

The colonel spoke quietly. He was sitting at a table, Major Johnson standing half-right from him. Brook had not seen the colonel at close quarters since the battle of Caen, and was shocked at how tired, worn and old he had become. His hair had been streaked with grey then, but now it seemed quite white: he had become an old man. There was a typewritten sheet on the table in front of him.

'I expect you know what this is about, Corporal?'

'Leaving my tank unguarded, sir?'

'Yes. This report says that neither you nor any of your crew were anywhere about when the Recovery people arrived. The tank was in possession of the Resistance. Is that right?'

'Yes, sir.'

There was a pause.

A little wearily, the colonel said, 'Well, is that all you've got to say?'

'No, sir. I know it was wrong of me. We were pretty tired and the Resistance chaps seemed very capable of guarding it. I knew it couldn't be moved, and we did take the firing-pins out of the guns.'

'What about the Mills bombs? What about the ammunition? Didn't you think what could happen if a pocket of Germans left behind had got hold of your tank?'

'I didn't at the time, sir. I have since.'

'I'm very surprised, Corporal. I had my eye on you, and I thought you were doing well and warranted promotion – but this has made me stop and think. I may as well tell you that Major Johnson had recommended that you be made a lance-sergeant and be given a troop, and I should have been glad to agree: but now I think we had better wait and see whether this was a momentary mental blackout or if you are really not to be trusted. That's all, Corporal.'

Brook saluted, and marched outside. Lieutenant Henderson came out a few minutes after him, and they walked back together.

As soon as they were out of earshot of R.H.Q., Lieutenant Henderson said, 'You were bloody lucky, my lad.'

'What – to lose my sergeant's stripes?'

'You might have lost them all. Fortunately for you the officer sent a confidential report instead of putting you on a charge. Anyway, you didn't know about your promotion.'

'No, but I do now.'

'Don't be silly. If you keep your nose clean and do well in this next show you're bound to get them.'

On reflection Brook decided it might have been a great deal worse. The troop congratulated him, and everyone seemed genuinely glad that he had not lost his rank.

ELEVEN

JUST BEFORE DAWN the tank crews were awakened by the roar of massed aircraft. They scrambled out of their blankets and stood peering up in the uncertain light.

Flying very low and filling the sky, flight after flight of heavy bombers towed strings of gliders towards the rising sun. The soldiers on the ground stood silently, thinking of the men packed in the gliders. Now as they approached the assault area, their throats would be dry and their hearts pounding.

'Rather them than me,' said Geordie. 'They must have bags of guts, those blokes.'

'Poor bastards,' said Taffy, 'floating down on top of Jerry and not being able to shoot back – I'm glad I'm in a nice safe tank.'

'But if it comes off,' said Brook, 'if they get the bridges over the Maas and the lower Rhine and the Waal all at once, it could be the end of the war, as the Major said. It's bound to catch Jerry on the hop – he might get some of them, but there are thirty-five thousand going down.'

For nearly an hour they stood watching the bombers going over like flocks of geese. Then the order came to pack up and start moving north.

'Our job is to move into the corridor made by the airborne boys,' Lieutenant Henderson told them. 'The Yanks and some of our armour are putting in an attack at the same time, and we'll probably be over the Rhine in a day or so. I shouldn't think we'll meet any stiff resistance until we've left Arnhem and swung round to the Siegfried Line. That might be a little sticky, but there won't be much fight left in Jerry by then.'

'There's *always* fight left in Jerry,' said Smudger.

But apart from a few pessimists like Smudger everyone felt that the end of the war was in sight. The unbroken advance from the Seine, the lack of any real German resistance, the strength of the airborne attack, all seemed to ensure quick success. That night many of them were unable to sleep allowing themselves to contemplate, almost for the first time, the possibility of getting away from the army, out of uniform and back to the lives they had left, and they felt reluctant to get killed 'in the last few days'.

They moved slowly north fighting a few short, sharp actions. Brook had become a good tank commander and his reactions were now almost automatic. In one village, defended furiously by about sixty German infantry, Lieutenant Henderson's tank was knocked out, and Brook led the rest of the troop in immediately, firing all their guns. This, combined with a determined attack by their supporting infantry, the tough little Welsh, broke the German defence.

Orders had come to let out one man from each tank to clear the surrounding houses. Sandy had brought in half a dozen prisoners, and had killed two who hadn't surrendered quickly enough for him. He was obviously in his element.

'You should be in the Commandos,' said Brook. 'Get back in the tank or we'll leave you behind.'

Lieutenant Henderson had baled out when his tank had been hit, and taken command of Lance-Corporal Cadey's tank. He looked haggard and exhausted, and as soon as they leaguered for the night he went to find out about his crew. Captain MacDonald, his brother-in-law, had just come back from the echelon.

'Did my driver get out, Arthur?' Henderson asked.

'I'm afraid not – the other three are all right, though. They told me they want to come up with you, but I think a couple of days in the echelon is what they need. You look all in, old man. Why don't you go back and wait for a reinforcement? It'll take a day or two, and you've earned it.'

'No: I'm all right. I'll take over Corporal Cadey's tank and send him back for another – he can bring it up with my crew and I'll change over then.'

'But, damn it – '

'Please, Arthur, shut up, will you – sir?'

'All right – have it your own way,' said Captain MacDonald. 'Have you heard from Alice lately?'

'Yes, I had two letters last time the post came up. She sends you her love. She says you're to take care of yourself.'

Captain MacDonald laughed. 'I'll do that thing.'

That night they listened with particular care to the B.B.C.'s nine o'clock news, from which they always seemed to learn more than they were told officially. The parachute action had been an overwhelming success. The bridge at Nijmegen had been captured intact, and three other bridges over the river Maas. The bridge at Arnhem was under attack and due to fall at any moment. The way was open for a drive through Holland.

They moved on, and late in the afternoon arrived at a small village which also happened to be on the line of advance of the division on their left, who were to cross over to their right at this point. It had of course been intended that they should pass through before the other division arrived, but a short, sharp action in the morning had disrupted the schedule, and both divisions' leading tanks arrived at the same time. The tanks were placed in conventional defensive positions while the top-ranking officers tried to straighten out the tangle. There were so many tanks that a squadron stretched out along each of the roads leading out into the country from the cobbled village square. It looked as though it would have needed a full-scale armoured attack to take the tiny village.

Brook's tank was next to Lieutenant Henderson's.

'Go down and get Corporal Cadey moved out to the flank a bit more,' Lieutenant Henderson ordered him, 'so that he can cover the bit of dead ground by those trees. Not that there's anything there, but we might as well do it by the book, with the Brigadier sitting over there – he doesn't miss much.'

The order could have been given over the air, but it would have drawn attention to the bad position Corporal Cadey had put himself in; and anyway, the air must be kept free for more important matters. Brook walked the seventy or eighty yards down the road and, climbing on to Lance-Corporal Cadey's tank, put him in the position the troop officer had indicated.

From the top of the turret he could see back to the village square, where Colonel Drayton and the colonel of their supporting infantry were conferring with the brigadier and his brigade major. They were all sitting in the colonel's jeep looking at the brigadier's very large map. The colonel's jeep driver was getting a brew going, and Brook decided it meant there was time for them to do the same.

He glanced over to the right, where B Squadron's tanks were stretched along another road, and suddenly he heard the distinctive pom-pom-pom of a light anti-aircraft gun firing. At the same moment a German half-track mounting a fifty-millimetre anti-aircraft gun came down B Squadron's road at full speed straight past the tanks.

There was no time for anyone to do anything, for the half-track was travelling at forty or fifty miles an hour. From the moment it came over a small rise and began firing its gun wildly at B Squadron's tanks until it arrived at the village square was no more than ten or fifteen seconds.

B Squadron tanks had placed themselves alternately to the right and left of the road leaving a narrow lane winding through them not much wider than a jeep. Suddenly every tank commander saw, for a few seconds, a half-track containing four young Germans, a small anti-tank gun and a machine gun, go rocking back and forth across the road with both guns firing indiscriminately. It went straight past all their tanks as a hard-kicked football sometimes goes past the players into the goalmouth.

In the square were the colonel's jeep and protecting tanks. The four young Germans must have known they had come to the end of their wild dash. Perhaps because they recognised the jeep as an important target, or perhaps just because it lay straight ahead of them, the anti-tank gun and the machine guns fired into it in their last few seconds: and at the same moment a number of tanks which had been bringing their guns to bear as fast as possible fired at the half-track, blowing it to bits.

When the noise of the firing had stopped – the whole incident had been perhaps half a minute – Colonel Drayton was dead, the colonel of the infantry was dead, and the brigadier and the brigade major were both wounded. The four young Germans were also dead, and could not know how successful their reckless effort had been.

The tanks went no farther that day. On the next they buried their commanding officer in the little churchyard, and were then pulled out for forty-eight hours to reorganise and do their maintenance.

Mid-morning the following day Lieutenant Henderson came back from the major's tank and saw Sandy stripping his Browning.

'Is Sergeant Brook about, Corporal Sanderstead?' he said.

'Sergeant Brook?' Sandy said.

'Yes – and you've been promoted lance-corporal.'

Sandy stood up with a big grin. 'I'm very pleased, sir.'

'So am I, Sandy. I'll be sorry to lose you.'

'Lose me, sir?'

'Get hold of Sergeant Brook and I'll tell you. And Sergeant Smith too, of course.'

Smudger and Brook, along with Taffy, Geordie, Sammy Cohen and Ben Lyon, were in a nearby farmhouse exchanging tea and sugar for eggs, when Sandy came up with the news.

Smudger said as he thumped Brook on the back, 'Welcome to the sergeants' mess, Brookie. When we get one, that is. It'll be drinks all round on you.'

Brook was delighted. 'What a drink we'll have!' he said.

'Come on,' said Sandy, 'he's got something else to tell us.'

Smudger handed over three eggs to Lieutenant Henderson as his portion, and the troop officer carefully put them in one of the boxes with crêpe rubber cradles inside intended to hold spare wireless valves.

'Here's the griff,' said Lieutenant Henderson. 'Sergeant Smith, you take over as Two Troop's Sergeant – there's a new officer and four tanks coming up tonight; Corporal Sanderstead will take over your tank as commander. Sergeant Brook takes over as One Troop Sergeant. Congratulations to all of you.'

'Not much promotion for me to go from One Troop Sergeant to Two Troop,' said Smudger. 'More like demotion.'

'The new officer hasn't been in action before, and the Major particularly wanted to give him an experienced troop sergeant,' said Lieutenant Henderson placatingly.

'Christ!' said Smudger.

The reinforcements came up that evening. Smudger packed his kit and went to take over one of the four new tanks, which had stopped behind one another in a line in the road. He introduced himself to the officer, a fresh-faced boy who had come straight from officer training school in England a few days before.

After returning Smudger's salute the young officer held out his hand.

'The Major has told me I'm lucky to get you, Sergeant,' he said pleasantly.

'Thank you, sir. Who have we got in the crews?'

'Here's a list. I don't know any of them, of course, but I understand some of them are old 33rd Battalion lads.'

Smudger took the list and glanced down the names. Six of them had been in tanks that had been knocked out recently and there were four who had been wounded at Caen. The rest were new, but he recognised the names of five who had been on the desert with him. He saw that he could have the kind of crew he wanted, and began to feel better.

'There's some good lads here, sir,' he said.

'Fine. Because we're going to have the best troop in the regiment.'

'Yes, sir.'

'I'm not just *saying* that, Sergeant, I mean it. The best troop in the regiment!'

Smudger looked hard at him and saw the brightness in the youngster's eyes and realised that he did indeed mean it. It looked as though he was going to have his work cut out, keeping this new officer alive for that critical period until he had learned caution for himself the hard way.

'We'll do our best, sir.'

'Right – now we've been assigned to that space over there. I want you to organise it, and I'll watch. I know I've got a lot to learn, and the Major says you're the one to learn it from.'

Smudger was a bit puzzled by this new officer; but he had seen many types come and go, and he got on with the job of putting the tanks into position, checking the oil, petrol, water, ammunition and food, and watching how the new chaps pulled their weight.

Sandy had taken over Smudger's old crew, who all knew and liked him. Turner, the driver, wasn't sorry to see Smudger go, for he had just about despaired of ever being able to please him. He knew now, that it was because Smudger had resented anyone taking Nobby Clarke's place; but it didn't help him, and he had become so jumpy with Smudger's constant criticism that he had begun making silly mistakes. He was glad of the opportunity to start with a new commander.

Ben Lyon, the wireless operator and one of the desert veterans, had realised for some time that Sandy was destined for promotion, and didn't begrudge him it.

As soon as Sandy had taken over, Ben Lyon said:

'Just one thing, Sandy, and then I'll shut up and do what I'm told.'

'O.K., let's have it.'

'No volunteering. We'll do anything we're ordered to and take our chances, but we don't want no medals. It's sticky enough in the Tanks without shoving your neck out too. You're a mad bastard – but this isn't the infantry, and there's four more of us in this tank with you.'

'What do you mean by volunteering?'

'You know – none of this "I think I can get a better view from the top of that hill" stuff. You'll get away with it a few times, but you're bound to get clanged if you keep it up.'

'Och, don't worry, I'm not bloody daft. But you don't win wars hull down, you know, and when I'm told to go forward then we'll go forward – is that understood? Because if it's not then you'd better go sick with a pain in your belly and I'll get someone else.'

'Keep your hair on, you barbary Jock,' Ben Lyon growled. 'I never went sick yet, and I'm not going to start now. I just wanted to get things straight, and then, as I said, I'll shut up. O.K.?'

'O.K.' said Sandy, cheerful and confident.

But that night Sandy lay awake thinking of all the things he didn't know about tank commanding, and then he wasn't so confident. He had never had a tank commander's course, but he had watched Brook, and had chafed sometimes at what he thought was undue caution, and had thought he could do as well. Now he began to be beset with doubts. In the morning he went to find Brook.

'Brookie,' he said, 'I've been thinking – there's a hell of a lot I don't know about tank commanding. Give me some tips, will you? Is it so difficult?'

Brook looked at him and saw he was serious.

'You learn as you go along, Sandy,' he said. He knew Sandy half hoped for some magic formula: but there wasn't one. 'I watched Paddy, and tried to learn from him.'

'Well, I've been watching you – but it strikes me there's a hell of a lot I don't know.'

'Like what? You've been a wireless operator and a gunner, so you know about that. Mostly you're told what to do – where to go. After that it's a question of keeping your eyes open. You see more every day. I can't tell you what to do, Sandy, but you'll be all right.'

'I hope so. I'll get stuck in and do my best, that's all.'

'I'll tell you one thing, though, since you've asked.'

'Yes?'

'You're too reckless. It mayn't be so bad when you're only risking your own neck, but it's not good enough when you're risking four other blokes'. Doing the job is one thing; sticking out your neck is another. Don't go in somewhere blind if it isn't necessary; don't stick yourself up against the skyline if you don't have to. And one thing always remember: If an 88 ever fires at you and misses – bale out. *Don't* try to find him and answer back, because he won't miss with his second shot. Get *out* and into the ditch, and when he brews your tank up the next minute you'll still be alive. There are always other tanks around and they'll fire at him.'

Sandy stared at him for a few seconds. 'You really mean that, Brookie?'

'Of course I do. The point is that they don't fire first unless they've got you dead in their sights, which means that they don't often miss; but sometimes they do miss – usually because they're a little high – and then they only need a few seconds to reload, and they won't miss the second time. On the other hand if you're not in their line of fire and you open up on them, even if *you* miss you're usually all right, because they're not going to hang about bringing their gun round to you either but will also get the hell out of there. I know it doesn't say so in the book, but that's the way it happens.'

'Well, God knows you're not windy, Brookie, and if that's what you say, then that's what I'll do.'

'I don't know about being windy – I'm bloody scared sometimes, though.'

Sandy laughed disbelievingly. 'What's your new gunner like?' he said.

'Bentley? He's the serious type, keen to get on. He's green as grass, but I think he's going to be all right. We'll find out up at the sharp end. Heard any news?'

'No. Let's go and find Henderson and get the griff.'

Lieutenant Henderson was marking up his map. He looked worried.

'I'm afraid we were a bit over-optimistic,' he told them. 'We haven't got the bridge at Nijmegen, *nor* at Arnhem. Jerry seems to have had a lot of stuff there and he's hitting back hard. The Yanks made an assault-crossing of the river in the teeth of everything Jerry could throw at them, and the Guards Armoured made a flat-out attack on the bridge at the same time; but I'm afraid they've been cut off by a Jerry counter-attack. They must be having a bad time.'

Brook whistled. 'Are we going to their help?'

'No – they don't need tanks. It's a very bad tank country, with too deep ditches and no cover. The infantry are trying to get through to them – poor bastards.'

It was a new experience for them to be miles away from the fighting, and they realised something of the helpless feeling that the rear troops have when things are going badly.

The next day it was confirmed that the airborne operation at Arnhem had failed, and they were ordered to advance to the Maas and stop the jubilant enemy from re-crossing it. Between them and the river were pockets of German troops, some of whom fought fiercely before being overwhelmed.

On the third morning of the advance to the Maas, One Troop were ordered to encircle a small wood where the enemy had been reported. They could see no activity, and Two Troop were ordered to go forward and confirm that the woods were empty. When Second-Lieutenant Graham, Smudger's new Troop Officer, was about three hundred yards from the trees, he came up on the air trying not to sound too excited.

'I can see a German tank at the far end of the trees! I think it's a Royal Tiger!' The listening crews in the other tanks smiled at one another: the first German tank anyone ever saw always looked like a Royal Tiger. 'We will engage – out to you. All stations Item Baker Two – advance. Get cracking.'

Brook and every other tank commander was searching the approximate position with binoculars; but the ground between them and Second-Lieutenant Graham rose slightly, so that only he could see the German tank.

'Hello Item Baker Two Able,' replied Smudger. 'Roger, but don't forget the woods on your right.'

It was tactless of Smudger to advise his troop officer over the air, and they knew he wouldn't have done so without a good reason. The rest of Two Troop acknowledged the order and began to move forward. The troop officer's tank disappeared below the hill, and the wireless went silent as everyone waited for his next report.

There was a far-off crack of an 88, followed by the noise of a tank exploding.

'One of my tanks has been hit!' the young officer's excited voice rose like a boy's. 'I don't know where it came from but I'll go over to him and see if I can spot it. Over.'

'No!' Major Johnson replied immediately. 'You'd better stay where you are for the moment. I'll get someone else up to you. Hello Item Baker One – get round the east end of the wood and back up Two.'

Lieutenant Henderson acknowledged the order quietly, and One Troop moved off, with him in the lead, along the edge of the wood. An 88 fired again, from a long way off.

'Item Baker Two has had it. Same gun, same place. It must be on the far ridge.' Smudger's voice was urgent, and they could hear the roar of his engines as he reversed his tank away from danger.

'Right. Come back. Watch your step, Item Baker One. Over.' The 88 was obviously very well sited, and the major didn't want it picking off his tanks one by one.

Brook, like the other tank commanders in the troop, kept his binoculars on the high ground over which Two Troop had disappeared, waiting for the remaining tanks to come back. All he could see were two columns of smoke rising from the knocked-out tanks. He glanced over at the woods on his right, but there was no movement. He guessed that there had been a self-propelled gun there which had pulled out and gone to a position where it could knock out anything that appeared over the hill. His head once again felt as big as a house as he pictured it in the sight of a sniper's telescope somewhere among the trees.

'Keep a watch on the woods, Bentley,' he said to the new gunner, 'just in case there's still some Jerries swanning about.'

'Right, Sergeant,' said Bentley, eagerly scrambling up on the turret. 'Can I use the Bren?'

Brook looked at him – he was going to be all right, thank God. 'Yes, but don't start blazing away until you know what you're firing at.'

Lieutenant Henderson was about fifty yards ahead of Brook, and he turned and pointed to the hill. Brook saw the top of the turret of Smudger's tank appear, and then the remaining tank of Two Troop. In a few moments they would be below the shelter of the hill.

A gun, which seemed to be on top of them, fired once. There was a tremendous explosion, and a great flame shot out of Lieutenant Henderson's tank.

Bentley had started to fire the Bren into the woods, when Brook saw two figures run from Lieutenant Henderson's tank towards the trees.

He pushed up the barrel of the Bren.

'Get back in the turret and man your gun!' he shouted to Bentley. 'Reverse on your left stick, Taffy. An H.E. up the spout, Wilcox...'

The orders were coming out of his mouth almost independently of his brain, and he felt detached, as though he were watching himself controlling the tank. He heard the breech of the gun clang open and shut, and the thud of the ejected armour-piercing shell as it landed on the floor of the turret. A bit dangerous, that – Wilcox should have known better.

He suddenly realised that he was in command of the troop now, and called up Sandy and Cadey: 'I saw two of our boys run into the woods. Put down some smoke and we'll advance under cover and see if we can get them.'

'Hello Baker One Able – what the hell is going on. Over.'

He realised that he hadn't reported to the squadron leader.

'Item Baker One has been brewed up by a gun in the woods on our right. I'm going forward to see if I can pick up any of the crew.'

Sandy and Cadey had fired their smoke cartridges, and all three tanks were moving into the smoke.

'... Stay where you are. We're coming up to you,' the major ordered. Brook was glad to be able to stop his tank; Corporal Cadey also stopped; but Sandy kept on going, and disappeared into the smoke. A minute or two later he came up on the air.

'I've found the gun – it's a wee one and it's abandoned.' Then: 'There's no sign of the lads.'

The smoke cleared, and Brook moved up next to Sandy. The gun was a small artillery piece, and could only have knocked out a tank at point-blank range. Their position right up against the trees was obviously not a good one, and they pulled back to where the rest of the squadron were. Brook stopped next to Smudger.

Smudger jumped over on to Brook's tank.

'Did Henderson get out?' he asked.

'I don't know,' said Brook. 'I only saw two and I don't know who they were. What happened to your new officer?'

'He was a death-or-glory boy. He didn't take any notice of the warning but went ahead to see if he could find the 88. It found him first. He'd have been a good bloke if he'd lived long enough to learn some sense.'

'Sergeant Brook?'

It was Captain MacDonald, Lieutenant Henderson's brother-in-law. He was standing in front of the tank.

'Sir?' Brook jumped down to the ground.

'Did Mr Henderson get out?'

'I don't think so, sir. I saw two running for the woods, but I couldn't see who they were. The ammo exploded in the turret, though.'

'I'm going up at first light to see if I can find them. I want you to come with me and show me where they went.'

'Yes, sir.'

Brook was dead tired, but hours later when he was able to get into his blankets by the side of the tank, sleep wouldn't come. He got up and climbed into the turret. Bentley and Wilcox were there listening to the wireless.

'I wonder what sort of an officer we'll get now,' Wilcox said. 'I liked old Henderson.'

'I don't know,' said Brook. 'I hope it's not a death-or-glory boy.'

He noticed that Bentley was cleaning his Browning machine gun, although it was after eleven at night. He was well pleased with Bentley, who had been first-class in his first losing action.

'How do you like tank fighting, Bentley?'

'I like it,' Bentley said. 'When I'm not frightened, that is.'

'Don't let that worry you – we're all scared of Jerry tanks and 88s.'

Bentley laughed. 'You, Sergeant. You were as cool as a cucumber. I wish I could be like that.'

'You did all right, Bentley, you all did.'

Brook was pleased that he had seemed cool and unafraid to young Bentley, just as Paddy Donovan had seemed larger than life to him, only four months before. He wondered if it was possible that Paddy Donovan had ever felt the sick fear that had been coming over him in action recently. He thought not – Paddy was one of those rare human beings born without fear.

'You'd better get some kip, lads,' he said. 'It'll be first light in a few hours.'

He wished them good night and walked down the column of tanks. He wondered whether he was sickening for something, or perhaps just tired. He knew that the reason he couldn't sleep was that he didn't want to go forward with Captain MacDonald at dawn to the wood, which might well be occupied by the enemy again. He knew also there was no way of getting out of it or of getting out of all the days that lay ahead, on one of which it would be his tank that the white hot armour-piercing 88 would hit.

He shut his eyes and thrust the picture from him – suddenly he would have given anything never to see a tank again.

Captain MacDonald himself woke him, when it was still dark.

'Get your tank ready, Sergeant, it'll be light in a quarter of an hour.'

He pulled on his boots and got into his tank suit, rolled up his blankets, tied them, and threw them on the back of the tank. Then he woke the others.

'Come on. We're going to see if we can find any of Henderson's crew.' As they were getting up he got the primus stove lit and the brew can on. After a mug of hot, strong, sweet tea they all felt better.

The two tanks went back along their tracks of the night before, and stopped as soon as the woods were in sight. The blackened hulk of Lieutenant Henderson's tank was still smoking a bit, but there was no sign of any activity. They moved across the fields to the woods, and Brook went to where the gun had been.

It was gone.

'Didn't you destroy it?' Captain MacDonald asked.

'No, sir.'

'Bad show. Where did you see them run into the woods?'

'Just up ahead.'

The tanks moved up.

'Just about here.'

'Right.' Captain MacDonald jumped down. He looked questioningly at Brook.

Brook swung his legs out of the turret. 'Wilcox – take over. Geordie, get the Sten gun and come with me.'

The three of them walked slowly into the wood. Some of the 88 shells of the night before had landed short and there were broken stumps of branches and gashes in the trees. They spread out a little to cover as much ground as possible, looking carefully for any bit of evidence.

Suddenly Geordie called: 'Christ! Here's Sammy Cohen.'

Geordie was standing white-faced pointing ahead of him. Fat Sammy Cohen was sitting up against a tree, with his revolver in his hand. His eyes were open, and for the first second it looked as though he was alive and playing a joke on them. Then they saw the grey death pallor on his face.

Captain MacDonald prised the revolver out of his hand.

'Three shots fired,' he said.

'I wonder what at?' Brook said stupidly.

Captain MacDonald bent over and looked at Sammy closely. He pointed to his middle, and they saw the dark bloodstains.

'Bled to death,' said MacDonald. 'Propped himself against the tree and made up his mind to have a go at one of them if he got the chance. He probably imagined they were all around him at the end.' He eased the body gently away from the tree and it fell over on its side. He took the paybook but left the identity disc, as regulations provided.

They searched the woods pretty thoroughly for several hundred yards, but found no sign of the others. They walked back to Lieutenant Henderson's tank. It was too hot to touch. It had burnt so fiercely that they knew there would be no sign at all of anyone who had been left inside.

For no particular reason Brook bent over and looked under the tank from the back. Resting casually against one of the track plates was a human hand. His heart and stomach turned over. He straightened up.

'Sir?'

Captain MacDonald looked round sharply at the tone of his voice and Brook pointed under the tank. Captain MacDonald walked round, bent over, and looked. For a moment he didn't move. Then he took a handkerchief from his pocket, and reaching forward picked up the hand gently. It had been cut off clean, an inch or two above the wrist, at about the place where a watch would be worn. The heat had dried it effectively and it was waxy white. On the little finger was a ring, which Captain MacDonald examined carefully. Then he wrapped the hand in his handkerchief.

'Mr Henderson?' Brook asked.

'Yes,' Captain MacDonald said, in a dry, tight voice.

TWELVE

LIEUTENANT KENTON, their new troop officer, was not the success that Grimshaw and Henderson had been. He was a small man with a sallow face and a permanent look of distaste. He didn't like Brook, and never missed an opportunity to be sarcastic to him.

Smudger had known him in the desert.

'He's a windy bastard,' Smudger said disgustedly. 'He always was, and he always will be. You want to watch the sod, Brookie, or he'll get you killed – he'll tuck hisself behind a wall when the stuff begins to fly and send you forward on your tod. And all the time he'll be hogging the air and waffling about being in front of you and telling you to come *up* to him. I thought after Caen we'd seen the last of him – I was sure he'd fiddle himself a cushy billet; but he must have dropped a clanger or something – I'm bloody sure he didn't *want* to come up to the sharp end.'

'Well, he certainly doesn't like me,' said Brook. 'He never misses a chance to take it out of me, and the lads know it – it's bad for troop morale.'

'Everybody knows he's windy, and *that's* bad for troop morale. You watch him, Brookie boy, and don't let him needle you into doing something silly. You've just about learned enough to keep alive, unless you're dead unlucky; don't go sticking your neck out.'

The first shell of their thrice-daily barrage landed some fifty yards away and the tank crews disappeared in a twinkling into the holes they had dug under their tanks. The shelling continued for three or four minutes and then stopped abruptly. Some of the bolder ones, relying on German routine, came out of the holes immediately, for the next lot of shells would not come for about three hours. The others, more cautious, waited for a few minutes to make sure.

They had been in the same position for nearly a month, occupying a deserted Dutch farm about a thousand yards from the German positions, waiting for the generals to decide on the next move. From time to time they shelled the Germans and were shelled back: their infantry went forward at night through the minefield and sometimes sniped someone on the other side; an evening or two later the Germans would return the visit. The strain of waiting for the next battle was beginning to tell on them all.

As usual, Lieutenant Kenton had disappeared when the shelling began, and was one of the last to come out from under a tank. When he did so he strolled over to Brook. Smudger saw him coming and pointedly left.

'They are starting day passes to Antwerp, Sergeant,' he said. 'Three per troop per day.'

Brook saluted. 'That's good, sir. The lads could do with a break.'

'It starts tomorrow, and it might last until everyone has gone and then again it might not – someone could be unlucky. I imagine you'll go first, won't you?' He knew perfectly well, of course, that it wasn't done, to take advantage of rank for a pass or other special privilege.

'We'll draw for the passes,' Brook said shortly.

'Antwerp doesn't appeal to you, Sergeant?' Kenton drawled. 'I hear the flying bombs are rather bad.'

'I'll probably win the draw.'

'I shan't be surprised. Let me know the three names as soon as possible.' He walked back to the farmhouse.

Brook got the troop together and all the names were put in a helmet. Taffy held it over his head and Geordie reached up and drew one out.

'Brook,' Geordie read out disgustedly. 'It's a fiddle,' he said.

The next names he drew were Wilcox and Ben Lyon, Sandy's wireless operator.

'Look out, Yvonne,' said Geordie, 'you're going to get it tomorrow.'

'Not me,' said Wilcox fervently. 'Never again.'

Brook found Lieutenant Kenton. 'Myself, Wilcox and Lyon, sir.'

Kenton smiled nastily. 'You wangled it then, Sergeant?'

'The hand is quicker than the eye, sir.' He smiled.

Kenton looked angry for a second. 'I'll hand in the names,' he said. 'I don't know if the Major is going to like a troop sergeant going first.'

'You'll let me know if he doesn't, won't you, sir?'

'That's all, Sergeant.'

Brook saluted, with unnecessary smartness. He hoped that when they got back to their proper role of a battle of movement, the tension between him and the troop officer would disappear. It would be very unpleasant for everyone if it didn't.

The next morning their own fifteen-hundredweight truck took the fifteen men of A Squadron back to brigade H.Q., where they changed into a brand new three-ton lorry. It was widely believed that all new vehicles went to division or brigade first, and Smudger, who had also drawn a pass, let anyone who was listening know what he thought about it.

A very smart sergeant-major from brigade H.Q. was in charge of their party, but apparently didn't hear Smudger's insulting comments. He rode in front with the driver. In an hour or so they were in Antwerp, and he called them all to attention.

'Report here to go back at ten o'clock tomorrow morning,' he said. He looked very smart in a new uniform. 'I warn you – I won't wait five minutes for anybody.'

'We'll be there, Sarnt-Major,' said Smudger. 'And take care of yourself. Don't get in the way of one of these Flying Bombs – we wouldn't want nothing to happen to you.'

There were a few indiscreet titters, and the sergeant-major glowered.

'What's your name, Sergeant?' he snapped.

'Ben,' Smudger replied innocently.

'Ben what?'

'Ben down and I'll wallop you,' Smudger said. This time there was a roar of laughter.

The sergeant-major went purple and looked around for support, but the lorry-load of men had mysteriously melted away. Brook stood next to Smudger but carefully looked the other way.

'You'll be on a charge, Sergeant, as soon as we get back.' He turned and strode away.

Brook took Smudger's arm.

'What did you want to do that for, Smudge?'

'I dunno. The sod looks too fat and shiny.'

Ben Lyon, who was one of the old desert rats, had taken hold of Wilcox and marched him round the corner so that they couldn't be called as witnesses or ordered to act as escorts to Smudger. 'You're a barbary sod, Smudge,' he said admiringly.

'Well, what now?' said Smudger. 'We got twenty-four hours – we don't want to waste any.'

'Let's go to the Piccadilly Bar,' said Wilcox eagerly. 'Maybe they've got some ham and eggs or something.'

'It's not ham and eggs you're after, you old ram,' said Smudger. 'What do you want to do, Ben?'

'Steak, egg and chips,' Ben Lyon suggested. 'I was three weeks here waiting for reinforcements and I've got me feet under the table in a caff down by the docks.'

The café was small and unprepossessing, but at the sight of Ben, the proprietor – an enormous ex-wrestler – beamed all over, hurried out and cleared a special table for him, greeting him as the son of the house. Ben took it all pleasantly but regally, as though it was no more than his due.

'How's Ma?' he asked.

'She's fine – but she don't like these bombs the boches keep sending over but she come down right away when I tell her Ben is here.' Ben looked modest and the others were suitably impressed.

A few minutes later a woman in her fifties, almost as big as the ex-wrestler, came in like an elephant under full sail and hugged Ben violently. He extricated himself without a trace of embarrassment, and gave her a squeeze, or at least as much of her as his arm would get round.

'Hell, Ma, how's tricks?'

'Ja, Ben, ja – steak'n cheeps, I know, steak'n cheeps.' She nodded vigorously and joined in their laughter. When the ex-wrestler came back with the knives and forks, he brought also a bottle of brandy and some glasses. Stiff drinks were poured out all round.

When they left an hour later they were full of food and brandy, and feeling relaxed for the first time in many weeks.

'Now can we go to the Piccadilly Bar?' Wilcox asked.

'All right, all right,' Smudger consented, 'we'll get lined up for later anyway.'

The Piccadilly Bar had evidently prospered, for there was a piano player and a fiddler even at that time of day, and half a dozen soldiers drinking at various tables. There were about six girls, none of them Greta or Yvonne; but the proprietor remembered the first night, and said that the two girls came on the night shift that started at six-thirty.

'But they are very busy,' he warned them. 'If you want one you must say now.'

'I'll chance me arm when the time comes,' said Smudger. 'What about the rest of you?'

'I think I'll book Yvonne,' Wilcox said, blushing like a girl. 'I wouldn't want her to be busy all night.'

Although they had had a tumbler full of raw brandy at Ben Lyon's café they ordered another one. Brook began to feel drunk and decided to stop drinking, as he didn't want to pass out and lose half of his leave. Smudger and Ben Lyon kept drinking it down and shovelling in food at the same time, but Wilcox also had stopped.

'You know what I'd like to do?' Wilcox said after the food. 'I'd like to go to the pictures.'

'Not a bad idea,' said Smudger. 'If we carry on like this we won't be no good for nothing tonight. I could do with a nice picture myself.'

They walked back to the centre of the town, where the huge modern cinema was showing films in English. Brook was not too enthusiastic about the idea, but thought if the film was one he wanted to see he would go. It was Errol Flynn in *Robin Hood*.

'Looks pretty good,' said Wilcox, looking at the stills outside.

'I always like Errol Flynn,' said Smudger. 'He's a man, he is. His pictures are always good. Bags of action.'

'Not for me,' said Brook.

'Nor me,' said Ben Lyon. Smudger and Wilcox tried to persuade them, but with no success.

'What are you going to do, Brookie?' said Wilcox.

'I don't know. Walk about. Buy some postcards and send them off to everyone I should have written to. I'll meet you here at six-thirty.'

'All right. I haven't written home in a long while. Get me a couple of postcards, will you? I'll write them in the café.'

'Right, See you later.'

Smudger and Wilcox hurried inside so as to miss none of the excitement of Errol Flynn fearlessly leading his merry men against the Sheriff of Nottingham.

Brook and Ben wandered through the centre of town, window-shopping. In a small shop Brook found a Scotch hand-woven jersey of a quality not seen in England since the war began. The shopkeeper had had a delivery from Scotland in 1940 and had put them away all during the occupation.

'I wanted to make sure they didn't keep a German warm,' he said, with an intensity that carried conviction.

Brook bought the jersey and put it on under his battledress blouse. Its fine quality felt good after the roughness of army uniform. While they were in the shop there was a louder, more violent, explosion than the flying bombs they had got used to.

'A V2,' the shopkeeper told them. 'A rocket.'

'They've been having them in London,' Ben said. 'My sister wrote and told me. Sounds like a gasometer going off. There was a terrible one near where I live in Camberwell. The only good thing about them is that when you hear it you're all right because they travel quicker than sound so you don't hear the one that gets you.'

As they walked up the street they heard a siren, and a minute later two ambulances flashed past.

'Looks like it might be nearby,' said Ben. 'Let's go and have a shufti.'

It took them ten minutes or so to find where the crowds were collecting. The civil and military police were already controlling them. They went up to an M.P.

'Where was it, Corporal?' asked Brook.

'The cinema. A direct hit. God knows how many of our blokes are inside.'

It was not until nine o'clock that night, after many rebuffs and much waiting about at the hospital, that they finally had it confirmed. There were over four hundred casualties, including many British soldiers. Smudger and Wilcox were both among the dead.

As they walked back along the badly lit road from the hospital Ben said, 'I don't know about you, Brookie, but I'm going to get drunk and then find myself a girl.'

A couple of hours later they were sitting at a table with two nondescript girls neither of whom spoke a word of English. Brook felt a little sick and very drunk. Ben filled the glasses.

'This is the last one for me and then I'm going upstairs.'

Another V2 somewhere woke Brook up just before dawn. He turned on the light and looked at the girl sleeping beside him. In repose, the hard lines of her face had disappeared, leaving her looking young, exhausted and unwashed. He left the money on the table next to the bed, dressed, and crept out. He didn't know which room Ben was in, but he knew he'd meet him at the lorry.

By the time he had walked back to the centre of the town the sun had risen. He walked past the cinema, and was surprised to see that the damage did not seem so bad. But when he got up to it he saw that the V2 must have landed in the centre of the roof and completely devastated the inside leaving the outside walls as a shell.

One café was just opening, and he sat at an outside table and ordered a *café au lait*, roll and butter. He asked if there were any postcards, and the waiter brought him three with the coffee. They were all photographs of the café. He addressed one carefully to his mother and father.

'*Just in Antwerp on a short leave. Am sitting at this café watching the world go by.*'

There were in fact one or two people now in the street. For censorship reasons, even if he had wanted to, he could not mention the bombing of the cinema.

'*Food very good here. Antwerp is a beautiful city.*'

He looked at the card. It wasn't enough.

'Bought wonderful all-wool Scotch jersey yesterday. All my love, MIKE.'

He got to the leave lorry at five to ten. The brigade sergeant-major was already there, but Ben Lyon wasn't. Brook walked up to the sergeant-major.

'Sergeant Smith and Trooper Wilcox were killed in the cinema yesterday, sir.'

'Yes, I know – I have the list of casualties. I'm sorry.'

He didn't sound such a bad bloke after all, Brook thought.

The others came in in twos and threes. Some of them had heard about the two blokes from A Squadron who'd got it in the cinema, and told those who hadn't. Death was commonplace, of course, but happening on a twenty-four-hours leave made it more of a topic of conversation than usual. At ten past ten the sergeant-major called the roll. Only Ben was missing. The sergeant-major said nothing, but went round to the front of the lorry. For a moment Brook thought they were going without Ben, but the lorry didn't move. Ten minutes later a taxi hurried up and Ben jumped out.

'I overslept, Sergeant-Major,' he said.

'Get in the back,' the sergeant-major said wearily. 'All right, driver, let's go.'

On the way back they decided that Ben should apply for Wilcox's job as Brook's operator. Sandy and Ben had not been getting on very well and Sandy would probably be glad to get a new wireless operator. Ben Lyon felt he would be safer in Brook's tank.

Lieutenant Kenton didn't oppose it, and the change was made smoothly.

Three days later Taffy and Bentley, who had been to Antwerp for their day's leave, came back with the latest rumour.

'We're being pulled out for refitting – right out. Right back into Belgium somewhere near Ypres,' said Taffy. 'Everyone at Brigade knows about it.'

'And we're getting a smashing new tank, as good as a Tiger,

mounting an 88 and with armour-plating the Jerries can't touch,' Bentley added excitedly.

'I remember the first time we were going to get a tank as good as Jerry's,' said Ben Lyon disgustedly. 'And you know what it was? A Honey with a pop-gun. Then we had Crusaders. They were supposed to be as good as Panthers, but he could still knock us out before we could get near enough to have a go, so they took away the Crusaders and gave us these bloody Shermans – Tommy Cookers – Ronsons – "always light first time". Don't talk to me about smashing new tanks.'

'Perhaps this time will be different,' said Bentley hopefully.

'Well, they're bound to be better than Shermans, and that's something,' said Taffy.

For once a rumour was right, and a few days later they handed over the farm to another armoured regiment and drove the tanks all the way back to Brussels.

They described the process of getting rid of their tanks as 'driving them on to the dust heap', but in fact the tanks had to be thoroughly cleaned and serviced first, and long complicated forms had to be filled in, before they finally stepped out of the little worlds they had lived in for months, and watched them driven away.

'That's the last time we'll ever see her,' Taffy said. 'I suppose I'm glad, in a way – she was just about worn out; but you know, I had a feeling she was a lucky one.'

'Give me a bigger gun and thicker armour and you can have the luck,' said Brook.

The transition from the tenseness of the constant shelling and sniping, at the farm, to the pleasant Belgian market town where they were all put in civilian billets, was quite remarkable. Brook, and many of the others who had been more or less constantly shot at for five months, realised just how tightly wrought-up they had been.

For the first few days of sleeping in a bed in a small room he was restless, waking many times in the night in a sweat, tense and listening until he realised where he was. The people he was billeted with were a woman of about sixty and her two daughters in their thirties. There had not been a man in the house since the father had died some fifteen years before, and after the first couple of days, when they treated Brook as though he might explode, their shyness wore off and they began to fuss over him like three mother hens with one cockerel chick. Brook scrounged bully beef, tea, sugar and coffee from the sergeants' mess, and these little luxuries made a great difference in the house. There was a good deal of drink in the sergeants' mess, and sometimes an evening would finish up in a general good-humoured roughhouse, rather like the rags at school, only a good deal more violent. Brook tried to keep up with the drinking, but without much success, and such evenings usually ended with his being sick or being carried to bed. He woke up one morning with a bump the size of a billiard ball on his head, and Marie and Clara and their mother were all, at first, rather cool to him. It seemed that he had been carried home and dumped on the bed and then had got up and fallen downstairs, and it had taken the combined efforts of the three women to get him back into bed. But their disapproval soon gave way to sympathy, and they plied him with black coffee.

The days were spent in classes. None of the new tanks had yet arrived, but they were being told all about them by sergeant instructors who had been sent over from England – solemn men who took their jobs seriously and disapproved of horseplay. They were pained at the ribald and sarcastic remarks that greeted some of their more poetic predictions about the new tanks.

One of them, a Sergeant Jenkins, told them earnestly that he had been trying for years to get out of the training centre in England and get up to the front, but the authorities simply wouldn't let him go.

'I'm too valuable, that's the trouble,' he said mournfully. '"You're doing more to win the war here, Sergeant," the Old Man always said to me, "than if you were up at the front. We can get plenty of tank commanders, but your uncanny teaching ability is rare – rare." So I do my duty, but you lads don't know how I envy you. Oh, you don't know.'

They sympathised with Sergeant Jenkins.

'Is it true, Sarge,' Ben Lyon asked, 'that sometimes you'd be sent out testing tanks and not see a pub for days?'

'Quite true, quite true. You want to spend a couple of weeks out on the range in North Wales in the rain to find out what misery is.'

'How about the bombing when you went on leave, Sarge? Bad, was it?'

'Funny you should say that. I remember I got a forty-eight and caught the night train to Bristol. I got out the train and there was no buses running and no taxis. "The warning's gone," they told me. "All right," I said, "I'll walk." Well, I started walking...'

'SSSSSSSSSS...' Some wag at the back of the room imitated a falling bomb. '*BOOM!*' He slammed his hand down on the desk. They all laughed.

Sergeant Jenkins stopped his story and went on sternly: 'The Comet is powered by a Meteor Mark Three liquid cooled normally aspirated sixty degree V12 internal combustion engine.' He turned to the blackboard and began to draw, and they all wrote laboriously in their notebooks.

Brook tried to ignore his hangover headache and pay attention to the technical description of the new tank which was on its way to them. It seemed, everyone had to admit, every bit as good as the Panther – Germany's third best.

Sergeant Jenkins began to describe the rigorous trials the tank had been subjected to in England. It had been raced over the roughest country and dropped eight feet at thirty miles an hour, and had come through with honours.

'We have done our best,' he said earnestly. 'The rest is up to you chaps.'

The door opened and the orderly officer came in.

'Class... *CLASS 'SHUN!*' roared out Sergeant Jenkins, bringing up a salute that would have done credit to the guard at Buckingham Palace.

'That's all right,' the orderly officer said as the class shuffled to their feet, 'sit down, everybody. There's a flap on. Pack up now and get back to your billets and prepare to move off. We go back to Brussels immediately, pick up our old crocks again and get trod in to stop Jerry. Get cracking.'

'Where's the flap, sir?' several voices asked.

'The Ardennes. Von Rundstedt has hit the Yanks and driven a bloody great hole through them. He's pouring armour through the gap.'

The orderly officer was understandably flustered, for orders had come through on the telephone at four o'clock in the morning. He had grabbed a pencil and written them down: '*The Regiment will receive its tanks, ammunition, food and petrol at Brussels and proceed to battle stations with the minimum delay.*' Since then things had been hectic.

The men threw their kit into their haversacks and piled into the waiting three-ton lorries, which moved slowly out on the road to Ypres. About every mile they passed a military cemetery of the First World War bearing names that were unfamiliar to them: Batt's Corner, Limon Cross Roads. They stopped for a few minutes by a huge arch across the road. It was the Menin Gate, and young Bentley memorised the inscription: 'TO THE MEN OF THE BRITISH ARMY WHO STOOD HERE FROM 1914 TO 1918 AND TO THEIR DEAD WHO HAVE NO KNOWN GRAVE.'

When it had been decided to pull them out of action for a rest it had not been only because their tanks were worn out by the six-month advance from the beach in Normandy, but because the men were too. They were not physically exhausted – they were mostly young, healthy animals, and a couple of good nights' sleep and a hot meal or two was all that was needed to restore their physical strength – but their nerves had been stretched taut for too long without a break. For, even when they had been pulled back, it was usually no farther than their own artillery. Then, because they had stopped attacking, their own big guns had begun a heavy artillery barrage. This had been answered by the enemy's guns, and night had brought out the bombers on both sides. It hadn't necessarily meant that they were either bombed or shelled themselves, but it had given them little opportunity to relax.

Most of them were unaware that anything much was wrong with them, for they were uncomplicated men not given to introspection. They knew they were frightened, but they knew that everyone else was frightened too, and had come to realise that wars are fought by a few frightened men facing each other – the sharp end of the sword, which would be useless without the rest of the weapon and the weight and skill behind it, but which nevertheless always got blunted first. In theory they were supposed to take turns doing the actual fighting, but it didn't work out that way: for battle experience was precious, and there was never enough of it for any to be held in reserve.

They did not think of it like this themselves. They complained that you always met the same blokes up at the sharp end and that they weren't bloody supermen – but most of them were proud because they were called on time and time again. Still, the long unbroken period of daily expecting to be shot at, of daily screwing up one's determination, of daily trying to keep in a state of intelligent alertness so that when the gun fired there was no hesitation that would imperil other men's lives, had eventually made itself felt. It had affected some more than others – the older men more than the young, the imaginative more than the stolid. In some cases it was not only the cumulative effects of six months' concentrated battle, but four or five years of getting ready for, fighting, finishing – sometimes by retreat and sometimes by victory – battle after battle.

When a man could stand no more he cracked. Usually he had not realised it was going to happen. Such casualties, which were not particularly dramatic, were accepted as part of the cost of fighting, and they normally didn't affect the efficiency of the unit of which the man was a part. It was much rarer for a regiment to crack, because it was usually possible to pull them out in time.

They had been a long way from actually cracking in Holland. At worst they had been getting stale, and, as they would be wanted for the spring offensive, it was thought best to take them right out for a month or two, give them the new, best Allied tanks, and then send them, as the spearhead of the attack over the Rhine, into the heart of Germany. They had not been told all this, however, and now the emergency had made nonsense of those plans and they were being sent back into action because there was no one else immediately available.

They got to the Exposition Grounds at Brussels at daybreak, and collected a tank, petrol, oil, water, food and ammunition, as quickly as it could efficiently be done. One Troop were out on the road heading south towards Dinant within three hours. The last few miles were made difficult by American lorries full of troops driving towards them at high speed. Every now and then one of them would stop, and several voices would tell them of the thousands of Germans pouring through the gap. Finally orders came to push on as fast as possible, forcing the retreating Americans off the road if necessary. When they reached Dinant on the river Meuse there were no more retreating troops to block their way: there was nothing between them and Von Rundstedt's advancing armour, which expected to cross the Meuse and go on to Brussels, only an hour away.

'Everything depends on our holding those bridges,' Major Johnson told them. 'It's a job for a brigade, but we haven't got a brigade. There is only this regiment. Therefore each squadron has a regiment's job to do, which means that every troop will have to be responsible for a squadron defence line. At least our orders are simple. We advance over the bridge; three troops go out and cover the three main roads approaching the bridge from the enemy sector; H.Q. Troop remains on the far side around the bridge itself to protect it from any other attack, and, in the event of the enemy breaking through our forward positions, to blow the bridge. If the bridge is blown we shall *all* be on the far side, and we shall no doubt still be able to deter the enemy for a bit longer. Now I don't know, but I am pretty certain, that reinforcements are being rushed here from all over the shop, so we won't be alone long; but for today, tonight, and possibly tomorrow, there will only be us. I want the tanks so arranged that as they get knocked out they will form a road block, so choose your positions with that in mind. Once you have chosen your position, there you will stay – for there's nowhere to retreat to. Any questions?'

'What about the Yanks?'

'They were overwhelmed by a vastly superior force. The ones you saw this afternoon were rear troops with nothing but their rifles and they were not intended to stop an armoured advance – that's your job. Over to the west they are holding well. The Yankee airborne boys are completely surrounded in a little town about thirty miles ahead, but they are holding out and causing the advance to flow round them, which has mucked up Jerry's plans. If they can hold out in that place – what's the name of it, Captain MacDonald?'

'Bastogne, sir.'

'Yes, Bastogne. Well, if they can hold out there until reinforcements get through to them the Yanks will be able to drive a wedge into Von Rundstedt's army. Don't worry about the Yanks – they've been caught off balance but they'll come back fighting – they always do.'

H.Q. Troop took over the task of mining the bridge and protecting its far side. One Troop was ordered to cover one of the approaches, Two Troop another, and the others subsidiary roads from those two. Lieutenant Kenton placed Brook across the road at a cutting where sheer rock rose up at either side of him.

'You know your orders, Sergeant. You won't move from here. You'll knock out anything approaching down this road and continue to engage until you are yourself knocked out. You'll make a very satisfactory road block here. Is that clear?'

'Quite clear, sir. And where will you be?'

'When I've put Corporal Sanderstead and Corporal Cadey in positions where they can cover you I shall go back to where I can cover them.'

'Sort of last ditch defence?'

'Exactly. Keep alert. Try not to go to sleep.'

He walked back down the road, fortunately not hearing Geordie's picturesque description of him.

It was a clear, cold night, and after the first two or three hours, when the excitement had worn off and the noise of tanks moving into position had died away, it became very difficult to stay awake. Brook kept looking up the road through his binoculars, and the moonlit shadows could have been anything. It was so still and quiet that he knew that his first warning of the approaching enemy would probably be the sound of their engines and the tracks.

Just before six a.m., as he was fighting off sleep, his ear picked up the far-off sound of a tank changing gear. He jerked himself wide awake. He shook Bentley, who was dozing with his head on the gun. He spoke to Ben Lyon, who was awake.

Ben pushed his head out of the tank and listened for the sound of the engines.

'That's them all right,' he said. 'Where d'you suppose the beggars are?'

They tried to get an approximate compass bearing on the sound, but it was so faint and the country was so hilly that it seemed to be coming from a pretty wide arc. They agreed it was approximately south-west from them, and probably between two and three miles off.

Brook reported it on the air and was answered by Major Johnson.

'Roger. Have you got a good view of the approach road? Over.'

'Yes, I'm hull-down at the top of the hill and can see the road well ahead.' He felt his palms begin to sweat.

'Good. Wait until you're sure before you fire.'

The noise of the approaching armoured column had grown louder, but nothing could yet be seen, though the leading units must soon show themselves. It suddenly occurred to Brook that as the tank was not going to be moved there was really no need for Taffy and Geordie to sit in the drivers' section waiting for them to be knocked out.

'Taffy? Geordie?'

'Yes?'

'Yes?'

'Look – we're not going to move from here, so you'd better jump out and get in the ditch. You can take the Bren gun and have a go from there.'

Neither of them moved, and he heard them talking quietly to each other.

'Bentley – we've got an A.P. up the spout, haven't we?'

'Yes, Sergeant.'

'Good. The place where the road bends is about seven hundred yards. Wait until you get him full in your sights.' He noticed that neither Taffy nor Geordie had moved. 'Come on, you two, hop out and get in the ditch.'

'We're staying here,' said Taffy.

'When you bale, we'll bale,' said Geordie.

'Now listen – what's the use of getting killed for nothing? You can't do any good stuck down there. Get in the ditch, and if we get brewed up you can probably help to pull us out, or something.'

'No,' said Taffy.

'Then I'll make it a direct order. Get out of the tank. That's an order.'

'And I refuse to obey it,' said Taffy.

'And me,' said Geordie.

Brook hesitated.

'Look,' said Taffy, 'if you're a tank crew, you're a tank crew. Either we all bale out or we all stay in.'

'He's right, Brookie,' Ben Lyon said.

'All right, you silly beggars... by the noise they'll be here any minute now.'

He turned round, and could just see Sandy about fifty yards behind, well placed to cover the road block Brook's tank would make when it was knocked out. He waved, and Sandy waved vigorously back. There was no sign of Lieutenant Kenton.

He turned back to his field-glasses, gluing them on the bend in the road where the first vehicle would appear. Christ, he thought, I hope we all get out.

Round the bend came a German tank. Brook could hardly believe his eyes, for the tank was travelling with its gun down and pointing to the rear.

'Got it?' he asked Bentley. He realised he was whispering as though the enemy commander could overhear him.

'Bang on,' Bentley said. 'What's the range?'

'Less than seven hundred, but wait. Don't fire unless he stops and starts to bring his gun round – he's a sitting duck. Let's see what's next.'

Behind the German tank was a half-track with a machine gun mounted for anti-aircraft, then a large lorry, followed closely by a motor-cycle tandem, followed by a staff car. They were all moving forward briskly, apparently quite unworried about possible resistance. Brook realised he had better report.

'A column of vehicles is coming towards us – only one tank – I think it's a Mark IV – and a lot of soft-shell stuff. Over.'

'Fire, for Christ's sake! What are you waiting for?' Lieutenant Kenton's voice had an hysterical note. 'Fire! Over.'

'All right, Bentley, but make sure of him. He's about six hundred, and coming at about twenty miles an hour. Aim for the centre of the turret ring. Fire when you're ready.'

They all held their breath while Bentley carefully placed the cross-wires of his telescope and set the range. Geordie and Taffy blocked their ears.

The gun fired; the empty shell clanged on the turret floor. Ben Lyon inserted another armour-piercing shell in the breech and clanged it shut in a matter of seconds.

'Put another in the same place!' Brook ordered. It was good to see the enemy, for a change, erupting from a tank like startled ants.

The gun fired again and the German tank began to burn. The rest of the column were trying frantically to reverse on the narrow road.

'H.E. this time, Ben,' Brook ordered. 'Move right down the column, Bentley, and get that last lorry quickly.'

Bentley traversed the gun rapidly and put a high-explosive shell smack into the lorry which was the sixth vehicle in the column. It was full of petrol and went up at once, making an impassable, blazing road block.

The men in all the other vehicles were tumbling out except the half-track, which was trying to come forward past the blazing tank to bring its light machine gun to bear on them. Bentley didn't have to be told: he put the next high-explosive shell into the half-track, skewing it round and probably killing the crew.

'Advance, Taffy,' Brook ordered. Their tank moved forward so that Geordie could see the enemy. 'Get in among them, Geordie.' The hull machine gun started to fire immediately. 'Have a go at the other lorry, Bentley.'

A gun fired a few yards from him, nearly blasting him from the turret. It was Sandy, who had come up alongside. In the next minute the other lorry, the motor-cycle and the staff car were knocked out.

They stopped firing. Brook reached for the wireless, but it was in use.

'...We are engaging enemy armour – out to you...' It was Lieutenant Kenton's voice. 'Hello, One Able, Baker and Charlie –

keep firing... Advance and follow me – over.'

Brook looked behind him. He could just see the top of Corporal Cadey's tank, which had moved up to Sandy's position. There was no sign of Lieutenant Kenton.

'Hello, One Able. Baker and I have destroyed one tank – I think it's a Mark IV – two petrol lorries, a half-track, a motor-cycle and a staff car. They are burning and nothing else seems to be coming on. Over.'

The major replied before Lieutenant Kenton had a chance to broadcast. 'Jolly good show – get in a good defensive position and wait and see what they bring on. Out to you...' He went on to report the success back to R.H.Q.

The last burning lorry, which had been sixth in the column and was just at the bend of the road, suddenly toppled over, and at the same moment a gun fired at them. The next German tank had moved forward and pushed the blazing lorry out of the way with its long gun but had fired too soon and the shell struck the road twenty or thirty yards in front of them.

Both Sandy and Brook gave the order to reverse and to fire back, and both gunners missed because of the erratic movement of the tanks. A few moments later Sandy was below the brow of the road and Brook was hull-down.

'A.P... range seven hundred... steady... on... fire!'

He heard himself giving the firing order as though he were outside listening. He saw a bright glow on the hull of the German tank where the shell hit, and expected to see it burst into flames: but instead there was a flash from the gun, and their tank quivered as the shell struck them.

'Bale out!'

He left the turret like a jack-in-the-box followed by Bentley and Ben Lyon and ran back down the road. A few moments later there was a roar as the 88 put its second shot straight into the turret and the ammunition exploded.

They threw themselves into the ditch and turned round to see their tank blazing. At the same moment Sandy's tank advanced slowly to the hump of the hill and his gun fired twice quickly.

Sandy turned round and waved to Brook, holding both hands

triumphantly aloft in the thumbs-up position.

Out of the smoke two figures came running. It was Geordie and Taffy. They thumped each other on the back, on the verge of tears with the effects of the shock.

BOOK TWO
LAST LIGHT

Last Light: When it is no longer possible to distinguish black from white. The tanks then begin to withdraw.

THIRTEEN

BROOK, GEORDIE AND TAFFY sat silently in the Dover to London train watching the countryside slowly unfold like an exhibition of landscapes. They were returning from abroad for the first time; never again would those calmly beautiful fields evoke quite so poignant an emotion as this first sight of England after the ugliness of the battlefield.

They shared the compartment with five soldiers from Divisional H.Q. but that was all they shared; in the years ahead such distinctions would be forgotten, but now, coming straight from the fighting, the three of them felt as far away from these other men in khaki as from the occasional man still working in the fields.

Two days after the loss of their tank they had drawn another at reinforcements and started back. They had spent the night at Regimental H.Q. The following morning on the way to breakfast Brook had stopped to read the day's orders. His own name had sprung out at him: '*Awards and Decorations. Cpl (Acting Lance-Sergeant) Brook, M. R. awarded the Military Medal.*' There had been three more, among which was '*Tpr Evans, D. W. J.*' – and it was several seconds before it dawned on Brook that this was Taffy.

They had tried to treat it casually, but each of them had felt several sizes bigger, and it was difficult not to show it. Taffy had been promoted to lance-corporal, which was automatic following a decoration, and shortly afterwards he and Brook had been put on the first leave party – two precious weeks in England before returning to the new tanks and the invasion of Germany. At the last moment there had been an unexpected vacancy and Geordie had got leave as well.

The three of them had been talking longingly of English beer all the way from Belgium, as though it had been years rather than a few months since they had tasted it. They made straight for the bar at Waterloo station and ordered best bitter. They concealed their disappointment and had another – it tasted as watered-down as the first.

'Drink up,' said Geordie. 'My round.'

'Not for me,' said Brook. 'It doesn't taste the same.'

'Nor me,' said Taffy. 'I'll wait till I get home – the beer's better in Wales.'

'It's better in Newcastle too,' said Geordie. 'Not like this muck.'

He picked up his pack bulging with mysterious objects.

'I'll see you in two weeks if I can still walk – my tart don't know what's coming to her.'

He adjusted his beret to a jaunty, non-regulation angle and swaggered off.

'The Cock o' the North,' said Taffy.

'One of the best,' said Brook.

They finished their beers and went on to whisky. Brook's train ran every twenty minutes from Waterloo, and he wanted to get home; but he felt instinctively that Taffy hoped he would wait with him until nearer the time of the train to Wales from Paddington.

'Let's get out of here, Taff,' he said. 'I'll show you a bit of London.'

They walked over Waterloo Bridge, then along the Strand to Trafalgar Square and up the Mall to Buckingham Palace.

'It's beautiful, Brookie,' said Taffy. 'I suppose you'll work here after it's all over. You don't know how lucky you are. There's nothing like this where I live. Just the pit and the slag-heaps, and the stone cottages with slate roofs, and the cobblestoned roads. It doesn't look so bad in the spring and summer, but it's pretty bloody awful in the winter. It's dark then when you go down in the cage and it's dark when you come up again. You count yourself lucky when you see a bit of grey sky on a Saturday afternoon.'

'London can be pretty grim in the winter, too, Taff. Fog and rain day after day – it's not always like today. Still, you could try it if you wanted to, couldn't you?'

'I don't think Mary – that's my girl – would want to come to London. I could get a job driving a bus or a lorry, all right, I should think, but it wouldn't be any life for her away from her people. I'll talk to her this leave and see what she thinks about it.'

'You could always stay with me,' Brook said. 'You know – until you get fixed up.'

'Thanks, Brookie.' Neither of them thought it at all likely. 'Well, I'll see you either on the boat or back with the mob.'

When Taffy had gone, Brook took the next suburban train. It was a slow one, stopping every few minutes at seemingly identical stations. It was only ten days since the Ardennes, and he could hardly realise that he would soon be home. He had wired from the leave camp, so his mother would be expecting him; otherwise he would have been tempted to spend the night in London.

Instead of taking a bus from the station as he had always done, he took a taxi. It was only six shillings, and he had more money in his pocket than he had ever had before. The taxi driver was an elderly man who took in approvingly his stripes and his M.M.

'On leave from France?'

'Belgium.'

'Ah – I was in Belgium in the last war...' He reminisced all the way to Brook's house.

The door was opened by his father, with his mother standing behind. Brook dropped his pack and was embraced.

'Your father stayed home from the office,' said his mother. 'Oh, you're so thin! Oh John, doesn't he look thin?'

'Nonsense – he's just lost some of his puppy fat, that's all. Come in, come in, Michael.' He took Brook's pack and put it on the sideboard. 'You're looking well, very well indeed. Do you feel fit?'

'You're taller,' his mother said, before he had a chance to reply. 'And you look years older. To think it's only been seven months! How white your stripes are – and that awful medal...'

'Don't be silly, Molly,' his father said sharply. 'Congratulations, Michael – we're very proud of you.'

'Thanks, Dad. It's good to be home. Nothing here has changed a bit.'

He let his mother lead him as though he was an invalid into the drawing-room.

'Would you like a cup of tea?' she said.

'Or a whisky and soda?' his father added. His mother looked a little startled.

'It's a bit early for that, thanks. I'd like a cup of tea, though.'

Later, when the excitement of his arrival had died down, he asked about Jennie.

'She's at school, of course,' his mother said. 'But she always comes to see us when she's home. She's very fond of you, Mike.'

'I'm fond of her. I want to see her. Don't they get an afternoon off once a week?'

'They wouldn't allow it, Mike,' his mother said reproachfully. 'She's only a schoolgirl, after all...'

'She's seventeen.'

'Seventeen! Why, that's only a baby. I remember the day she was born – it was the day Lindbergh landed in Paris. Do you remember, John?'

'Yes, I do, but seventeen isn't a child, Molly. Is there some... er... understanding between you, Michael?'

'No, of course not! Ye Gods! Just because I want to see her doesn't mean that we're going to get married.' He got up impatiently. 'I think I'll go up and have a look at my room.' As he went up the stairs he could hear his father's voice raised and his mother's soothing tones.

The room had been left just as it was when he went off to report to his training regiment in 1943. He looked at the hodge-podge of books, and smiled at some of the titles he had had since he was a small boy: *The House at Pooh Corner*, *With Lawrence in Arabia*, and half a dozen Arthur Ransomes.

The room seemed smaller than he had remembered it. He opened the cupboard. All his civilian clothes were hanging just as he had left them, but there was a strong smell of mothballs. He took out his school blazer and tried it on – the sleeves were too short and it was tight across the shoulders. He hung it up carefully again and put on his dressing-gown.

On the wall opposite the bed was 'The Boyhood of Raleigh' – given to him by an uncle, and, he now saw, not a very good reproduction; a chart of enemy aircraft silhouettes – more familiar to him now; a map of Europe cut from a newspaper in 1940 when the British Army had first arrived in France in force. It was intended for recording the quick defeat of the enemy, but instead it bore the red crayon arrows where he had tried to follow the smashing advance of the Germans that summer of the blitzkrieg.

He remembered clearly coming out of a cinema and seeing a newspaper seller's board: 'THE GERMANS CLAIM AMIENS ABBEVILLE AND ARRAS.' He had made a note of the names in order to find them on his map. When he saw what a great gash across France it made he had thought he must have been mistaken, but that night his father confirmed it and said that things were grave, very grave. He had wondered about those unfamiliar names. And now what had been lines and printed words on a map had come alive for him. . . AMIENs – the Maquis walking steadily ahead of the tanks as they rumbled into the sleeping town; the surprised Germans being cut down by the Bren guns. CAEN...

The door opened quietly and his mother came in.

'Are you all right, dear?'

'Yes, of course I'm all right.'

'Why don't you have a rest before tea?'

'I don't want a rest – I'm perfectly all right, Mother.'

'You're terribly tense, Mike. Don't you think if you saw someone in England and told him that you'd like to teach or something that they might find something for you here?'

'Oh God, Mother...'

He began to protest, to say that he wanted to go back; but he knew she had seen through him already and could tell that he was afraid.

'I think I'll put away some of these things,' he said. 'I'll get a box down from the loft. You know – the kids' books, and some of this stuff that's been lying around for years. You'd better give away my clothes too – they'll be too small for me when this is all over.'

She looked at him with a mixture of worry and fear on her face. 'All right, Mike. Tea will be ready soon – I've made some lemon curd tarts.'

He dragged a wooden box down from the loft and packed it with the boys' books, the collection of cigarette cards, the model plane that had taken so long to construct, a photograph album and a box of penknives, magnifying mirrors, a horseshoe magnet and a half-made crystal set. He added three scarred cricket balls, his cricket bat and pads, and, at the last minute, his stamp collection.

On his next leave, he decided, he would bring home a Nazi dagger or other souvenir to hang on the wall where 'The Boyhood of Raleigh' had been.

After supper he walked over to see Jennie's parents. They greeted him almost as effusively as his own had done.

'She's fine,' Mrs Winterton said. 'And she's coming home this weekend – I told her headmistress that her uncle was only here for a few days. It was a lie, of course, but Jennie begged me.'

'That's marvellous. I'll ask Dad to lend me the car and we'll go to London to the theatre.'

'Well – all right, but you mustn't be too late. She's only a child, you know, Mike – she's two years younger than you.'

'Mike will take care of her,' Jennie's father said. 'And tell your dad I can let him have a coupon for two gallons of petrol.'

He met her at the station on Saturday morning. Jennie too had changed in seven months, and her school uniform looked incongruous – as though she was an actress dressed for the part. She surprised him by kissing him on the platform.

'I didn't want you to come and meet me. I didn't want you to see me in this awful uniform.' She slipped her arm in his.

'Why not? I've seen it enough times before.'

'That's just why – you're not the only one who's been growing up, you know. I've had experiences, too.'

'What kind of experiences?'

'Never mind – only don't treat me as though I'm a child, like you did on your last leave, that's all.'

'All right, I'll treat you as a woman of the world – but don't say you didn't ask for it.'

'I can take care of myself,' she said airily. 'What are we going to see?'

'I've got tickets for *The Dancing Years*.'

'Marvellous. The girls'll die when I tell them. Oh, that reminds me – I told them that you were a captain, and that you'd just won the M.M.; and Agatha Holroyd, whose father's a major, said that for an officer it was the M.C. Is that right?'

'I'm afraid so. Why did you say I was an officer – I'm very proud of being a troop sergeant.'

'I don't know – it just came out. I shall think of something to put a spoke in her wheel, though, don't worry.'

When he called for her late that afternoon she was completely transformed. She had put up her shining black hair and had made up her face with surprising skill, using a dark red lipstick and rather too much eye shadow. Her eyes, so dark they were almost black, were her best feature and she was evidently determined that they should be noticed. She wore a low-cut, white dress which showed off her dark skin. She was not much more than five feet in height, but already her body was mature, with small but firm breasts. She had quite lost her puppy fat.

'Well?' she asked, with a trace of anxiety.

'You're lovely, Jennie – where did you get that dress?'

'Never mind where I got it – you like it, don't you?'

'Of course I do, but isn't it a bit old for you?'

'Oh, Mike, you are an idiot – anyone would think you were about forty. Of course it's not too old. Come on, the theatres start so damned early these days.' She had never in her life been to a theatre in London at night.

The evening was completely successful. They were both in the mood for a musical comedy and enjoyed it uncritically. After a meal at a Soho restaurant Brook drove back. The blackout and the screened headlights meant they had to drive very slowly, but he didn't mind, for the sensation of having her sitting next to him in the dark was exciting.

They sang the choruses from the show. Brook put his arm round her shoulders and she moved in close to him. They drove in silence for a bit.

About two miles from where they lived, he swung the car off the main road and turned off the engine.

'Not here, Mike,' she said quietly.

'Why not?'

'Oh, Mike – Lovers' Lane? It's so sordid.'

He started up and drove off without replying. She had made him feel ashamed with a few words.

'Let's go up on the common,' she suggested, 'and get out of the car and walk.'

'It's damned cold,' he protested, 'and those shoes are hardly made for tramping about the common in January, you know.'

But she insisted. Ten minutes later they had parked the car and were walking hand in hand along the sandy path.

'What were you going to do back there?' she asked.

'Kiss you.'

'Is that all?'

'I don't know – I didn't get beyond that.'

He stopped, and so did she, turning to look up at him. They kissed chastely, but almost at once he felt an ember inside him begin to glow as though she were blowing on it gently.

He gripped her more tightly and kissed her again, fiercely, with his eyes shut. She reached up to him with her arms behind his neck, pulling down hard. The kiss seemed to last for minutes, before they had to break apart to breathe. She pressed her cheek against his tunic.

'Oh Mike...' she sighed. 'Oh God! Mike...'

'Jennie,' he said, kissing her hair, 'Jennie, Jennie, Jennie.'

He slipped his hands under her coat and felt her knobbly spine and her warm body through the thin dress, pressing the muscles of his thumbs against her breasts. They kissed again.

'You're cold,' he said thickly. 'Let's go back to the car.'

They stumbled back along the path, clinging to each other, and got into the back of the car without another word.

Only once did she try to stop him, but by then he was ablaze and wrenched his wrists free from her hands and kissed her again and again. She pulled her mouth free from his and pressed their cheeks together.

'Don't hurt me, Mike,' she whispered. 'Don't hurt me.'

Geordie was the only fighting man among the eight passengers in the Newcastle train, though there were three other soldiers also going on leave. But two were Ordnance and the third was an elderly Pioneer, so Geordie had no competition. There had been one or two half-hearted attempts to get a bomb story in, but Geordie had squashed them, considering it his duty to enlighten people about the horrors of tank warfare. He had told the story of the Normandy village four times in the three days of travelling from Belgium. The newspaper cutting was beginning to fall apart, but it never failed to deal with anyone who might have doubted his stories.

He took back the cutting from the plump girl travelling with her mother. At first she had been quite chummy with one of the Ordnance blokes, until Geordie had turned the conversation away from Vera Lynn into more important channels. The Ordnance bloke had taken to reading a book rather pointedly, but Geordie didn't mind.

'There's some talk about the French giving me a medal or something – you know, what they call the Legion Donner!'

'The what?' asked the plump girl.

'The Legion d'Honneur,' said the elderly Pioneer. 'A great honour, sir.' He smiled at Geordie.

Geordie felt that perhaps he was being laughed at. 'Have you got one or something?' he asked.

'No, alas,' said the elderly Pioneer as he got his kit-bag down from the rack. 'Only the Iron Cross – second class. Good day.' He stepped out into the corridor.

'Whatever that may be,' said Geordie.

The train was slowing down as it approached Newcastle in the blackout, and the soldiers all helped each other to load on the various packs and webbing equipment and adjust their bulky gas masks. Geordie's large pack was hoisted on to his shoulders by one of the others.

'What you got in there, mate – gold bars?'

'Loot,' said Geordie with a grin. 'Lots of lovely loot.' He gave the plump girl a buccaneer's wink, and struggled out into the corridor like an overloaded camel.

On the platform the porters ignored him, looking for better prospects; but Geordie, with over fifteen pounds in his pocket and conscious of being a returning hero, grabbed one of them and unloaded all his equipment.

'A taxi,' he said in his lordliest manner.

'Right you are, Sarnt-Major,' said the porter, who was no fool and thus got half a crown instead of a shilling.

Geordie gave the taxi-driver his grandmother's address. It was on the other side of the Tyne, where they didn't see many taxis. The fare was four shillings, but Geordie gave him three half-crowns and waved away the change. The taxi driver normally didn't take a tip at all from soldiers, but he was a perceptive man and saw that it was important to Geordie. Even he didn't guess, though, that it was the first taxi Geordie had ever taken.

Between twenty and thirty people lived in the house. Geordie had known many of them all his life, but he saw no one as he climbed the stone stairs to the two small rooms at the top that had been home to him. The stink of the communal water-closet filled the air as always, but it didn't offend Geordie. It reminded him of the countless freezing mornings he had been sent down to the ground floor to the only tap, to fill the bucket which would serve his grandmother for all her wants until he came home at night.

Sweating, he put down the heavy packs on the floor at the top of the stairs. He opened his grandmother's door.

'You there, Gran?' he shouted. 'It's me – George.'

Old Mrs Brunch had been listening to 'ITMA' on the one valve radio given to her when she left service. When she heard Geordie she took off the earphones and waddled over to him, throwing her arms about him happily.

'I knew you was coming, I knew you was – I told your mum only last week, I said "Mark my words they'll give him leave one o' these days and he'll just walk in." God strike me blind if I didn't say it. But you could of written, you could of – you write very nice now. Why didn't you write and I would of made a black pudding for you?'

'It all happened so quick, Gran – one day I was spud bashing and the next I was on me way. It wouldn't of done no good to write because I would of got here before the letter, see?'

He extricated himself, dragged his packs inside the room, and kicked the door shut.

The big double bed that she had hung on to even though she

had had to sell everything else in the years following her husband's death, took up nearly half the room, leaving barely enough space for her chair, the table they ate at, and a small table for her greatest possession – the one-valve wireless set.

Geordie had slept in that bed with her until he was twelve years old, and then she had got him a mattress which he rolled out on the kitchen floor every night and poked under her bed during the day. The kitchen, he suddenly realised, was really a large cupboard with the doors removed. She saw him looking around.

'Good to be home, ain't it Georgie?'

'Yes, Gran,' he said quickly. 'I see you still got the old wireless, then?'

'Of course I have, I wouldn't never sell that. I was just listening to such a lovely programme – would you like to hear it?'

'Yes, but what about this?' He opened his large pack and struggled for a minute, finally pulling out a blanket-wrapped bundle which he put on the bed. He untied the blanket and revealed it. It was a black and gleaming silver Telefunken radio that looked like the instrument panel of an aeroplane. She gasped. 'Oh, George, where did you get it? You didn't knock it off, did you?'

'O' course I didn't,' he replied testily. 'I liberated it. It's for you.'

'It's lovely, Georgie, but I'd be afraid to touch it.' She stroked it gently. 'I never seen one so beautiful – it's too good for me.'

'Oh no it ain't,' said Geordie. 'It works lovely – you can get any station in the world on it almost – America, Australia, Paris... anything what you want to listen to. Here, let me show you.'

He unwound the aerial, which he had carefully preserved, and got out the electric lead; but the only source of electricity in the room was the bulb which hung from the roof, so he promised to get it going for her the next day. He was going to wrap it up again in the blanket, but she stopped him.

'It's a lovely blanket,' she said, 'and you'll need it tonight.'

She got him a piece of old sheet instead.

'You must be hungry,' she said, 'and I've got nothing at all except a bit of potato and cabbage from me supper.'

'That's all right, Gran, I'll get some fish and chips for tonight.' He put his hand in his pocket and peeled off one of the notes in it. There was no use her getting the idea that he had a lot of money. 'Here you are – to get grub with, tomorrow; and when that's all gone, I'll give you some more.'

She took the note and stared at him. 'Why, you're a man now, George,' she said. 'You was just a snot-nosed little boy when you went away and now you're a man. Look – see what I've got on the wall here?' She pointed to the wall above the head of the bed.

She had glued on to a piece of cardboard the write-up in the paper, and a photograph he had had taken of himself after they had removed his bump, and the cardboard occupied the place where formerly her wedding picture had hung.

'Here,' said Geordie, pulling out his wallet. 'Here's another one of me and the rest of me crew what we had taken in Antwerp – that's in Belgium. There you are: the best tank crew in the army!'

It was the five of them standing rather stiffly in front of a street which had been renamed in honour of their colonel.

'That's Brookie there in the middle; he's the tank commander and he don't give a damn for nobody. And that's Taffy – the driver, and me mate – well they're all me mates. And that's Sandy – he really *likes* fighting – and that's old Wilcox – he's dead. 'Ere – you 'ave it.'

After the picture had been stuck on the wall next to the others, she made him a cup of tea, and he took her bucket of slops down and the water bucket and brought her fresh water. He had a wash, and changed from his army boots and gaiters into brown civilian shoes he had bought in Brussels. It was then about half past eight.

'Where's Mum, do you know?'

'In the pub, I expect. That's where she is most nights. In the one opposite the fish and chips or the other one. Anyone'll tell you – they all know her. She calls herself Sandra now – Katie wasn't good enough for her.'

He put his mother's present in the inside pocket of his battledress blouse, and felt the roll of pound notes in his pocket. 'All right, Gran, I'll just go and have a drink or two with her and some fish and chips. Don't wait up for me.'

There was a queue outside the fish and chip shop, so Geordie pushed into the pub opposite.

The publican recognised him immediately. 'Hello George,' he hailed him heartily. The rest of the public bar looked round, and those who knew him greeted him.

Geordie moved to the bar and ordered a pint. In the past he had scarcely been noticed, and this new treatment was balm to him. He asked about his mother.

'She goes up the road to the Crown with her new bloke,' said the landlord's wife. 'We're a bit too rough for her down 'ere. You'll find her in the Private.'

The Crown was a large pub on the edge of where the district started to get respectable. Geordie remembered it as not doing much business, but in these boom times it was evidently flourishing. When he had got past the blackout curtain he found himself in a blaze of light, in a room packed with people and filled with tobacco smoke.

Almost immediately he heard his mother's scream-like laugh. She was one of a party of four, sitting at a table in the corner. She was dressed in a shiny, bright-green dress so tight that it showed every fold of her body. Her hair was blonder than he had remembered it, and piled in curls all over her head; her lipstick was a bright red, and she had long eyelashes. She wore silk stockings, and several men were looking slyly at her legs. She was very beautiful, thought Geordie, and he was filled with pride.

When he was a few feet from the table, she saw him.

'Georgie-boy, Georgie!' she shrieked with pleasure.

'Hello, Mum.'

He stood awkwardly in front of them. The bloke on her right was obviously the new one. He was much smaller than they usually were, and older, too – he must be about forty, thought Geordie. The man was looking at him sourly.

'This is Mr Butt, George. Johnny, this is my boy, Georgie.'

'Your mistake,' said Mr Butt, and laughed. 'The time you slipped.'

'Oh come on, Johnny, don't be nasty. George, this is Veronica, and this is Mr Goldman. Buy him a drink, somebody.'

'No,' said Geordie. 'Let me get this round. What you drinking?'

'He's a big boy now, Mum,' said Mr Butt. 'And he's in the chips

– is that right?'

'I asked you to have a drink,' said Geordie. This one didn't look as tough as most of his mother's blokes. He saw his mother put her hand on Mr Butt's arm.

'I'll have a gin and lime, love,' she said quickly. 'What about you, Veronica?'

'I'll have a gin and lime too.'

"I'll have a whisky,' said Mr Goldman. 'You want another pint, Johnny?'

'You're bloody well right I want another pint, *and* I'll have a rum to go with it.'

Geordie got the drinks, including a pint for himself, and was surprised to see how little change there was out of a pound. His money wouldn't be too much for fourteen days' leave at this rate.

When Geordie finally got back to their table Mr Butt seemed to be in a better mood. He even moved round so that Geordie could get in on the other side of his mother, between her and Veronica.

'Haven't they taught you to drink dog's nose in the army yet?' he asked. 'Here – have some rum in your beer: it'll put lead in your pencil. You look as though you need it.'

'I do all right,' said Geordie.

'That's right – you stick up for yourself,' his mother approved. 'He's not a kid any more, you know, he's a man now.'

'What – that?' said Mr Butt.

'Well, he's doing a man's job, anyway,' his mother said.

'What are those French girls like?' asked Mr Goldman hurriedly. 'Are they as hot as everyone says?'

'You bet they are,' Geordie boasted.

Both the women shrieked. Veronica slapped Geordie's thigh playfully. 'You're going to have to watch him, Sandra,' she said. 'The women won't be safe around here.'

Mr Butt said, 'He wouldn't know what to do if a real woman – like his mother – got hold of him.'

Geordie realised there was going to be trouble between him and Mr Butt unless he left. He was half inclined to get up and go, but just then Mr Goldman got a round of drinks, including a rum for

Geordie's beer, and Geordie began to feel there was no reason to go. He didn't want to fight his mother's bloke, but if he had to he would. He wasn't a snot-nosed kid any more, and Mr Butt wasn't so big.

Someone was asking him to tell the story about the village, and he told it again, ignoring the interruptions of Mr Butt. His mother and Veronica were a good audience, and gasped in all the right places. He went on to tell of other battles, and paid for another round of drinks, and someone kept pouring rum into his beer, and suddenly he felt sick.

He found his way to the lavatory and was able to vomit, after which he felt a bit better. He splashed some water in his face and dried it off with his handkerchief. He realised that he had had nothing to eat since sandwiches on the train, and that it was probably too late to get anything now.

When he got back inside the pub he could hear the row going on and he knew that his mother was in it. She and Mr Butt were standing up and screaming at each other, and the landlord was trying to quieten them down. Just as Geordie came up his mother slapped Mr Butt's face hard, and he knocked her sprawling with a swinging backhander.

Geordie took careful aim and hit Mr Butt as hard as he could on the jaw. Mr Butt didn't go down, but instead flung himself at Geordie. The burly landlord stepped between them.

'Not in here you don't; not in my pub. Get outside if you want that lark. Come on now – OUT!'

Geordie found himself bundled outside into the street, and then pushed into the centre of a ring of people. The only light came from the open door of the pub, and Geordie with his fists clenched and held in front of him looked towards it. Mr Butt came at him like a wild man. Geordie felt a blow on his mouth and tasted blood, then one in the pit of his stomach that made him want to die. He swung wildly, hitting something, but with no effect, and another blow on his ear deafened him. He slumped to the street and felt Mr Butt's boot thud into his side. He covered up his face with his hands, knowing that that was where the boot would come next.

But his mother threw herself, biting and scratching, on to Mr

Butt, and Geordie was able to get to his feet. Mr Butt was trying to hit his mother, who was clinging to him, Geordie leapt at him and got his hands round his throat, and the three of them fell to the ground. Geordie squeezed as hard as he could, ignoring the kicks he was getting, until his hands were torn away and he found himself held by a policeman. Another policeman was holding Mr Butt, and still another his mother.

Everyone started explaining at once, and in the end they were taken to the police station. Geordie was laid out on a table like a corpse, until they were able to stop his nose bleeding. Mr Butt, promising loudly to kill the little bastard, was taken away and locked up. Geordie's mother explained that her son had come home on leave from the army in Belgium and they were having a quiet drink when Mr Butt whom she knew slightly began abusing her and her son George had naturally come to her rescue. The police sergeant looked cynical at all this, but decided to let them go. A taxi was called and Geordie helped into it, holding a bloody handkerchief to his nose.

One of the policemen patted him on the back and said, 'You want to take some boxing lessons, my lad.'

Sandra lived in one room, but she had a sink and a gas ring, and there was a water-closet on every floor. Geordie lay on the bed with his eyes closed while she got him something to eat. It was only tea, bread and butter, and the kipper she was going to have had for her breakfast, but he felt much better after it.

Sandra was beginning to show the effects of the night's battle and looked quite ill.

'I've got a drop of gin put away, love,' she said, getting it from under some clothes in a drawer. 'That's what we both need.'

The bottle was nearly half full and she poured a couple of large ones into two tumblers, adding about half as much water from the tap. She drained hers in two swallows, and immediately the colour came back into her face. Geordie sipped his. At first his stomach threatened to reject it, but then he felt better.

He remembered the present he had brought her, and fished it out of his inside pocket.

''Ere you are, Mum, it's for you. It's worth a packet.'

She opened the small parcel eagerly. It was a necklace of dark green stones set in gold. When she held it up admiringly the stones seemed to glow in the reflected light.

'Oh, Georgie love, it's lovely! Where did you get it?'

'I found it on a dead Jerry officer. It was wrapped round his middle in a bit of flannel. I should of told the other blokes but I never. I was going to flog it but I'd rather you 'ad it.'

'It's too good to wear, Georgie, somebody'd cut my throat for it if I was to wear it some of the places I go. And I don't dare leave it in here.'

'Why not? Nobody's to know you've got it,' Geordie said. 'And if you ever need the money you can always get some from the pawnshop for it.'

'All right, I will.'

She put it on her neck and looked at herself in the mirror. She held out her hand and put on a look of great hauteur.

'Now,' she said, 'I look just like a lady!'

'You *are* a lady,' said Geordie stoutly.

'Yes, I know I am – but I mean a real lady with furs and a car and things.'

'Perhaps I'll find a lot of money, when we get into Germany. A bloody great bagful hidden in a house. Then I'll come back and get a car and buy you whatever you want.'

'No you won't,' she said cheerfully. 'You'll spend it all on some girl. Never mind – your old mum'll get herself a rich man yet. Old Buttsy's knocking back over thirty quid a week now – but I don't suppose I'll see him again.'

She caught Geordie's doleful look, and crossed over to him.

'Anyway,' she said, 'it's a lovely present, and you're a good boy.'

She kissed him full on the lips.

Geordie couldn't remember when she had kissed him last. He sat on the bed tingling, and watched her move away. She filled up their glasses with gin again, adding even less water this time.

'This damn dress is killing me,' she said. 'Turn your face to the wall while I get it off. Go on – turn right away – you're getting too big to watch your mother get undressed.'

Geordie lay on the bed and faced the wall. When he shut his eyes his head spun, so he kept them open. In a few minutes she told him he could turn round.

She was dressed in a bright-red silk dressing-gown with what looked like green butterflies all over it.

'It's pretty, isn't it?' she said. 'It was brought from Hong Kong for me by a friend.' She whirled round.

'How old are you really, Mum? Jannock, I mean. I won't never tell nobody.'

'I'm thirty-five. But everybody thinks I'm thirty-two, and I'll kill you if you ever tell. I don't know why I told you. I suppose it's because I'm a little drunk and you gave me that lovely necklace.' She sat down unsteadily on the bed.

'But, Mum, I'm nearly twenty! How can you be thirty-five?'

'Well I am! – I was sixteen when you was born. Below the age of consent I was, he should of gone to jail – and he would of too if they'd found him.' She finished her drink fiercely.

'Who was he?' said Geordie.

'He was the chauffeur in the house where my mum worked.'

'What was his name?'

'George – that's why you're George.' She giggled.

'What was his other name?'

'Never mind what his other name was,' she said craftily. 'I don't want you getting yourself into no trouble.'

'Did you ever see him again?'

'No, and I don't want to. If it hadn't been for 'im everything would of been different.'

'Is that what your bloke meant when he said I was your mistake?'

'What? Oh, you don't want to listen to 'im, love, he was just jealous, that's all.'

She put her arm round him and pressed him to her.

'Sometimes when I'm drunk and feeling miserable I say things that I don't really mean, to get people to feel sorry for me and to try and make myself believe that I'm not what I am. You see I know really that if it 'adn't been 'im it would of been somebody else. I've always been bad – ever since I was eleven years old I've liked getting men worked up. I couldn't help meself – as soon as ever I saw some man – no matter who he was – getting in a state about me it seemed to bring out all the bad in me and I'd play up to 'im until he didn't know if 'e was on 'is arse or his head. You'd be surprised if I told you some of the big men it worked on.'

She poured some more gin in her glass and sipped it slowly.

She said, 'I'm just rotten, I suppose.'

'No, you're not,' said Geordie, putting his arm round her. 'You never 'ad no bloke to take care of you, that's all.'

He felt suddenly dizzy, and lay back on the bed and closed his eyes. He was conscious of her lying next to him, and turned and nuzzled her like a puppy. She pressed his face into her breasts as though he was a baby, and stroked his hair. They lay quite still for several minutes.

Suddenly she pushed him away and struggled to sit up.

''Ere, come on – we'll both go to sleep if we don't watch out. I don't know what time it is. Where are you staying – with Mum?'

Geordie sat up with difficulty. 'Yes – but I don't want to go all the way back there. Can't I stay 'ere? I'll kip down on the floor if you've got an extra couple o' blankets. I don't mind – I done it thousands o' times in the army.'

'Well, I dunno.'

She looked at him uncertainly.

'I suppose if you don't feel right, you'd better stay. There's extra blankets in the cupboard.'

Geordie made up a blanket sleeping-bag, army fashion, and took the seat cushion of her chair for a pillow. Then he took off his battledress blouse and trousers, shirt, boots, and socks, and worked himself carefully down into his cocoon.

'Good night, Mum,' he said cheerfully.

She was still sitting on the bed in her dressing-gown sipping her drink and looking at him quizzically.

'Good night, love.'

He pulled the blankets over his head and prepared to go to sleep.

She drained her drink and then put the light out and finished getting undressed, feeling under her pillow for her silk pyjamas, which had also been a present from her friend from Hong Kong. Then she pulled the blackout curtain and let the moonlight flood into the room. She lay in bed and tried to sleep.

But sleep wouldn't come to either of them. Geordie found the floor much harder than usual, and soon his hip began to ache. He turned and turned, but it seemed more and more uncomfortable.

'Mum,' he whispered hoarsely. 'You asleep?'

She didn't answer immediately, and he thought she was. Then she said wearily, 'No – why, what's the matter?'

'I dunno – this floor seems awful 'ard. I can't get comfortable.'

There was a long pause, and he thought perhaps she had gone off to sleep. Then she said:

'All right. You'd better come in 'ere with me.'

FOURTEEN

SQUADRON COMMANDERS had taken the opportunity offered by the rest and refitting in Belgium quietly to get rid of the old soldiers who they judged had had enough and the new men who had not come up to standard. Commanders were always trying to shift their worst men off on to someone else – it was a well-known game; but there was also a certain priority which was understood, and in the case of a crack tank regiment there was usually no trouble in getting anyone posted to another unit.

When Brook returned from leave many changes had already taken place, and he found himself, as troop sergeant, responsible for the welfare of eighteen men, six of whom he knew well, six more whom he knew by name and reputation, and six new faces.

They were a mixed crowd ranging in age, background and experience from youngsters like Billy Bentley, who had still been in school when the rest of them were on their invasion schemes in Aldershot, to regular soldiers like Corporal Tim Cadey, who had joined in 1935 after two years as an unemployed shipbuilder. There was Nick Ems, twenty-one, Sandy's co-driver, whose occupation was given as 'pugilist' (which the enlisting clerk had spelled for him) and who had spent three years in Borstal for shop-breaking in his native Stepney and nine months in the glasshouse at Aldershot for breaking the jaw of the corporal of the guard. Then there was Gordon Page, twenty, who had had a year at Cambridge and would still have been there if the authorities had not sent him down for spending too much time in London – he had got a small part in a West End play during term time, which he now admitted was pushing things a bit far. He was well-built and handsome, with fair, wavy hair, and maintained that he had volunteered for the tanks because he thought it would look well some day in his entry in *Who's Who in the Theatre*. He was Lieutenant Kenton's gunner, which he declared meant that he had a good chance of finishing the war not only alive but with his beauty unimpaired. They were above average intelligence, because that amount of sorting out had taken place before they reached the regiment. All in all, Brook was well pleased with the troop, deciding that it was pretty well balanced between old sweats who might be too cautious and youngsters who might be a little reckless.

In action, a new man was absorbed into the crew quickly, for he was with them twenty-four hours a day, most of which was spent in the close confines of the tank. But now they were not in action, and still had no tanks – which meant that the new men tended to keep to themselves. It was not good for troop morale, and Brook was impatient for the new tanks to arrive.

There were all the delays they had learned to expect, and a month was spent on classes, fatigues and guards before the first Comets arrived from England. The new tanks were heavier and better armoured and carried a bigger gun than the old ones. A Squadron had the first issue, so One Troop were among the earliest to be fully equipped. Almost immediately they were ordered to fire them in on a range which had been set up on the sea-shore.

The range was on a desolate bit of coast so that the shells went out to sea. One Troop drew haversack rations and used the move as a practice operation for wireless operators to sharpen up their rusty procedure and for co-drivers to get a chance to drive the new tanks.

Lieutenant Kenton, in the leading tank, seemed to be in a good mood and pleased with the wireless operators and the standard of driving. The Comet had foot-operated brakes like a car, whereas the Sherman had been braked by pulling back both sticks at once: so it took some time for drivers to learn to react instantly to the new system. However, Taffy soon mastered it, and enjoyed the feel of the powerful engine and the heavy vehicle's responsiveness to the lightest touch of the sticks.

When they got to the range another troop had not yet finished firing, so they decided to eat their lunch first, and got their primus stoves going in the lee of some sand dunes.

It was a bright, cold February day with a few wispy clouds racing out across the Channel towards England. The noise of the guns firing on the range was dulled by the sand dunes. After their lunch they lay about in their grimy tank suits, smoking, and feeling, almost for the first time, like a troop again.

The conversation turned, as it often did, to plans for after the war.

Geordie was pessimistic. 'It's all right for you blokes who know what you're going to do, but I'm blowed if I know what I'm good for.'

'You could stay in the army,' Sandy suggested.

'Yes and I could cut me throat too, but I'm not gonna. "For the duration," it says, and for the duration is what it's gonna be. The day after Jerry packs in I start for Newcastle.'

'Och, there'll be plenty of work for everybody after this lot's over,' said Sandy. 'Think of all the building there'll have to be done, for a start…'

'What do I know about building?' said Geordie. 'What do I know about any bloody thing?'

'Well, you can learn, can't you?'

'What!' said Geordie indignantly. 'At my age?'

There was a laugh at this, and somebody threw a cigarette at Geordie, who caught it expertly.

'All right, Sergeant,' said Lieutenant Kenton, getting to his feet. 'That's enough waffling. Get packed up and bring the troop over to the range.' He walked away towards the firing butts.

'You never know where you are with that sod,' Corporal Cadey said. 'One minute he's all chummy and the next he'll bite your head off.'

It took nearly two hours for all the guns to be fired in. The officer in charge of the range kept a careful score.

'Congratulations,' he said to Lieutenant Kenton. 'That's the best performance of any troop that has shot here so far. Now to finish off, the *piéce de reststance* so to speak, we have a demonstration to convince any of your chaps who may still be sceptical about the ability of this gun to knock out a Tiger. We've got a tame one over here.'

He led them to a knocked-out Tiger tank which had already been holed several times. Its 88-millimetre gun was pointing skywards, looking as long as a telephone pole. Brook felt his throat go suddenly dry and the hairs on his neck rise. It was like a cat sniffing a dog, he thought. He was not the only one who felt the aura of menace, for they had all gone quiet.

The Artillery officer pointed to the holes, which had been outlined with chalk. 'That's so you'll know that yours are new ones,' he said cheerfully.

'I say, how about a peep inside?' said Gordon Page. 'This is the first monster I've ever seen.'

They clambered up and peered inside the turret. The Tiger had burned as fiercely as any of theirs, and the insides were twisted and discoloured by the heat.

'For God's sake let's get on with the job,' Lieutenant Kenton snapped. 'We all know the damned things burn.'

One tank was to fire at it. 'You'd better do it, Brook,' Lieutenant Kenton said shortly.

'All right, sir, but wouldn't it be better if one of the new gunners had a go? Bentley has been in.'

'Right, put Martin in under Corporal Sanderstead.'

Sandy was always glad to fire at anything, and put his tank into the position indicated, about five hundred yards from the Tiger, which was then broadside on to them. Jack Martin fired an A.P. into the centre of the turret ring, and they all trooped off again to see if the shot had actually pierced it. It had.

'You've convinced me, sir,' said Sandy, 'but if I ever get that close to a Tiger I'll just put a wee match under his tail instead.'

On the way home they stopped to brew up a dixie of tea. When it was ready, Brook looked round and noticed that Lieutenant Kenton was missing. He filled a mug and walked back towards the troop officer's tank to find him. The rest of the troop were engaged in a loud argument about football, which covered the noise of his approach, and he came suddenly round the end of the troop officer's tank.

Lieutenant Kenton was standing with the nozzle of his Sten gun pressed against his left foot. There was a clip of ammunition in it.

Brook froze, but before he could say anything Lieutenant Kenton saw him. They looked at each other for a few moments, then the officer put the Sten gun down on the back of the tank carefully and took the tea.

'Thank you, Brook,' he said quietly.

Brook felt a sudden sympathy, and wished that he could say something; but of course it was impossible. He walked back thoughtfully to the others.

January and February passed quickly. They completed their training and were brought back to peak efficiency. When March came they daily expected the spring offensive to start, but nothing seemed to be happening on any of the fronts.

Early in March the entire regiment was ordered to parade at Ypres where Field-Marshal Montgomery would address them and the other two regiments in the armoured brigade.

'That's a sign things are moving,' Corporal Cadey said. 'Remember he gave us the griff just before the invasion do?'

Every man was inspected three times; by the squadron sergeant-major, the troop officer, and the squadron leader. Field-Marshal Montgomery always said he didn't want too much attention paid to spit and polish, but commanding officers knew better than to accept that, and the regiment was turned out looking as nearly as possible as they would for an important inspection in England.

They filled every seat of the ground floor and balcony of the large cinema, and fidgeted and talked for twenty minutes or so. Suddenly, and dramatically, Montgomery walked to the centre of the stage.

'*ATTEN ... SHUN!*' bellowed a regimental sergeant-major in a parade-ground voice that bounced off the farthest corners of the theatre. About two thousand men scraped noisily to their feet and tried to stand at attention between the seats.

The field-marshal gave a sign, and they were ordered to sit down again. He cleared his throat and the noise died away completely.

'You may smoke,' he said, and instantly, it seemed, the air was full of lit matches and then glowing cigarettes. He began to talk about the war, about how everything had so far gone according to plan and how it was going to continue that way, carefully and methodically until Germany was finally beaten. He punctuated his lecture with little stories, at one time suddenly imitating General Eisenhower's accent to lend point to an anecdote. He did it very well and got an explosion of pent-up laughter. Gordon Page, as a student of dramatics, gave him full marks. His voice was a little dry, perhaps even schoolmasterly, but that was soon forgotten as he talked about the part of the war they knew nothing about. He brought generals, prime ministers and kings before them, and they had a sudden inkling of the war as it would be written in the history books.

Suddenly he stopped talking.

'Stop coughing,' he said, pleasantly but firmly.

The coughing, made worse by the tobacco smoke which now filled the theatre, had sounded like the zoo at feeding time; but at Montgomery's words it stopped completely.

'There'll be an interval for coughing later,' he said firmly, and carried on.

'Very soon now – I can't tell you when, of course, but it will be very soon – we are going to cross the Rhine and take the war, for the first time, deep into Germany itself. We shan't stop this time until we reach Berlin, and we *shall* reach Berlin, for we are going to bring such a weight of armour and shells and bombs to bear on the Germans that they will not be able to withstand us. I promised you before the Invasion that when it came we should have so many more guns, more tanks, more aeroplanes, more men, that they could not possibly stop us. That is what happened, and that is what is going to happen again. We shall smash them, and we shall make certain that they will not be able to start all this again in twenty years or so.'

He paused for a cheer, which came dutifully.

'I know that you're fed up with waiting, and it won't be much longer. You're probably a bit fed up with your food too, aren't you?'

There was a roar of agreement. 'Well, you'll be going through some of the richest farming land in Europe when we get into Germany, and, as you probably know, Hitler said that whoever else starved it wouldn't be the Germans; so I expect that you'll find them well stocked with hams and sausages stored in the cellars and tender little pigs and fat chickens running about...'

He waited again for the delighted laughter to die down.

'Now remember – there is to be no looting – '

He paused until they were quiet.

'But – if one of those chickens should happen to walk into your pot, I suppose the only thing you could do would be to cook it.'

That was his curtain line, and they applauded and applauded, and some wit shouted 'Encore!'

As they marched back through Ypres, Gordon Page said admiringly, 'The man's a bloody marvel. What a loss to the profession – what timing!'

'Perhaps he'll go on the stage when this is all over and he's unemployed again,' said Sandy.

'Give a copper to an old soldier – no pension, no dole, and fought all the way from Alamein to Berlin,' Ben Lyon added in a passable imitation of Monty's voice.

'Ol' Churchill went to see the King abaht 'im the uvver day,' Jackie Martin started. ''e said – "I'm a bit worried abaht Monty, your Majesty." "Ho!" said the King. "Wot's 'e been up to nah?" "Well, to tell you the troof, Your Majesty," said Winnie, "I fink 'e's arter my job." "Thank gawd for that," said the King. "I thought the feller was arter mine."'

After a few more Monty stories, Monty no longer seemed quite so big nor they so small, and they felt better.

A few days later, when the results of all the courses were in and troop officers and troop sergeants had decided on any men they wanted to get rid of, a list of final tank crews was posted on the notice board. There were no last-minute changes in One Troop, which was a good sign.

Tanks were made ready to move off at short notice, and were fully loaded with ammunition for all their weapons, spares for the guns, the wireless set, the noisy little motor inside the tank that charged the wireless batteries, equipment for cooking, for cleaning the guns, and for many other things which ran to a four-page mimeographed list for each tank.

It seemed to Brook that every day he was required to submit a return in duplicate of something or other, including all the serial numbers.

'I won't go so far as to say I wish we were up at the sharp end,' he said, 'but in some ways life's a lot easier when we are.'

'Och, you bet it is,' said Sandy. 'All you've got to do if you're short of something is either help yourself off a knocked-out tank or report it "lost in action". Let's get stuck in – that's what I say.'

Every morning tank engines were warmed up, wireless sets netted in, guns stripped and put back together – all of which took an hour and a half. For the rest of the day those of them who weren't on fatigues kept out of the way. As it was expected that they would move the next day or so no special routine was laid on. Their only news of the war was the B.B.C., and the newspapers which came from England daily. They knew that the offensive was opened and that the Rhine had been crossed: and they guessed that as soon as bridgeheads were established they would be sent in for their attacking role: but they couldn't have any idea when that would be. The fine edge of their preparedness began to wear off.

At last, orders were posted that they were to move to another area in Belgium. However, tanks were to be fully loaded with ammunition and stores. Lieutenant Kenton sent for Brook.

'Any idea where we're going, Sergeant?'

'Over the Rhine, sir?'

'How do you know that? – it's supposed to be Top Secret.'

'It was a lucky guess.'

'Really? Obviously the Intelligence lost a good man when you joined the Tanks.'

Sarcasm, Brook remembered from his N.C.O.s' course, was one of the unforgivable sins towards one's juniors: but it was one of Lieutenant Kenton's favourite weapons. Brook ignored it, because to have done anything else would have been foolish.

'Where are we going, sir?'

'Across Belgium and part of Holland to the Wesel bridgehead, where we cross the Rhine into Germany. Then, I take it, we break out. I should think it's going to be bloody grim when we run into Jerry's armour a few miles past the bridgehead.'

He stopped, and neither of them spoke. Brook felt awkward, for they both knew that a troop officer didn't say things like that. The morale of a troop of four tanks was a delicately adjusted thing like a tuned musical instrument. It depended largely on how the crews felt about, first, their own tank commander, and, second, the troop officer. These two were the only ones who were able to make the decisions upon which the lives of all of them depended. Confidence and an attacking spirit were transmitted to all of them and made them almost forget their fears; uncertainty and a preoccupation with defence ran through the troop like a shiver, and reminded them that they were imprisoned in large, slow-moving steel boxes full of explosives and gallons of readily inflammable petrol – and when they thought about that too much they changed from a hard-hitting asset to a slow-moving liability and were in even greater danger.

'That's all, Sergeant.' Lieutenant Kenton sounded suddenly tired. 'You can tell the men – but they're not to chatter about it in their billets.'

When Brook got back to the tank he told the others.

'We're going into Germany over the Rhine at a town called Wesel, where we've been building up inside the bridgehead. When we've got everything we break out.'

'Just like that, eh?' said Ben Lyon dourly.

'Well, it won't only be our division: there's another a few miles up the Rhine on our left, and old Blood-and-Guts Patton on our right. The Air Force has been softening Jerry up for weeks, and I expect they and the artillery will lay on such a stonk before we move off he won't know what hit him.'

'He didn't know what hit him at Caen either,' said Ben lugubriously. 'And a few hours later we didn't know what hit us.'

'That's right, Brookie,' said Geordie. 'They ought to send in the infantry first to winkle out them anti-tank guns.'

'Don't be bloody daft, Geordie,' said Taffy. 'That's not footsloggers' work and you know it – it's our job. You might as well expect the Navy to sail up the Rhine and sink Germany for you.'

'I never said it wasn't our job – I just said I wished somebody would knock out a few of them 88s first, that's all,' Geordie protested. 'But I don't care, if you blokes don't – roll on death, and let's have a crack at the angels, eh Brookie?'

'Damn that,' Brook said as cheerfully as possible. 'We're not going to get clanged – we're bullet-proof and we'll all go back home and grip our kids rotten with stories of the great war. See if you can get the Forces programme, Ben, and let's have some cheerful music.'

A few minutes later they were all yowling mournfully and happily in unison with Vera Lynn.

They reached the Rhine just after dawn the next day. As they came off the bridge on the other side and on to German soil for the first time all they could see were buildings, not so much wrecked as pulverized. The bomb damage had been so devastating that when the assault troops took the town and made the bridgehead it had been necessary to bring bulldozers over to mark out new roads, for the old ones were lost beneath the rubble.

Their route was marked for them. They moved slowly through the wrecked town and continued for a few miles beyond, stopping at a cluster of small cottages, where they waited for supplies to come up to them.

Some old people were moving quietly about, avoiding coming into contact with these first enemy soldiers or even looking at them. They were the first ordinary Germans most of the troops had ever seen, and they looked surprisingly like the Dutch, the Belgians and the French.

About an hour later the order came to stay there for the night. The Germans were turned out of their houses and warned not to be seen out after dark. Some asked to be allowed to take one or two personal possessions, but this was refused and they were ordered to leave immediately. They walked back along the road in an uncertain cluster, stopping every now and then to argue among themselves, until someone fired a shot from a revolver in their general direction and they broke into a trot.

Each tank took over a cottage, and almost immediately began looting. They ripped mattresses and pillows looking for hidden money or valuables, but found nothing. It was obvious that the owners of the houses were poor.

Young Billy Bentley was the first one in an upstairs bedroom. He saw there was something hidden under the sheets on the bed. He pulled off the sheets eagerly. An old man, quite dead but with his eyes open, had been laid out in a shroud with his hands across his chest. Bentley put the sheets back quickly and fled downstairs.

'There's a dead man in bed upstairs, Sergeant,' he said, a little breathlessly.

They all went upstairs and looked at him. He looked waxen, like a tailor's dummy.

'You know,' said Ben Lyon thoughtfully, 'it would be just like them cunning swine to hide their money under him or in his mattress. Come on, Geordie – give me a hand with him.'

'That's all right, mate,' Geordie said. 'It was your idea and if there's any money there – it's all yours.'

'All right. Bentley – you take his feet and I'll take his shoulders,' said Ben. Young Bentley gulped, and then, pale-faced grasped the old man's cold feet firmly. He weighed not much more than a child, and was quite stiff, and they had no difficulty in lifting him and putting him down on the floor. They cut the mattress and searched it, but found nothing. When they left the bedroom the old man was covered with a layer of feathers. They closed the door on him.

'I bet they'll get a shock when they find him there,' Ben laughed.

Petrol and food came up about ten o'clock that night, and with them a terse order: *'Tanks will petrol-up and prepare for Battle. Tank Commanders' conference at 2300 hrs at R.H.Q.'*

FIFTEEN

REGIMENTAL H.Q., who were in a village about a mile away, sent jeeps round to the other squadrons to bring in tank commanders for the briefing. Maps had been issued, and Brook folded and fitted his into the map case and made sure he had a supply of chinagraph pencils for marking on the transparent cover. He also got out a virgin notebook he had been saving – this time he was resolved to keep up with all the changes and new information as the campaign progressed, so that he would know what it was all about. He had tried before with other campaigns, but always after the first few days it had come down to concentrating on his own job. The larger picture had always become blurred, and all he had known about was the next objective.

One Troop were almost the last to arrive, and a few minutes later there was a check to see if everyone was there. There were four troops of four tanks in each of the three fighting squadrons and four tanks in H.Q. Squadron, making fifty-two tanks in all. Of these, sixteen tanks were not intended primarily for offence – the four of R.H.Q. Squadron and the four in each squadron's headquarters troop; the remaining nine troops, of four tanks each, formed the regiment's main striking force.

Colonel Stillwater, tall, thin, wearing the M.C. and several campaign ribbons, came in. They were all called to attention by Major Arnold, the second-in-command.

'Sit down and make yourselves comfortable,' said the colonel.

He walked over to a blackboard almost covered with an elaborate map in coloured chalks, and waited until there was absolute quiet.

'Now we're here...' he began. He tapped the map with his swagger stick. 'Our other armoured division is up here on our left, and our friends the Yanks are down here. Now, at first light tomorrow we are all going to move forward and knock Jerry for six. Then we'll press on as fast as we can, ignoring anything but organised defence in depth – that is, leaving the odd S.P. or anti-tank gun or any small groups of the enemy to be taken care of by our support troops. Our role is to get *on* and *into* Germany, as far as possible and as *quickly* as possible. The other two divisions on either side of us will be doing the same thing, and a small bet has been made that we'll get farther than they will.' There was some laughter at this, but it came mostly from the officers. 'We'll keep to the roads as long as we can, and the form will be to advance with a squadron up, a troop leading, and a point tank.' He paused and a cold wind seemed to blow through the room. 'Point tank will of course be alternated. Now the order of march will be: A Squadron leading, C Squadron following, then R.H.Q., with B Squadron in reserve. Take this down, please: A Squadron will form up at the crossroads here at 0430 hours and move off at first light, C Squadron will move from their leaguer to the crossroads at 0500 hours, and then the rest of us will move off as the opportunity occurs. Any questions so far?'

'Air support, sir?' someone called out.

'Yes, we've got a squadron of Canadian rocket-firing Typhoons, if we need them, but I don't want to whistle them up unless we run into something very sticky. Make sure that you've got your coloured identification panels where they can be seen, or you'll be shot up by the Typhees yourselves.'

'How about the artillery, sir? Will they lay on a stonk before we go in?'

'No, we don't really know what's up ahead. As far as Intelligence has been able to find out, the ground immediately in front of us – for the first two or three miles anyway – is very lightly held, so bombing or shelling would be wasted. That's our job – to go and find out where Jerry wants to make his stand – we'll worry about the artillery and the bombing then.'

'How about our infantry, sir?'

'There'll be a Bren-gun platoon following up behind the leading troop, to be used only if we run into infantry or machine gun defence.'

There were no more questions, and the colonel stepped a little forward from the blackboard.

'Mr Churchill said some time ago that we had come to the end of the beginning. I think tomorrow may well mark the beginning of the end. Just how long it will take depends on many things, and in no small measure on us – on how determined we are not to let Jerry stop us. We know he's a damn good soldier, and there's no doubt that now he's defending his own country he'll fight even better; but we also know he really hasn't got a chance. He is being attacked on all sides and he is giving way. The time has come for a last, all-out push. If we make it with our maximum effort the war can be over very soon – the alternative is a long-drawn-out campaign which could be worse than a short, sharp action.'

He paused.

'That's all, except that on our record we have been given the honour of leading the British Army's attack into Germany. I know you are going to add to that record tomorrow.'

He turned abruptly away, and the crowd broke up into squadron groups.

Brook, Cadey and Sandy walked over to where Lieutenant Kenton was talking to Major Tommy Johnson.

'"Press on regardless",' said Corporal Cadey. '"Remember I'm behind you" – a bloody long way behind.'

'Today is called St Crispin's Day...' Sandy quoted with a grin.

Brook had had one thought uppermost in his mind for the last five minutes – who was going to be point tank? He knew somehow that it was to be him, and it seemed as though he was sitting and watching the film round again as Major Johnson said cheerily:

'Well, we're leading the first day, which I think is probably a bloody sight better than the second. One Troop up – at least at first.'

He looked Brook in the eyes, and smiled, and Brook knew what was coming next.

'I want you to take the lead, Sergeant...'

'Yes, sir,' Brook said automatically.

'Er... there's been an order that troop officers are not to do point tank, or Lieutenant Kenton would have done it himself, of course.'

'Yes, sir.'

'Yes – right. I shan't be telling you to push on tomorrow, Brook, because I know you will be – just as fast as you can. Keep your eyes peeled and don't take unnecessary chances: if you don't like the look of anything, put an A.P. and an H.E. or two and a few rounds of Besa into it. Your job is to make contact with the enemy – not to get yourself knocked out.'

Brook nodded, then realised that he had to say something.

'I'll do my best, sir.'

'Can I be second tank, sir?' Sandy asked.

'That's up to Mr Kenton,' the major replied. 'But don't worry, Sanderstead – you'll get your chance to lead.'

When Brook got back to the little cottage it was well past midnight, but his crew were all up and still systematically emptying drawers and cupboards looking for valuables.

'For God's sake pack that in and get some sleep,' he said irritably. 'You'll get all the bloody loot you want before we're finished.'

'But look, Brookie,' Geordie protested. 'Look what I found wrapped up in an old blanket!' He held up an ormolu and marble clock that might have been modelled on the Albert Memorial. 'I bet that's worth something!'

'Well, pack it in anyway. Here's the griff.'

He opened his map case and they gathered around.

'We move out of here and along this road at first light tomorrow. A Squadron up, One Troop leading, and us as point tank.' He hurried on, ignoring their groans. 'But the Old Man says there is very little just ahead of us and we are going to alternate as point tank, so we'll probably do it for the first hour or so and then hand over to someone else.'

'I've heard that one before,' said Ben Lyon. 'But I've never seen it happen – you do point tank until something happens – it stands to reason that everyone would tick if you just tootled along for a couple of hours without seeing anything and then somebody else took over and got clanged.'

'You're getting to be an old granny, Ben,' Taffy said with disgust. 'You'd think you'd never been up the sharp end before.'

'I've been up the sharp end more than anyone else on this tank,' Ben said angrily. 'Even if I haven't got no medals.'

'Don't worry, Ben,' said Brook. 'First opportunity for a volunteer to stick his neck out I'll give it to you.'

'Oh no you won't. Never volunteer – I learned that my first week in the army.' Ben grinned at the recollection. '"Anyone want to learn to ride?" the sergeant said. "Yus – me," I said stepping forward like the silly bastard what I am. "Well ride this," 'e said giving me a bloody great long broom.'

They swapped stories of their recruit days until after one o'clock in the morning. Finally Brook had to order them to shut up.

'We're being wakened by the guard at four o'clock,' he said. 'Now get to sleep or you'll be dozy tomorrow.'

There were a few rude remarks and noises in the dark but the talking stopped.

Brook lay awake in his blankets like most of the others. The minutes had ticked relentlessly by since the major had told him they were to lead. He knew he should try and get a couple of hours' sleep, but it was almost impossible: his mind was racing, jumping from subject to subject – imagining one minute that he was engaging a Tiger and the next back in England at school – at home – with Jennie. He wondered where Jennie was, and what she would be doing tomorrow – Good Friday, 1945. He shut his eyes.

A few minutes later he felt himself being shaken by the guard.

'Come on, Sarge, wake up, it's four o'clock.'

He struggled to wakefulness and propped his head on his hand.

'All right, thanks, I'm awake now.'

'Sure?'

'Yes. Any char about?'

'I think there's a drop left in the guard room – give me your mug.'

The guard disappeared, and Brook allowed himself the luxury of a few more minutes in his warm blankets.

When the mug of hot tea came he sat up and sipped it.

'Thanks,' he said to the guard.

'That's all right.' The guard, who was an infantry man from a brigade H.Q., didn't leave, but stood leaning on his rifle. 'Is that right, Sarge,' he said, 'that you're leading tank today?'

'Yes – at least to start off with.'

'Rather you than me. I wouldn't get in one of them things for a thousand pound.'

'Every man to his job.'

'I suppose so – well, good luck, eh?'

'Thanks.' Brook was not sorry to see him leave. He finished his tea and rolled out of his blankets, pulling his trousers on over his long underwear, which he slept in.

'Wakey! Wakey!' he shouted. 'Roll out, roll out, out of your sacks and on to your feet. Come on, my merry men.'

'Nark it!'

That was Geordie. Brook crossed over to him and pulled up the end of his blanket bag, dropping him out on the floor. Geordie tried to crawl back in, like a rabbit going underground.

They struggled out of their blankets and within a few minutes they were dressed and had their bedding rolled up in their ground-sheets and tied. They had fifteen minutes to get in position at the crossroads a hundred yards or so away and in that time they cooked and ate their breakfast, stowed away their cooking and eating things and their bed-rolls, netted in the wireless, and warmed up the tank engine. At four twenty-five they were in position, waiting for the order to move off.

It was a cold morning, and not yet light, but the inside of the tank soon warmed up and they began to shed some of the scarves and Balaclava helmets they had put on. The wireless was crackling with last-minute messages from R.H.Q. to squadrons and from the squadron leader to troops.

'What's our call sign, Ben?'

'George Howe, and it's wireless silence when we move off.'

'Right – we netted in O.K.?'

'Bang on.'

'Hello – all stations George Howe.' It was Major Johnson. He sounded worried, as he always did at the business of getting the squadron rolling. 'Move off now – move off now. Over.'

The air now belonged to One Troop. 'Hello, George Howe One Able – Advance – Over.'

'George Howe One Able Wilco Out,' Brook replied, and then switched to the tank's internal telephone system. 'Righto, Taff, straight up the road – how far can you see?'

'It's not too bad – I can see about fifty yards.'

The tank moved along the road. When it had gone about thirty yards Sandy's tank began to follow, then Corporal Cadey's, then Lieutenant Kenton's, and so on until all the tanks were moving forward in a snakelike line.

As it got lighter Brook could see that the country was flat and uninteresting, mainly fields with an occasional house or two. They passed through the forward infantry positions half a mile or so ahead of their start line, and waved at the antitank gun crews who had pulled off the road. Brook stopped at the last one and took off his headset.

'Seen any Jerries?' he shouted over the roar of the engine.

'Not a sausage,' a big sergeant replied. 'We heard tank engines most of the night, but they were obviously pulling back.'

'Thanks.'

'Good luck.'

Brook waved an acknowledgment, and the advance continued. Brook went on at a steady clip, but stopped before any ridge or other natural anti-tank position and had a good look before he went on. He always reported what he was doing, and Major Johnson always replied with a short acknowledgment, keeping his promise not to push. But about ten o'clock, when they had advanced several miles and there was still no sign of the enemy, the colonel began to get impatient.

'Hello, George Howe. We've got to get on quicker than this. Our tail is still coiled up behind. Tell your leading boy to push on. Over.'

'Hello, George Howe, Wilco – out to you. Hello, George Howe One Able – can you get on a bit quicker? Over.'

'Hello, George Howe,' Brook replied, 'we'll try – out.'

He looked at the country ahead. It climbed gradually to a high ridge, and he would know in the next few minutes whether or not there were tanks or anti-tank guns hull-down behind it.

'You heard that, Taffy,' he said, 'we might as well get up to that ridge smartly, because if he's there we can't avoid it now anyway.'

'O.K., Brookie.' Taffy put his foot down and the tank speeded up from the five or six miles an hour they had been doing to about twenty. The ground between them and the ridge closed rapidly. Brook kept sweeping the top of the ridge with his binoculars but could see nothing at all.

'Aircraft!' Ben Lyon shouted, pointing up.

Three planes were coming in low and fast, from behind them and to their right. Before they could do anything the planes had shot past, only a hundred feet over their heads. Brook could see clearly the Allied markings and the rockets underneath. The tanks' bright pink plastic identification panels had ensured that they weren't chosen as targets. The Typhoons flew on and over the ridge, just clearing it, and then began to climb steeply in formation.

'Obviously there's nothing over the ridge or they would have had a go at it,' said Brook. 'O.K., Taff, get up on top of it as fast as you like.'

As they moved quickly along the road Brook glanced back. Sandy, who was no more than twenty yards behind, waved gaily at him. Corporal Cadey was the agreed fifty or so yards behind Sandy. Lieutenant Kenton was a long way back.

'Here come the Brylcreem boys back,' shouted Geordie pointing ahead. The three Typhoons had climbed to a couple of thousand feet, but were now coming down in screaming dives straight towards them. Brook glanced back to make sure that their identification panel was still there. Sandy had caught up with him just as they reached the top of the ridge and was pointing to the diving Typhoons. Brook made a 'don't know' gesture with his hands and at that moment the leading Typhoon fired his rockets. They could see them leap forward from the plane leaving puffs of smoke and streak down at something on the other side of the ridge. As they got to the top they saw what it was.

Three Tiger tanks had been waiting for them not a thousand yards down the other side of the hill. They had come out of a small clump of trees after the Typhoons had passed the first time but they had been too eager and had been spotted. One was already burning fiercely, and from the other two the men were erupting like angry ants and running for the cover of the trees.

Both Geordie and Ben Turner, Sandy's co-driver, opened up with their hull machine guns without being told. Brook and Sandy got their tanks rolling down the hill and their turret gunners firing at the fleeing enemy tank crews too. In the same minute or so the other Typhoons fired their rockets and both scored direct hits: so within a few minutes of the tanks breasting the hill there were three Tigers blazing and a number of dead and wounded crew. Having done their job the Typhoons streaked for home.

Brook had been too busy to report on the air. Now he heard Lieutenant Kenton's voice.

'Hello, George Howe – we have engaged three Tigers and they have all been brewed up. We are now mopping up the crews. George Howe One. Over.'

Brook looked round and saw Lieutenant Kenton's tank just coming over the top of the ridge. He caught the eye of Corporal Cadey, who had come up to him, and grinned.

Cadey shouted: 'I bet that sounded good back at Brigade H.Q.'

The message had been passed back and congratulations were being exchanged. They passed the burning German tanks, and Brook saw that some of the crews were still alive but wounded. One had had most of his clothes burned off and was crawling blindly forward.

'Hello, George Howe – there are a number of badly wounded Jerries here,' he reported. 'Can you send the blood wagon up?'

'Hello, George Howe One Able O.K. Out to you. Hello, George Sugar – did you hear that? Over.'

'Hello, George Sugar, yes we're coming now. Out.' The medical officer had a reputation for travelling up as near the leading units as possible, and many times during an action they had been surprised to see his jeep darting among burned-out tanks while shells were still dropping.

'Hello, George Howe.' It was the colonel's voice. 'There's a routine laid on for casualties, as you well know. Now we can't stop here all day – push on. Out.'

Brook confidently waited for a new tank to be ordered to take over the lead. It was now about twelve o'clock, and they had been leading since half past four.

'Hello, George Howe One.' The major couldn't keep a trace of annoyance out of his voice. 'Push on. Push on.'

'Hello, George Howe, Wilco. Out to you. Hello, George Howe One Able – get moving forward again – same order as before. Over.'

'Hello, George Howe One advancing now. Out,' Brook said grimly. 'All right, lads, it looks as though we're still leading. Let's hope the Typhees have put the wind up any more of them there may be about. Advance, Taff.'

As they moved off he saw that Sandy was driving level with him. He appreciated the gesture, but it was foolish, of course, to present two targets to the enemy, and he waved him back. Corporal Cadey was about fifty yards behind and to the left, where he should be, and Lieutenant Kenton was still behind the burning German tanks. As they moved off again they saw the ambulance coming, and Brook pointed it out to one of the German soldiers who was asking for water.

They ran into no more resistance during the next hour and they were ordered to stop while certain changes and adjustments were made to the tail of the armoured column. Brook stopped in a hull-down position from which he could see a small town about a mile ahead. He spent most of the waiting time examining it in his binoculars, but saw absolutely no sign of life at all. This was bad, for if it was not held there would almost certainly be someone about – some foolhardy civilians trying to save their treasures or even to spy in an amateurish way.

After about an hour, during which they had something to eat, the column was ready to move again.

'It can't be us any more,' said Geordie. 'We've had a go, now let some other bloke take over.'

'I should think they will,' said Brook.

The wireless began to crackle again as move orders came up. They listened anxiously for the words that would give them a respite, but as division spoke to brigade and brigade to regiment, the colonel to their squadron and the major to Lieutenant Kenton, it seemed as though there was no more chance of avoiding it than of stepping out of the way of a bullet.

'Hello, George Howe One Able.' There was a noticeable quaver in Lieutenant Kenton's voice. 'Advance now. Advance.'

'Hello, George Howe One.' It was Sandy's voice. 'Can I take over the lead? George Howe One Charlie. Over.'

Sandy should not, of course, have volunteered, and his crew would not thank him for it. Anyway, it was obviously not possible to allow that sort of thing, and Brook quickly seized the air before Lieutenant Kenton could reply.

'We are moving towards the bridge now,' he reported unnecessarily. 'Shall I stop for the sappers to examine it or cross it anyway?'

'No. We can't stop for that,' the major answered. 'Push on and we'll see if it's mined.'

'Hello, all stations George Howe.' The colonel sounded annoyed. 'For God's sake get on and stop this damned waffling. Get on! Out.'

The bridge had not been mined – or at least it did not blow up as they crossed it. Brook stopped on the other side and tried to detect any sign of a defensive position, but there was nothing except a stillness that was unnatural. The road sloped gently up from the little river to the centre of the town, turning sharply to the right about three hundred yards from them. Brook could see that there were two crossroads between him and where the main road turned. The houses were admirable cover for snipers or machine guns, while an anti-tank gun could be to right or left at any crossroads. It was not really very sensible to send in a tank alone among buildings, but there was no evidence to justify his calling on the infantry except his own feeling that there was someone there. He continued to look through his binoculars as though they could see through the bricks.

'Hello, George Howe One Able – have you spotted anything?' It was the major.

Brook wished he could see something – anything – to delay matters, but the town was as dead as a plaster model.

'No,' he replied, 'but I'm just having a good shufti before I move in among the buildings.'

'All right. If you don't see anything, move up the street – we're all covering you.'

Brook licked his lips. No one in the tank spoke; everyone was straining to see through his own particular peep-hole. Geordie and Taffy had their hatches shut and were looking through their periscopes. Geordie held his finger on the firing button of the machine gun; Taffy kept the engine running a little faster than usual with the clutch disengaged ready to move at a split-second's notice. Brook knew he could wait no longer.

'All right, lads, I'm afraid this is it.'

He was shocked to hear himself say the words aloud, and ashamed of the note of dejection in his voice. He cleared his throat and spoke more briskly:

'Advance up the street to the first crossroad, Taff.'

The tank was moving before he finished speaking.

They crawled between the buildings and he remembered the German soldier who had thrown the potato-masher grenade at him from the farm window. His head felt enormous, and he wanted to duck down inside the turret and shut the hatch: but it would have been madness. There was no use in looking at the houses as they passed, for obviously he would not see anyone before they fired. He slipped the Bren gun from its mounting and held it, heavy with the drum of anti-aircraft bullets, cradled in his arms. If he saw anything move he would fire, and so would Bentley and Geordie.

They reached the first crossroads, Taffy stopping the tank with the gun poked across the street. If there was an anti-tank gun sitting in the road, to either right or left, they would only see the long gun-barrel. Brook heard the noise of Sandy's tank, which had crossed the bridge and was coming up behind.

'Traverse left, Billy.' His voice was croaking again and he cleared his throat. 'When we go forward, if you see anything to the left, fire at it. I'll be watching the right. Advance, Taffy.'

He pointed the Bren gun off to the right ready to rake anything there with fire. It wouldn't knock out an anti-tank gun, but it might well unnerve infantry for the time it would take the tank to cross the road.

They crossed in a few seconds. There was nothing to be seen

down either road.

At the next crossroads they did the same thing, and again there was no sign of any enemy or preparation for them. The streets and the houses were apparently completely empty. They reached the bend in the main road and saw that it led into the village square.

The clock on the town hall said half past three, and Brook automatically glanced at his watch to confirm that it was right. He could hear the noise of the rest of the tanks crossing the bridge.

The road entered the square at a corner, so that if he got well over on his right-hand side as he approached, the rest of the square, which he couldn't yet see, would become visible more quickly. He told Taffy, and Taffy immediately put the tank up on the pavement and scraped along the old red-brick houses as they crept forward with the gun at half-left covering the whole square as it slowly came into sight. Brook was still clutching the Bren gun, watching hidden ground become uncovered. Just before they reached the end of the road and entered the square itself – just as Brook had decided that there was no room left for an anti-tank gun – a German soldier stepped out from behind the last building on the left with a bazooka in his arms.

Brook's scream, the firing of his Bren gun without his aiming it, and the firing of the bazooka, were simultaneous. The range was not more than twelve feet, and the target must have looked as big as a house: but either because he was nervous, or because Brook's scream made him point the weapon at Brook instead of the tank, the German missed, and the bazooka went just over Brook's head, struck the house the tank was pressed against, and exploded.

Brook was swatted to the floor of the turret by the shock, and at the same moment most of the wall collapsed on top of them. As the tank backed frantically away, the rest of the house fell into the street.

In the few seconds that this took, Brook thought first that he was dead, and then immediately that he was badly wounded in the head: but even while these thoughts were in his mind he was getting to his feet and putting on his headset to direct Taffy, who was reversing blind, and might well take them, rear end first, through one of the houses opposite.

'Left stick... right stick... left stick...'

Sandy's tank roared past them at full speed and straight into the square, where it slewed round looking for trouble: but there was nothing. The extremely courageous young German had not been touched, and there was no sign of him.

'Halt, Taffy... that'll do,' said Brook. He put his hand to his head and felt a bump where a piece of brick had hit him. His ears were ringing, and his mouth and eyes were full of brick dust.

A calm voice asked, 'What are you doing?'

Brook looked down, and was amazed to see the colonel, standing up in an open jeep next to him.

'We've just been bazooka'd,' he said stupidly.

'I know that – I should think everyone in the army knows that by now – you've been broadcasting for the last five minutes.'

Brook dropped his hand microphone as though it were hot.

'Are you all all right?' asked the colonel.

Brook picked up the microphone again and asked each of them if he was hurt, and the reluctant admissions that they were not came back.

'No, sir, we're all right.'

'How about you? Is that blood on your face?'

Brook wiped his face on his sleeve. 'No, sir – only brickdust.'

'Is the tank all right?'

'How about it, Taffy?'

Taffy moved it forward and back a foot or two. 'She seems all right, Sergeant.'

'Well then, what are you waiting for?' The colonel sounded genuinely puzzled 'Push on – you can't hold up the entire British Army for a bazooka wallah, you know.'

Brook stared at him in disbelief. 'It only takes *one*, you know,' he said.

'I'm well aware of that, Brook, but don't worry – I should think you've frightened any others off with all the row you were making. Now come on – push on; we've wasted enough time here already. You go along and I'll follow right behind you to give you support.'

'Yes, sir. Advance, Taffy.'

Brook was surprised to find that the awful feeling of dread had quite left him. It was not that he was no longer afraid, but that he felt detached – as though what was happening was unreal. He passed Sandy's tank in the centre of the square and moved along the road leading out of town. At the town's edge he looked back and saw Sandy behind him, and immediately behind Sandy the colonel, sitting in his open jeep and waving some of the infantry on to flush out the buildings behind.

'Thank God the light won't last much longer,' he said to his crew. 'We've got away with it this long – maybe we'll get away with it altogether.'

'Hey, Brookie?' Geordie sounded worried, and Brook hoped he wasn't going to have trouble with him.

'What do you want, Geordie?'

'Would you look and see if my clock is all right?'

Relieved, Brook glanced back at the mound made by their bedding rolls – Geordie had wrapped his treasure lovingly in his blankets. The tarpaulin was covered with bits of brick and plaster, but otherwise seemed quite whole. He reassured Geordie.

The three tanks of One Troop arrived all together on top of a hill. Sandy got off the road and moved down the slope some fifty yards ahead, and Brook fell in behind, determined to pass him as soon as possible and tell him he must not assume the lead. Corporal Cadey, waiting for Brook to put the proper distance between them, was perched on the hill against the skyline: and it was probably for this reason that he was selected as the target.

The crew of the 88 had had plenty of time to adjust their sights, and they scored a direct hit. Both Brook and Sandy saw the gun fire.

'Traverse right... steady... on!... fifteen hundred... there! Can you see it, Bentley?'

'Got it!'

'Fire!'

The shell was an armour-piercing, which meant that it would have to score a direct hit – and it didn't.

'Up two hundred... try an H.E... fire!... another H.E... have a go with the Besa, Geordie; range seventeen hundred... fire when you're ready, Bentley...'

Fifty yards ahead of him Sandy was firing; he was dimly aware that they were being shelled again by another gun; several more A Squadron tanks had taken up positions on the ridge and were firing back; high in the sky he saw another three aeroplanes and hoped fleetingly that they were coming in with rockets; Corporal Cadey's tank was blazing and the ammunition was going off like giant fireworks. They knocked out the second 88.

Through all this, Brook had a detached feeling. He could hear his own voice as though it belonged to someone else. It sounded clear and unemotional, and the necessary orders came out as though they were on the range; but he looked closely at himself and saw that his knees were trembling and that his hands were running with sweat. There didn't seem to be any connection between him and the person in the turret giving orders and reporting 88 positions.

The short sharp action was over in ten minutes and Brook took the lead away from Sandy again to the next small village beyond the knocked-out 88s. There they were told they would stop for the night.

Brook sat in the turret stupid with fatigue while the rest of the squadron came into the village. Lieutenant Kenton called him and Sandy over to his tank.

'Right – we'll take over that big house there. If there are any Germans inside, turf them out. Tell them to get out and stay out of sight. I've got to go to a griff conference, so get me a billet.'

'Who got it in Corporal Cadey's tank, sir?' Sandy asked.

'Stone and Owen – the other three are wounded or burnt – Corporal Cadey badly.' He avoided looking at them, and swung out of the turret and walked towards the major's tank.

SIXTEEN

THE BIG HOUSE turned out to be the mayor's. They swung their tanks in across the pavement, knocking down the iron fence and making nonsense of the neat little garden, and parked them up against the side of the house.

'Come on, Sandy,' said Brook, making sure he had his revolver. They walked up to the big carved wood door and knocked loudly. It was opened almost immediately, by an elderly and sick-looking German.

'Ja?'

For a moment they stared at each other. Then Brook realised the complete impossibility of making himself understood, so he moved the old man gently to one side and went in. There was a large, dark hall with several rooms off it. Brook and Sandy went into one, obviously the family living room used only for important occasions. It too was dark, but they put on all the lights, pulled the curtains, opened the windows. There were a large old horsehair sofa and two matching chairs.

'We'll only get one room to a tank,' said Brook, 'because this town will be filled up by midnight when supplies come up. Let's find the best bedrooms and drag any spare beds or mattresses in while we've got the chance. Better get the rest of the troop in.'

Sandy went off to bring them, and Brook started upstairs. The old man had been hovering about muttering to himself, and now he put his hand on Brook's arm.

'Private house,' he said carefully in English. 'This private house – not soldiers.'

'No,' said Brook, searching for the few phrases of German he knew. 'Keine dein Haus. Not your house.'

'Keine mein Haus?' the old man said incredulously.

'Nein. Der Haus ist der alliedkomandatten Haus – alles ist.' The old man followed him upstairs. There was an equally old woman in bed in one room, with a girl of about sixteen sitting pale-faced beside her. He stood awkwardly in the doorway.

'What do you want?' the girl said in English. 'You cannot come in here – my grandmother is sick. Get out!'

'It is you who are going to get out,' Brook said angrily. 'I'll give you ten minutes to get out of the house – all of you.'

He walked out of the room and down into the hall, where the rest of them were gathered.

'All right, find yourselves somewhere to sleep. The bedrooms are upstairs, but there aren't enough beds to go round. I've bagged the one the old lady's in, so don't anyone try to get that. When you've claimed a bed, Taffy, see what there is in the kitchen, will you? Bentley, get some water hot for a brew and a wash.'

Some of them dashed upstairs and the others went into the large rooms downstairs, already looking for loot. The old man stuck close to Brook, still protesting. Brook ignored him.

'How about having a look in the cellar for some food?' Sandy suggested.

The house was a solid, stone-built, nineteenth-century one and the cellars were large and clean. The old man followed them downstairs, and when they found his small wine store he cried out as though he had been stabbed. In another part of the cellar there were several dark hams hanging from the roof, and fat sausages. Brook tucked under his arm one of the hams and a string of sausages, and told Sandy to bring the wine.

'With no permit from the commander to take the food it is forbidden,' the old man said firmly.

'Raus, Jerry,' Sandy said fiercely. 'Go on – raus!' He pushed him. 'Schnell!' he added, which was about the extent of his German.

'He's got a granddaughter who speaks English,' said Brook. 'I told her to get out with any of the rest of them in ten minutes. Come on – we'll find them and see what's happened.'

They delivered the ham, sausages and wine to Taffy in the kitchen, and the smell of cooking reminded them how hungry they were.

The girl was standing in the hall with her arm round her grandmother, who was sitting in dressing-gown and slippers. There were two more girls standing behind, obviously servants – young, plump, red-faced and red-handed. They looked frightened and were holding hands.

'Excuse me, Sergeant,' the mayor's granddaughter said, 'but my grandmother is too ill to go into the street. If you want her bed you can have it, of course, but will you please let me take her upstairs to the attic?'

'Who are these two?' Brook asked.

'They are our servants – they are not Germans but Polish girls.'

'Slave labour!' Sandy said excitedly. He stepped forward towards the two, who moved away from him. 'You're free now – free,' he said. 'The war is over for you – you can go home. Understand?' They realised instinctively that they were in no danger from Sandy, and they giggled foolishly.

'They are *not* slaves,' the mayor's granddaughter said. 'They volunteered to come and work here.'

'Well, tell them they're free anyway,' Sandy said. 'Go on – in German.'

The girl turned and said something to them, to which they replied. She turned back to Sandy triumphantly.

'They say that they want to stay here with us.'

'All right,' said Brook, 'that's enough. Take your grandmother back into her bed, and go with her – and don't show your nose out of that room again, or by God I'll put you outside and keep you out.'

'Thank you, Sergeant.' She helped her grandmother up. 'And my grandfather?'

'Take him with you and keep him in there too, for God's sake.'

'Thank you.'

All five of them went back into the room.

'Where are you going to kip?' asked Sandy.

'I'll find somewhere. Come on, let's see what Taffy's got to eat.'

The ham and sausage tasted very good, washed down with wine.

'Save some for Mr Kenton,' Brook ordered.

'Why?' someone asked. Brook ignored it.

'Where were you when Tim Cadey got it?' Sandy asked Gordon Page.

'Down below the ridge where we couldn't see a damn thing,' said

Page. 'I'm the last man in the world to stick my neck out, but I did think Kenton would move up and have a crack. We could hear yours and Brook's guns firing, but we didn't budge until Three Troop had passed us and were firing back. Then the Major came alongside and blistered him.'

'What did the Major say to him?' Brook asked.

'Asked him what the hell he was doing, and Kenton said he'd had engine trouble.'

'Had you, Sweeney?' Taffy asked the lieutenant's driver, who was an old sweat.

'Had we hell! He's so windy he's useless.'

Gordon Page said, 'Did you know that the Colonel caught us behind a house back in that town where you were bazooka'd, Brook?'

'No. What happened?'

'Well, when we heard the noise of the bazooka we thought you'd had it, and Kenton ordered Sweeney to go between two houses. There was only just enough room to get a tank in there, and of course he could see damn all. A minute later the Colonel stopped in his jeep – that took guts, didn't it – coming up like that to the sharp end in an open jeep – well, all he said was "This way, Mr Kenton" – but we got out of there quicker than we went in.'

A messenger from H.Q. put his head in the door.

'Petrol, oil, water and ammo will be up at eleven o'clock,' he said. 'Wireless net at eleven too – here's the new frequencies and call-signs. Move off fifteen minutes before first light, which is about four thirty. Rations'll be here in about half an hour. O.K.?'

Two or three voices asked, 'What's the order of march?'

'Three Troop up, Two in reserve, then H .Q. and One doing rear-guard.'

'Three bloody cheers,' said Ben Lyon fervently.

'Sergeant, the Major wants to see you and Sandy at his tank in about half an hour.'

'Right,' said Brook.

The messenger turned to go, but before he could do so the kitchen door opened again and Lieutenant Kenton came in, looking white and tired. The talking stopped dead.

'Any food left?' he said.

'Yes,' said Brook, 'there's some ham and sausage we found, and we made a bully beef stew.'

'Good show – I'm starved.' All the places at the table were taken, and he hesitated. Before Brook could tell someone to get up Taffy did so.

'Here you are – I'm finished,' he said. 'I'll just take a look at the tank.' He left the room.

Lieutenant Kenton sat down, and Brook served him. One by one the others got up and went out, until only Brook and Lieutenant Kenton were left.

The officer ate quickly, and Brook sipped his wine in his mug. He sensed that Kenton was near his breaking point.

Suddenly Kenton said, 'I've had it, Brook. It's no use pretending – I've had it, and everybody knows it.'

Brook started to protest, then stopped, because any protest would so obviously have been false.

'Why don't you see the M.O., sir?' he said.

'I have – he refuses to do anything. He says it's just nerves and that everyone's got them, and he gave me some codeine. I couldn't make him believe that I can't help myself – there's nothing I can do about it.' He stared straight ahead of him.

'Don't say that, sir, you just need a rest, that's all…'

'What – after the first day? I've just had three months' rest and it hasn't made a damn bit of difference.'

'Well, what *is* going to happen, then?'

'I don't know – I'll think of something. I shouldn't be talking to you like this, Brook, I know. Forget it, will you?'

'Of course I will,' said Brook. He saw his opportunity to get away, and added, 'The Major wants to see me and Sandy, so I'd better get along.'

He retreated from the kitchen, leaving Lieutenant Kenton still sitting at the table.

The major was dog-tired, hunched over his maps with a plate of bully beef in his lap. He squinted as they came up, and rubbed his red eyes.

'You two did bloody well today,' he said, 'and the Colonel asked me to tell you that he's pleased with you. I'm promoting you to full Corporal, Sanderstead, and you'll be taking over Tim Cadey's place as troop corporal.'

'Thank you, sir.' Sandy was exultant.

'Any news of Cadey and the others, sir?' Brook asked.

'Nothing recent – the 88 went right through the driver's compartment and into the ammo. They were all pretty badly burnt.' He changed the subject abruptly. 'I've got another tank coming up to replace Corporal Cadey's – they should be here before we move off. But there's one more thing – Lieutenant Kenton is ill and is being sent back to the M.O. for medical treatment; I think he'll be up with us again in a day or two. I don't want to lose his tank – do you think you've anyone capable of commanding it, Brook?'

'Only Taffy – Corporal Evans, sir. I should hate to lose him.'

'It'll only be for a day or two, and we're doing rear-guard tomorrow. I shouldn't think we'll be leading again for some time. Get hold of him, will you? You go, Corporal, and send him back.' Sandy saluted and doubled off.

'Good man, eh Brook?' Major Johnson said as soon as Sandy was out of earshot.

'One of the best,' said Brook warmly. 'I wish he wasn't so reckless, though – he takes unnecessary chances.'

The major looked sharply at him. 'I could do with a bit more recklessness like that.'

Taffy came up and saluted.

'I want you to take over tank commander of Lieutenant Kenton's tank, Evans. It'll only be for a few days.'

'I'd rather not, sir.'

'Why not?'

'I'm a driver, sir, not a tank commander. I know what I can do and I know what I can't do.'

'Everyone does something else before he commands, Evans. You've been promoted, and this is an opportunity to earn another promotion. If you do well it will be noticed, and you might get a shot at a troop sergeant.'

'Thank you sir, but I don't want it. I just want to carry on driving a tank – Sergeant Brook's tank if I can, and as a trooper if necessary.'

'You're as stubborn as a bloody mule,' Major Johnson exploded. 'All right, you can carry on as before.'

'Thank you, sir. Can I say something?'

'What is it?'

'I think Trooper Page could do tank commander, sir.'

'What do you think of that, Sergeant?'

'It hadn't occurred to me – what makes you think so, Taff?'

'When you've driven tanks for as many tank commanders as I have, you get so you recognise the kind of bloke – I knew you were, as soon as I saw you.'

'All right,' said the major, 'double back smartly and send Page up here.'

Gordon Page came up smiling.

'Well, Page, your tank commander is being sent back for medical attention. Do you think you could take over as tank commander – at least for a day or two?'

'I'm sure I could, sir,' Page replied promptly.

'Oh you are, are you? It looks like a pretty easy job, does it?'

'It looks like a doddle to me,' said Page cheerfully and with his charming grin.

'Well, you'll have a chance to find out tomorrow. That's all.'

Page saluted and started to leave.

'Corporal Page!' the major called, and Page whirled round, surprised.

'You'll have to have a rank, you know; if you can get hold of a tape, sew it on tonight. If you can't, chalk it on.'

'I've got one in my pocket, sir.'

Page grinned, and pulled out a single lance-corporal's stripe.

'I always carry it with me.'

He saluted again, and left.

'Maybe he will make a tank commander, at that,' said the major.

When Brook got back they were all working, taking on petrol, oil, water, food, and ammunition, and he pitched in to help his crew. Bentley handed down the twenty-four bright shell cases they had fired that day, and he passed up the loaded replacements. Taffy stood on top of the tank pouring in petrol from the four-gallon jerricans handed up to him by Geordie. Ben Lyon was drawing rations, and later he and Bentley would clean the gun.

It was after midnight before all the jobs were done. Brook walked round to take a last look at his four tanks before going to sleep. Support troops had arrived, and a guard had been mounted, so the responsibility was no longer his.

He was just going in, when a voice hailed him from a lorry. He walked over and saw that it was the quartermaster.

'Do you want a drop of rum, Brookie?'

The quartermaster reached for a bottle behind the driver, and poured a generous dollop in a mug.

Brook leaned against the high mudguard of the three-ton lorry and drank the rum slowly. He felt it all the way down, and he felt his deep fatigue too.

'I was hanging on the wireless all day,' the quartermaster said. 'We all do, back in reinforcements – it's bloody awful sometimes, too, listening to you blokes and waiting for it to happen and never knowing who's going to get it next. Some bloke you've known for years like Tim Cadey, for instance. We were in the same recruit squad nine year ago.'

He poured some more rum in his own mug.

'Or maybe somebody like you that I still think of as just another civvy in uniform. I remember when you got put on Paddy Donovan's crew – you were so pleased anybody'd have thought you'd got a medal.'

He took a long drink.

'And now you bloody well have. More rum?'

'Just a drop – this is strong stuff.'

'You bet it is – this is the real stuff, with no water in it – like you never get to taste. Here you are – it can't hurt you. Anyway, what I was going to say was that when I was hanging on to that wireless listening to you – at the end when we took on the S.P.s – I wondered how the hell you could keep your voice so calm with all that going on.'

'I don't know,' Brook said. 'My knees were knocking and my voice didn't seem to belong to me.' He finished his drink. 'I suppose that's what training comes down to in the end.'

'Yes – I suppose it does make sense after all – all them schemes. I've never been in a tank, you know, and I don't want to go in one – is that jannock about your knees wobbling?'

'They were wobbling, all right.'

'You all right now?'

'Yes – it's fine once it's all over.'

'It is at first – then it changes. Old Tim Cadey had had about enough.'

'Have you heard any news about him?'

'Yes – didn't you know? I went back to Casualty Clearing tonight – he died an hour after they brought him in.'

He poured some more rum in his mug and held the bottle out to Brook.

'No – that's enough for me. Thanks, Q. Good night.'

Brook turned and walked back to the house.

The hall was dark, and he could hear all the noises of sleeping men around him. The rooms downstairs were full, now, as the tail of their column had come in. He heard someone in the kitchen and went in. Gordon Page, Sandy and Taffy were sitting at the table.

'We've just put a brew on,' Taffy said. 'Want some wine while you're waiting?'

'No, thanks. I'll have some char, though. I've just been talking to the Q – Tim Cadey's dead.'

He told them because he had to tell them. They said the conventional things for a minute or two, and then changed the subject. It was not the time to recall the small details about Tim Cadey, or 'Tich' Wilson his driver, or Owen and his singing. It was best to try and forget them all immediately.

'Has Lieutenant Kenton gone back?' he asked.

'Yes,' said Taffy, 'the M.O. came himself and took him off in his jeep.'

'I bet we don't see him up at the sharp end again' said Sandy. 'And good riddance.'

'He'd just had enough, that's all – it could happen to anyone,' said Taffy.

'Nuts,' said Sandy cheerfully. 'If a man's a man he stays a man.'

'All right – have it your own way,' said Taffy. 'Char's up.'

Even though they were in a kitchen with a kettle and a teapot they still made tea as though they were in the tank, by boiling water in a big dixie, dropping in a handful of tea, adding tinned milk and sugar, then allowing the brew to boil for a few minutes. It was an acquired taste, Brook had decided.

By the time he had finished his tea it was ten past one. The effects of the quartermaster's rum had worn off, and fatigue crept through his body like paralysis. He dragged his feet upstairs to where he had dropped his bedding roll outside the main bedroom.

As he stooped to pick up his bedding roll he heard low voices. He opened the door.

Billy Bentley and the mayor's granddaughter were sitting in two wicker chairs by the side of the bed, talking earnestly. The old man and the old woman in a deep sleep in the bed looked like corpses. Over their heads was a large picture in bright colours of a buxom blonde mother looking down on an enormous blonde baby.

The talking stopped, and Bentley and the girl looked at him.

'You'd better get some sleep, Bentley – we move off in about three hours.'

Bentley got to his feet, embarrassed. 'All right, Sergeant,' he said.

'Well – finish your natter if you want to.' Brook closed the door on them again.

He picked up his bedding roll and looked around. There were bodies sprawled in the hall, and he knew that all the other bedrooms were full too. He hoisted the roll of blankets on his shoulder and plodded upstairs to the attic. There was a small door, which yielded to his push.

By the light that came in the tiny window under the eaves he could just make out two beds and a table. He struck a match and lit the stump of a candle on the table. In the two beds, apparently asleep, were the Polish servant girls.

There was a space under the window, and he dropped his bedding there and struggled with the knot. His body shrieked with tiredness. He suddenly stopped trying to untie the rope, and went over to one of the beds and shook the girl's shoulder.

Her eyes flew open immediately and she drew the rough sheet up to her neck. She was obviously frightened, but she didn't make a sound. He pointed to the other bed. She slipped her feet out, and in one movement leapt across and into it, putting her arms round the other girl, who snuggled up to her.

Brook pulled off his heavy tank suit and battledress, but left on his shirt, underwear and socks. He took his pistol out of its holster and put it under his pillow.

The mattress yielded to his weight and he felt a wonderful relaxation start to flow into his body. He blew out the candle and let his head fall on the pillow. The pistol felt big and hard. He took it out, and feeling under the bed for his boots, dropped it in one.

'Gute Nacht, Fräulein,' he said, more to reassure her than for anything else. She didn't answer.

SEVENTEEN

GEORDIE LOLLED BACK in the remains of the haystack. He had taken off his boots and grey woollen socks, rolled his trousers up to the knees, and washed his feet and legs; now he was letting the midday sun warm them. There was a pleasant smell of sun-warm hay, and an even pleasanter smell of fresh pork cooking.

'This is the life,' he said, and smacked his lips. 'I don't care if we never move from 'ere – sleeping in the 'ay, sunshine, and bags of scoff. What more do you want?' No one bothered to answer him, so he lay back and closed his eyes contentedly. 'Don't forget to wake me up when the pork is done,' he said.

With a German bayonet Taffy was turning over the large, crude cuts of pig in the frying-pan. Now and then he cut off a small piece and ate it, to make sure it was cooking well. Billy Bentley was concentrating on frying a huge pan of eggs in the pork fat and brewing tea for the whole troop. The rest of them had made themselves comfortable like Geordie.

The four tanks of One Troop were in a circle facing out like the points of a compass: inside the circle were two broken haystacks, most of the kit off the tanks, and a clothesline stretched from one tank to the next on which khaki shirts and woollen underwear fluttered. The only evidences of war were the smoking shell of the farmhouse and a knocked-out enemy anti-tank gun a couple of hundred yards beyond them.

The sky was a pale blue with a few small white clouds, the trees were just beginning to bud, and the whole farm looked ready to burst into spring. The pigs that had escaped being slaughtered for an unexpected meal of fresh meat were nosing hopefully around the trough where their food had always appeared in the past; some chickens scratched in the yard near the back door of the farmhouse; a black and white cow grazed contentedly, for someone in H.Q. Troop had milked her. One of the German anti-tank gun crew who was now a corpse had been lifted up and draped over the gun to keep him away from the pigs.

All their dixies had been washed in clean well-water and were lined up on the tarpaulin with each man's ration of biscuits, butter and jam and his mug. The smell of frying pork became almost unbearable, and there were one or two moans – but Taffy wasn't to be hurried.

They had been advancing steadily into Germany for the past month, never meeting any defence in depth, but fighting a few short, sharp actions, which usually followed the knocking-out of their leading tank. In one or two places they had run into tough, determined resistance, but often when they had overcome this they were able to advance again for several miles.

They had discovered that in close country an unaccompanied tank was helpless against concealed enemy infantry armed with bazookas – the weapon handled by one man and costing only a few shillings, which by the use of a hollow charge could blow a hole through the thickest armour. Now the tanks carried infantry on their backs who went in to search out the enemy lying in wait for the armour.

They had been attacked at dusk two nights before, and the infantry had disappeared into the woods in pursuit of the Germans, leaving the tanks alone in the forest. Co-drivers had been ordered out to guard against any enemy who might slip back. When the order to move had come again Nick Ems had been missing, and the rumour had gone about that he had deserted.

A jeep turned off the road and came rapidly up the farm track. Lieutenant Wilfrith Moore, their new officer, got out and came over to them.

'They've found Nick Ems,' he said. 'About fifty yards inside the woods – he'd been quietly knifed by one of their Commando types – they were probably all around us.'

No one said anything, and he went on:

'We're waiting for the boundaries of the cease-fire area up ahead to be agreed with Jerry, and then we'll move on. We'll still be carrying infantry on our backs – Shropshires...'

'The Welsh have been pulled out, then?' Brook asked.

'Yes – they had very severe casualties attacking up the slopes of

Teutoburger Wald; they lost thirty-eight killed in one day, including a major, a captain and half a dozen N.C.O.s. I believe one of their corporals has been put in for the V.C.'

'He can have it,' several of them said firmly.

'What do you make of this cease-fire proposal of Jerry's, sir?' Brook asked.

'They say they've got a large hospital area filled with infectious cases like typhus, and if there is fighting there, many of the patients will get away and we'll have an epidemic on our hands. Apparently there are sixty thousand prisoners...'

'Prisoners? I thought they were hospital patients?'

'They are, but they're prisoners too – civilian ones. Anyway, once the boundaries are agreed we fight up to them, and then have a free passage across the area, until we reach the agreed line and then fighting starts again.'

He smiled at them, suddenly looking very debonair. He was wearing one of the old-style, black tank suits, which Gordon Page maintained he must have had made for him because no army issue would have had quite such narrow hips and waist. But then Gordon Page was obviously jealous of someone who looked more like a film star in a war film than he did himself.

'What have you got cooking there?' asked the officer. 'It smells jolly good.'

'Young porker,' Brook replied. 'We've got bags of it – stay and have some with us. Is it ready yet, Taffy?'

Taffy tasted it judiciously. 'Well – all right. Come and get it.'

Half an hour later Lieutenant Moore licked his fingers clean and sighed with satisfaction. 'I'm glad I've got a troop who know how to scrounge, at any rate.' He climbed into his jeep, waved cheerfully at them, and drove off.

'If you ask me he's a bit of a bloody V.C. wallah himself,' Ben Lyon grumbled. 'I'm glad I'm not on his tank.'

'He's all right,' said Sandy. 'A change from that windy bastard Kenton, anyway.'

'Cut that out, Sandy,' Brook said wearily. 'Kenton's paying for it now.'

'I don't know why you make excuses for him.'

'I don't – I just know how he felt, that's all.'

'Well I knew how he felt too, but...'

'No, you don't, Sandy – and I hope to hell you never do,' Brook said vehemently. 'Now stop harping about Kenton – he's gone, and we've got Moore, who should be bloodthirsty enough even for you.'

'I wonder what you have to do to win a V.C. in a tank?' said Gordon Page. 'I shouldn't mind getting one. I don't think there's ever been a V.C. actor in London – not that I'd allow them to use it, of course.'

'The hell you wouldn't,' laughed Sandy. 'You'd have it embroidered on your pyjamas.'

It was C Squadron's turn to lead, and their leading troop had arrived at a point where from hull-down positions they could watch a bridge across the next river. The far side was heavily wooded, but all seemed quiet. The tanks were supposed to meet Royal Marine Commandos here and try to seize the bridge, but something had gone wrong and the Commandos were nowhere to be seen.

The troop officer examined the country ahead through his field -glasses.

'... I'll just go down and have a closer look,' he reported over the air, sounding excited at the prospect of seizing the important crossing himself.

A minute later he was dead. The enemy guns concealed on the other side had waited until they could get two tanks and had fired simultaneously: in another few seconds the bridge was blown up.

The Marine Commandos came, and, with C Squadron's tanks supporting them with shellfire, swarmed down to the river and across in their little boats. They were swept by heavy machine gun fire, but pressed home their attack and established a small bridgehead at dusk. The Marines were repeatedly attacked during the night but refused to be dislodged, and at dawn the tanks were ferried across. As soon as there were enough, they attacked and broke out of the bridgehead, and slowly the Germans fell back before the weight of tanks, infantry and shelling.

By eight o'clock in the morning Brook was moving up a road with infantry on either side of him, both his machine guns and the infantry's rifles firing almost continuously. Once again his head felt as big as a house, sticking out of the turret. Sandy was on his left and almost level with him.

Suddenly an infantryman shouted and pointed his flame thrower to one side. A young German had been lying on top of his bazooka, evidently covered with leaves or dead branches, until the tank was almost on him, and had then suddenly jumped up in a desperate attempt to knock it out. He screamed as the flame hit him, and tried to turn, but was knocked down and instantly covered with the thick burning liquid. He had dropped his bazooka, which rolled to one side looking like something contrived by an amateur inventor in his cellar workshop.

An armour-piercing 88 screamed over the top of Sandy's tank, missing by inches. Brook saw that a Tiger had come out of the woods about a thousand yards up the road and fired at them. It was facing them, and Brook knew that any second it would fire again.

'Fire, Bentley, fire!' he shouted, not bothering to give the range or direction, for it seemed to be right in front of them.

Bentley fired at the same time as the Tiger got off its second shot, which hit the front of Sandy's turret. Bentley's shot hit the Tiger but did not knock it out, for it immediately backed into the woods again.

As soon as they had reversed twenty or thirty yards Brook ordered Taffy to stop, and looked towards Sandy's tank. With tremendous relief he saw that it was not burning. Sandy suddenly got up from the ditch and spoke to someone. Then all five of the crew ran, half-crouching, back down the road.

Brook reported the Tiger's position, and the squadron leader called Lieutenant Moore.

'... Send one of your boys round through the woods to see if he can come up on the Tiger from the side while the rest of you are keeping him busy. Go forward with your other boy and try to draw his fire. Is this understood? Over.'

'... Wilco,' said Lieutenant Moore. 'The infantry support have gone to ground though – hadn't we better have some more?'

'We are sending some up to you with piats,' the major said. 'Wait for them.' Piats were the British Army version of the bazooka, but there had been little opportunity to use them, for so few enemy tanks had been seen at close quarters.

A few minutes later Brook heard the sound of a tracked vehicle approaching from behind, and then it shot past him. It was a half-track full of infantry, and it kept right on going, up to Sandy's abandoned tank. Brook yelled at the top of his voice but couldn't be heard over the sound of the engines.

Someone stood up in the half-track and began looking up the road where Brook had seen the Tiger. Brook turned to one of the infantrymen lying in the ditch.

'For God's sake run up and tell them to come back!' he said.

The infantryman got to his feet, but at that moment the Tiger's commander decided that as no better target was likely to offer he would take that one. The half-track exploded as the shell hit it, throwing men out like dolls.

'Advance, Taffy,' said Brook. 'Slowly, and keep in to the side. Have you got an armour-piercing up the spout, Ben?'

'Yes, but you're not going to show yourself to that damned Tiger, are you?' There was a note of near-panic in Ben's voice.

'We've got to, Ben. If we don't go after him he'll come looking for us.'

'Then the infantry'll get him with the piats,' Ben said urgently as Taffy got the tank moving.

'There aren't any infantry with piats – they were all in that half-track. Now shut up, Ben, and stop arguing. We know we're coming and he doesn't, so we should get our shot off first. Keep on your toes.'

As they got closer to the half-track, which had been spun round by the shell's impact, Brook saw that there were two infantrymen in it and one on the road, all evidently dead. No others were to be seen, which meant they were probably lying in the ditch. He looked back and saw that his own infantry support hadn't moved.

He stopped the tank and shouted for the infantry. One of them got up and ran to him. He was a large, red-faced corporal.

'What are you going to do, Sarge?'

'Have another go at the Jerry tank. You've got to bring your lads along – as soon as I get past the half-track any of your mob who were in it and are still alive will get a chance to get back. See?'

'Yes, that's right,' said the corporal slowly. 'Wait a minute, then.'

He ran back and got his men up on their feet, and they started to come forward again. Brook glanced down. The body of the young German who had been killed by the flame-thrower was directly beneath him. It was still burning, and Brook saw with horror that the man's hip-bone had made a shallow container in which his fat was gently bubbling. He jerked his eyes away at once, but he knew it was something he would see for the rest of his life. He heard Lieutenant Moore calling for a report and he answered automatically.

'... The Tiger has knocked out the infantry vehicle. We are going up to see if we can get a shot at it. Over.'

He suddenly realised that he wouldn't be sorry if he were told not to go. But Lieutenant Moore approved, and ordered him on briskly. Gordon Page had disappeared into the woods on the right, and now he came up on the air cheerfully.

'... We've found a sort of track and we're moving along it more or less parallel with the road. We should be getting fairly near to where the Tiger was, soon. Out.'

Then, as sometimes happened through a faulty microphone, Gordon Page continued to broadcast when he thought he was talking to his crew on the internal telephone. 'That ought to satisfy 'em. We'll just sit nice and quietly here and wait for them to catch up with us... If they think I'm going to try and creep up on a bloody great Tiger when he's not looking they've got another think to think... ooooh nooooo... not Mrs Page's little boy...'

He began to whistle 'Lili Marlene', while every other tank listened to what he would say next.

'Have you got any of that cold pork left, Greggsy? Cut me off a slice will you, and hand me that bottle of... *FIRE!* for Christ's sake *FIRE! QUICKLY YOU CLOT! RIGHT IN FRONT OF YOU!... YOU HIT HIM! AGAIN! FIRE AGAIN! REVERSE, PORTER, REVERSE FULL THROTTLE! HOLY MOTHER OF GOD HE'S*

STARTING TO BURN! WE'VE KNOCKED OUT A TIGER... WE'VE KNOCKED OUT A TIGER!...'

He stopped broadcasting, as he jogged his microphone or the short circuit cleared itself; but in a second or two he came up again, in a strong, calm voice.

'Hello, Baker Charlie One *Charlie*. We have sought out the enemy and destroyed him. The Tiger has been brewed up. It is safe for you to come forward now. Over.'

'Hello, Baker Charlie One Charlie. Good show. Push on now to the main road and re-join us.' The major was obviously pleased. 'Congratulations – have another piece of pork all round. Out to you – Hello, Baker Charlie we've knocked out the Tiger and are pushing on now. Over.'

'Hello, Baker Charlie.' It was the colonel's voice. 'Thank you – we were most interested to hear how your boys work. But do not advance yet – I am sending up some more infantry to you. Over.'

Brook had moved round the bend of the road and was now past Sandy's knocked-out tank. He could see smoke rising from the woods well to the right, and he realised that the Tiger had been withdrawing when it suddenly presented itself side on to Gordon Page's gun. There was no sign of any other defences, but the woods ran as far as he could see on either side of the road. He was glad that they were to have infantry in front of them.

The ambulance had come up and was taking care of the wounded men who had been in the half-track.

Brook jumped down and climbed up on Sandy's tank. There was a perfectly symmetrical hole through the three-inch steel shield in front of the gun. It then carried on straight through the four inches more of the turret. The shell was nestling in the remains of the wireless set. Brook lifted it out. It was still hot and of a mottled blue colour. The point of the nose had been very slightly flattened, but otherwise it looked as though it had never been fired. He carried it back and it was handed round his crew.

'So much for our 88-proof tanks,' Taffy said.

'What did you have to bring it for?' Ben complained. 'I don't want to see the damned thing.'

The Tiger was the last resistance they met before coming to the cease-fire area. B Squadron had taken over the lead, and reported that everything was quiet; the prison guards were still on duty and had offered no resistance. They pushed on past the buildings, and a few minutes later A Squadron arrived.

They moved in fits and starts, and Brook's tank came to a stop just opposite the main gate of a large enclosure. There was a sentry-box manned by a German soldier with a rifle, who stared at them curiously. A huge, fat N.C.O. came out of a small building and stood in the road not twenty feet from Brook's tank. He wore a Luger automatic and had on shiny black boots.

'He looks a cruel swine, doesn't he?' Taffy said.

'I wish I could tickle him with a burst of m.g.,' said Geordie. 'I wonder who'll get that Luger? One of the brigade H.Q., I bet.'

Brook looked up at the nearest watch-tower and saw that it too was manned by German soldiers with machine guns. It gave him a prickly feeling in his scalp to see them looking down on the tanks. A few hundred yards along was another tower also manned: between the two ran a high wall crowned with barbed wire.

'They certainly don't intend to let their prisoners escape,' said Bentley. 'What's the name of this place, Brookie?'

Brook reached for the map on top of the wireless and found their route. 'That village the Tiger was in front of was called Walle... and the town up ahead is Bergen, so this must be... Belsen. Yes, that's right, it's called Belsen.'

'Never 'eard of it,' said Geordie jokingly. 'But I wouldn't want to live 'ere.'

The column moved again. They were not sorry to get away from the grim-looking towers with machine-gunners on them. B Squadron's leading tanks passed out of the cease-fire area and within minutes were engaging the enemy again. They lost a tank, knocked out some enemy guns, and moved on. By four o'clock in the afternoon they were pinned down by well-sited tanks and guns supported by infantry. A Squadron was called up to put in an attack on the flanks, as B Squadron would try once more to get up the road.

They moved up to a small clearing, where Brook saw the colonel talking to the major and B Squadron's commander. They were poring over a large map, and after a few minutes Lieutenant Moore was called over. Brook and his crew, and Gordon Page and his crew who were just behind them, watched the informal conference, waiting to see what their role would be.

The colonel pointed off to the right and Lieutenant Moore nodded.

''Ere we go again,' said Geordie. 'Any time the war gets 'eld up, just send for us.'

'It looks as though we're not going up the road, at any rate,' said Taffy. 'And that's good, because I pity the poor beggars who do.'

EIGHTEEN

THE ROAD WAS raised above the marshy countryside, which meant that anything moving on it could be seen for miles. This was why the Germans had chosen to site their guns on it. Two B Squadron tanks were burning only a few hundred yards from where the road emerged from the cover of some woods.

'Brookie... Brookie.' Ben Lyon was tugging urgently at his trouser leg. Brook put his head down inside the turret to see what he wanted.

'I've had it, Brookie, I can't go on any more,' Ben said in a hoarse whisper. His face glistened with sweat and he looked ill.

'Are you sick?'

'I just can't go on, Brookie. I won't be no good to you like this. Let me out, will you, please?'

'I can't let you out now, Ben. Get a grip on yourself – we've only got a few hours' light left, and it's not likely we'll cop anything before then. I'll let you go sick tomorrow – I'll report you sick tonight as soon as we're pulled out. I give you my promise.'

'Look, Brookie, if I *could* go on I would, but I can't damn you!' He punched the breech of the gun with his bare fist, and then went on more calmly: 'I'm sorry, Brookie, I know it's not your fault – but you've got to let me out, you've got to.'

'Well – I'll have a word with Lieutenant Moore. Now, get a grip on yourself, Ben.'

Brook grasped him by the shoulder and felt his body trembling.

'Come on, Ben!'

Ben made a great effort, breathing in deeply. Then he picked up the spent 88 shell Brook had taken out of Sandy's turret.

'Will you get rid of this goddamned thing? I've been sitting and looking at it until it's nearly driven me off my rocker. Here.' He handed it up to Brook, who threw it into the side of the road.

Lieutenant Moore left the colonel and walked back to his tank. He turned and looked towards Brook and Gordon Page and tapped the top of his head with the flat of his hand – the signal for them to go up to him for a briefing. Brook waited for Gordon Page to reach him, and then walked with him.

'I dropped a clanger, didn't I Brook, old boy?' said Gordon ruefully.

Brook laughed. 'You would have, if you hadn't knocked out the Tiger; but you're all right now. You were lucky, though.'

'What do you suppose we're on now?'

'I don't know – put in an attack across the fields, I should think, though they look pretty marshy.'

It was a good guess.

Lieutenant Moore pointed out a narrow blue line that ran across the map between them and the enemy guns. 'This stream looks like a fairly effective tank barrier,' he said, 'but an infantry patrol has been up ahead and reports that it's pretty shallow with a sandy bottom, so we're going to try to get across in a line. Jerry won't expect an attack by tanks across there. You, Brook, will be on the extreme right, then me, and you, Corporal Page, on my left. We will advance up to the bank of the stream, which is lined with trees and ought to give us some cover. Then the infantry will cross and put in an attack to take the far woods where the Jerry guns are. At the same time as we cross the stream B Squadron will have another shot at getting up the road. Is that clear?'

He sounded calm and confident. They murmured that they understood.

'Right, that's all – get back to your tanks and we'll move off in a minute or two. Six infantrymen on the back of each tank.'

'Just one thing, sir,' Brook said.

'Yes?'

'It's my wireless operator – Lyon – he's in a pretty bad way.'

'What's the matter with him?'

'He says he can't go on, that he's had enough. He's been very shaky lately, and I don't think he's much good to us as he is.'

'Well, we can't do anything about it now. He'll have to stick out this show – there isn't anyone else, and you can't go in without a wireless operator.'

'I could use Geordie Brunch and do without a co-driver.'

'No, of course not. Brunch is not an operator, and anyway you know we can't do that sort of thing. Tell Lyon I'll get him out tomorrow but he's got to carry on for the rest of today.' He turned and climbed up on his tank.

When Brook got back to his tank he heard the sound of arguing coming from the turret. He clambered up and dropped down inside: Ben was shouting at Bentley.

'Shut up,' said Brook. 'You sound like a couple of women over the back fence...'

They both started to explain but he cut them short.

'I don't give a damn what it was about. We've got a job to do. Now both of you concentrate on yours – get some ammo out from under the floor, Ben, and fill up the bins.'

Ben got down and began traversing the turret so as to get at the store of shells. Brook pretended to concentrate on his map, though there was nothing much it could tell him that he couldn't see with his own eyes. To the right, the way he was to go, were flat fields about three feet below the level of the road they were on. The fields extended to some trees about half a mile away, which ran parallel to the road, across the country, down to the stream, and up the other side to join the main forest, which was their objective. He could even see where the main road went over the stream perhaps half a mile ahead. The stream was too narrow for a bridge, and the water had been led through concrete culverts under the road.

The order came to move into their attack positions, and they swivelled on their tracks and went off the road, dipping down at a steep angle until they reached the field.

'It's soft underneath,' Taffy warned. 'It'll be low gear all the way.'

'O.K., but keep going as fast as possible. Move along away from the road until I tell you to turn left – we're going to be the extreme right-hand tank.'

'Brookie?'

'Yes, Ben.'

'Did you ask Mr Moore about me?'

'Yes, he promised to do something about it tomorrow.'

'Tomorrow won't be any bloody good,' said Ben in a low voice.

'We're going to get clanged and I won't see tomorrow.'

'All right, that's enough of that, Ben, do you understand? Not another word...' He waited, but Ben turned to his radio set and made some adjustment.

When they had gone some two or three hundred yards Brook looked back. Lieutenant Moore was a hundred yards behind him and Gordon Page about the same distance again. Lieutenant Moore waved his arm and his tank began to turn left.

'Left stick, Taffy...' The three tanks were now advancing towards the stream line-abreast, and a few moments later reached the trees lining its banks. Taffy picked his way through them and came to the stream.

To Brook's dismay the bank was some six or seven feet above the water here, but before he could report, Lieutenant Moore came up on the air.

'Hello, One Able and One Charlie. Get the footsloggers off your backs and cross the stream *now*.'

Brook passed the message to the infantry N.C.O. and they jumped off the tank and formed up on the bank.

'You going to be able to cross here?' the N.C.O. asked doubtfully. Brook shook his head, waiting for an opportunity to use the wireless; but the major was now telling B Squadron to start moving up the road, and at the same time came the roar of Lieutenant Moore's engines as his driver put the tank down the bank and across the stream.

At last Brook got a chance to report.

'... It is impossible for me to cross here. Shall I come round to where you are? Over.'

'... Cross now! Cross now!' Lieutenant Moore shouted. 'Advance!'

'... I say again – it is impossible to cross the stream anywhere near where I am. I will come back and come down to where you crossed. Is this all right? Over.'

The sound of gunfire and shells exploding could be heard, interrupted by the ripping noise of the machine guns. Lieutenant Moore came up again.

'Hello, One Able – I don't care how high the bloody bank is.

Advance now, advance now – is this understood? Over.'

'What do you think, Taffy?' Brook asked quickly.

'It's too steep – she'll dig her nose in,' said Taffy.

'... If I advance here we shall get stuck in the stream.' Brook tried to sound calm. 'It is not possible to get across here. Over.'

'Advance!' Lieutenant Moore said angrily. 'I don't want excuses – advance in low gear full revs and keep on going. Don't come up on the air again. Advance now. *OUT* to you. Hello, One Charlie, keep on going... keep on going and make for the cover of the trees. Don't stop. Out.'

The infantry N.C.O. was still looking questioningly at Brook. The noise of the fighting grew louder. 'We ought to be getting on, Sarge,' he said.

'All right, Taffy, take her steady and give her full revs when she touches the bottom.'

The tank started forward, and the bank crumbled and let them down at a steep angle. The tracks went into the water and were followed by the nose. The stream was about three feet deep and the water swirled up and flooded over the tracks, which ground round helplessly, digging them in deeper.

'It's no good, Taff, reverse and let's see if we can get out.'

The tracks chewed up the bank until the belly of the tank was supported on the ground and it was then quite helpless. The tracks spun uselessly.

Taffy said quietly: 'That's it.'

The infantry stood on the opposite bank looking at them.

'Sorry,' said Brook, feeling foolish. 'You'll have to go on.'

They started off at a trot towards the sound of the firing.

'It's getting deeper in here – can we get out?' Taffy asked.

Brook looked down and saw that the stream was running into the tank and Taffy and Geordie were sitting waist-deep in it.

'Yes, of course. We'll all get out – we're not much use here. Bring the hull machine gun with you, Geordie. Get an extension lead on the wireless, Ben, and hang my earphones over the back.'

A few minutes later they were all out of the tank and had removed the Bren gun, the hand grenades and their revolvers. Brook tried to assess the situation. The first thing was to find out how the attack was going, for if it were successful the forward tanks would sweep on, the rear tanks would soon be up to them, and they would be pulled out of the river. He put his earphones on, standing up against the back of the tank.

'... Our Big Boy has been knocked out. I am taking over. Out.' It was Captain MacDonald's voice, and it was followed by confused reports and jamming. Major Tommy Johnson had been killed and B Squadron had lost another tank and had then plunged off the left-hand side of the road. They were now behind the embankment, where they couldn't be seen by the enemy's guns but couldn't see anything themselves either. There was nothing from Lieutenant Moore or Gordon Page, which was strange.

Brook realised he ought to report, and waited for an opportunity. When it came, he said, as briefly as possible, that he was bogged down in the river.

'Be on the alert for possible Jerry infantry attacks,' Captain MacDonald told him. 'And if you have to abandon your vehicle, brew her up first. Our own footsloggers may be coming back, so don't fire on them.'

A few moments later Gordon Page's voice cut in. 'I've taken Mr Moore's crew on board and will try and reverse out of here – give us some smoke cover.'

Captain MacDonald acknowledged the message and ordered the rest of the squadron to start shelling the woods where the anti-tank guns were concealed.

'What's happening?' Ben asked anxiously.

'They're coming back again – it didn't work. I think Moore must have copped it.'

'Oh my God!' Ben screamed like a child. 'Let's get the hell back while we can. Come on.' He started to run.

'Stop. Ben!' Brook drew his revolver. Ben kept going, half stumbling, and Brook fired a shot in the air. Ben collapsed on the ground. Brook put his revolver back in its holster and went over to him. He was sobbing like a wounded animal and took no notice of Brook's attempts to rouse him.

'Taffy! Geordie! Give me a hand.'

They picked Ben up and half-dragged him back to where they had dumped the bedding rolls, and he lay on his back with his arm across his face. Brook looked at the other three: Bentley and Geordie were pale and had obviously been shaken by Ben's breakdown; only Taffy looked back at him calmly.

To the front of them there was a sound of men running.

Brook dived for the Bren, which he had loaded and placed with its tripod to cover the other side of the stream. He saw someone coming towards them, and recognised the khaki uniform.

'It's all right,' he shouted, in case any of the others hadn't seen. 'It's our blokes.'

There were three of the six who had ridden on the back of their tank. The N.C.O. was not with them. They scrambled up the bank and stood behind the tank panting.

'What's going on?' Brook asked.

'There were more machine guns than there were of us,' one of them said. 'Snipers too – it was a sniper got your officer in the other tank and I don't know how many of our blokes.'

'Were you ordered to fall back?' Brook asked.

'Yes – the tanks have already pulled back.' He looked at the other two. 'All right – let's go.'

'Wait a minute,' Brook said. 'I've reported that we're stuck here, but if you should see any of our mob, tell them exactly where we are, will you?'

'All right – you going to stay here, then?'

'Yes – if we leave we'll have to brew up the tank, and I don't want to do that unless I have to.'

The infantryman nodded, and then spotted Ben, who was still lying motionless.

'Is he hurt?'

'No,' Brook said. 'Just resting.'

It seemed very quiet when the infantrymen had gone. The firing had largely died down and the wireless had stopped its confused spluttering.

'Brookie?'

It was Taffy.

'If we're going to stay here shouldn't we have a guard posted out front? We can't see much from here, and Jerry could be up on us before we knew it.'

'Yes, Taff, of course. We'll do an hour at a time. Come on – let's find a spot.' He stood up. 'I don't think you'd better take the Bren – what about one of the other machine guns?'

'They're not much good without a tripod or mounting,' said Taffy. 'I'll take about four grenades – one of those going off will probably make them keep their heads down long enough for me to get back.'

They moved to the bank and Taffy slid down. Just before Brook followed him he turned to look at the other three.

'Geordie – you're in command until I get back.'

Geordie straightened his shoulders.

'Right, Brookie – don't worry about us. We'll give him a burst of Bren if he comes.'

'Well, make sure you don't give me a burst when I come back...'

'You ought to have a password, then.'

Brook laughed. 'O.K., Geordie, we'll make it – "Newcastle".'

'Right,' said Geordie seriously. '"Newcastle" it is.'

When they climbed up the bank on the other side they lay flat on their stomachs for a few moments while Brook looked at the country ahead through his binoculars. The trees were not very thick and came to a stop a hundred yards or so ahead, where open ground ran for perhaps another thousand yards to the next, denser trees. Any infantry would have to come across the open ground unless they went well over to the right where the two woods joined and came back along the stream in the cover of the trees. But, Brook thought, if they did that it didn't seem likely that they would come right over to where their tank was. There would be no reason for them to do so. After he had satisfied himself that the woods immediately ahead of them were clear he started to get up.

Taffy said urgently, 'Get down, Brookie.'

Brook dropped flat, thinking Taffy had seen something.

'If there are snipers over there they'll have telescopic sights...

we'd better crawl forward, hadn't we?'

'Well, it's quite a long way, Taff...'

'You could have seen *them* in your binoculars, couldn't you?'

'Yes, I suppose you're right. Come on, then.'

After a few minutes of trying to drag himself forward in the way the infantry could, keeping flat, using his arms and toes, Brook gave up and got on all fours. They crawled to the edge of the trees and lay down behind a fallen log. Brook used his binoculars again, but could see no movement from the woods beyond.

Half-left from them, some three or four hundred yards away, was Lieutenant Moore's abandoned tank. It had been knocked out by anti-tank guns, but deserted when Lieutenant Moore dropped inside the turret with a bullet through his head. It looked strangely derelict with its gun pointing up in the air, and through the binoculars Brook could see the rolls of bedding still on the back and a large black frying-pan strapped to one. Inside the turret was a dead man in a black tank suit that looked as though it had been made for him.

'This'll do, Taffy,' he said. 'I'll leave my binoculars with you. If you see them coming, don't wait or start slinging grenades about but get back as quickly as possible to us.'

'Shouting "Newcastle" at the top of my voice.'

'Yes, that's right. Good old Geordie – I'll have him come out and relieve you in about an hour.'

When Brook got back Geordie told him that the colonel had been calling him, and he got on the air immediately. He reported that he had a man posted out ahead of him and there was no sign of any enemy near them.

'... Good show. We'll try to get a recovery vehicle up to you as soon as it's dark. You're better off where you are, because if you came out of cover you'd be fired on. You may have to stay there for the night – if you do, keep a good lookout.'

Brook acknowledged the message and turned to the others.

'They'll try and get somebody up to pull us out as soon as it's dark. Jerry doesn't know we're here, so this is the safest place to be.'

He tried to sound confident and cheerful.

'We'd better have something to eat. Get on with it, will you,

Bentley? Give him a hand, Ben.'

Ben had been sitting up quietly but not moving. Now he got to his feet and walked over to where they had put the stoves and food. He still hadn't said a word, but he was obviously better.

Brook carried the Bren gun about fifty yards away, as it occurred to him that the tank would be the first target if the Germans did send a patrol forward to find out where their line was. He set it up on a small knoll commanding a sweep of the bank opposite the tank. He got down behind the gun and made himself comfortable. It was on single shot, which meant it would fire as fast as he could pull the trigger – which was about every second.

The earphones hanging over the back of the tank were making a noise.

'See if we're being called, Bentley,' he shouted. Bentley put them to his ear.

'No – it's all R.H.Q. to Brigade.'

'Jump in the turret and shut it off, then, or we'll have no batteries left. We can come up every hour or so.'

Bentley climbed on the tank and disappeared inside.

'How's the char coming, Geordie?'

'Won't be long, Brookie. We got some bully beef and sardines too.'

'Right – you'd better have yours, because I'll be taking you up to relieve Taffy soon.'

'O.K.,' said Geordie cheerfully. 'Only no whistle this time, eh?'

A few minutes later Ben brought him over a mug of tea and an army biscuit with a slab of bully beef and two sardines on it.

'Thanks, Ben. All right now?'

'No,' said Ben. 'I've had it. We're not going to have to stop here all night, are we?'

'We might have to, Ben. It's probably the safest place. Jerry thinks we've all pulled back, and if he has a go at anyone it'll be at them.'

'To get to them he's got to go past us, hasn't he? We'll get shot in the night like bloody birds.'

'He doesn't have to come this way. He'd probably go down the road or along the line of the woods. Come on, Ben, you'll be all right

– you're an old soldier.'

'Too old – ten years I've been in the army – over five years of tank fighting – and I've walked away from a lot of them – and now I know I'm not going to walk away from this one.'

'For God's sake shut up Ben. You're enough to put the wind up anyone. We're all right, I tell you.' He watched as Ben walked morosely back and threw himself down behind the tank.

The light was going fast, and he thought it would be best to get Geordie up to Taffy before it was quite dark.

'Ready, Geordie?'

Geordie nodded but didn't speak.

'Bentley, come and take over the Bren while I'm gone,' he shouted.

Bentley showed his head out of the turret.

'Come on – that's a damn silly place to be, anyway.'

As Bentley swung his legs out they heard Taffy shout, and Brook saw him running towards them through the trees. The next instant there was the angry rip of a German machine gun, and Taffy went down. The bullets hit the leaves and branches above their heads.

Brook flicked the lever to 'Automatic' and fired the clip in an arc aimed at the far edge of the trees, knocked off the empty clip, and put a new one in.

'Come down, Brookie, *down*!' Geordie was shouting from behind the tank. 'You haven't got a chance up there.'

Another burst of the unbelievably fast German machine gun ripped through the trees, some of the bullets hitting the turret of the tank and ricocheting off with a whining noise. Bentley had dived from the top of the turret to the ground and rolled behind with Ben and Geordie. Brook realised he couldn't stay up on the knoll. He picked up the Bren and ran for the shelter of the tank. As he wasn't fired on it was probable that the Germans couldn't see them.

A few minutes later the Spandau fired again and they heard the bullets hitting the tank.

'They must be able to see just the turret,' said Brook. 'We can't sit here blind – it's just asking for it.' He saw the earphones and microphones dangling, and grabbed for them, before he remembered that Bentley had just switched the set off.

'Damn!' he said.

'Do you want it switched on again, Brookie?' Bentley asked quietly.

'No, not that badly, Billy. We'll think of something. Get your Stens and follow me.'

The machine gun fire had seemed to come from somewhere to the right, so he slid round to the left of the tank and followed it down to the water. He looked cautiously round the end of the tank, but could only see the stream stretching away.

'I'm going to try and get up the other side and see if I can spot Taffy,' he said. 'You come with me, Geordie: Ben and Billy stay here and keep your eyes open. Ready, Geordie?'

'O.K.'

Brook picked up the Bren and waded across the stream, followed by Geordie holding the little Sten gun. Slowly they pushed themselves up the other bank until they could see the trees. Instantly a long burst of machine gun fire ripped through the woods and they both ducked down.

'Do you think they saw us?' said Geordie.

'No, I don't think so – I don't think they'd have missed if they had. I wonder if Taffy's alive? I can't hear anything, and he wasn't far away when he went down. Come on, let's have another go.'

They pushed their heads up cautiously again, and this time nothing happened. Brook pulled himself up, keeping as close to the ground as possible, and Geordie followed suit. They wriggled forward and lay flat.

'Shhhht! What was that?' whispered Geordie.

They listened for ten seconds or so but heard nothing.

'I didn't hear it,' said Brook. 'What was it?'

'Somebody groaning over there.' Geordie pointed slightly to the left. 'It must be Taffy.'

There was the sudden sound of the Sten guns firing just behind them, and forgetting about concealment they pushed themselves up and dropped back down the bank. A long burst of Spandau ripped the bushes where they had been.

Ben Lyon was standing out in front of the tank with his Sten, and for a moment Brook thought he had cracked and was firing wild; but then he looked where Ben was pointing, and saw a figure slumped in the water not more than fifty yards from the tank.

'He had a bazooka,' said Ben. 'The cheeky so-and-so was going to creep right up on us.'

Brook ran back across the stream with Geordie behind him. 'Come on,' he said to Ben, 'there's more where he came from – don't stand out there asking to be shot.'

They got round to the left of the tank again, for the bazooka man had come downstream from the right. It looked as though a small party, probably a patrol, had come down the line of the woods on a general reconnaissance and had spotted the tank. It must be a small party or they would have attacked.

Brook stood Ben up behind the turret with the Bren propped against the top of the track, from where he could see right down the river but was fairly well protected by the tank. He put Geordie round the back of the tank from where he too could see the ground to the right.

The earphones were gently sputtering again; Bentley had climbed up and switched on the wireless. Brook got hold of the microphone and took a deep breath to keep his voice calm. Another stream of bullets hit the tank, but because it was bellied into the ground it formed a perfect protection for them. They pressed themselves against the sides. Brook realised that a determined rush by the Germans with bazookas, if done under cover of the machine gun, couldn't fail to knock them out, and that he and Bentley should take the Bren to where they could cover the approach to the tank.

He pressed the switch on the microphone. As he hadn't been on the air for some time he had to use precious minutes calling for a reception report to make sure someone was listening. Fortunately the duty operator was on the job and came back to him immediately.

'... We are being attacked by a small party of infantry who have got us pinned down with m.g.' Brook said carefully. 'They had at least one bazooka, which we have knocked out. One of my men is lying out ahead wounded. Can you send assistance? Over.'

'... We'll try and get some infantry up to you but it may not be possible. If it gets too much for you you should destroy your vehicle and then come back to us,' Captain MacDonald replied tersely.

The only way they could destroy the tank would be to pour petrol from one of the spare jerricans all around the turret and then throw in a burning piece of oily rag, or possibly a grenade, which would perhaps set off the H.E. shells. There was no chance that the Germans would let them get away with it, but it was obviously no use explaining all that, so Brook merely acknowledged the message. He turned to Bentley.

'That was a good effort getting the wireless on, Billy. Now I want you to come and help me man the Bren. Do you see that small depression between those two trees?' He pointed to a spot about thirty yards behind the tank. Bentley nodded. 'Well, we'll run for that. I'll carry the Bren and the spare clips. As we pass our gear, pick up the drum.'

The drum of ammunition for the Bren contained two hundred and fifty rounds and was used for anti-aircraft, but if the Germans did come in at a rush it might stop them.

As they ran the thirty yards Brook had a horrible feeling that machine gun bullets were going to cut across his back between his shoulder blades: but nothing happened, and they threw themselves into the shallow depression made by the trees' roots. Brook got the Bren up on the lip of the hole.

They were a few feet higher now, and could see the woods on the other side of the stream quite clearly. Brook set out methodically to examine every tree and every bush from as far right as he could see, looking for some sign of the enemy. He wished he had his binoculars. There was no sign at all that there was anyone there. He tried to find the spot where Taffy had gone down, but couldn't. Then suddenly he saw an arm come up and wave feebly, and his heart gave a leap.

'There's Taffy!' he said. 'He's alive.'

Geordie turned and shouted. 'Have you seen Taffy?'

'Yes – he's about fifty yards in, about ten o'clock from the tank,' Brook shouted back. 'He's waving his arm.'

'I'm going to get him,' said Geordie, and started to move round left of the tank.

'Wait a minute, Geordie!' Brook shouted. 'Wait until it's dark – we can't do anything for him anyway.'

'If those bastards see him waving his arms they'll give him another burst,' Geordie said. 'I've got to go, Brookie. I've got to.'

'No, Geordie – it's mad.'

Geordie started to move across the stream.

'Wait, Geordie – if you're going we'll try and keep them busy. Now *wait* until I tell you.'

Geordie sheltered by the rear corner of the tank, and Brook shouted Ben's name.

'Yes?' Ben shouted back from his post near the front of the tank. His voice sounded loud and clear.

'When Geordie crosses the stream, take some grenades and go with him. When he's ready, sling one as far to the right as you can. When it goes off I'll start firing the Bren. Then you, Geordie, try and get to Taffy. Keep slinging grenades, Ben as far to the right as possible. Got that?'

He had shouted the words slowly and clearly, and Ben and Geordie both acknowledged the instructions.

'O.K., Geordie, go ahead.'

Geordie put his Sten gun down and walked into the water, and Ben followed him. They pulled themselves up the other bank and slowly pushed their heads up. Brook kept his eyes ranging along the area where he thought the machine gun might be, but nothing happened. Ben turned round with a grenade held in his right hand and waved to Brook.

'Keep looking over to the right, Bentley,' Brook said, 'no matter what happens to them – because that's where the fire will come from, and we have to spot it.'

Ben threw the grenade and it sailed through the air into the trees. The seven seconds seemed a long time, but then the grenade went off, throwing up dirt and leaves. Brook began firing the Bren in short bursts, sending the bullets through the woods at about three feet off the ground.

When the grenade went off Geordie launched himself out of the defile of the stream, stood up for a second or two, then saw Taffy and ran towards him, throwing himself flat on the ground as another of Ben's grenades exploded and the Bren continued to fire.

'That you, Brookie?' said Taffy. 'Thank God.'

'No, it's me – Geordie. You hurt bad, Taff?'

'I got it in the stomach and I can't move my legs. It hurts like hell, Geordie.'

'All right, mate, I'll drag you out of here back to the tank. We'll get you some morphine.' He wriggled round and got his arms under Taffy's, and locked his hands across his chest.

'Brookie copped it, then?' Taffy asked.

'No, 'e's all right – he wanted to come and get you hisself only it was better for him to stay there, see?'

'Good old Brookie – I knew he wouldn't leave me out here.' Taffy closed his eyes, and Geordie sat up, dug his heels in, and heaved. Taffy screamed like a wounded animal and Brook and Bentley both looked over involuntarily.

'Sorry, Geordie,' Taffy gasped. 'I won't do it again.'

Geordie heaved and dragged him a few feet, rested, and then did it again. Ben threw a grenade every minute or so and Brook kept firing the Bren in bursts of five to eight shots. Taffy didn't scream again, but when Geordie stood up and dragged him the last ten yards he fainted with the pain. Ben stood up and clutched for Taffy's legs.

A single shot fired, and Geordie pitched off the bank into the water.

Brook saw the movement, in a tree not two hundred yards from them. The sniper started to climb down in a desperate hurry. Brook pointed the Bren at him and squeezed the trigger, holding it for three or four seconds, and he crashed twenty feet to the ground.

Ben had slid Taffy down the bank and turned to pick up Geordie. Brook and Bentley raced across and jumped down, and together they lifted the two of them and stretched them out on the ground behind the tank.

Geordie's eyes were shut, but he was still breathing. The front of his tank suit was wet with blood.

'Get some blankets round them,' said Brook. 'I'm going to see if there's any more.'

He ran back, picked up the Bren, and climbed on top of the tank, straddling the Bren on the hatch.

Someone shouted, and he swung the Bren towards the sound. It came from a tree not far from where the sniper had been, and as he looked a rifle clattered down through the branches. Another German soldier was holding his hands up.

Brook pointed the Bren at him and closed his finger round the trigger. The German shouted something. A wave of nausea went through Brook, and he let up the pressure on the trigger.

'Kommen Sie hier!' he shouted. 'Schnell... schnell!'

The German climbed down the tree and, stepping over his rifle, came towards them with his hands level with his head. As he got closer Brook saw that he was very young. He was smiling in a frightened way.

'There's a prisoner coming in, Ben,' Brook shouted.

The young German jumped off the bank and walked through the water to them.

Ben had pulled his revolver out. 'Let me shoot the bastard, Brookie,' he said.

'No, Ben.' Brook jumped down. 'He gave himself up. Put your gun away.' He pushed the German down and placed his hands on top of his head. 'Sitten Sie,' he said. 'Watch him, Ben.'

Taffy had recovered consciousness and was groaning. Geordie seemed to be sleeping but was breathing heavily. Brook got out the morphine that every tank commander carried and gave them both injections.

'Is the M.O. coming?' Taffy whispered. 'I don't want to die, Brookie.'

'Yes,' Brook lied. 'He's coming. I'll just jog him up.' He got hold of the microphone again. It was now quite dark and there would be no moon – he didn't have much hope that they would try and get the ambulance across the marshy fields to him before first light.

The colonel answered his call himself.

'Find out from your prisoner how many there were in his party – frighten him so he'll tell the truth. If there were a lot more get your wounded away from the tank under cover if possible and sweat it out until first light, when we'll get the M.O. up to you. I'm sorry we can do no more for you, but any movement forward is impossible now. You will be relieved in the morning. Over.' Brook acknowledged the message and went back to the others.

'They'll try and get up to us,' he said. 'Meanwhile I think we'd better get away from the tank – we're sitting ducks here.' Bentley and Ben carried Taffy, and Brook told the young German to pick up Geordie's legs. He chose a spot in a hollow among the trees well back from the tank, and Taffy and Geordie were made as comfortable as possible. Then Brook remembered that he was to interrogate the prisoner.

He drew his revolver and walked over to him. The youngster stared at him disbelievingly.

'How many soldiers? Wieviel Soldaten?' Brook asked. 'Mit Sie – how many?'

'Fünf,' the German said quickly, holding up five fingers. That meant the one with the bazooka in the river Ben had shot, the sniper Brook had shot, the prisoner, and two probably farther back manning the Spandau, which hadn't fired for some time. There could hardly be less and it wasn't likely that there were more or the attack would have continued. He was probably telling the truth. Brook put his revolver back, and told Bentley to keep an eye on him.

Ben was squatting next to Taffy. 'He's out of his head,' he said. 'He keeps talking about his engine.'

Brook leaned over and put his ear down to Taffy's mouth. He was mumbling something that seemed to be worrying him.

'What is it, Taff?'

Taffy opened his eyes and said in a stronger voice, 'Every week top up the bevel box, the gearbox, the final drive, the suspension reservoir and the power traverse gearbox…'

He clutched Brook's tank suit.

'Don't forget to grease the control cross shaft,' he said earnestly.

'Don't worry about it, Taffy,' Brook said, and Taffy went off mumbling again, going over the theory that had cost him so much effort to learn.

The night passed slowly. About two o'clock in the morning there was noise of rifle and machine gun fire well over to their right, and they thought they were going to be found by German forward patrols. They lay still on the ground, Brook holding his revolver against the prisoner's head; but after half an hour or so the firing stopped.

About four, Bentley called Brook.

'Geordie's conscious, Brookie, he wants to talk to you.'

'All right. Come over and sit next to the prisoner.'

They changed places.

Geordie's breath sounded as though he was blowing bubbles. Brook risked turning on his torch for a second, and saw that he was breathing out bright red bloody froth.

'They won't be long now, Geordie. Hang on, chum.'

'Write to me mum, will you Brookie?'

Brook could hardly make out the words.

'Of course I will, but you'll write to her yourself.'

'Tell her I'm sorry…'

'You're sorry?'

'Yes – just say George said he was sorry – that's all…'

'All right, Geordie,' Brook promised. He held his hand, which was cold and clammy. Geordie closed his eyes, and Brook thought that was the end: but he opened them again.

'Brookie?'

'Yes, Geordie, I'm here.'

'You could tell her how you left me in command for a bit if you want to…'

'I will, Geordie.'

Geordie didn't speak again. He died just before first light.

Half an hour later their own infantry came across the ground and swept past them. Not long after that the ambulance arrived, and took Taffy back to the casualty clearing station.

NINETEEN

HIS OFFICERS COULD tell that the brigadier was feeling very pleased, by the way he was flicking his fly-whisk about. He had had it ever since the desert, and it accurately reflected his mood. Now he had come back from a Corps Commander's conference at which some complimentary things had been said about his brigade. The Corps Commander himself had had a most satisfactory meal with Field-Marshal Montgomery, at which it had been demonstrated that everything was going exactly to plan and that Germany was collapsing.

'Of course,' the brigadier said, 'we've been damn lucky, I know. The resistance has been light all the way and we haven't had to fight one set-piece battle. Still, it hasn't all been plain sailing...'

'The Teutoburger Wald...' murmured an infantry colonel, whose regiment had spent three days and nights trying to dislodge the Germans from those wooded slopes.

'Yes – and there've been one or two other sticky patches, but nothing that really worried us...'

They agreed that nothing had really worried them.

'The resistance has been so light that I think we're justified in taking rather more risks. We've led the way so far and we're going to keep on leading. Our friends on the left are coming up fast now, and once they get on the autobahn they'll go like a bomb for Hamburg and get there first. The Field-Marshal says we can't have that – that won't do at all.'

There was admiring laughter – the Field-Marshal was a tartar, and they all understood about the keen rivalry between divisional commanders. After all, they were professional soldiers, and their careers would be largely determined by the success or otherwise of their divisions now.

'... And so we're going to stick our necks out.' Bang went the fly-whisk on the map. 'We're going flat out for the Elbe. We're not likely to run into any organised defensive positions – just the odd self-propelled gun or an occasional Tiger, which needn't cause us much trouble...'

The shelling had continued at intervals throughout the night, but the tank crews were either in shallow trenches under their tanks or curled up inside the turrets with all the hatches shut tight, so no one was hit. Sleep had been difficult, though, and they were not as reluctant as usual to get up at first light.

Brook and his crew had spent the night in a hole under the tank. They had been too tired to dig it well, and the sides had been gently crumbling on them for the five or six hours they had tried to sleep. Brook had slept only fitfully, and had been awake for an hour before the guard roused them by banging on the tracks with an iron bar. Although he had been unable to sleep he had dreaded the coming of day, as he always did now.

He had tried to shake off the deep depression that was like an illness, and he kept hoping that he would have a long night's sleep and wake one morning with it gone and his confidence restored. But every morning when he opened his eyes and knew where he was, a feeling of sick dread welled up from his stomach and he wanted to shut his eyes tight and stay in his blanket cocoon while the tanks and the war went on without him.

Now, like the others, he wormed out of his blankets, rolled them into an untidy ball in the cramped space, and pushed them ahead of him as he crawled out from under the tank. As he stood up the loose earth fell down inside his shirt.

A cluster of air bursts not far away put out of his head any idea of getting his shirt off and washing, and he scrambled hastily up on the tank and into the turret. Bentley and the new operator followed him, and his new driver and co-driver jumped into their positions and closed their hatches on top of them. They listened to the sharp crack of the air bursts now right overhead. When they had died away Brook switched on the wireless set and the turret light.

'Get some char on, will you Billy? Have we got any water?'

He had tried hard not to let them know how he felt, and they put his moroseness and irritability down to losing Geordie and Taffy.

'Yes,' Bentley said. 'Matthews filled the water can last night.'

Matthews was the new driver – young, and trying desperately hard.

'Well, let's have a brew first, and then we'll all have a cat-lick wash in here.'

Someone banged on the hatch and he opened it. It was the driver of the ambulance.

'I got a letter for you, Sergeant. It came up with the supplies.' He thrust it at Brook and jumped off the tank.

It was from Taffy, written on a piece of ruled paper in the round, childish writing Brook remembered from their course in Belgium.

'It's from Taffy,' he said. He suddenly wanted to read the letter somewhere in private, but it would have seemed strange to do so.

Taffy wrote that he was going to be all right. They had told him only one of the bullets had done any real damage – the one that had grazed his spine – and they had taken that out and he was getting better. He would have to wait until the nerve grew before he could move his legs, but the medical corporal had told him it grew a sixty-fourth of an inch a month; he didn't know how much there was to grow but it looked like it was going to be a long wait…

Brook stopped reading the letter. The other two in the turret were self-consciously not looking at him. He felt his eyes smarting, but he knew it was not what had happened to Taffy and Geordie that made him want to cry like a baby, but the state of his own nerves. He felt Taffy's bullet in his own spine now, just as, when he thought of Geordie, he could taste the blood in his own mouth.

They were going to fly him back to England that day, Taffy went on – his first flight. I'll think of you, he wrote, when I'm drinking my first pint after a nice double order of fish and chips. He finished with the old warning – keep your head down, it won't be long now.

Brook folded the letter and tucked it in his top pocket. Bentley looked at him questioningly.

'He's going to be all right. They're flying him home – the lucky beggar.'

They pretended to agree that they thought he was lucky.

It had been cold in the tank when they first got in, but with the hatches closed, the petrol stove burning, and the heat of their five bodies, it soon got warm and unhealthy-smelling, like a barrack room. They began to loosen their battledress blouses and tank suits, but they preferred the fug to the cold, fresh air. The new operator netted in efficiently and Lieutenant Mudie, the new troop officer, came up and ordered all tank commanders to his tank. Brook gulped down his hot tea and pushed open the hatch and heaved himself out. His crew groaned as the cold air came in, and he shut the hatch on them again.

It was just getting light. The sun, a blood orange, was moving up some narrow black clouds lying in long bars across the sky; the trees were sharp silhouettes cut out of black paper. Brook dropped to the ground and waited for Gordon Page, who had elected to sleep in his turret, to come up. He was bent over like a hunchback.

'Well, did you get any sleep?' said Brook.

'Of course, old boy, we slept like tops – all curled up like puppies – each bloke with his feet on the next one's neck. Oh it was lovely – of course, I don't suppose I shall ever be able to straighten up again, but no sacrifice is too great for a Page to make for his country.'

Lieutenant Mudie was waiting for them by his tank. He was one of the officers who had been wounded at Caen; he knew his job but didn't take unnecessary chances. He turned to his map and tapped it.

'Now here's the picture... the Jocks are over here on our right. They are going to put in an attack on this town today. Our job is to push straight on up this main road, by-passing the town, and, turning in right, to seize the crossroads north of the town here... You'll see that's the only escape route, and we should get a chance to brass up Jerry as he tries to bolt. Is that all clear?'

'Yes,' said Brook slowly, 'but it's rather a long way, isn't it? What about where our road runs through the woods there for three or four miles – how do we know we won't get held up there?'

'Well, Jerry's pretty well disorganised, you know. The recce boys have been swanning about all over the show, and they haven't seen any sign that he's digging his heels in anywhere.'

'The form is to shove the leading tank on until it gets knocked out, then?' said Brook.

There was an awkward silence.

'Until it finds the enemy, Sergeant. It doesn't follow that it has to be knocked out.'

'No, sir – are we leading?'

'No – Two Troop are...'

'What – Sandy again?' Brook asked unbelievingly. 'That will make three times in a week...'

'Major MacDonald has promised that we'll get a crack later. There are odd pockets of barbary Jerries off the centre line, and we'll probably be sent to sort them out if they decide to be troublesome, so Sergeant Sanderstead won't be getting all the shooting, Sergeant.' Lieutenant Mudie dismissed the subject by folding up his map. 'Right, that's all then, if you're quite pictured...'

'Yes, sir,' said Brook.

'All clued-up, sir,' said Gordon Page.

'Good – good – well, "press on regardless"...' He laughed. 'As soon as you're all teed up we'll move out in the road and take up our positions behind Two Troop. I'll lead, then you, Sergeant, then Corporal Cleethorpes, and Corporal Page doing rear-guard.'

Brook walked slowly back to his tank thinking about Sandy. He had taken over Two Troop as sergeant when he came back with a new tank, and had been given his chance to lead the next day. He had rushed ahead recklessly overrunning infantry positions and knocking out two anti-tank guns which had unaccountably missed him. He had been held up as an example to the other squadrons, and Captain MacDonald, now promoted to major, and their new squadron commander, was very pleased with him. As long as Sandy was willing to advance at that speed, Major MacDonald was willing to keep him out in front.

That day was no exception. Their centre line led through a large forest which seemed a natural place for some anti-tank guns or even a tank, but Sandy went bowling through the woods with the infantry hanging on to his bumping tank. The tanks at the rear of the column had to go flat out to keep the gaps closed up, and clouds of dust marked their approach. Two Troop officer came up on the wireless to report their success cockily.

'Good show, push on – push on,' the major replied. 'All stations Mike Nan we're moving on again – keep up, keep up.' The advance continued.

'It can't last,' Brook said. 'It can't. Jerry's bound to make a stand somewhere, and when he does he'll brew up half a dozen tanks at one go.'

They were rocking along the road, and he turned to look at his own infantrymen, who were hanging on precariously.

'Your blokes all right?' he shouted to the N.C.O. in charge of them.

'We're O.K. This is better than footslogging,' the N.C.O. shouted back.

'... It's a pretty fair-sized town,' Sandy was saying, 'but there's some lovely hull-down positions we could paste it from.'

'Is there any sign that it's being held?' the major asked.

'No, I can't say I've seen anything, but the road approaching it has no cover at all. We'd be sitting ducks to any gun in the town.'

'Push on slowly down the road and we'll see what happens. Hello, Mike Nan One – get your boys up right behind Nan Two and cover Nan Two Able as he goes in. Over.'

'Mike Nan One – Roger – Wilco – Out!' Lieutenant Mudie replied breezily. He turned to wave to Brook, and then moved rapidly up the road to where Sandy was hull-down at the top of the hill with the rest of Two Troop just behind him. When they arrived, Two Troop officer waved Sandy on.

Brook got out his binoculars and carefully examined the road ahead. There was one house on the left-hand side just off the road, but otherwise only open fields. Brook saw nothing but Sandy's tank moving alone some three hundred yards ahead of the rest of his troop. He tensed himself waitmg for a gun to fire.

Suddenly, when Sandy was not more than a hundred yards from the house, he stopped and quickly traversed his gun left. It fired a shell straight into the house. A moment later the tank moved towards it at full speed. Sandy stopped and fired once more and they saw the shell burst inside the house and the lines of tracer bullets from his machine gun converge on it. Nothing seemed to be coming back at him. He advanced again and the tank struck the house, hesitated, and then, climbing slightly over the debris, ploughed straight through it. As the back of the tank disappeared into the house the whole thing seemed to settle down into the ground.

A cluster of shells ringed the house, another burst among the tanks on the ridge, and a third among the rest of Two Troop. The infantrymen went to ground and the tanks started to fire back at the flashes of the guns sited in the town.

Forty-five minutes later the town was a smoking ruin. They had called on the artillery for help, and the hundred-pound shells of the 5·5s had forced the German light anti-aircraft guns to withdraw.

Sandy had been hauled out of the cellar of the house he had tried to drive his tank through. The anti-tank gun found under his tracks, although not manned, had been sitting in the living-room and sited up the road.

'If it had been manned they would have got you,' Brook told him. 'What the hell is the use of charging an anti-tank gun? Do you think you're in the cavalry or something?'

'What would you have done, then?'

'I'd have put an A.P. into it while I was reversing to some less exposed position and I'd have reported it to get some help... I might even have baled out. But I certainly wouldn't have charged at it like a bloody silly bull!'

'Och, Brookie, you're not yourself these days,' Sandy said sadly. 'You're beginning to sound like an old woman...'

'All right – get your fool head blown off, then,' Brook snapped, and turned and walked back to his tank.

They had halted in the market square and were waiting for the infantry to flush out the few remaining Germans from the houses. The only resistance was coming from a few who had holed up in the railway station, and the mortars that were being brought into position would deal with them. Brook climbed back into his turret and swore he was finished trying to pound caution into Sandy's head; obviously Sandy was determined to get himself killed.

None of Brook's crew spoke to him; they went on talking quietly among themselves. He leaned forward on the hatch cover with his chin in his hands and looked round at the smashed and smoking buildings that had been a small, prosperous town. Some of the infantry were drinking tea, and some were poking about in the houses that had been cleared, looking for portable loot. Four German dead had been dragged off the road so they wouldn't get under the tracks, and laid head to feet in a neat line alongside a building; a small car that looked as though a giant had stepped on it was squashed in the road. Some tank driver had been unable to resist the temptation to drive over it.

An hour or so later the order came through for them to stop where they were for the night, and they took over the least damaged buildings as makeshift billets.

By ten o'clock that night, when all the jobs had been done and his troops were bedded down, Brook found once more that although he was exhausted he could not sleep. He didn't think he was actually ill, but the feeling of nausea seldom left him for long, and he had a persistent headache – which was a new experience for him. He had often heard his mother complain of a headache, but he had never had one before this last year. Now it was as though a little man with a pneumatic hammer was working away steadily inside his skull. It was no use lying in his blankets in the darkened room listening to the snoring of the men around him, so he got up and slipped outside.

He called out to the infantryman on guard, to let him know he was there, and walked to the tank and climbed into the turret.

'Don't you get enough of that, Sarge?' asked the guard, who had walked over.

Brook made some non-committal reply, and the other, realising that he didn't want to talk, went back.

Brook sat on the commander's seat, and stared ahead at the black shadow of the long gun.

'What is wrong with me?' he whispered. 'What the hell is wrong with me?'

He knew the answer, and he forced himself to say it:

'I'm afraid. I'm afraid. I'm afraid.'

But he felt no better for having brought it out into the open.

'What can I do about it?' He knew the answer again – 'Nothing, nothing, nothing.'

He thought of his first battle on the hill in Normandy and

remembered his terror when through his periscope he had first seen tanks burning. He had wanted to get out and run but the stocky figure of Sergeant Donovan had blocked the way. Now he was the tank commander, and he still couldn't get out and run.

There had been a long period when he wasn't afraid, when like Sandy, he had felt that he couldn't be killed; but now he felt he was going to be. Perhaps tomorrow, perhaps in the next few days, but he was sure it wouldn't be long. He had scoffed at other men's premonitions, but now he understood how they had felt. It was like coming to the end of anything – there was nothing you could do about it except wish that it hadn't gone so fast.

It seemed almost certain that the war itself was coming to an end too; but that didn't help, for in the last minute of the last hour a gun would fire and someone would die. He could go to the M.O. and say he had had enough, but as long as you could go and say that you'd had enough you were still able to direct your mind and your body and you hadn't had enough. He could refuse to get into a tank again, and be arrested and court-martialled and live with that for the rest of his life. Surely death would be better than that? No, death wouldn't – death wouldn't be better than anything – not really; and if the choice was certain death or refusing to go on and taking the consequences, he knew he would not choose death. But of course, it wasn't, for there was the chance that he would get away with it – there was *always* the chance that he would get away with it – even after the 88 or the bazooka hit his tank. He wasn't afraid of pain – he looked down at his legs and wondered if that was what was going to happen to him. He stretched out one – would it be that that he would leave behind to rot in the German earth? If he knew that that was the worst, he could face it: but he didn't want to die.

He had never written the kind of letter to his parents that he'd read about. It had always seemed a small thing to set beside so large a thing as death, but now he realised that there were some things he had never said to them that if he were dead he would want them to know.

He tore a leaf from a notebook and wrote rapidly. He didn't write about freedom or Hitlerism or even the concrete reasons for his being where he was, for none of that seemed important to him then: he didn't mention his fear, for that would add to their pain without relieving his: the things he said were simple and private, not well expressed, even clumsy – it was not a letter that would ever be published or that would interest anyone if it was.

He folded it carefully and put it in his paybook. There was a compartment in the back cover into which it fitted snugly. The page opposite was labelled 'WILL'.

'SOLELY FOR USE ON ACTIVE SERVICE' it said. *'This will page must NOT be used until you have been placed under orders for Active Service.'* There was a blank space, and lines underneath for his signature, rank, regiment and army number. On the back of the sheet were short specimen wills... *'In the event of my death I give the whole of my property and effects to my mother, Mrs Mary Bull, 999 High Street, Aldershot, signed* GEORGE BULL, *Fusilier No. 1973, Royal Fusiliers,'* he read, and then the date – 5th August, 1914... Evidently Fusilier Bull hadn't believed in wasting time.

He smiled to himself – somehow this evidence of the army's trying to think of everything had brought his feet back on the ground. He took out the letter to his parents and read it through again. He wasn't proud of it, but he didn't tear it up: it said, however clumsily, some of the things they wanted to hear and it was little enough to do.

He put the paybook and letter back in the little envelope of gas-proof material hanging around his neck. Of course if it was to be a bazooka and he didn't get out, everything would burn... He shut his eyes and put his hands to his pounding head.

He got out of the tank and started to walk back into the house. When he had gone only a few yards he heard the scream of shells. He threw himself back on the ground beside the tank as three shells burst in a line across the street. The nearest was twenty or thirty yards away, and the concussion jarred him. He kept his eyes shut and stayed where he was.

'You been hit, mate?' The guard was bending over him.

He opened his eyes and pushed himself upright. 'No, I'm all right.'

'Sure?' asked the guard doubtfully.

God, how I wish I was hit, he thought – just a nice piece of shrapnel in the leg.

'No, I wasn't touched,' he said. 'Did they do any damage?'

'No, I don't think so – they just lobbed them over on chance, I should think. Is there something wrong with your head, Sarge?'

He realised that he was holding his head in both hands and he took his hands away quickly. 'No – I've just got a hell of a headache, that's all.'

'Why don't you walk down to the blokes on the blood wagon? They'll give you something for it.'

'Good idea – thanks.'

The ambulance was parked a few hundred yards behind. When he got there they were dealing with a casualty who had been brought in earlier – an infantryman who had stepped on a mine. There was another ambulance waiting to take him back to the casualty clearing centre as soon as they had done what they could for him. Brook waited for the medical sergeant to finish, but when he walked over he saw that it was the M.O. himself.

'Doctor…?'

The M.O. glanced at him and then stopped. 'Oh, it's you, Sergeant Brook. What do you want?' He sounded brusque and unsympathetic.

'Can you give me something for a headache, sir?'

'Yes – had it long?'

'Yes – on and off for two or three days.'

'Mmmm. Well, I'll give you some codeine – don't take too many or they'll put you to sleep.' He shook out some white tablets from a large bottle. 'Is that all?'

'Yes, sir.' Brook turned to go. 'I suppose you haven't any more news of Corporal Evans, sir?'

'Yes – he's going to be all right. It may take a bit of time, but he's pretty well out of danger.'

'I'm very glad to hear that.'

'Yes, of course you are. Well, now take a couple of those and then get some sleep. Good night.' He turned and climbed into his jeep and drove off.

Brook got back into his blankets, and shut his eyes and tried to sleep. The codeine finally dulled the pain of his headache, but he couldn't sleep. About once an hour a few shells came over, and each time he went rigid, waiting for one to come in the room somehow. All around him men were sleeping and none of them seemed to wake. He fell asleep at last, to dream that he was tied up inside the tank, which was filling with smoke. He fought his way awake and lay there with his heart pounding. The room was very stuffy, and he got up again and went to the window. Light was just beginning to appear, so he didn't try to go back to sleep again.

But it all seemed like a dream that morning. A voice inside him kept chanting 'Today's the day, today's the day,' and the rhythm was repeated by the tracks rapping on the road –

'Today's the day, today's the day...'

He knew he was doing his job inefficiently. Gordon Page had quietly taken most of it off his shoulders, and when Lieutenant Mudie had to repeat a question to him twice, Page tried to cover up for him.

'I think One Able is having trouble with his set,' Page had reported, and had tried to attract Brook's attention by shouting; but Brook's new operator had reached over and tugged at his headset.

'The troop officer's calling you, Sarge,' he said. 'Something about the ground on the right.'

Brook came up on the air and asked for the question to be repeated. Lieutenant Mudie sounded irritated.

'I say again – I saw something move on the road about figures fifteen hundred half-right from you. Can you spot what it is? Over.'

Brook acknowledged the message and brought his binoculars to focus. He saw two or three green figures running, half-crouched, down the road.

'Enemy infantry,' he reported. 'I will engage – Out.'

He brought his gun to bear and put a shell on the road where he had seen them, and then another a few yards farther up. When he looked again there was no more movement to be seen. One Troop was ordered to go up and have a look. When they got there there was no sign of any enemy, and Lieutenant Mudie reported it and waited for orders.

The road was tree-lined, and high, and they could see a good deal of the country off to one side. It looked a pleasant farming land, with tall churches sticking up here and there to mark the villages.

An excited voice on the radio got his attention – it was a strange one to him.

'A Tiger has been reported in among some houses at map reference figures five one three four four six...' The reference was repeated, but Brook, like every other tank commander, was quickly finding it on the map. It was off to their right. Brook found it and marked it, then marked his position and oriented his map, and followed the extension of the line from his tank, as he had been taught to do so long ago on the sandy heaths round Aldershot.

He was looking at a group of seven buildings, one a tiny church, one a hall or school, the rest unimposing houses. They were along a road at right-angles to the way he was looking, and were not much more than fifteen hundred yards from him. He trained his binoculars on the buildings. There was no sign of life at all – the whole scene looked like an illustration for a calendar.

'All right...' the colonel was saying. 'Out to you – did you get that map reference, Yoke Able?'

'Yes,' Major MacDonald replied quickly and efficiently. 'I've got some of my boys not far from there and we'll have a look at him. Out to you. Hello, Yoke Able One – did you get that map reference?'

As soon as he had heard the word 'Tiger', Brook had known that this was it, and now he heard the machinery moving relentlessly. It was as though he was being marched to the wall and the firing squad were loading their guns. He heard Lieutenant Mudie's voice reply, and he knew what his next words were going to be as surely as though it had all happened before.

'... Yoke Able One *Able*, you've found that reference, haven't you? Over.'

All his life had been moving towards this: his tank had traced its way through the maze to this point. The Tiger had been reported by civilians sick of the war to divisional headquarters, and there someone had looked at a map and called the brigade, who had looked at a map and called the regiment, who had called the squadron, who had called the troop, and now it was coming to him and it could go no farther.

'Brookie... Brookie.'

It was young Billy Bentley looking worriedly at him.

'You'd better answer, Brookie.'

He pressed the switch on his microphone. 'Yes, I've found the map reference.'

'Good. Well, advance on the houses, then. Don't hesitate to fire if you see anything at all. We'll support you from here. Over.'

Brook looked again. The sun had come out and the houses looked harmless. Behind, or even inside one of them, was a Tiger. Its commander would wait to fire until he couldn't miss. Brook answered automatically and then switched to the internal telephone.

'All right, Matthews, hard right stick and advance.'

The tank pivoted on its track and moved across the road. It nosed between two trees, pushed down an old wooden fence and emerged out into the sunlight.

'Stop, Matthews.' He started on the left with his binoculars – a house. He couldn't see inside, of course, but he tried to – the windows were black holes. Next, another house about the same size – the Tiger could come between the two. Next, a third house a little farther away and smaller. No sign of life. Next the church; a house behind the church, then the larger building, evidently the village hall or school or both; another house, and a bit apart from the rest a bigger house with a barn. All around were fields and trees – there was not another house anywhere near.

'All right, Matthews, advance as you're facing, towards that group of buildings about fifteen hundred yards ahead.' He tried to think of the co-driver's name but it had gone. 'Co-driver, be ready to fire your machine gun when I give the word.'

'All ready now, Sergeant.' He was a nice lad; Brook wondered if he would get out.

The tank slowly closed the distance, crashing through hedges and going down and up ditches. For a thousand yards nothing happened. Brook's belly felt tied in a knot.

'Stop, Matthews,' he said.

Again he started to examine the buildings with his binoculars, when suddenly the wireless, which had been silent waiting for his report, broke into excited speech.

'I s-s-saw the sun glint on m-m-metal by the big house on the right...' Lance-Corporal Cleethorpes shouted. 'Look out, Brook, look out!'

'Traverse right... steady on... fire!' Brook said.

'What at?' Bentley asked.

'At the house – put one straight through it... quickly!'

The gun fired and an armour-piercing shell went straight through the house.

'Now the m.g.s... lace the whole house from side to side... top and bottom...'

The tracer bullets made a long curving line into the house.

'That's right, that's right... now the barn, the barn!'

Brook heard himself screaming, and clamped down hard to control his voice. The house was beginning to burn and the barn burst into flame almost immediately. He suddenly knew that the Tiger was in one of the other houses – getting ready to pull away but not before he'd put a shot through Brook. He had to get him quickly.

'Traverse left... fire!'

Bentley hesitated.

'Fire, damn it, fire!' Brook shouted. 'Then right up the row – put a shell in every house – fire, fire!'

The machine guns kept up, and one after the other the houses began to burn.

'Advance Taffy,' he said. 'Advance slowly.' He caught a sob. 'I'm sorry – I mean Matthews – advance Matthews.'

'That's all right, Sergeant,' Matthews said gently. 'You often say that but I know you mean me.'

They reached the road a few yards from the first blazing house and he silenced his guns. He took the tank round the backs of the houses, around the church which was also burning, and the school inside which the shells had burst. Finally he came back to the road and moved down to the last, big house, which he had fired on first.

There was no sign of any living thing anywhere: there was nothing but burning houses.

Suddenly he felt completely exhausted.

'There's no one here,' he reported. 'No tank – no one at all.'

'Good show,' Lieutenant Mudie laughed. 'I'd hate to see what you would have done to that place if there had been something there. Come back and re-join us now.'

A movement caught Brook's eye and he swung round with his Bren gun. It was the wooden cover of an air-raid shelter exactly like the one in the farm in Normandy that Nobby Clarke and Smudger had lowered him into above the dead family. Slowly the cover lifted and fell off. An old woman crawled out and smiled uncertainly at him. She was followed by an old man, who touched his head in a half-salute, and then a young woman carrying a baby, then two younger children who clung to her, and last of all two young men. Brook's finger tightened on the trigger, but one of them stepped forward.

'We are French,' he said, speaking in English. 'We are forced labour. We have been here since 1940.'

'Now you are free...' Brook started to say, but his voice was a croak.

'Why did you do it?' the Frenchman asked quietly. 'Why?'

'German tanks,' Brook said. 'Tigers...'

The Frenchman shook his head. 'We have not even seen any German soldiers for two days. There have never been any tanks here – no soldiers, no guns – just the old people and the women and the children. They are good people – why did you destroy their houses – why?'

Suddenly Brook dropped his head on his arm and started to cry uncontrollably. Bentley eased him off the commander's seat and let him sit on the turret floor.

Bentley moved into the seat, put his head out of the turret, and adjusted the headset.

'My commander has been taken ill,' he reported, 'and I am now in command.' His young voice sounded confident. 'What are my orders? – Over.'

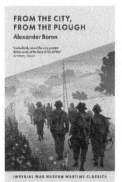

ISBN 9781912423071

£8.99

'Alexander Baron's *From the City, From the Plough* is undoubtedly one of the very greatest British novels of the Second World War and provides the most honest and authentic account of front line life for an infantryman in North West Europe.'

ANTONY BEEVOR

ISBN 9781912423095

£8.99

'Takes you straight back to Blitzed London... boasts everything a great whodunit should have, and more.'

ANDREW ROBERTS

ISBN 9781912423156

£8.99

'When a man has been a soldier and seen action, he writes of war with true understanding, and with authority. When that man writes with wit, elegance and imagination, as Fred Majdalany does in *Patrol*, he produces a military masterpiece.'

ALAN MALLINSON

ISBN 9781912423088
£8.99

'A tremendous rediscovery of a brilliant novel. Extremely well-written, its effects are both sophisticated and visceral. Remarkable.'

WILLIAM BOYD

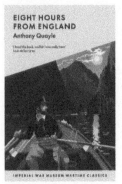

ISBN 9781912423101
£8.99

'Much more than a novel'

RODERICK BAILEY

'I loved this book, and felt I was really there'

LOUIS de BERNIÈRES

'One of the greatest adventure stories of the Second World War'

ANDREW ROBERTS